10001 10002 FRA

OVER THE MOUNTAINS

Books by
PAMELA FRANKAU

NO NEWS

THE DEVIL WE KNOW

A DEMOCRAT DIES

SHAKEN IN THE WIND

THE WILLOW CABIN

THE OFFSHORE LIGHT

THE WINGED HORSE

A WREATH FOR THE ENEMY

THE BRIDGE

ASK ME NO MORE

ROAD THROUGH THE WOODS

PEN TO PAPER

SING FOR YOUR SUPPER

SLAVES OF THE LAMP

OVER THE MOUNTAINS

Over the Mountains

A NOVEL

by

PAMELA FRANKAU

THE BOOK CLUB
121 CHARING CROSS ROAD
LONDON W.C.2

First published 1967 by
William Heinemann Ltd
This edition 1968

Printed in Great Britain by
Cox & Wyman Ltd,
London, Reading and Fakenham

For GEOFFREY VICKERS, V.C.,
because of Lisbon, 1940

The Author acknowledges, with deep gratitude, these sources of help and information:

Mrs. Muriel Oakes Ames, Mrs. E. Taylor, Mme. Ginette Spanier, Major-General J. C. Haydon, Captain John Moore, Mr. Peter de Polnay and the late John Lodwick.

The lines from *Goodnight, Mrs. Astor* are quoted by permission of the authors, Nancy Hamilton and Morgan Lewis.

The lines from *Disgustingly Rich* by Rodgers and Hart are quoted by permission of the copyright owners, Chappell & Co; Inc.

CLOTHES OF A KING'S SON

A Trilogy

Over the Mountains

LONDON

Now it was early afternoon; an old lady's time for sleeping and bright dreams. Not that one could think of oneself as an old lady; one simply became used to hearing other people say so.

For oneself it was no matter of ageing but of living every year inside an envelope that was wearing out, inside a framework whose dilapidations could no longer be checked or repaired. The person who lived here was – naturally – irked by the increasing restrictions. This person remained obstinately young.

Marion Murray thought of saying as much to Percy; then decided against it. Though he himself must feel an approach to the same emotion, being in his sixties, he would snap. The statement of a problem invariably made him snap. A problem, for Percy, was something to be solved. If it couldn't be solved, it shouldn't be mentioned. So long as it wasn't mentioned, it didn't exist. "The male is an ostrich, an ostrich, an ostrich ... which is precisely what he thinks of me at this moment, of course. He thinks I am refusing to face facts. He fails to understand that one can always face facts (nothing easier when, as today, they are inescapable) without feeling obliged to do anything about them."

Marion Murray lowered her heavy lids, to let a deliberate mist come down over the room; the big room furnished with its many little treasures, sacred and profane; the room sun-dusted through its tall window that gave on to the gardens outside. An old lady's ground-floor flat in Kensington. Few places were safer (they said) than a ground-floor flat in a solid Victorian house.

As though any true safety existed in England on the afternoon of May the Twenty-Fifth, Nineteen-Forty. That was Percy's argument. But one needed to contemplate the situation, alone and steadily; this was all one needed. This was, for the time being, forbidden.

"The world in flames," she thought, "and my bullfrog of a son-in-law a fixture on my carpet. Poor Percy; not only is he wasting his time and delaying my afternoon sleep; he is clouding the issue. So much to contemplate . . . The German Army almost within speaking-distance: Boulogne; they might as well be in Brighton. I daresay they will be next week; no, more likely Folkestone. A shorter sea-crossing." She was only aware that she had spoken aloud when Percy clasped his forehead, saying "What's Folkestone got to do with it?"

"As a landing-place, I mean."

"I don't believe you've been listening to one word —"

—"No, I haven't. But then I've heard it before. Twice," she reminded him, "Once at the time of Munich and once last September."

This he took very badly indeed. A busy man like myself, said Percy, a dozen things to do, people to see and you won't even take the trouble . . . Mrs. Murray wondered once again how and why Percy had become so important, so military, so central. She had but the vaguest notions of his significance in this war. He had done well in the last one, but that was a long time ago, and the years between had made him a successful business-man. Connections, she remembered; Percy always had Connections, Influence and, of course, his Old Regiment: high-ranking friends with nicknames like Buffles, Piggy and Gasper.

"How old are *you*?" she asked suddenly.

"Why on earth do you want to know?"

"Curiosity."

Percy's lips made a blowing sound.

"Never mind, you needn't tell me. And you can save yourself the rest of the argument. I am staying where I am. What? No, not foolishness and not courage. Curiosity again. If this is the end of our world then I must see the end come. Besides I have always wanted to be in at my own death. What? Yes, of course one is, but I prefer to be present with all my faculties – or as many of them as remain at my age. A sudden death would be dignified. And interesting, given

2

just a few minutes. Let me be clear; I haven't the slightest intention of being packed off to Scotland like a crated antique."

"You used to be fond of Scotland," he grumbled; he went on grumbling; the words faded out of her ears, murmuring a little way off as though a bee were buzzing against the sunlit window.

Her thoughts went down into darker places. They hunted after Thomas, her grandson Thomas, over there in France; somewhere in the middle of the sudden furious fighting. One did not know where, one could form no picture, one knew only that it would have to be Thomas and not any of the others. The others were all safely in America.

Except for Rab, driving her ambulance: Rab too must be somewhere in the thick of it. But, as a member of the family, Rab, the imported stepsister, did not ring true. "And one knows for certain that she passionately wanted to be where she is. With Thomas, one feels it's just a matter of conscience and duty."

"As it was in the beginning," said Mrs. Murray, "*Somebody's* got to stay . . ." She felt the twitch of a sorrowful smile at the corners of her mouth.

"Meaning yourself?" Percy, pop-eyed, showed a blink of respect.

"No. I was quoting. I meant Thomas."

Percy pounced. "Yes, well, Thomas, now. That's a thought, isn't it? How would *he* like to think of you here in danger? Hate it, wouldn't he? Simply hate it."

"Hate . . . hate . . . hate . . . I don't think he knows much about hating."

The bullfrog didn't listen. Though the name of Thomas had set him off again, his words gave Mrs. Murray no image of her grandson. He was talking about the British Soldier. The only thing likely to sap the morale of the British Soldier, Percy explained, was anxiety for his Womenfolk at home. (Womenfolk . . . a word with echoes of Kipling; distastefully German, too.) "That's what gets the average chap down, my dear Marion."

"Then it will scarcely trouble Thomas, will it?"

"Ug?" said Percy; it sounded like ug; one was, of course, growing a little deaf.

"Didn't your friend Gasper – or was it Buffles – complain of

3

Thomas's failure to conduct himself like an average chap?" A mischievous reminder; she couldn't help giving it, couldn't help holding on tightly to the odd, beloved young man she knew; to her grandson as he was, not as Percy wanted him to be. "At Sandhurst, remember?" she said, "'Though appearing to take kindly to discipline himself, he is somewhat prone to excuse the lack of it in others'." She was pleased to be word-perfect with the quotation. Percy, obviously wishing he had never shown her the letter from Gasper at all, turned away his head.

"Teething-troubles; teething-troubles; nothing unusual. You'll admit the boy has shaped remarkably well ever since." His pink forehead ceased to frown; he stroked his chin and smiled. Now he wore his stockbroking look; the look of the Thomas-owner, the wise investor. He had owned Thomas for months; or so it felt.

How many times had she heard the proclamatory clauses? "My young nephew. Joined up last summer. Put himself down for my Old Regiment. Luckily. Obvious officer-material. But nowadays – as you know . . . A bit of wangling. Old Buffles. Old Gasper. Old Piggy. Short course at Sandhurst. Commissioned in January."

Percy was accustomed to glow upon the achievement as if Thomas were a block of shares shrewdly bought and sharply risen in market-value. She saw him glow again, but not for long. Mercifully, he was looking at his watch.

He squared his shoulders and raised his chin for the last sermon; she hoped it was the last. It was the one about consideration for other people. The other people to be considered were, as usual, her daughter Flavia – Percy's wife – and the family in America. Flavia came first: Flavia frantic, Flavia telephoning to the North, Flavia ready to act as escort. Then the family; Philip, Paula, Sarah . . . how would *they* be feeling, six thousand miles off in California? And Gerald in New York? Agony it must be for them all, mustn't it?

"With the news as it is this week I can't think the agony will be much reduced by a cable saying Flavia has taken me to Forfarshire."

Percy's elbow knocked two small china owls off the mantelpiece. He replaced the owls and stayed where he was. Had she, then, no consideration for the Air Raid Wardens and the demolition workers?

Their heaviest problem, once the bombing began, would be that of elderly people living alone.

"I have heard it said," Mrs. Murray admitted. "But I have never understood why. Is it more difficult to dig out old corpses than young ones? In any case I shan't be living alone. There are the second-floor tenants. And Blanche is moving in."

"Blanche? Nanny, you mean? Nanny?"

"It can hardly have escaped your notice that I call her Blanche. I've been doing it ever since she came to work for me."

"Well, I always call her Nanny. So does Flavia." An odd bone of contention, but Percy appeared to seize upon it with enthusiasm. "Nanny," he repeated in a grieved way, "She's always been Nanny."

"Well she's not my Nanny, dear, is she? And the children are all grown-up," said Mrs. Murray. Percy snapped his fingers: "Nanny's moving in? Into this house? When?"

"As soon as she's packed that hysterical sister of hers off to the Cotswolds. I should have thought she'd be here by now."

"Today? Oh. Oh . . . I see. It's all arranged, eh?" Percy – she reflected – was having quite a horrible afternoon: he liked to be the one who did the arranging.

"Well but she can't sleep here," he said. "Can't share your room. Can't sleep on *that*," he added, with a disparaging glance at the huge, velvety sofa.

"Oh yes she can. Once the raids start. Till then she can stay on the top floor – in Mr. Dutty's room. Keep all her things there and use his bathroom. For the duration; it won't cost her a farthing."

Percy, faintly appeased, began to say that this was extraordinarily generous of the fellow, whoever he might be; posted overseas or what?

"He has been arrested under this new Emergency Powers Act," Mrs. Murray explained. "Very prompt, the police were. And they all went off quite amicably together, no sign of a scuffle. I have had my suspicions of Mr. Dutty; so much typewriting in the evenings, and always that trench-coat. Have you any idea – you who know everything – why Nazi sympathies inevitably bring people out in trench-coats?"

And now the trumpets of relief were sounding: Blanche's latch-key in the lock; Blanche herself butting determinedly through the clashing beads of the portière. She carried a suit-case, a brown paper parcel and a bulgy string bag that dated from the Twenties. ("But perhaps it is not the same bag, merely one in the line of succession . . .") A flat package was lodged precariously between her right upper arm and her ribs. Percy sprang to help her unload.

Blanche beamed at him as though this were an ordinary day. She beamed and prattled. "Yes, sir, thank you. I saw her off from Paddington this morning. Gracious, the train was crowded, lucky to find a seat. Such a nice couple got her in, I'd never have managed it. There was a man with a pram. He'd got his wife and baby in, but not the pram. Nobody would help – I felt so sorry for him."

"Your sister all on her own?" Percy asked.

"Only as far as Kemble. Frank, that's her son, meets her there with the car. He gets plenty of petrol, being agricultural, like. Well, that's one load off my mind," said Blanche, smiling at Mrs. Murray. "Isn't it time for your rest, M'm?" Easier not to answer than to say "Long past it." Percy was suddenly awash with good-humour, patting Blanche's shoulder, no doubt thinking Gallant Little Woman as he gazed down into the bony face with its bright blue eyes and severe nose: Blanche more gnomelike than she used to be . . . how old now? Sixty-something, it didn't matter.

"Well, then I went back to Battersea, just to collect my things – have a last look round. We've put dust-sheets over everything. It isn't as if I won't be looking in once or twice every week. Promised Mary I'd keep an eye."

Percy's attention was deflected. By what? Raising her lorgnette, Mrs. Murray saw him absorbed in a study of the flat package brought by Blanche; it was sewn up in greenish canvas and appeared to be coming to pieces. Percy went on handling it, reading the labels.

"That belongs to Thomas," said Blanche, her voice grating a little.

"Looks as if it's given the Field Post Office a headache," said Percy. "What's inside?"

Blanche, now chilling off to zero, replied "I don't know, I'm sure. Excuse me, sir." She twitched it out of his hands. "Something he asked me to keep safe for him."

Safe. The word, Mrs. Murray thought, made a mark on the air.

Silence followed it. She saw Percy's face wiped over with solemnity, she felt all three of them looking stonily at the battered green parcel, the entrusted thing.

We are making the wrong vibration; we are inviting the worst. At once she began to say a prayer in her head; not that one stopped praying for more than a few minutes at a time nowadays. Everybody was praying. Every day the *Times* letter-column carried a new suggestion for prayers suitable to the hour. Mrs. Murray, having the habit, did her best not to take a cynical view of the belated, unanimous rush to God.

Percy was shaking hands with Blanche; he was spouting hearty, victorious words. He came to kiss her, to say "Best of luck – I admire your pluck," and to look surprised at the unintentional rhyme before he strode off. The portière rattled behind him; the door banged.

"What has Thomas sent, Blanche? Obviously you know."

Blanche laughed. "Well, he's such a one for minding other people's business, isn't he, Mr. Percy?"

"That," said Mrs. Murray, "*is* his business. I think it must be very tiring."

"It's just Thomas's notebooks in here, M'm. The ones he's been keeping since he went to France. Quite a time they've taken, must be a month now since he wrote to say they'd be coming."

Always the notebooks, Mrs. Murray thought. She remembered Thomas buying six of them at Straker's on the last day of his embarkation-leave; making the choice most seriously, as when he was a child. Red covers, he had chosen; foolscap paper, with lines.

"Does anybody know what he puts in them? Has anybody ever known?"

Blanche hesitated. "He used to call it 'doing today' when he was small. Sort of diaries, they are. I know he uses them for his drawings sometimes."

"If he had sent them to me I should yield to temptation and read every word. Which proves how wise he is to send them to you."

"Yes, M'm."

Blanche was guiding her inexorably towards the bedroom. Blanche was turning back the coverlet, settling the three small pillows into their triangular nest; drawing the curtains across the

7

sunlight. "Just ring when you wake up, and I'll bring your tea," said Blanche, as though it was an ordinary day.

Fade far away, dissolve and quite forget . . . This was the ritual phrase, spoken as regularly as a prayer, once her corsets were off and she was lying flat, with the chiffon scarf across her eyes; the old body aching less, the slower breath beginning. *Fade far away, dissolve and quite forget.*

Delicious magic. And a moment's flicker of surprise that she could embrace the sleep with such fervour when there might be so little time left.

Mr. Dutty's room was sparsely furnished. "All the easier to keep clean," Blanche Briggs told herself with determination. Dust in the corners; tomorrow she would face the task of carrying Mrs. Murray's vacuum-cleaner up three and a half flights: tomorrow, not today. The room seemed more abruptly bleak today than yesterday. It held a narrow divan bed, a small bedside table with a lamp on it; a chest of drawers and an armchair that canted sideways, having lost one castor. The black-out material was nailed along the top of the window frame. Mr. Dutty had made a careless job of it. Given time, Blanche decided, she would get it down and make it into proper linings for the flimsy curtains.

Plenty of space; a big wardrobe, full of old wire coat-hangers. The bathroom was across the landing.

Blanche bobbed to and fro, settling her possessions. The sense of freedom and relief was dwindling down. When the train drew out from Paddington Station, bearing with it the burden of Mary, Mary's nerves and Mary's panics, she had found the air suddenly, blessedly quiet. But the quiet had become forlorn, once she reached Ramillies Terrace. She had, most oddly, found herself missing Mary as she went from empty room to empty room. Foolish: Mary was quite impossible these days, poor dear. And it was foolish, also, the feeling of eviction from the Battersea house, her home for nearly twenty years. She was lucky to have this room; lucky in having the old lady to look after. (Though the old lady's extreme independence and love of organization made her a difficult charge. It was easy, taking command of the helpless Mary.)

Mrs. Murray professed to look forward to the air-raids. She maintained every precautionary device; sand-buckets; buckets of water; the stirrup-pump; the regulation shovel for dealing with incendiaries. She had bought what they called a siren-suit last September. These were not her only preparations. She had ordered three dozen bottles of red wine on Mr. Percy's account, the day Hitler invaded Holland. They were taking up two shelves and all the floor-space in the linen-cupboard.

One had to laugh.

Blanche dumped the string bag in the corner of Mr. Dutty's wardrobe. Certain items lived in the string bag from week to week. There was the gas-mask in its cardboard case. She had long ago forgotten how to fit the silly thing and – but for Mary – would have thrown it away before this. There was a small first-aid case, bought at the time of Munich and never yet opened. There were some candles in a box and some spare matches.

Where to store the package from Thomas? The notebooks would, obviously, be safer downstairs; safer from bombs, that was to say: in considerable danger from Mrs. Murray. "One day, when she's out, I'll find somewhere to hide them; some place where she wouldn't dream of looking." As Blanche lifted the package off the bed, the battered green canvas fell apart, a shell of corrugated paper yawned open and the foolscap books in their red covers spilled on to the floor.

No point in trying to wrap them up again. Best, perhaps, to put them in the string bag, to be seized quickly at the moment of emergency. She stooped and gathered them. One lay wide open: the two exposed pages were blank. A discreet flutter with finger and thumb showed that this notebook was quite empty. "No time to write in it, I suppose," she said to herself.

A grey melancholy came in with the thought; a gloom out of all proportion to the fact of an unwritten notebook.

Briskly rejecting the shadow, Blanche stored Thomas's property and dealt with the rest of her own. No room for her Bible next to the

9

bedside lamp. She put it on the mantelpiece. The photographs could go there, too. At Ramillies Terrace, she had made a severe selection; packing away most of her records; framed snapshots: the Hale family on the lawn and the little Mattingleys in the dog-cart: a dim dark face in a gilt oval, the boy she had promised to marry, dead at twenty-one: her father and mother on their silver-wedding-day: and of course, a whole gallery of Westons, from babyhood onwards.

She had brought the little one of Mary and Frank at Kenilworth. She put this on one side of the Bible and, on the other side, the folding leather frame that held three Weston pictures.

In the first panel there was the old honeymoon picture from Sawcombe, Devon, 1926: Mrs. Philip at the wheel of her car and Mr. Philip posed with his foot on the running-board. The second panel showed a newer one – though not so very new; it dated from the 1929 summer in France: Gerald, Sarah and Rab after a swim, perched on the rocks, with a bright sea behind them; three wet heads and three laughing faces, three angular young bodies darkened by the sun. This snapshot, like the honeymoon picture, had enlarged very well.

Into the third panel, after some careful trimming, she had fitted the studio picture of Thomas. It was quite new; reluctantly acquired on his last leave, because his father was badgering him for one in uniform. Thomas seldom emerged successfully from the photographers. Here his hair disappeared into a whitish blur; he looked as though he had no eyelashes at all and he was grinning lop-sidedly above the loosened battledress collar.

THE UNWRITTEN NOTEBOOK

THE JOURNEY BEGAN IN THE DARK, IN THE WOOD.
The wood had made itself important to me before this. Seen from
our position south of the river it was, I'd thought, like a mediaeval
design in tapestry: a neat little wood on a sudden hill, with a white
road curling round the base. It went up into a point; a cone of green
larches. You could see the silvery turrets of the château near the top.
The poor old château was just a shell of broken walls, but you
couldn't guess that from the river view. On a fine morning there was
the perfect tapestry. It reminded me of a dream I used to have as a
child; the gold men marching under bright banners; I could half-shut
my eyes and make them be there, on the road.

Not now. Not any more. We were patrolling the lower slopes of
the wood, picking our way through the trees, waiting for first light.
If anything came down that road it wouldn't be my army of little
gold men. I found I could go more quietly crawling; there was a
splendid smell of moss and fern and damp earth.

Through the trees, over to the North, the gun-flashes came like
summer lightning; I could hear the gentle thunder from time to
time. There was a quiet, final feeling in the air. End of a phase, as I
used to write in my notebook. It didn't take any gifts of prophecy to
know this today. The effect was to make me feel rather sleepy; the
last way you're supposed to be feeling when out on rearguard patrol.

The night-walk, I said to myself; this is the night-walk; prep
school again; prowling the forbidden dark just because it is the dark.
The Army had been reminiscent of prep school all along; well, no,
not quite; I was removed from prep school ages before I could
become a prefect. And subalterns were prefects, weren't they? Yes,
they were. A sobering thought. Despite Uncle Percy, I still felt I

wasn't genuine prefect material. I was playing some sort of game, obediently but without real concentration; I was doing that now, crawling through the wood, having light-hearted, sleepy fun. Roughly speaking, I was happy.

I tried to think about the matter in hand, but here I found thinking difficult. Easier just to wait and feel. Nobody knew anything, anyway. Rumours and orders amounted to much the same confusion. We were pulling out, we were getting back to the coast, we must go North by way of the bridgehead. Whoever gave that order hadn't seen the bridgehead: column after column converging on it in the dark, a shambles of men and material, an insane traffic-jam. Taking all day to shift, not shifted by nightfall. No more orders from Brigade H.Q. either; H.Q. appeared to have lost itself.

With any luck we'd find the last of the traffic-jam on the move when we got back. If we got back. The "if" didn't worry me. Every time I looked at the prospect of being killed I thought "Oh well" and went on to something else. *Not* a prisoner, though, I said to myself, couldn't be taken prisoner – wouldn't . . . Would not, could not, would not, could not, would not join the dance . . . There was a dragon rattling somewhere on the road, I could hear him; an iron-coated, heavy dragon. *"Don't dream, Thomas!"* echoed sharply from a long-ago classroom.

This was it.

As I moved abruptly, Rayner came close, making very little noise; he's a countryman, he moves like a cat. "Here they are – *sir.*" Always that little pause before he came down hard on the "sir".

"Sure it's them?" I asked him.

Rayner said " 'They'," on a note of pained correction, reminding me of Romney Butler, my King Charles's Head, as you might say: Rayner often did this. He added "Sure enough. Aren't *you?*"

"Better be safe than sorry. Get cracking; pick up Marrs and get back. Go like hell."

Of course he had to waste the seconds asking "Not you. – Why not?"

We'd worked it out ahead. But no tactic, no orders, no strategy would stop Rayner putting up one more question. I said "Because I say so," and this sounded so much like Nanny that it made me giggle.

He swooped off as silently as if he wore skis; the branches hardly moved behind him. I envied his smooth co-ordination, being clumsy myself except on a games-field.

(Clumsy as an owl flapping home half-blind, that's why you always got caught at the end of the night-walk, remember?)

No match for the dawn. I never was. And here it came. First light was the better description, I decided, watching the greyness filter the black. The first light ever, the beginning of light over the whole universe when God said the word. That must have been like this.

I pulled back, crawling a little higher up the slope. (Wait for it, wait for it, you won't have long to wait.) I fished my field-glasses out of their case. This was like any other blank, empty minute in that it gave my thoughts the danger of moving over to London. To London. Not to Rab. They, the thoughts, couldn't move over to Rab any more. I just couldn't get through. Often in these last weeks I had told myself stoutly, "Rab is my love, Rab is my girl and everything is all right." But I didn't believe it. Nothing was right, nor had been right since our one stolen meeting at Amiens. It was no use fooling myself and it seemed somehow dishonourable to try. (But keep your mind off London now, or you'll be into that old nightmare: the bombers black on the sky and you running through the ruins to get to Nanny before her house is hit. Don't go there in your head, just pray.)

I pray with one side of my head, automatically. Not sure if this is right, but it's become a habit. I engaged the other side with Rayner: that bastard Rayner, by the platoon's christening; not mine. Rayner's gentleman-ranker act bored the troops to death, but it made me rather sorry for him. I knew about his wife who left him and I knew the way he'd lost his money farming.

Gentleman-ranker, gentleman-farmer, gentleman-misfit (any misfit will always remind me of Romney). Gentleman-shit, said my Company Commander who mourned in my presence that there was no effective penalty for the bad boys out here. Tick them off, put them on fatigues, take away their stripes: all you could do, said the Company Commander with a groan.

Well, this morning at least I'd found a use for Rayner, bad-boy

Rayner, the man with the quick feet. Perhaps he'd get his stripe back. It had fallen to my lot to take it away.

One minute I was thinking about Rayner; alone among the trees in the silence and the greyness. The next minute they were there; I was looking down on them. The dragon's head and crest lay on the curl of the road below.

My first sight of them, ever. The Wehrmacht; right under my chin. It wasn't in the least alarming; just surprising. Head of the dragon, head of the column, halted. The dimness and the curl in the road together made it impossible to know what their strength was. Two motor-bikes, I could see, two armoured cars; a small solid mass of men; behind these, and high over their heads, what looked to be the snout of a gun, mounted. Then the hillside cut off the view. I couldn't be sure of the gun; through my field-glasses the picture danced and blurred in a film of grey gauze.

It was the crackle in the wood itself that got me moving; a crackle behind me, coming roughly from the point where Rayner had vanished. If it meant an advance patrol I was caught for fair. That was my way home. I couldn't imagine how they'd penetrated the wood on our side, but it might just have been possible in the dark. I didn't think beyond there. I went straight on up; aiming for the place where the trees were thickest, in the direction of the château.

A steep climb, but I managed it less clumsily than usual. I kept going with all the speed I could, until my breath gave out.

No sound behind me now. I strained my ears. Absolute silence. I went on again; the moss was soft and slippery but I felt safer and safer in the grey, sweet-smelling forest. I began to think I'd imagined the advance patrol; a deer or even a large-size rabbit could have made that noise.

Then the trees thinned out; too quickly for my liking. I peered ahead. I was standing at the edge of a grassy jungle; a wild, waist-high jungle that stretched for about fifty yards. The dim bulk looming beyond it must be a part of the château itself.

How the devil would I get down from there? I didn't know.

There was the brief, lonely chirrup of a bird waking in the trees; and then the shout. This sounded more like a dog barking than a human voice, but it was human all right. It brought me down flat on my face. I hadn't a clue where it came from; somewhere down the hill; I wished I had Rayner's country-trained ears. I began crawling as fast as I could through the jungle.

Old, stunted rose-bushes grew there, half hidden; they snatched at my belt, at my respirator, at the strap of my field-glasses; they whipped my face; they jabbed my hands. I wallowed and butted, knowing only that I was through the jungle at last when my tin hat struck hard against a stone. Nice loud clang it made, too. But nothing happened. I saw three worn steps. I went crawling up them; there wasn't a door at the top, just an open arch. It led into a shadowy passage that ran between solid walls; surprisingly solid, blessedly dark.

Safe again, for the moment. I sat on the floor, leaning against the wall, getting my breath back. I had nothing to worry about, except me. Rayner and Marrs would be there by now with the signal.

Better explore, I told myself. I took off my tin hat and my boots; I crept along the passage close to the wall. The stone floor felt like ice under my feet; there was a chill, abandoned smell here. I stepped on something soft and dead; a rat, I thought. Every few minutes I stopped to listen.

My groping fingers felt the wall come to an end: a cornerstone on each side: the passage led into a huge darkness. I stumbled down a step and stood still. It was safe enough now to flash my torch around. I saw the channel of a stone sink running along the wall; an enormous rusty stove, with a pile of rotted sacks beside it. Hanging next to the stove there was some kitchen stuff that looked mediaeval in the extreme; a great iron hook, a pan, an old spit: cobwebs wreathed them over.

The beam of my torch found a door in the far wall. The door was big; solid wood, studded with rusty iron. Leading where?

I switched off the torch, put on my boots again, adjusted my tin hat and gave the door a shove. It yielded at once, swinging open with a loud creak to let the sunrise in. I stood dazzled, blinking at a red dawn. Before my feet the smooth coblestones began to shine.

Down to my left I could hear the barking voices. They came up very clearly; now a motor engine roared and bubbled; there was a grinding of gears, the crunch of brakes before the engine cut.

I dragged the door to. It creaked abominably.

Yes, then. I was going to be caught at the end of the night-walk, as I had somehow expected. I felt a deep responsive sigh shaking me inside. *All over; and you knew it.* How had I known? Not, I thought, from any magic message. Those messages, I'd noticed, seldom came through to me on the background of war. This was straight hunch. I'd gone out on patrol with a wry, cold feeling; the feeling the Northerner had before Gettysburg, in that book Rab loves so much: *What have you got today for a man with my name?*

In here, the dark wasn't dark any more; the sunrise came through little windows. Slot windows, thickly cobwebbed, high up. I retreated to the pile of sacks behind the stove. As I pulled my gun from its holster this seemed to me the strangest of all the strange games I'd played since last year: squatting on sacks behind a stove, in the corner of a mediaeval kitchen, pointing a pistol.

I could hear nothing. No voices. The engine hadn't started up again: all quiet. At least, as the minutes drew out, I could assume nobody had heard the door creaking. I kept my eyes on my watch; the luminous dial shone pale green. The first watch I ever possessed had luminous figures and some pleased echo was still sounding from the first time while I looked at this one.

I began to list the other things that kept that echo. Wet brown banners of seaweed on a sandy beach; a clump of red and white daisies in a cottage garden; any new penknife, particularly those set up on a card in a shop-window. I always have to be careful to distinguish between sheer nostalgia and the authentic pleased echo, which is – I suppose – more like the survival of a recording made on wax. I only catch it in a blink when my mind's loose and wandering.

What else? The taste of Devonshire cream; the smell of hay and the smell of a tennis-ball.

My conscience couldn't prod me with "Don't dream, Thomas!" (My Training-Sergeant's version was, I recalled, "Wake up – you dozy individual!") There were only three things to do. I could get back down the passage by the way I'd come, and out into the grass jungle again; I could make a dash for the unknown, by way of the cobblestones: or I could stay here. Staying here was obviously a dead loss, but so, I thought, were the other two choices.

End of a phase . . . Everything coming to an end? Including – possibly – the little list of first-time echoes in my head? Oh, well.

The door creaked and swung. A man stood there, looking in. He left the door open behind him and as he tramped slowly through the shaft of light I could see the details of his uniform: all highly familiar to me from the flat coloured poster on the wall of the platoon hut last autumn: private soldier, German, and the insignia to be noted. Quite an old friend, the uniform.

The man inside it was about my own age. His face was sleepy-eyed and thick-lipped. He carried his rifle slung. He was a sitting duck as he loitered there to gobble something out of the palm of his hand. What was he eating? Cherries; a handful of cherries; he spat out a stone.

Everything slowed up. The only thing I knew for certain was that I could no more shoot him than I could fly.

The knowledge came quite flatly, a revelation if you like, but there was no suddenness: it seemed to join on to other knowledge, making a logical full-stop to a sequence already begun. I was neither surprised nor shocked. I cradled the revolver, watching him as he spat out the last cherrystone. Then he raised his ugly helmet to give his head a good scratch: his hair was pale straw-colour, the same as mine. He settled the helmet back again.

I don't think I made any sound at all, but I saw him get the feel of my presence, like an animal made aware. He whipped his rifle up to his shoulder and came straight for the sack-pile. Then I was looking down his barrel and he was facing mine. The two barrels wavered. There was a kind of "Will you – won't you?" hesitation about us both. It made me laugh. The laugh seemed to shake him; he stared, pop-eyed, and I didn't see his foot come up to kick my wrist because I was watching his funny face. The kick hurt like hell; the pistol clattered on the floor. He got to it before I did.

"*Auf!*" he said. "*Raus!*" I was on my feet with the point of the rifle pressing between my shoulder-blades. He marched me out into the dawn.

The first person I saw was Rayner; Rayner with a lop-sided smile and blood trickling from the corner of the smile. "Sorry, *sir*," he said, "but I think Marrs made it."

My immediate reaction was disappointment. I heard myself murmuring "Marrs – not you. Why's that, do you suppose?"

The truck was the worst. It was a captured French truck, encumbering the column, moving at a crawl. Rayner and I were the only Englishmen aboard and because I'd got a bump on the head in my last struggle with the two privates who shoved us inside, it took me a little while to realize that all these cursing French soldiers were cursing us. Nothing personal: we were the sons of *Perfide Albion*, but those weren't the words used. The British, and only the British, had got them into this mess; they didn't say mess. French being my second language I could have cursed back, but I paid them no attention until the man who was groaning to relieve his bladder unbuttoned himself and did it against my leg. Rayner clunked him hard on the head, but that didn't stop him. Two Frenchmen got Rayner down on the floor; their bodies closed over him: he was shouting to me, but I couldn't hear what he said. My neighbour went on peeing. The corporal in charge of us, hanging on to the back board, laughed heartily as the hot stream of urine soaked my trousers and pattered on my boots. The corporal went on laughing: he was talking to me, not to any of the others; a jocular, one-sided conversation. As far as I could understand, he was offering me apologies; something about an officer being treated with more respect once we were clear of the column.

Lucas, I thought, would probably kick him in the face. The hatred of Lucas for Germany and all things German is a passion. It interested me because I never before met an all-embracing hatred. I had heard *'Les Sales Boches'* from childhood onwards: my father always called them Huns. But Lucas, now . . . "I loathe their music, I loathe their cities, I hate their bloody Black Forest. I hate Heidelberg. I hate Einstein. I hate Kant and Heine and Wagner. I hate their dreary, boring efficiency and I hate every one of their Goddamned refugees. As for their language . . ."

He had once, he told me, been persuaded to take a ski-ing holiday in the Austrian Tyrol. When he got out of the station there was a horse-drawn sleigh standing in the snow; two rosy-faced old men wearing fur caps sat there side by side. According to Lucas he was just finding the sight rather picturesque and amiable when one old man said to the other *"Ja, ja, natürlich."* At the sound of the language Lucas had turned straight back into the station to wait for the next train home. "It's a phobia – like snakes or spiders," he explained merrily.

I wondered if I hated the corporal. Or the officer up at the château. I didn't think so. I had fought the officer for my wallet; the rest of my property I'd told him he could have, with my love and a kiss, but not the wallet with the snapshots inside. I'm sure if I hadn't got into a rage and punched him he would have given it back. But those rages come too fast; I can't stop them. Something about his fingers meticulously turning the snapshots over set this one off. And after that there was plenty of rage left for the two men frog-marching us downhill to the road and shoving us into the truck. (A bad example to Rayner. I'd told him often enough to learn the art of self-control.)

Now rage was out of me. I was too dazed, too sore, to summon it back. I simply wanted the corporal not to be there; just as I wanted the peeing Frenchman not to be there. The only solution, of course, was for me not to be there . . .

Our driver suddenly cruised into a ditch and we were still. Those of us who could get our heads out craned to watch the stuff go past. I saw two gunners aloft, with little bunches of corn and poppies stuck in their buttonholes. They looked happy, excited.

I heard Rayner's voice again: "You all right, *sir*? No end to this bloody column, is there?"

Certainly it seemed to be going on forever. Odd, I thought, the unreality of the grey-green and the swastika; the tanks and the guns. Here I was in the middle of their armour and I couldn't assimilate the thought. They had nothing to do with anything, somehow; I couldn't take them seriously.

"Of course you can't. They're the hostile tribes."

The whisper came from childhood; from the game Rab and I used to play, long ago. One never got caught by the hostile tribes; by adults at the end of the night-walk, yes; not by these imagined enemies; they lurked, but one could always dodge them, or dissolve them with a lethal sprinkling powder. The hostile tribes, I murmured to myself, only the hostile tribes: I began to feel better. I didn't believe in any of this. If Rayner chose to believe, that was his business. He had worked his way back to my side. As usual, he seemed to know a great deal. He knew where we were headed; back to the base-camp, to a prison camp, to be shot, to be rounded up for transport to the Reich; and nobody need think we'd have the assistance of this fornicating cattle-truck for long. At the crossroad (which crossroad?) before the village (which village?) we should be turned out to slog it on foot.

A motor-bike careened sideways and crunched to a halt behind the truck. The rider growled at the corporal, the corporal swung himself up beside me and we were on the move again. We moved fast. Once free of the rear of the column, the driver went hell-for-leather; the truck jounced and swayed. The motor-bike roared along behind us and Rayner cursed the bumps.

As we took a bend the truck rolled in a skid and we all went slithering. The corporal, knocked off balance, fell backwards and I was hurled past him into the gap his body left. I could hear him swearing down by my feet; I could see, below me, the movement of a yellow-green cornfield in the wind, the field itself pouring past. Now. There was just that one word. *Now.* I never looked at Rayner: there wasn't time. I jumped for it. Over and out with the wind in my face before the ground flashed up at me. The last thing I heard was the shot.

The shot went on and on. It was chasing me through the darkness, a swift, pursuing pain. After I had outrun it, I slept sound.

HOLLYWOOD AND NEW YORK

AROUND THE BRIGHT BLUE SWIMMING-POOL THERE LAY the bright brown bodies: the radio crackled behind the voices, the loud, inescapable voices.

"This is the end of it."

"Looks mighty like the end of it."

"End of Europe – Europe signing off."

"Paris tomorrow."

"Paris tomorrow – London in seven days. That's my estimate. Anybody want to bet?"

"Lousy sons of bitches."

"Mean the French or the Krauts?"

"You can have them both for my money."

Philip Weston, deciding that he could take no more of this, arose from his chair beside the pool. He sauntered along the patio, aiming for the bar. Idiotic to come to the Country Club today, he was telling himself. The sound of feet was padding after him. "Mr. Weston, excuse me —"

Philip turned to see one of the boys from the pool; a tanned youngster, pudgy and smooth all over, his stomach like brown rubber cut by the white belt of the swimming-trunks.

"I'm Billy Tucker – a friend of Sarah's. I just wanted to say Hello."

"Well, hullo," said Philip flatly, dreading a word of sympathy. But the boy didn't mention Thomas. He said "Sarah won't get to drive that ambulance in France now, I guess."

"Doesn't look like it."

"And she was hell-bent to go, wasn't she?" Tucker said. "I tried to talk her out of it."

"Well now you won't have to do that again, will you?"

"I never thought they'd fold so fast. I'd have bet on them. I was in France two years ago. What would *you* say Britain's chances are if France goes?"

Oh, he was too stupid and puppyish to arouse this cold anger. But Philip could find no civil words and so said nothing at all.

"One thing – this'll make a whale of a difference to the American attitude." He looked as if he expected Philip to reward him with a bone. The phrase had been in regular use since the invasion of Holland. "No more anti-war talk, I mean," the boy said eagerly. "Everybody's waking up around here."

"About time, too."

"She won't try to get to England, will she, Sarah? Wouldn't make any sense." (Wait for it, Philip told himself. Here it came.) "She'd only be another mouth to feed."

"Why, so she would. D'you know I never thought of that."

The sarcasm went over the curly dark head.

Billy Tucker said he would call Sarah now; maybe she would like to go some place this evening, take her mind off things. At which point Philip ceased to be angry and felt sorry for him, because Sarah was surely dated and the brown rubbery boy seemed to care.

Escaping, he crossed the patio and found the cool dimness of the bar an immediate consolation. The sunshine was inimical just now. Nobody here; all quiet save for the little drilling torture of the radio-announcer's voice: the barman had the set turned low but Philip could still hear it as he walked between walls of mirror-glass to a table in the corner. He saw himself reflected many times, a sequence of Philip Westons, and his thought was the repeater-thought of many years: "Nobody could take me for anything but an Englishman." He sat down gracefully opposite himself sitting down gracefully. And he looked upon an ageing actor whose jauntiness was a mask, whose sad brown eyes stared, without hope, from the mask.

Not one of the chosen roles of a lifetime, the Gay Cavalier, the Lucky Fellow or the Laughing Philosopher could meet this hour. He had disowned them all. Far away in distance, far away in time, the young Philip Weston who fought at Loos and Mons gazed reproachfully down upon his successor in Hollywood.

"You'd only be another mouth to feed . . ." The prize cliché of the moment.

Philip lit his pipe and focused his thoughts sternly on the ballade he was writing: he had begun it between takes in the studio yesterday. Had they been shooting this afternoon he would doubtless have finished it, instead of loafing around at Bel Air, going crazy thinking about Thomas. The opening stanzas had earned their laughs from the British Colony last night.

> I thought it must be time for me to go
> – with better men – to serve my country's need.
> But sympathetic voices told me "No.
> You'd only be another mouth to feed."
>
> I sought the Consul with my tale of woe,
> He shed a tear, but gloomily agreed:
> "You're over age and out of training, so
> You'd only be another mouth to feed."

With Paula, he had begun to score the number of times they all said it. Not for Billy Tucker's ears – that he had in fact caught himself saying it to Sarah last night. Well, any father could, he decided, be excused for saying anything to Sarah as she was last night. Doggedly he pursued the theme.

> The patriot who yearns to face the foe
> Must first of all divorce his belly's need
> and learn to live on air until – good show! –
> at least he's not another mouth to feed.

Hardly satisfactory. He used to be a good lyricist; in his own view; Paula had never thought so.

Deserting his muse, he wandered to the table where the newspapers and the magazines lay out, arranged in a wide, orderly circle. There was a consecutive rank of *Life* magazines, neat as a hand of cards overlapping each other on the green cloth. May the Sixth was the one he wanted – and didn't want. His fingers moved in spite of him: here it was: the cover-photograph showed an R.A.F. gunner in uniform.

Philip turned the pages. He read the words THE LAND OF FRANCE and, below, the sub-heading: For It A Devoted People Gladly Live And Die. All over, now – or nearly over. Had *Life* chosen the theme in salute, or in prophecy of imminent doom? The photographs were heartbreaking: Normandy, the Loire, Vezelay; the Gorge de Daluis, familiar road to the south. And one, the first, set above the headline, more heartbreaking than all the rest. *Pavés de Flandres*, with the rain-wet cobblestones, the small sparse trees, the glimpse of dark, patient roofs and poplars in the distance, under a cloudy sky.

I was there – once.

Thomas was there.

Where is he now?

You didn't, if you valued your reason, go further. But you went on trusting. Or tried to. Just as you tried not to take a drink too soon. He loped across to the bar and the barman said at once "Hello, Mr. Weston. Any news of the boy?"

"Still missing," said Philip curtly. "That's all we know. Mind if I use your telephone?"

"Help yourself."

Paula's voice said "Where are you?"

"Out at Bel Air. Anything from England?"

"Nothing. There's a letter from Portugal; Miles."

"I don't think I want to hear about Miles," Philip said pettishly.

"You don't have to. But I'd come home if I were you." She meant "Come and drink here, not there." She was right, which he tried not to resent. He said "On my way. Let's dine somewhere magnificent."

"Oh my love. I can't. I'm on again at six."

"Damned if you are. Why are you?"

"Pinch-hitting for the redhead. The war-news has gone straight to her stomach."

"I like that," said Philip, "I like that."

"At least," said Paula, "You'll agree it shows a healthy change in the American attitood."

He chuckled. Sometimes she was expert in soothing him. "Where's my neurotic daughter, do you know?"

"Walking the dogs. Morale slightly improved. She's dining with a Britisher."

"Englishman," he said. "You're slipping, aren't you?"

"I beg your pardon; Englishman. Hurry now; this is no time to be alone."

She was right again. But just for the minute ("that's as long as we are in it" and how long was that?) he couldn't feel anything but alone.

Paula hung up. She sat on the sofa in the shabby, chintzy room whose windows looked out on a sprawled garden. The garden, like the room, was not strictly within the Hollywood convention. If your eyes skipped a yucca, and a humming-bird lancing at the lilies, you could almost make it an English garden.

Within the room some signs of the expatriate were present; among them the 'English Castles' calendar, the beer-barrel, the war-map, and the silver cup won for sports; engraved with the school crest. ("The one thing I never tried to pawn," said Philip.) This, the ground-floor apartment of a two-storey house, had turned itself gradually into home. Here, Paula thought, their past and their present had lived at comparative peace until the world exploded. From last September onwards she had felt the walls cracking, and the floor. Today her own insanity of restlessness was unbearable.

A fleeting look in the glass gave her, as always, the decline of beauty. She no longer cared. She only looked to make sure that her face needed no fixing for Philip's return. She saw the touched-up hair, metallically gold; she saw the lines and the hollows; the square-set blue eyes with the blue shadows beneath. Her sustained verdict "Elegant, but haggard" still held good. It was disheartening, though, to find such a total, if temporary, lack of interest in oneself. It made her feel like a ghost haunting the room.

She deserted the mirror for the round, glass-topped table that stood under the window. Below the glass there lay a kaleidoscope of snapshots; the children from different times and places: Gerald,

Sarah, Thomas and Rab; with a few of Nanny and one of the Grandmother. There was less and less comfort in this pilgrimage to the table, this ritual round-up. But one went on making it just the same. There were two sorts of heartbreak here; Thomas and Rab.

Rab at least was safe; so far. Rab's laconic "Okay" had followed the cable telling them Thomas was missing; "And is it an exaggeration to feel Philip has hated me just a little since that moment?" Paula asked herself, not waiting upon the answer. She had never been happy delving below human surfaces; she found the practice worrying and slightly indecent. But the question hung around.

Her eyes stayed on the snapshot of Rab in uniform; the cocky, boyish face and the cropped fair hair. Every day now she caught herself wishing she hadn't drummed the lesson of courage into her child quite so consistently. The Book of Golden Deeds, Knights of the Table Round – this was where they got you. Rab the crusader was all her own work. "And at Rab's age, damn it, I'd be doing the same thing. Don't I wish I were?" She walked around the table until she came to Thomas the small boy, sitting on the sands at Sawcombe, with his arms around his knees, knees hunched up to his chin; grinning widely at the camera.

"You've got to be all right, d'you hear?" she said to him, "For all of us – see? And you will be. You were always the one who knew the answers."

Beyond him, overlapping the corner of the beach, set at an appropriate angle, was the one who looked as though he knew the answers: Gerald, glossy-headed, nonchalantly posed with his ukulele. "You louse," said Paula and felt better.

She hadn't said it on the telephone half an hour back. Not because she feared her elder stepson; simply because he embarrassed her into silence. Speaking from New York, Gerald had sounded more than usually clipped and purposeful. "Mary and I have decided to fly down to Bermuda as soon as the show closes. I feel it imperative to go and sit under the Union Jack."

"And if that's all you feel, I guess it's your affair, chum," she thought. "Not mine." Here, below the glass, she met the eyes of Sarah, looking up thoughtfully from a manuscript-book on her knees, Sarah at twenty-one; a dark and dreaming beauty; contriving somehow to look like a tragedy-queen before tragedy ever hit her.

"And I'd rather have Sarah, for all her threshings, than Gerald keeping cool," Paula decided. The sight of Philip on the garden path gave her a guilty, separated feeling. Spying upon his children . . . Plainly ridiculous after fourteen years, but the thunder in today's air shook all sure foundations. Though she had said "This is no time to be alone," she could still feel lonely in his company. "Maybe that always happens when it comes to weather as rough as this."

She saw him now smiling at her determinedly, acting away with all his might. He was still a good-looking man; some traces of the dark dazzler endured. Since his current picture demanded a moustache, he was very much the English gentleman. Across the years an old voice sounded: "Every *American's* idea of the English gentleman" and something about his needing a toupee after twenty years. (It was the voice of the impresario Chester Groves; Chester's diagnosis had been correct. The silky hair-line was receding fast and the toupee was mandatory now.)

Some blazing plan had occurred to Philip. His kiss was given on the run as he shot towards the drink-tray. "Bumped into Nigel just as I was leaving the club. He thinks it'll be quite easy to get Nanny over. She'll be a godsend with the children on the boat, and earn her keep looking after them here."

"What children?"

He snapped his fingers; she knew all about the scheme; the Actors' Orphanage scheme, didn't she? "Yes, you do. Well then you weren't listening. We're bringing over more kids, as many kids as we can." He went through the details again and she still wasn't listening. She interrupted him – a habit she had never lost, a habit which still made him angry. "Better find out Nanny's views before you start anything."

Over the rim of his glass he gave her a look of pure hatred.

"Oh darling, use your head. Nobody her age can possibly dig up roots and come to Hollywood *now*. She'd think you were crazy. Said that before. You can tell from her letters – and Grandma's. They wouldn't dream of moving. Bombs or no bombs. There's only one place to be at the minute – and that's where they are. And that's where we ought to be."

"Oh, is it?" He was furious. He had begun to twitch and shiver. "All ready to pack up and go, are you? *'All change here'*" he flung at her. "Good, sound commonsense view. You'll be quoting Sarah next. 'If they're killed, *I* want to be killed.' Is that the notion?"

"Don't let's quarrel tonight," she said. She went to him and hugged him. "I'm sorry, sweetheart, I'm sorry. I love you."

He was, thank Heaven, adult enough to turn off a temper in time: quite a trick, she thought while he kissed her hair.

"Trouble is," Philip said reluctantly, "I know how you feel – and how Sarah feels. God, what I'd give to be there."

"But what sort of war-jobs could we get? What use would we be?" She could take the other side, the sensible view, though her heart wasn't with it.

He murmured, "A fine is imposed here for the first one who uses the word 'another', 'mouth' or 'feed'."

"Oh certainly," said Paula.

"If I were Gerald —" he groaned.

"If you were Gerald you'd have your wrist in a steel handcuff, attached to a stout length of chain. At the other end of the chain you'd have Mary Castle. Suit you? He called, by the way. They're off to Bermuda next week. To sit under the Union Jack."

Philip said "Damn it, is he a man or is he a mouse?"

"He's Mary's breakfast, lunch and dinner. Believe me, I once said she wasn't a husband-eater. I must have been crazy."

Philip went roaming around the table with the snapshots, glass in hand. "Thomas was always the pick of the bunch," he told her. "Taken me long enough to realize it." He sighed, a low, rattling sigh. For a moment she thought he would break down; instead he groaned at her "Why the hell aren't there any grandchildren? That's what we ought to have – grandchildren." He sounded as though it were her fault. "And I don't believe Rab'll ever marry Thomas, even if he does get through all right," he added, on a continued note of blame. It would be foolish to tell him not to take another drink. He took it. She glanced at her watch.

"I must go, my love; sorry."

"You can be late."

"No, I mustn't be."

"It's iniquitous – expecting you to —"

"Yes, I know, just can't be helped."

"My God, why do you always have to interrupt? Well, all right, if you insist on going I'm coming with you."

"Darling – the dogs. Sarah'll be bringing them back any minute."

"Damn the dogs . . . where's Miles's letter – you said there was a letter."

(And you said you didn't want to read it.) Picking up her bag, she found the letter. At the door she turned to watch Philip reading; he was wearing the expression reserved for Miles, eyebrows lifted, lips set in supercilious distaste. It was the distaste from long ago, accelerated. Miles the eccentric chauffeur had been headache enough for Philip. Miles grown ample and prosperous, living in Europe, was an object of horror.

"Hasn't heard about Thomas," Philip said, throwing the letter aside.

"How could he, in the time? I did write to him; think maybe I ought to write again, to the new address."

"Sold his farm and bought a canning factory – fellow's one great bluff, if you ask me. D'you believe a word he says?"

"I did believe that. Canning. Portugal, after all. Sardines. And anchovies," said Paula vaguely.

"No need for him to talk like a bloody tycoon."

"He always did. I'm off, darling."

"I see you are." Suddenly he smiled: "And I can't do without you. Think I'll come up to your slave-galley and eat there. If Sue doesn't want the dogs she knows what she can do about it. Bless you, my sweet."

Paula walked up Harper Avenue, passing the Garden of Allah Hotel on her right; crossing Sunset at the junction that faced the Château Marmont. She turned left, walking two more blocks down the Strip.

The place to which she had given most of her energies in the last ten years was a fake log-built cabin called Sue Brown's. Inside there were the bar and the griddle; small tables and an atmosphere so cosy you could choke. Sue herself dated from Paula's schooldays. Having divorced three Californians to Paula's one, she was in a strong financial position. Just after the crash in '29 Sue had proved herself a good friend, offering this job to Paula the amateur. Now the institutional phrase was, "Anything you like to ask, honey, just so's you don't leave me. I'd be lost without you."

"Me too, without this," Paula thought now. "More than ever, these days." The work made for an old, a constant, fight with Philip. "All very well when we were broke – when I was still free-lancing. Now I'm under contract what's the point of wearing yourself to the bone?"

He had forgotten her lifelong compulsion to fill every minute, to crowd the time. And he still overspent like a drunken sailor. Her salary helped.

(Two-eggs-once-over-lightly-bacon-and-French-fries-one-hamburger-with-medium-rare-one-tuna-on-rye-toasted.)

Sue's clients were mostly the writers, small-part actors and minor executives. She had made the place into a virtual club. A mad Anglophile, she gave the visiting foreigners cut rates. At one time Philip had resented this patronage and loathed Sue. A convinced man-hater, she was always telling him to get wise to himself, laughing at his act. After the third Scotch they would cease to be on speaking-terms. Not any more. He fed Sue the Scotch to light up her anti-American fireworks. She had the noisiest contempt for her own country's neutrality.

Which was all very well for Sue, thought Paula. It came badly from Philip, who had made his home here.

Everything, at this moment, came damn badly from one's nearest and dearest. Didn't it? She listened to the uproar at the bar; not a fight; just the crescendo of talk that made Philip declare all drinking Americans should be fitted with silencers. The noise, the crowd, were consoling, somehow. She had heard the old cliché about feeling lonely in a crowd, but for her it had never rung true.

"Hi, Paula — Any news?"

"Not yet."

Unlike Philip, she was grateful for the sympathy. Carrying a plate of sandwiches past one table, she heard a voice explaining "Not *her* son – Philip Weston's by his first wife – Paula's stepson."

Life at the moment might be simpler had she and Philip achieved a child of their own. How old would he be now? Twelve – thirteen, maybe. A focus and an anchor for them both. Returning to the griddle, Paula found herself looking a long way back, to her dream-family: a bunch of little boys with large fair heads, like Thomas.

Having chosen her companion simply because he was British-born, Sarah now found him all the more infuriating. He was Walter Ash, the composer; a large gentle Jew with a calm of manner that brought one Dick Abrahams to mind. Walter Ash had worked here for two years now. In movies, of course. Was there anybody, in-habiting this circus-tent, this World's Fair encampment of plaster and parking-lot, Neon and palm-tree, Drive-in and swimming-pool, who was unconnected with movies? Walter Ash said he liked Holly-wood. "Why not? It's a convention to pretend one hates it."

"I think you must have a happy nature." She studied him care-fully. Late in his thirties; going bald too soon; velvety eyes, charm-ing smile, bluish jowl. Slightly over-civilized and a person respected at Chasen's; they had one of the better tables. He was, obviously, intending to invite her into bed later on; meanwhile, as the argument warmed up, he adopted a manner of affectionate punditry.

"My darling child, as far as the war-effort's concerned, people like you and myself have no significance. Do you really feel Churchill pointing a finger all the way across from there to here, saying ENGLAND NEEDS YOU? I don't."

"I hate you," said Sarah.

"Of course you do. Because I'm making sense. For you at this moment it's indecent to make sense."

"Don't you care at all?"

"Of course I care. But I'm allergic to hysteria; particularly Holly-wood hysteria, which is what you're suffering from, along with several thousand others. This is the moment of storm," he said, dealing tidily with a soft-shelled crab: "One must simply sit it out."

"In comfort and safety?"

"Why not? Could I stop Hitler tonight? No, I couldn't. So I

31

might as well stay where I am and enjoy my dinner. So might you. Make an effort, now. No wonder you're so thin."

"If you had a brother —"

Walter Ash wagged his head at her. "I'm also allergic to the *argumentum ad hominem*. I had it all last winter, taking the blame single-handed for the phony war at every party. A forest of wagging American fingers and one theme-song: If You Were The Mother Of A Dead Finn . . . Suggesting to me nothing so much as a counter at the Mac Fisheries. You must have been on the receiving end for some of that too, weren't you? Forgotten? The unattractive Russians beating the gallant little Finns?"

"Well, whose side were *you* on, for Heaven's sake?"

"I wasn't there," said Walter Ash. He leaned over to refill her glass, adding as he did so that drinking didn't help.

"Don't be absurd, of course it does. Why else does anybody drink?"

The affectionate pundit said "People as beautiful as you are should be protected from the bottle."

If they save Thomas I'll never take a drink again.

But they wouldn't save Thomas. Of this she was sure. That was the next thing waiting. Almost a year of the wild dark walk begun when Romney died; and the wild dark walk was leading only to there.

Steadily she drained her glass. What was so damnable about this stage of the walk was to look back with deep nostalgia to its beginning; to the purity (it seemed now) of her own grief. To the simplicity of that: one was clean and brave with that. She saw herself in far perspective: Sarah in her trance of tragedy, sailing from England; Sarah the stunned, the stricken. She saw Sarah back in America with Romney's ghost for company; talking to him aloud, stretching out her hand in the pretence that his hand was there to hold; still wearing his watch on her wrist. She saw Sarah waking to the hopeless tears left by a dream of him; Sarah kneeling at her bedside every night, praying the crude prayer: *If there is anything I can do for him in this world or the next, tell me, please tell me.*

The person who prayed looked – from here – to be good and lucky. That one had said to herself again and again, "Thomas was right; you can't be angry with Romney. No anger – no resentment. Nothing but pity, nothing but sorrow." Saying, "He did it for me – not for himself; he refused to be a burden to me." Steadfast in mourning, that one, and faithful to God. (Not to the God of any one church, though. To the church, suicide was a sin and Romney damned.)

She went on gazing enviously at Sarah the widow; come to California to be with Paula and Philip, the sad, privileged guest.

All that was betrayed. The simple pattern had begun to break as the New Year came and the pull of England grew stronger. That was the time, of course, when one should have gone home. Yet one had lingered, trying to write a book, striving to dredge up the old, lost talent; forever delaying the return to a London without Romney. There was the switchback move from one side of her head to the other; stay-here, go-home, stay-here, go-home; the onset of the drinking and the threshing.

It was always the arrival of letters from England that switched her to the Go-Home side. Nanny's round handwriting from Battersea; the grandmother's resolute mixtures of the pious and the practical: "This is the thirty-fourth day of my Perpetual Novena and Blanche flatly refuses to carry her gas-mask any more." The letters from Thomas had beckoned. (That hurt the most now; one's own idiocy for missing all the chances of seeing him again.)

"But you wrote to him; he wrote to you," Walter Ash persisted. "You'd made your peace."

"I can't get over being so mean, so bloody; it's unbelievable now – that I left England hating him."

"Why go back to there?"

"I always had to say I was sorry again – every time I wrote. Guilt doesn't stop just because you've said you're sorry."

"Well in that case I can't see the point of saying it again and again, can you?"

"Please don't be so sensible."

"Then please don't be so stupid. Try to stop lashing yourself, there's a good girl."

"At least I thought I could shoe-horn myself out and get to France. Drive an ambulance, like Rab."

"That's decided for you now."

"If I had to earn a living, it would help. I've got too much money – Romney's money. And I ought to send all the dollar-assets back, not just half."

"Do you imagine you're the only person out here who's dodging Treasury regulations?"

"I'm the only one I think about. Thomas said I had the rare habit of contemplating myself all the time without getting the smallest pleasure from the process."

"Meanwhile, I get considerable pleasure from contemplating you."

The steady approach begun, she thought. Did it matter, the trivial journeying from one bed to another bed, this growing easier after the first time? Oh yes, it mattered. (Talking about Romney in other men's beds; he had become a routine stage property in the act of fornication: a cardboard figure, the true figure diminished now; she had lost the right to mourn him.)

"The night I met you was the night before I met Romney," she said thoughtfully. "Remember? Mary's and Gerald's party?"

"Of course. I remember leering at you across the top of the piano."

"The beginning," said Sarah, drifting with it, drifting back. "The day before the beginning. *Love Is Nothing New*. Whistle it for me – will you please?"

The composer didn't whistle his tune. He looked meditative: "I'm told I ought to conduct a survey to find out how many people I put to bed with that one."

"After Romney died I used to stop my ears when I heard it."

"But you want it now."

"I want anything that can remind me of being *honourably* sad."

"That," said Walter Ash, "strikes me as masochism carried to its most exquisite point of precision."

"Other people's misery always looks like masochism."

"*Touché* . . . It does. When we go back to my apartment I'll sing and play for you. The whole score, if you want it."

When we go back to my apartment . . . Not 'if'; not 'perhaps you would like . . .?'; just 'when' . . .

34

"And let me make it quite clear that I haven't the slightest intention of trying to seduce you, much as I should enjoy it if I succeeded. Why not? Partly because I'm far too arrogant to want to rank as just one of your sins. Partly because you're something of a wandering star at the minute. One should leave wandering stars alone."

"You're very intelligent, aren't you?"

"Very. Some strawberries? Or just coffee? Would you like your friend Morris Ward to join us? He's all by himself."

"Not my friend, really. Gerald's friend. Or he was," she said.

Walter Ash murmured, "Yes, darling, we all know about *that*," as the dramatist came up to the table. Large, pale and silver-haired, he loomed beside it, refusing to sit down.

"I can't, I must go to bed. I've a six a.m. start tomorrow. Sarah darling, is it true about Thomas? How utterly bloody. I'm so terribly sorry. God, I hate this war." He went dejectedly away.

"Why are you laughing?" Sarah asked.

"He contrived," said Walter Ash, "to make it sound like a persecution directed solely at Morris Ward."

The last of the tunes rippled gently off the piano. Walter Ash sat on, looking at her.

"And now," he said, "I'm going to drive you home."

"Thank you."

"And remember – though it may sound like heresy, you'll get over Romney's death. You're too young to live in the grave with Ophelia. I know, because I had it happen to me."

"To you."

"Yes. When I was twenty-one."

"Why didn't you say so before?"

He laughed. "Perhaps I should have said it before. I thought I was sounding rather too knowledgeable about everything. We'd been married almost a year, same as you and Romney. She was killed in a car-smash. I was driving; I wasn't hurt much. The mistake one makes, you know," he said, "is in running away. That's the mistake you made. Inevitable when one's young."

"Where did you run to?"

Walter Ash looked benign. "My first step was towards the gas-oven. Fortunately I was sharing a friend's flat. He came in and turned the taps off."

Sarah said, "You're braver than I am."

"Why?"

"I just can't do it. I've thought about it, but I get no further than thinking."

"Which proves, *I'd* say, that you're braver than I am. But there's nothing brave about rushing off to Europe and impaling yourself on the war. That," said Walter Ash, "would be just another runaway. From this."

"Then what," she asked humbly, "should I do?"

"My knowledge doesn't extend that far; one day or another day you'll wake up and find you're alive again. You can't see it coming, it just happens."

"How?"

"I can remember quite clearly. I lost my temper. Up till then I didn't think I had one left to lose. I suddenly minded. I saw a woman hitting a child on Hampstead Heath. I just remember thinking 'By God, that won't do!' and being surprised at the sound of my voice yelling at her. That was the moment. Yours may be quite different. But it strikes like lightning," he said, "when it comes. Wait for it."

Dear Sir,
  My prophecy is that Hitler will blitz Great Britain into submission in three weeks, and then we shall hear what loud-mouthed Mr. Churchill has to say.

"I thought," said Gerald Weston, "I had forbidden any publication of the Hearst press to intrude under this roof." Carrying the newspaper between finger and thumb, he walked to the window and dropped it out. He watched it part into flapping disorder, blown this way and that across the gulf of Sixty-First Street down below. The apartment being on the fourteenth floor, the newspaper took its time.

"How nice it would be to do that with Anne Morrow Lindbergh," he murmured, returning to the breakfast-table.

"I wouldn't," said Mary, "start quite so early in the day, my darling. Bad for your insides."

Gerald gazed upon her, wondering again at the power of his hatred for so exquisite a creature. Mary wore apple-green pyjamas and her new hair-rinse was russet-gold. Idly he contemplated slapping that face, the triangular face, the archetype with the wide grey eyes, the magic smile, the skin of a baby. Slapping hard . . . There was a pleasing touch of blasphemy in the project. Were she another sort of star, a queen of classic drama for example, one of the theatre's great ladies, the blasphemy would somehow be less. Mary was the darling, the honey, the sweetheart, just about everybody's favourite girl. To say you hated Mary Castle would be on a par with saying you thought Abraham Lincoln a son of a bitch.

How long had he hated her? He reckoned it up, lifting a sliver of crisp bacon in his fingers, biting it delicately. How long now? Thirteen months. He could remember the exact moment, the exact place, where hatred began. (Or perhaps, his mind said now, the place where it had been first acknowledged.)

It was the night before the summer closing of Jay Brookfield's *Call For Caviare*. The two of them were walking away from the stage-door, to supper at Sardi's. As ever, the fans had milled around them; and the last of the autograph-books he signed was held out to him by a willowy, white-faced boy with dyed hair. Gerald could not now remember what he had said to the boy, but this had provoked Mary's small, deep chuckle, a squeeze of his arm as they walked off; and then the lapidary words: "Sure you wouldn't rather take *him* to supper?"

One moment after, she had been all grave eyes and tender, loving apology; apology so complete that it cancelled itself out. "Unpardonable; ungentlemanly, can't imagine what made me say that. I don't deserve to be forgiven. I love you so."

37

She had never known the truth of it; the truth was standing alone inside his head, a sentinel saying, "I hate you. I shall hate you forever."

It was a moment of power.

It had given him the illusion that he could escape: that he could run away to star in the movie of Morris Ward's *Little Victims*. He remembered the London reunion with Morris; a brief encounter and a happy one. All over, as soon as he saw Mary again. When he blamed the war, and the movie's cancellation, for his failure in escape, he was lying to himself. He had been defeated by Mary alone: by the absolute iron below the honey.

So, back to Broadway, and – last January – their second smash hit and here they were again; poised for the summer closing, linked as the perfect lovers.

One half of a headline romance hating the other half; interesting. In the detached compartment of his mind he studied the notion.

He thought of Romeo hating Juliet, Abelard hating Heloise, the Duke of Windsor hating the Duchess and presently of Darby hating Joan. The team that was Mary Castle and Gerald Weston could never split. Cast as perfect lovers, perfect lovers they must remain. In these roles they belonged not to themselves but to their public, their backers, their business-manager, and their tax accountant.

It was idle to fool himself that he fooled Mary. She knew. Never a word, but she knew. She was, in this situation, far cleverer than he; putting up a performance of great skill, a non-stop, night-and-day performance. This obliged him to follow on, to compete; reluctantly admiring, pledged and committed to match her skill, just as he was pledged and committed while onstage.

There was no quarrel, ever. Even in these suddenly hideous weeks with Europe alight, there had been no quarrel. Her mood was steady. Mary took no all-American line, the line some British actors were taking. She said simply, "God knows I'd go home – if I could."

She worked like a slaving angel for War Relief. She was on every committee and every platform. But she felt no shame, as he felt shame, for being here. When he strained at the shackle, there it was again, the iron below the honey. "My darling, I know what you're going through. Me, too. But our duty's here. We owe this country so much. You can't quit any more than I can." And then the sad laugh; the laugh she used in public to usher the same phrase: "Not exactly a heroic war-effort – earning dollars for Britain, but one that's mighty useful."

"Mark you," Gerald said to himself, eating another slice of bacon, "she's kept a lot quieter since we heard about Thomas." There he had to cut the reverie. His last meeting with Thomas stood out too sharply; his own voice, imitation-Brookfield: "Would I be plagiarizing anybody if I called you a bloody little prig?"

For want of something better to say, he said "I love you."

"And I love you," said Mary. "And I love Sunday in New York. And this time next week we'll be in Bermuda. Fellow here's written a terribly moving poem about Paris. *Open City* . . ." She began to read from the paper:

> Now take our last salute, the sunset gun
> firing on darkness. We remember, we
> who watch your lights departing one by one
> along the river into history.

There were tears in her great eyes. Gerald said "'Your lights departing' strikes me as a touch visceral. Why not 'your liver'?"

As always, she caught up with his mood. "That dressing-gown's dreamy," she told him. "If we weren't closing, I'd suggest you wore it in the bedroom scene instead of the black and gold one."

"Saks," Gerald said. "When my morale sags, I go to Saks. Sags. Saks." He poured himself another cup of coffee. He sang cheerfully, from the musical *Higher and Higher*:

> I'll buy everything I wear at Saks,
> I'll cheat plenty on the income tax.
> Heavy with highballs,
> stewed to the eyeballs,
> just – disgustingly rich.

but he broke off, depressed at once. There was a boy who died a long time ago, a boy called Gerald Weston, who had thought money meant freedom. The foolish fellow. Perhaps not so foolish; that one would never have married Mary Castle.

The telephone rang. When the operator said "Hollywood calling Mr. Gerald Weston" his nerves prickled. The subject of the possible Hollywood assignment was delicate in the extreme. Though of course Mary had handled it beautifully so far: "My darling, if they really want you, don't imagine for a moment I'd stand in your way." A British wartime picture; of course it wouldn't happen: only a few months' escape, but it wouldn't happen. Somehow she would manage to outwit him; he had to fight to prevent himself looking forward, dreaming the days of solitude and freedom, down to the last luxurious detail.

There was some sort of hold-up on the line. He could hear the operator saying "Go ahead please" and "I have your party for you" and still silence at the other end. Then there was Paula's voice saying, from a little way off, "I'll tell him, darling; give it to me," and before she spoke again he knew what there was to be told.

"Gerald. This is the worst," she said, her voice light and level. "We've just had a cable."

"Thomas?"

"Yes. Taken prisoner and then shot, trying to escape."

Now Gerald heard himself saying to Mary in a formal tone, "I hope you won't mind if I ask you to leave the room."

THE UNWRITTEN NOTEBOOK

"EH BIEN, IL VA MIEUX, NOTRE EMILE, NOTRE PAUVRE Emile?"

Two voices. Who's poor Emile, I asked myself, and who are they? They had, it seemed to me, said this before, and it must be a joke because now, beyond the dark, somebody chuckled softly. I heard a door shut. It was a very long time since I had heard anything at all. Wasn't it?

In a moment I should remember. The dark was solid, the dark was a bandage across my eyes, keeping them shut; I could feel it pressing the lids. There was still somebody in the room.

"*Essayons – donc.*" he said and there came a small rattling noise; curtain-rings, I guessed; then the sound of his feet. Fingers groped at my face; a hand slid under my neck. The bandage was unwound. I looked out through a double blur as though I were using badly-adjusted field-glasses. Above me I saw a duplicate head and shoulders. Behind these there were four pale squares of window, weaving together, then sliding apart.

"*Clignez. Clignez encore.* Bleenk," the duplicate head instructed me. I blinked; the binocular focus began to improve. Two fingers waving became one finger near my nose. I followed the finger's progress while it drew slowly away. It prescribed an arc and at the top of the arc I saw a ceiling that sloped with exactly the same slope made by the ceiling above the bed in my attic room at Ebury Street. Gradually there assembled about me the early-morning shape of a different attic room: cloudy but certain; a little room with a huge dark cupboard pressing up to the end of the bed. Two tiny windows moved in. The man had only one head now. Since he stood with his back to the grey light I could barely see his face, but it seemed to be smiling.

"Lucky boy."

That's a ringside-seat, lucky boy . . . Up you come, lucky boy . . .
Words out of an old dream, my dream of the two theatres, usually
most difficult to recapture, and I chased this memory until it
vanished, the way it always does.

"All the same," he said, speaking French, "I should have liked an
X-ray."

Obviously he was a doctor. I knew now what must have happened. I had got myself run over. It was always going to happen.
Nanny and Paula had warned me again and again. I had the habit of
straying across any road without looking either way. Several near-
misses on the cliff-road at Sawcombe, I remembered, when the bus
came by. And since this was a French doctor I must have done the
trick at last on the road outside our villa, between Anthéor and St.
Raphael. Not very clever. And the ruination of a summer holiday.
Oh well . . .

"I don't mind being X-rayed," I assured him, "But I suppose it'll
have to be done in hospital. Can I go in the car with Miles or must it
be an ambulance?"

I didn't hear his answer because the double vision had shifted; it
was inside my head, not outside. The villa, the Twenty-nine summer,
I said to myself – but I've *had* that, and the sloped ceiling in Ebury
Street comes afterwards, quite a long time afterwards: goodness, I'm
mixed up, and the thing I am afraid of is beginning to happen, what
is the thing? Pain, yes, that is the thing.

I knew about pain. Once I thought I had the power to take it
away, didn't I? Surely. But when and where? Something to do with
Romney. *Pain was Romney's property and Romney is dead, so I've
inherited the property. It lives between my shoulders; quite a small cross of
pain; I don't want it to grow bigger and grow claws and turn into a
swastika.* I knew it was liable to do that.

"Can't we have an X-ray? It feels as if something's broken,
nothing grave, you know, but something small – at the back –
here."

"Lie still. *Bougez-pas.* You speak French marvellously well," said
the doctor. "Do you know your name?"

"Of course. Thomas Weston."

42

He repeated *"Veston,"* and this brought back a joke from the Twenty-nine summer . . . The Waistcoat Family.

"But now," he said. "Your name is Emile, you are called Emile."

"Why am I?"

He didn't answer; he was explaining my injuries; a cracked shoulder and two broken ribs; these were no cause for anxiety. It was the head-injury that still troubled him a little, since he had the reputation of being a fusser. He became highly technical, telling me why he would have liked to X-ray my skull and my dorsal vertebrae. He had thought, originally, that my skull might be fractured, though there was no bleeding at ears or nose: no paralysis. A very severe concussion, an unusually long period of unconsciousness and I had been slower than he expected coming out of the semi-coma.

"But your vision is perfect. Once more now, try again." The finger wove around and I followed it with my eyes; the light was stronger at the little windows. I could see the doctor's face, a long face, amused and melancholy at the same time; a Jewish face; he reminded me of Leo Clyde, but I couldn't place Leo Clyde . . . Didn't I mean Abrahams, Dick Abrahams? That was somebody I used to work for . . . *Don't dream, Thomas.* First things first.

"What on earth have I been doing to myself? Was I run over?"

"You don't remember? Nothing at all?"

"Well I remember a lot of things but they won't settle down."

The cross between my shoulders was widening out.

"You can't remember how it happened? No. You don't know how you got here? No. Nor where you are? No." Every time he said the "No," he nodded.

"It's a month ago, now," he told me. "Four weeks and three days."

"Honestly? *Sans blague?*" The right arm of the cross was growing a claw; I could feel it dig into my shoulder-blade; a sharp, metal claw, hotting up.

"They found you in the ditch. At the foot of the field."

"Who did? The family?"

"Yes, the family. They thought you were dead; later, when it was dark, they went out to bury you. And when they realized you were alive they carried you up here."

"What a funny way to do it. I mean no proper funeral . . ." (Brigstock, I thought, would have been furious about that.) "And why wait till it was *dark* to bury me?"

The doctor gave me another melancholy smile. *"De peur des Fridolins. Naturellement."*

It was the word *"Fridolins"* that rang the bell. And about time too. Perhaps because that word had been buzzing around in the truck, it latched on to my last memory before the lights went out. I remembered my leap through the air, and the cornfield. I remembered the shot running after me through the dark.

"Good God, yes. *Yes*." The truth made my head go round like a gramophone-record. Questions came hurtling out of me:

"What happened to Rayner? Did Marrs get back? Did they blow the bridge? Where are they now – the Battalion?" The doctor shook his head each time. "But you must know – *somebody* must know," I said and then I began to groan because the pain had suddenly become the most important thing. All four claws of the swastika were eating into my back.

"Quiet, quiet, please," he said. "One little minute." He knelt down, out of my sight. Then I became aware of an old, established pantomime; the tinkling sounds, the flame, the syringe lifted up. The movement of the plunger. I had wept for the pantomime, I remembered, implored and wept, while somebody's hand across my mouth choked my sobbing. He made the casual jab high up on my naked shoulder. I remembered this too. His face watching me while I waited for the glorious moment became as familiar as Brigstock's face, bending over me to say good night.

This was familiar too; the doubt; the feeling of sentry-go; waiting for it to work. Then it began, the camphorated warmth flowing wide under my skin, sinking deep. The kind invasion swept over the swastika, there was no more swastika; the claws let go; the cross vanished away. It was a miracle of happiness. As I mumbled a thank you to God, the doctor laughed and I knew this, too, had happened before.

"Toujours pas Catholique?" he asked. Then he kneeled on the floor, which was where he kept the tin box that held the drugs; under two loosened boards. He bobbed up again; he looked quite stern and cross.

"I must tell you, that's almost the last of the private stock – and I can't get any more. But you don't really need any more. This is in the nature of an indulgence. A treat to celebrate the return of your wits, I trust undamaged, I believe undamaged – though, as I have told you I am by nature a fusser."

I lay bathed in clear, light-headed peace; peace resounding; funny place to find it.

"What's happening in the war?" I asked.

"Finished, the war," said the doctor. He drew the curtains across the little windows and went out.

Held up, triumphant, drifting on the gentle tide, I considered these words. My mind was lucid; more than lucid; it was like a burning glass held over the moment of now. *Finie, la guerre*. He meant for me, of course; finished for Thomas *Veston*, lying in the attic room. Was I as badly hurt as that? And why had he called me Emile?

"Don't think," my voice said aloud. "Don't think. Thinking is a waste of the miracle. You're in the magic zone; don't waste a second; sail on while it lasts."

I shut my eyes. The way was open all across my world. I could go where I pleased: to London, to Sawcombe, to the Twenty-nine villa; to Miles's restaurant above the Vence road; anywhere. It was easy: not so much a journey as a beckoning of the map to come to me, knowing it would obey. In the golden hunting of the past made present, I could find them all again; Brigstock, the Grandmother, Gerald; alive and vivid. Now I hit a boundary off Taylor's bowling; now I swam with Sarah from our red rocks. Neither the living nor the dead were barred to me. Here was Romney, with his look of a querulous eagle; his wild eyebrows. He smiled at me; the voice was authentic, strong in my ears. He said, "I was always going to do it, you know."

"Going to kill yourself?"

"Oh, yes. It was always waiting for me, that. Not your fault, so don't you think it."

"I do think it, though. Sometimes."

"Because you couldn't heal me? Quite absurd." The harsh, metallic note came into the voice.

"I shouldn't have tried."

"I made you try. You didn't want to. Foolish young man. Listen – if I hadn't the intention, why should I have carried the morphine with me all that time?"

"I've wondered."

"You needn't. People like you don't know about people like myself. *Accidie*. You wouldn't understand." He twitched one eyebrow.

"But is it all right now?"

Silence.

"*Romney* – is it all right now?" My voice was loud; no answer came and I knew he wasn't there; nobody was. One question too many and each would vanish like that; leaving me heckling the air. But the next minute there would be another voice, another landscape.

Blue water, a harbour basin with small boats rocking, and I had come to Rab's island; the island I've never seen except in photographs. I saw it now. I went up the grass knoll towards the little white house with the pointed roof. For a moment I thought it was Rab coming down the knoll to meet me, Rab in a white shirt and blue dungarees, with the yellow feathery dog Tylo bounding after. But this bright vision flew away. They were not there any more, neither Rab nor Tylo; the island house had vanished. Amiens now, grey-brown city with the snow still hard on the rooftops and the March wind blowing. I turned away from this. The golden hunt was at an end. I slid off to sleep. Presently, with a dry mouth, I awoke and remembered. Our single afternoon, Rab's and mine, stolen out of war.

I had never expected it to go wrong.

I'd built up the prospect to a tremendous peak; to a childish, first-day-of-holidays peak. I'd lain awake for it; I'd sweated for fear it wouldn't happen after all. Our last-year slogan was still sounding: "If you see me before I see you, just whistle and I'll be there." We'd written "Just whistle," at the end of every letter since July.

I was lucky to get to Amiens. It wasn't easy; in fact damn' difficult. Lucas, our Adjutant, German-hating Lucas, was the one who fixed it up for me. He knew there was a girl involved and this amused him because he had, he said, earmarked me as a virgin. (Some of Lucas's talks with his junior officers would give Uncle Percy's kind of soldier a go of apoplexy.)

So, thanks to Lucas, I got my twenty-four hours and a railway warrant. Rab failed to see this as an achievement. She was not, apparently, subject to army regulations. The exact purpose of the American drivers' unit remained mysterious to me (and, I thought, to her. "A raft of keen, dedicated girls in khaki milling pointlessly around" she wrote.)

All the vehicles, including the ambulances, were allotted for service to the *Comité de Quatorze*: which suggested to my mind the Grandmother's Fourteen Holy Helpers, but was in fact a welfare organization, founded during the '14–'18 war. Its headquarters were at Vaillancourt-sur-Aisne, fifty miles north of Paris. Once Rab reached Vaillancourt, she began threatening to descend on Battalion H.Q. as though I was at boarding-school and she was a parent coming to take me out to tea. Distance, regulations and petrol no object. (But we laughed about this in our letters. Shall we ever laugh again? I wonder . . .)

At the last minute but one, Rab ran into trouble with her Commandant, the Emily-Brontë type, Lisa Groves. I got this information in a tangled-up telegram and plunged into the gloom that makes people go out and get drunk; I only don't do it because drink deepens the gloom. Then there was the last-minute telegram saying everything was fine again; thanks to an American reporter. I'd no idea what she meant and I didn't care.

I was on top of the world. Amiens under the lingering snow was Samarkand. The town and the cathedral were familiar from one of our excursions in the Twenties. The hotel was familiar; the whole doomful scene came back as I walked into the foyer. My father having a row with Gerald because Gerald owed him five hundred francs and refused to admit this; Sarah having neuralgia; myself knocking Paula's Café Liégeoise off the table with a clumsy movement of one elbow; there seemed to be far more of it on the carpet than could ever have got into the glass. Rab, I recalled, had missed the doom; she was off somewhere with Miles.

But we'd called it the Doom Hotel. I only remembered that now, walking in. Perhaps the hotel would deny having reserved a room for me. Some Priority type would have pinched the room. No. All well, but I couldn't go up yet; not before two o'clock; the room wasn't ready. I made grateful noises and signed the register.

We had said the bar. I was an hour ahead of time and something told me I'd have a longer wait than just the hour. For all her current privileges, Rab would continue to be late. It's a gift. She inherits it from Paula. Once you know that's how people are made, you stop worrying. I pushed my way happily through the crowd in the foyer; all uniforms except for occasional *fonctionnaires* carrying those oddly inscrutable briefcases that belong only to the French and look as though they had nothing inside.

I walked down a pinkish-painted corridor; to where a glass panel said AMERICAN BAR. I tried to be cool and collected; pretending it wasn't Rab whom I should meet here, but somebody quite ordinary. Who was the dullest person I knew? I picked the A.E.C. Colonel who gave us a lecture at Sandhurst. Then I got sorry for him so I switched to the nearest problem in sight: why were all bars in European hotels called American bars? "Why's that, do you suppose?" I was saying to myself as I walked in; my heart pounding away.

The bar was jammed: uniforms again, but the drinkers were mostly standing up, crowding the counter; I found an empty chair that faced the door. I would sit here and cover the door.

I didn't want to blur the impact of Rab with as much as one drink. I wanted to stay quite still and watch the last minutes that separated us, drawing off, going by. Defeated minutes, I thought, falling back in disorder. Time had defeated us for eight months: today we were the winners. I piled up my greatcoat, respirator and tin hat on the floor beside the chair. I lit a cigarette.

Then I saw her. Two French officers moved away from the bar; and there was Rab sitting on a stool talking to somebody just out of my sight. She wore khaki uniform; she looked even more like a boy than I remembered. This much I took in, as I plunged through the dazzle of the moment to find her. I was thinking "If you see me before I see you" (but she hadn't done that; it was the other way round). I put my hand on her shoulder.

She turned her head; she jumped down off the stool and there before me was the face I loved, grinning at me: the wide blue eyes and the short nose, the bumpy cheekbones, the unpainted mouth. The collar and tie fitted her neck precisely. As a rule I think women look rather odd in uniform, but Rab didn't. The clothes simply removed her a little from the girl I was waiting for, the girl I used to know. Her comical stare reminded me that she hadn't seen me in my fancy-dress, either. I don't know how long we stood and stared, grinning, holding each other's hands.

I hadn't noticed the second girl. Rab introduced her as Virginia Something, the war-correspondent. She was dark and thin and lively; she wore battledress and she was based on Vaillancourt for a week; with her own allotted car; this was how they'd managed to outwit Rab's Commandant. (Too much talk of Virginia Something, I thought in a dazed way. Did I care if she worked for Grant Parker, the New York publisher of three great magazines, *Point*, *Steer* and *Democrat*? I didn't. I only waited for her to get cracking and leave us alone.)

"Champagne-cocktail? On me," Virginia Something invited us.

Still holding Rab's hand I looked for the ring. I'd bought it two weeks after she left London; having searched stubbornly for one that would suit her, for a stone the colour of her eyes. I'd got it at last from Cameo Corner; an aquamarine, in a thin, antique gold setting. I thought it was beautiful; it cost a mint by my standards and I worried for weeks in case the shop had made a nonsense of posting it to America. It was an enormous relief when her letter came, saying she loved it.

But where was it now? Perhaps uniform ruled it out. I would have to ask her as soon as Virginia Something left us.

Things . . . the importance of Things had always been inclined to haunt me. Not necessarily things of my own. The Grandmother says I've no sense of property, but I have in my time become deeply attached to an old shirt, to notebooks of all shapes and sizes; likewise to my scruffy little toy animals, which I packed up most carefully and lodged with Brigstock before I came overseas. Idiotically, I worry about things that don't belong to me at all; things that stay in shop-windows unbought; things people throw away. (The minute when Sarah threw a gold pencil into the sea was so agonizing that I had to go diving after it.) Crackers, I've said to myself time and again, you're crackers. But it still goes on. My worry now was for the ring itself because Rab might have lost it. I saw it lying somewhere in a field or a dark place and nobody coming to look for it.

We clinked our glasses. Virginia Something joined in. Rab said "Well, we made it," still holding my hand.

Then it was all talk of time-the-present; it had to be. We swopped our local logbooks, we traded rumours and grumbles and funny stories. I thought that women at war sounded much like men at war: this waiting stage suited neither. The crusaders merely marked time, grew bored and lost sight of the crusade. The icy winter had lowered their spirits. In the absence of shot and shell, they gave room to illnesses and personal problems. Women were undoubtedly worse there, Virginia said, and Rab agreed.

We arrived somehow at leadership. They talked of a woman called Noel, head of the Vaillancourt outfit, always at odds with Lisa Groves and an *enfant terrible* in her own right. But a leader, so to be admired. Not by me, I said, I mistrusted a Führer who could also be a rebel: it sounded stupid.

We might never have had any other existence, Rab and I. The whole of last summer with its dark ending, Romney's death and the hateful inquest, our final goodbye in the rain; these things, I thought, might never have happened. (And I might never have been your lover, nor you promised to marry me: this shining, precarious today is all we possess. But good enough, once Virginia leaves us. Oh Rab, I love you so.)

Virginia stayed to eat lunch with us. By now, on two drinks and the news that she was off to an assignment with a French unit some twenty miles away, I felt better. And very hungry. Lighting into the first really glorious food I'd eaten for ages, I would, I said eat myself to a standstill. "Always the champion eater," Rab explained to Virginia. "First day we met he stole my ice-cream. Swallowed his own in no-time-flat and then grabbed mine."

"No, I didn't," I said placidly.

"You did, too. A fudge-sundae."

"I know that. But you've got it wrong."

"Come again?" said Rab.

"Completely wrong. What happened was that you didn't want your ice, you were bored with it, so you gave it to me."

"Oh so that's the way it was, was it?" She had forgotten; she was laughing at me; she really did believe I'd taken her fudge-sundae.

"That *is* the way it was. I distinctly remember your saying 'Have mine' and Tubby Whittington telling me I wouldn't be hungry for the picnic if I ate two ices. And I said I could eat tons and tons of absolutely anything. Which is still the case," I added, loading up with *coq au vin*.

Rab winked at Virginia; the wink made me quite cross and when Virginia winked back I was crosser still. I thought "I don't like the way she smokes or the way she moves her elbows; and her cuff-links are enormous" (though why this last should be irritating, I couldn't imagine.) Rab was saying "Okay, Thomas darling, just so's it makes you happier, I gave you my ice-cream: proof of a beautiful nature."

"But that's what happened. And nothing to do with a beautiful nature, you just didn't want it."

"Okay, okay," she patted my hand. "Let's leave it right there, it doesn't matter."

It didn't, of course, matter. But the next thing mattered very much. Rab wasn't staying overnight. She couldn't: old Emily Brontë Groves would raise hell. Virginia was coming back for her after dinner and they would drive through the black-out to Vaillancourt. This, when Rab had laughed away all obstacles; especially mine. I wished she had told me at once, in the bar. And then I remembered – across several years – my having to break news of the same kind to my girl-friend Carola. Carola had said I chose the wrong moment to tell her and I'd said, "There isn't a right moment for telling those things." Correct. I sat silent, trying hard to be good about it.

But there is, I thought, a casual intimacy between these two now, as Virginia rises, pushing back her chair; the See-you-later, the

Got-enough-dough? The dark eyes and the blue eyes meeting; this I do not like, nor Rab's head turned to watch her go.

"She's fun," said Rab, "don't you think?"

"I haven't really thought."

"Such a bad liar, you always were. You've been hating her guts from the first minute."

"Oh well . . . Not hating, just wishing she wasn't there."

"I couldn't have made it without her. Sorry, darling." Her tone was dejected, lifeless and at once I was sorry too. I ordered the coffee. We held hands while we drank it and soon we were slipping back easily, our past closing over the No-Man's-Land between Vaillancourt and Battalion H.Q. Family talk. We grieved for Philip and Paula's long-distance worrying; and for poor sad Sarah drifting around Hollywood. "Sort of appointed penance," I said, "Sarah's the one who was always homesick for England. Not Gerald." Gerald, said Rab, would be all right any place, any time; self-sufficient, he was.

"But lonely."

Rab stared at me. "Nobody married to Mary Castle could be lonely – be illegal, wouldn't it? Why do you say that?"

"I just think he is. But Sarah's the one I wish would come back."

"Maybe she will. Once the blitzkrieg gets going."

"She sounds sort of mixed-up. Does she write to you?"

Rab shook her head; adding "I don't blame her."

"Why not?"

"I told you I called them to say goodbye, before I sailed. When I talked to Sarah I made her quite mad. I said to snap out of it all and do something useful. Not very kind of me, I guess."

"No. Not very kind."

"Well she would play her old record – the one about being cruel to you. That girl eats remorse the way kids eat candy."

"Oh Lord," I said. "As if I hadn't told her again and again. It was absolutely natural for her to hate me. In her view I'd killed Romney. And sometimes that's my view, too."

Rab let fly, as I knew she would. But it was a loving fury. Afterwards we swopped our letters from Brigstock, which were very good as always, and Rab took the one-eyed silver lion out of her breast-pocket, setting him up beside the sugar-bowl. I'd given him to her so long ago; the first, the only present I ever gave her; before the ring, that is.

"Where's your ring?"

"I left it with my bank on the Vineyard. So scared of losing it, my finger's just too thin; it did slide off once or twice and I nearly went crazy."

This annoyed me. "You could have it made smaller," I said, "Couldn't you? Perfectly easy to do that."

"The jeweller takes weeks. He'd have had to send it off-island. I couldn't bear to let it go."

"Well but you've let it go now, haven't you?"

Here she became plaintive and wide-eyed, saying she'd hoped I would be pleased with her for doing something so sensible. And here, belatedly, I remembered Carola's rule about making love first and talking afterwards.

The room was huge; all dusky green brocade and marble and mahogany; with a yellowed chandelier hanging from the ceiling. The windows were swaddled in black-out stuff. There was a gilt-framed mirror above the mantelpiece; a marble hunting-dog at one end of the mantelpiece and a marble goddess at the other. Rab hung her cap on the goddess.

Was it really all right? Afterwards we swore it was, and we've sworn it since, in letters, but I still get the feeling that it wasn't. In retrospect our love-making looks like a one-sided business, just me being selfish, because the first time I didn't hold on long enough. I simply couldn't – I had been without it for eight months and I came too soon. It was splendid, but only for me. And then I could have slept forever beside her. I kept saying I was sorry and then going to sleep. The second time it was all right. After this I remember lying in each other's arms, curled up, warm and drowsy; talking about marriage and fixing a date in April, skipping over all the things that stood in the way. Here, we said; we'd be married here and take our honeymoon in Paris and go to London and we didn't believe in the Blitzkrieg, we thought nothing to this war anyway, no future in it, we said, and no fighting. Then she slept, and so did I. It was her voice that woke me; she was saying "Do you mean that? *Really* mean that?"; she seemed to be shocked.

"I was asleep. Was I talking?"

"I'll say." She switched on the bedside lamp and stared at me.

"What about?"

"About the Army. All about the Army."

"Not very surprising. If I'd talked about the Navy, now . . . You look so *alarmed*."

"Prison, you said; prison, and then prep school."

"Oh well, it is rather like prep school."

"You went on and on about judging people. Who asked you to judge?"

"I don't know, I'm sure," I said, imitating Brigstock: "I suppose a certain amount of judging has to go on."

"But you sounded as if you were in agony. You said you couldn't judge anybody: nobody must ask you to. Something to do with the witness-box. Don't tell me that old witness-box is still on your mind?"

"Ho," I said. "It is, you know. Sometimes. I'm a perjurer. You're going to marry a perjurer." I tried to make light of it because I'd obviously worried Rab.

"Who's Rayner?" was her next question.

"Rayner . . . Bad-boy Rayner. He's one of our problem-customers. I had to take his stripe away last week."

She said in a muffled voice, "Wish you didn't have all these dreams. I never dream."

"They're quite fun as a rule. What else did I say? Come on, darling, why was it all so terrible?"

She lay with her face in the pillow. "Said you were going to be shot," she mumbled.

"Did I? Truly? There now, fancy that."

"It isn't funny."

"A firing-squad, was it?"

"Oh honest to Pete," said Rab, exasperated. She turned over on her back, but when I put my hand on her she only sighed and held the hand in a close grip. She said, in a vocal-cord-gloom voice, not unlike my father's voice when he quotes:

54

"There is no future.
There is no past.
There is only this hour and it goes fast.
Hurry, hurry, this is the last."

Rab not being one for quotations, I was interested.

"John Brown's Body. Stephen Vincent Benet. It's gotten to be my Bible," she explained.

"Doesn't sound a very cheering Bible."

"I've brought it for you anyway," she said. "I want you to know it too. It's important."

There was an overtone here. I said "Why is it important?"

"Because it's all of war – all of everything." She sounded unlike herself, making me ask "Who put you on to it?"

She paused before she said "I found it at Vaillancourt."

The worst thing didn't happen until we were dressing; at some speed because the hotel had turned off the heating; outside the bed the room was icy. When we voyaged up to the mantelpiece to look in the glass and get our ties straight, Rab gave the marble goddess a slap on the bottom. I stroked the hunting-dog's nose.

"What's the news of Tylo?" I asked her. "Tylo all right?"

Rab didn't answer. I was looking at her reflection in the glass. It was a smoky kind of reflection, the glass being old and flawed. I turned to look at her real face. She had put a vizor down.

"Skip it," said Rab. "Will you, please?"

"Has something awful happened?"

"I said skip it."

I put my arms around her. Leaving Tylo had been her King Charles's Head. All last winter's letters were full of Tylo. He was a one-man dog and he'd starved himself nearly to death during the weeks she spent in Europe. This time she'd given him to an Island chum, who loved him. She herself had seemed quite happy about it when she wrote to tell me.

But I could guess now that Tylo was dead. I hugged her. I said "We won't talk about it. But I do know, I do understand."

"No, you don't." She pushed me away. She walked into the middle of the room; she stood there, buckling her belt. Then she stiffened, with her arms at her sides, lifting her chin. It was the attitude of one ready for punishment. I remembered it, from our childhood, whenever she got into trouble. Philip used to call it The Boy Stood on The Burning Deck.

"I lied to you," she said.

"All right, darling; that's your business, don't worry."

"But you'll find out. That darned wave-length of yours, or you'll dream it or something."

"Rab, I don't want to know."

"Well, you're going to know. It wasn't true about giving him away. I shot him."

That silenced me. She went on standing there, rigid, with her arms at her sides; her face was expressionless; so was her voice:

"I played with him on the shore all morning; we had a good time. In the afternoon when I took the gun he thought we were going after rabbits. He didn't know a damn thing about it; I'm a good shot. He wasn't looking my way; he was barking at a squirrel in a tree. I buried him under the tree."

She still wouldn't look at me. Her face was very white. "Hot or cold," she said, "it was the only thing to do."

I'm so damned slow and stupid sometimes; I was now. There isn't much difference, if you come to think about it, between having a dog 'put down' and killing him yourself. Rab had talked of having Tylo 'put down' and although it saddened me, it had never shocked me. This shocked me. I couldn't see anything in my mind but Tylo, alive and happy, barking under the tree, and Rab pointing the gun at his head, firing, smashing the life out of him. The life, I thought. Nobody has any right to take life away, not like that.

Under the light from the yellowed chandelier I saw her face. She was looking at me as though she were afraid of me.

"You're angry, aren't you?"

I didn't know what I was; I just couldn't say anything.

"Guess I ought to have had the guts to tell you long ago. Why not? Easy, why not. I knew you'd hate me for it. Well, say so, for the love of Pete."

Still I said nothing.

"Never told you I could shoot. Every time it came up, every time it *could* have come up, all I could think of was you being sorry for a lot of rabbits. So I kept quiet. I was right, wasn't I? Shooting Tylo was the toughest thing I ever had to do, but you don't care about that, you don't give one good goddamn about that." She had begun to pace about the room, hands in pockets, not looking at me. "So you can't judge people?" she said, "Fine. Absolutely fine. What else are you doing – right now? Judging me, aren't you?"

It was no moment for a rage. When the rages come, they leave me out, I'm not there any more: this one was a tornado taking over.

Not until long after, not until I had finished cursing her and we were both in tears, did I realize how completely I'd wrecked our only day.

The wrecking was to last.

For all our vows, our *written* vows, our reassurances, each of us taking the blame and each swearing we'd forgiven and forgotten, the thing was still there. It would be there, I knew, until I could see her again. I began to understand what Sarah had meant, writing to me from America: "I read your letters over and over, and I ask myself why absolution on paper somehow doesn't take. This isn't your fault. They are all of comfort and kindness, the letters; but I shan't feel truly at peace until I've looked you in the eyes and heard your voice."

To look Rab in the eyes, and hear her voice; that was all I had wanted, as the snows went and spring came with a rush. Here was April, my old friend April turned enemy, because Rab wrote less often. I wrote more often. I spent most of my spare time with the book *John Brown's Body*, loving it as she did and getting much of it by heart. The book was my April adventure. I began to wonder, sorrowfully, what hers might be.

Now the question was haunting me again. Odd, perhaps, that it could still torment the new, battered survivor who was myself; here alone in his attic room:

What happened to you in April, Rab? Shall I ever know?

IN APRIL

RAB CRAWLED OUT FROM UNDER THE TRUCK. SHE WIPED her oily hands on a rag and lit a *Caporal bleu*. She sat on the step of the truck; relaxed, sleepy, at ease in the spring sunshine. The tune was playing in her head: no tune at all, really; a home-made melody to which some familiar words had set themselves.

> This is the last,
> This is the last,
> Hurry, hurry, this is the last.
> We dance on a floor of polished sleet
> But the little cracks are beginning to meet
> Under the play of our dancing feet.

It was the talisman tune; holding off the future.

A glorious, unusual quiet surrounded her. Nobody here. Not a sound, now that she had ceased her own tapping and tinkering. From the old stable yard where jeeps, trucks and ambulances had moved in (their wheels quickly wearing the moss off the stones, their ugly backsides protruding from converted horse-boxes) she looked out through an archway, across a flagged terrace, to the main door.

The main door of the Château de Vaillancourt was given a certain wistful importance by its height from the ground. A double stair-way led up to it: a lyre-shaped stairway with a curving iron balus-trade. From where Rab sat, the arch precisely framed the door and the two flights of steps: there was, on each side, a width of purple-red brick, making a border. The shadow of the chestnut-tree (the tree itself invisible from here) flowed across the steps on the right-hand side. There was, Rab decided, something highly satisfactory about the view. Why? She tried to think why. Because the composition was neat? Because of the light and the gently-moving shadow? Not entirely. These things were outside and some of her content came from inside. She paused here, not wanting to think nor look too deep.

That particular danger was new. Reverie was a habit gaining steadily, gaining but still to be mistrusted. (One used, automatically, to do what one was begging oneself to do now: sprawl in plain physical enjoyment, the job being done; taste the tobacco, look at the view, lazily, with eyes that were only lenses; think – if it could be called thinking – about a bath and a change of clothes, all in good time.)

All in good time.

The tune subsided; a phrase from the same book, the book that had become a Bible, came instead:

You had a good time in this funny war.

A good time, for Heaven's sake, Rab said to herself; in this world of women; set about with women, drawn into the pattern, one of the crowd? She had shied away so long (it seemed so long) from close company. She had made a policy of escape, of skimming surfaces; she had preferred things to people; she had liked doing and not talking . . . That Vaillancourt should prove to be the end of the cool way, the solitary way . . .

"Vaillancourt – are you crazy? Nothing to do with Vaillancourt. That way finished last year, with Thomas."

She was shocked. The part of her mind being used at the moment had managed to leave Thomas out completely. It had linked Vaillancourt to the Vineyard, ignoring the stage between.

There was no time to absorb the discovery; nor could she run from it, back to the view. The view was off. Through the arch the silent, sunny perspective had broken up. There were figures on the stage; the main door opening, Lisa Groves walking down one flight of steps, Noel down the other.

This Rab had seen often enough and still found diverting. "They never go down the same flight. They part outside the door, Lisa takes the left and Noel the right as though it were a marching-order.

Even when there's a car waiting for them both and they get into the car together, they go down by the different steps."

She watched them joining up again on the flagstones, standing together, talking; the talk was, one could see, an argument. As usual. "Or maybe," Rab thought, "it isn't an argument. It is just the look of them; their two egoes colliding; plus one's own knowledge."

She watched Lisa go out of sight; catching a glimpse of the falcon profile under the khaki forage-cap, the tidy shape in uniform, two paces of the loping walk. She heard the car door shut with a little slam; then the sound of the engine turning over. Noel waved a lazy hand. Alone, Noel kept her act going; there was some light-hearted wickedness of defiance in her attitude, standing there, looking after Lisa. She was, of course, improperly dressed. She wore no cap; the jacket of her uniform was slung on her shoulders, the sleeves hanging. Khaki slacks took the place of a skirt. It was possible that her dress had been the subject under argument. Except, Rab thought, Lisa must be used to Noel by now.

Immediately there began the Noel reverie.

It was difficult to realize that she must be forty. She had a boy's figure, the manner of a boy and a boy's head. Her hair was bright brown, solidly curling, cut short above her pointed ears. The hair sprang back from a wide forehead with lines on one side, no lines at all on the other. That was preparation for the shock the whole face gave you, its two sides differing entirely. A slash of the knife at a Caesarian birth had given Noel this face. That was what people said.

In thought, Rab looked away, as everyone looked away, seeing the peculiar imbalance for the first time; as she herself had looked away. The reverie took her past Noel's face to the rule and domination of Noel here at Vaillancourt. As head of the *Comité de Quatorze*, she ruled by right over the French welfare-workers. A magician who could direct other people without seeming to do a stroke of work herself, she organized her devout band with smooth efficiency: they were posted in charge of *foyers* and medical centres; they had completed the orderly evacuation of families from Alsace to the Dordogne: they were, in Rab's view, a string of busy little women dotted over the landscape, operated by remote control. She would, she knew, have no interest in their needs were it not for Noel. The rest of the drivers' unit felt the same way. It was Noel and not Lisa who inspired what enthusiasm they possessed in these waiting weeks.

"She is the Pied Piper," the reverie continued, "Follow – follow – follow. When she laughs, you laugh too. When she takes something seriously you go after it." (The book, *John Brown's Body*, was a case in point.) "She puts on no airs, she's completely without swagger. She has, I guess, no dignity. Lisa has dignity. Lisa is nobody's chum. Noel is everybody's chum and nobody's friend. Nobody's enemy either. She is like a top, spinning around all alone."

The path of the reverie being well-worn, she was undisturbed at its interruption by Noel herself, strolling in through the archway. This had happened before; one's private enquiry pursuing its way, detached from the person who was its subject standing before one's eyes: "As though one were not thinking about her at all, but about somebody quite different."

Rab shot quickly to her feet as the rule (Lisa's rule, not Noel's) dictated. Presumably Noel too was off somewhere else in her own head, for she looked startled, saying "Good Lord, what are *you* doing here?"

"We just got in from Paris, with the truck. Roberts and I."

Nothing surprising about this; why was Noel surprised? Snapped out of reverie, Rab gazed into the crooked face; at one time a difficult thing to do.

On the left side, under the lined half of the forehead, the eyebrow arched and the nostril flared; the corner of the mouth went up (this profile, with the pointed ear and the narrow blue-green eye giving Noel a demon look.) On the right, under the smooth-skinned forehead, there was a straighter eyebrow, a wider eye and a flatter nostril. The lips on this side met in a level line. The effect of the right-hand profile was serious, thoughtful, almost sad: the pointed ear didn't wholly suit it although the right was the intended original, the demonic side merely the result of the cut muscles.

The full-face view being taken for granted now, Rab saw the colour of the springing hair, the light on the skin, the clear-water eyes and the laugh.

"You look," said Noel, "as if you'd had another stand-up fight. With the truck, I mean."

"Only the fuel-pump," said Rab, glancing down at her stained shirt and her arms blackened to their elbows.

"*Only* the fuel-pump . . ."

"I fixed it. Roberts hasn't a clue."

"Madame la Commandante Groves was searching for you."

"She must have *heard* me," Rab said. "Couldn't not have."

"She thought it was Marny on the truck today," Noel flipped a cigarette from the back of her hand to her mouth, a trick they all tried to imitate, usually failing, "and she didn't want Marny to drive her after that little episode with the lamp-post. Fortunate for you."

"Fortunate?"

"You might even now be racing her back to Paris to meet the American Ambassador. Would have given you a night in Paris, though; she's staying over. You'd have liked that – no?"

"Not so crazy for Paris, known it all my life," Rab murmured, bragging instinctively. It was vital, in Noel's presence, to distinguish oneself from the others; not to be written down with the Americans seeing France for the first time; the wide-eyed girls. These were akin to the uninitiated sightseers on Mr. and Mrs. Bigley's tour of Europe last year.

Any attempt to measure up to Noel's knowledge of Europe was, however, ridiculous. Noel belonged here. Noel belonged to Vaillancourt. Half-English, half-French, she was the last of the family line. It was, by all accounts, a crazy line; inbred, cross-bred and congenitally doomed; the heirs either killed in battle or by shocking, gratuitous accidents. For Rab, who found few studies more dustily intimidating than a study of the past, it was impossible to arrive at the true history of the Noels. There were portraits of former Noels to be seen in the château. There were old prints and framed citations, adding up to the Entente Cordiale, to La Gloire; to a vanished parade of remarkable soldiers and their remarkable ladies. In the vaults of the forlorn Gothic chapel generations of turbulent Noels now lay quiet, giving nobody any trouble. Noel's mother, looking like a cross between Boadicea and Florence Nightingale, gazed grimly down upon the long dining-room. It was she who had founded the *Comité de Quatorze*. Her only son had killed himself in an aeroplane. Noel remarked on occasion that she had never expected to inherit the *Comité* along with the family seat and would have preferred to inherit neither. She gave the impression of a prince who had meant to abdicate and forgotten to sign the necessary papers. Even the pavilion, her private quarters, now shared with Lisa Groves, had something moodily royal about it.

She was also said to be bankrupt (which seemed appropriate to the prince) and Vaillancourt the property of the French Government. There were other Noel properties in France, one near Aix, one south of Limoges. The last survivor – seemingly – cared for none of them. Her pre-war reputation was frivolous; that of a play-boy rather than a play-girl. She was an expert fencer, a ski-champion, a gambler and a driver of fast cars.

Or so it was rumoured. The Noel reverie ran out, as ever, in a forest of question-marks.

The low voice with the impeccably British accent was saying, "Well, off you go and enjoy yourself. There's nothing on earth happening around here. My plan is to paint every one of the pavilion shutters before Lisa gets back. *And* the door," she added with a wink.

Rab gave the return wink. To paint, or not to paint, the shutters had been an issue fought between Noel and Lisa since the fine weather came. The paint was a requisition; destined for the new dormitories. It must be odd to see your own home turned into an institutional barrack. Rab wondered if Noel could remember it free of outbuildings, huts, wire-netting and asphalt; free of the crowd. As the cradle of the *Comité*, Vaillancourt had perhaps looked much like this in her childhood.

The paint was kept locked in a shed. Rab hesitated while Noel moved in that direction.

"Miss Noel —"

"Not 'Miss Noel', please. There's a good chap . . . 'Miss' is strictly for shop-girls."

"Ma'am?"

"And for God's sake not Ma'am."

"What then?"

"Call me Noel."

One couldn't now call her anything.

"I was only going to ask if you wanted the key to the shed."

"Certainly. If you know where it is. I was all set to kick the door down in my quiet way."

"I'll fetch it for you," said Rab.

There was no reason, Lisa Groves reminded herself, to take Vaillancourt along in her head. She need not see the place until tomorrow. It lay ten miles behind her already. She was alone in the April afternoon, driving fast towards Paris.

Driving fast; hating Noel. This was becoming an obsession or dislike, a violence within, an all-day devil. There was no aspect of Noel that could fail to infuriate her. The jokes, the jig-saw puzzles, the sleeping-pills, *John Brown's Body*; the cigarette flipped from hand to mouth; the smell of lemon-verbena. Noel's laugh, Noel's walk, Noel's casual rule over Vaillancourt; the fever of Noel-worship; no matter where she looked, she saw Noel or Noel reflected.

The attachment of the unit to the *Comité* was – as Lisa had foreseen – her own particular plague and doom.

She had said this to nobody; nor wanted to say it. She was used to facing a problem alone. In what she had come to call 'real life', the time before the war, she had striven a long time against the emotional disorders arising from herself as she was made.

Did one see in Noel, perhaps, the sort of person one might have been had one ever succeeded in stifling the serious impulse to be good?

"Be good," Lisa thought, "A smug way of putting it. It is not goodness. For goodness, read order, read discipline, read going to bed before midnight and liking to have a clear head in the morning. Read a sense of responsibility: worrying, as opposed to 'Couldn't care less', worrying and taking constructive action."

There was no constructive action to be taken at this moment; therefore it was foolish to worry; to be fussing because Noel was left in charge. "Will she sleep at the Château tonight, as she should, as one of us must, according to the rules, or will she hang around at the pavilion, playing 'J'attendrai' on the gramophone and doing that damned jig-saw until three a.m.? If she does decide to keep a rule instead of breaking it, will she put out the pavilion lights, see to the black-out, remember the fireguard?

"What about Rab? Where's Rab today?"

Another worry, only a small worry; she had no proof that Rab, with the rest, had succumbed to the fever. She would feel, always, more responsible for Rab than for any of the others. "Because I let go, because I cut my love down by the roots; because I welcomed her back to the Vineyard and grew up at last ... with an effort, without having hurt or harmed her. I fired my last shot of bad behaviour (I think and hope) the night I heard she was going to Europe without me last year."

It is the way that Noel looks at her when she walks past the window.
"Quiet, now. You imagine it. Why think about it?"

"Because, I suppose, I am not yet old enough – this may come in one's fifties, perhaps – to detach myself completely from a manner of life against which I revolt."

She stared at the straight road ahead; at the poplars and a magpie flickering up from the grass. One's love of France was so much a love of the land itself.

She saw the neglected, undrained pastures of Vaillancourt, the ravaged garden and the dead trees fallen in the woods. Vaillancourt again; Noel again . . . the all-day devil.

The pavilion, nearly a mile from the château, was a bizarre little structure with an onion-shaped roof like that of a mosque; the onion covered with shabby, silvery tiles, the two wings stuccoed in yellowish white. Somebody's Folly, Noel said; that was obvious; all by itself on a mound at the edge of the woods.

They had ridden down in a jeep, Noel making the jeep do acrobatics while the paint-cans clashed about the floor. She had left the jeep at an absurd angle on the grass slope; it looked as though it were standing up, begging.

There was no more sun. Rab saw the light move off the young leaves, her own shadow move off the wall. She said in her heart 'Don't let it rain,' aware of threatened happiness. She went on painting, with a swoop of the brush across each flat surface, with conscious dexterity when she came to the corners. She heard an occasional oath from Noel, slapping the paint on, making splashes. They passed and repassed each other, not talking much.

"Germans here in '17," said Noel. "German General's billet. Funny if we were painting it up for Nazi occupation."

"Are we, d'you think?"

"I'm inclined to think so, yes."

"Honestly?"

"This country's not at war. Not in its mind anyway. I've enough French blood in me to know. Pay no attention, I'm a pessimist." She stepped back, looking at the shutter. "That crack's been there since I can remember. Mad Aunt made it for a bird-table; she lived here after the Germans. Do you run to mad aunts?"

"No aunts," said Rab, "Not even sane ones."

"She wasn't really much madder than my mother. My mother used to wear her medals on her nightgown. What do we do about the door?"

"You said we'd toss for the door."

"Shouldn't have kept it to the last," Noel said, scanning the sky: "Rain, any minute now."

"Oh don't. If one says it aloud it comes quicker."

"Let things out into the air and then they happen, eh?"

Rab made no reply. She cleaned off the brush and stared at the scaling door. "Wants sand-papering; wants an undercoat," she said.

"Want must be its master. For the moment, anyway. Here it comes."

Hopelessly, Rab watched it come; the wind skirling across the trees, the leaves shivering in the first shower.

"I like it," said Noel. She sauntered off through the quickening downpour to the jeep: she fastened its mackintosh flaps at leisure. Strolling, loitering, she called "Take our stuff inside, will you, please?" as though she had an urgent appointment there with the rain. Rab collected the cans and brushes, the rags and the bottle of turpentine. Carrying them to the door she could still see Noel walking around the jeep, getting drenched.

"Crazy," she said to herself.

The door opened upon the salon; a long low room smelling of Noel; which was to say of tobacco and lemon-verbena. There were some amusing things here; the fencing foils crossed above the mantelpiece; a kaleidoscope; the inevitable jig-saw laid out on a long table; a parade of toy soldiers on every shelf in sight. The furniture mixed spindly gilt with solid pieces. There was an unexpected angel on one wall; made of gilded wood, a small, flying cherub who suggested somehow that he had been caught with a butterfly-net. Rab gazed at him; his devout eye and solemn underlip reminded her of Thomas.

Since the floor was parquet, well-polished, she spread a newspaper for the painting equipment. She stood looking about the room, her head and shoulders damp enough to be uncomfortable; her muscles suddenly stiff, aching; she remembered that there had – long ago – been a plan for a bath and a change of clothes.

Here he stood waiting, in the strange room, with the rain drumming on the windows.

He stood . . . That was what you thought: that was the way you had always thought, not knowing you thought it: yes, knowing, but not admitting. You had always been a boy inside. You had never thought "She". It was "he" in your head, every time. The child had thought "he", the girl had thought "he", the young woman still thought "he". But the boy as thought was no more masculine than feminine: he was you, without a sex, without a name.

(You were glancing at this in your mind, brushing past it as you had done all your life. It was nobody's business but yours.)

Behind Rab the door banged. Noel walked in, with dripping hair and a shirt that had turned from khaki to black.

"Of all the ways to get pneumonia . . ."

"Nonsense. A *volupté* . . . To be followed by a hot bath."

"I'd like a bath, too," Rab said. "All right with you if I take the jeep?"

"You can have a bath here."

"I want to change."

"Shouldn't be difficult. Care for a pair of Lisa's pyjamas? Or there's a fancy-dress belonging to the Mad Aunt somewhere around. It's *L'Aiglon*." Noel moved away, chuckling to herself. Rab heard the sound of taps running. The scent of lemon-verbena grew stronger. Noel reappeared in a white towel robe.

"I'm off," said Rab. "You won't be eating with us tonight?"

"Certainly not. I've a date with some red caviare."

"Well, if it's still raining after supper, would you like me to come down and fetch you?"

"Fetch me?" Noel looked surprised, then laughed: "I'm not spending the night up at the old mausoleum, if that's what you mean. And don't remind me of the rule, Lisa's reminded me already. How about sharing the caviare?"

"Thanks. I'd better eat with the others."

"Comme vous voudrez," said Noel indifferently. She was rubbing her face with a tissue. She crumpled the tissue and shied it accurately into the wastepaper-basket. She seemed, suddenly, to present her crooked mask for inspection. There was no accompanying gesture; there was simply the face, rubbed free of make-up and Noel standing with her arms folded.

"Which side do you like best?" she asked. "When I was a child I liked the right one. Now I think I prefer the left." With the palm of one hand she pushed up her right cheek and her right eyebrow until the face became symmetrically the demon. "How's that?."

"Are you trying to embarrass me?"

"Well of course," Noel said.

"You don't, you know."

"I see I don't. Why don't I?"

"Because it would be babyish and bad-mannered; and I hope I'm neither."

Though Noel's look was one of congratulation, she did not speak. She played the cigarette-trick again, flipping it into her mouth, lighting it.

"Thanks for a nice afternoon," Rab said. She saw the hand held out. "My French upbringing," Noel explained, "The handshake is always imperative, even if the parting is only for half an hour. I'll have a drink ready for you."

The one who had described and forecast this technique was Virginia, the third person at Amiens; the girl whom Thomas had instinctively disliked. Had Thomas not made her so miserable that afternoon, Rab would, she knew, have stopped Virginia talking. On the long drive through the dark to Vaillancourt she had listened gratefully to the tortuous prattle. Concerned with Noel, it was the pull-back into the world of women, acting as a lifeline. (But it was not the beginning of the Noel reverie; that was already begun. Thomas's antennae had picked it up. "Who put you on to it?" he asked of the book *John Brown's Body*, and you hadn't spoken Noel's name.)

Aloft in her own small cubicle on the château's top-floor, Rab looked back over a year; to the lost time of innocence. Innocence, like solitude, seemed to belong to the island. To have lived in that time with Lisa; untroubled, untouched, she thought: "Nobody would believe it. Hell, nobody did believe it. But I neither saw that nor cared."

What has woken you up?

Noel – only Noel.

Do you have to find out more? Can't you leave it all alone?

Somehow I have to know.

Why?

This thing has been with me too long. It's always waited for me. When I think about me I know it.

And when I think about men . . . Not about Thomas, about men.

Men in your childhood; picking you up, swinging you around, slapping your haunches, straddling you across their knees. You had never told anyone how much you hated that. You had never told Thomas of the hate and the fear. Saying you had been afraid of the sexual act, you had told him only half the truth.

The secret horror you kept to yourself; at its worst on the beach in summer: horror of hairiness, bulges, jock-straps, knotty muscles and craggy toes. Noses snorting, mouths spitting in the water. Huge noisy laughter.

Men as fellow-workers you liked; tougher and simpler than women. (That was proved here at Vaillancourt.) You liked the truck-driver, the builder, the fishermen, because you never saw them without their work or without their clothes.

All others you despised. You despised the jocular male, the drinker, the pipe-smoker and the pouncer. Male arrogance was so complete that to be a man was enough. (Lisa's teaching.) A man could grow a paunch, lose his teeth, turn bald and still be utterly content with himself, surprised – even shocked – that you refused the proposition, the honour he had done you in making it. Men, Lisa said, should be kept in the stables, like animals, brought in for sexual intercourse as required and quickly dispatched again afterwards. Years ago she had said all this; you could remember laughing, remember being careful not to go along with it.

What's all this got to do with anything now?

It has to do with me.

Not any more. Thomas put an end to that. There is Thomas who loves you.

Pulling on the yellow sweater, flicking her hair with the comb where the sweater had rumpled it, Rab thought 'he' again. She gave a last look at that pale, bewildered boy's face in the glass. She ran down the stairs; she went through the gallery where the Noel portraits hung; she did not look at them; she came to the hall and met Brousse, sad-French-governess Brousse who had charge of the household staff, looming up the long stone passage from the kitchens, to ask "You will be in to supper?"

"Yes: just going for a drink."

"Oh I'm so glad. So many people away this week-end, I didn't realize, no one ever tells one anything till the last minute and I have got such a nice supper."

Rab walked out to the jeep, with the image of Brousse on her eyes; the sad smile on the fat white face, the round body that should never wear uniform. She was sorry for Brousse, sorry for the supper. Certainly she would come back for the supper. One quick drink with Noel – and away.

The rain had slackened; the twilight over Vaillancourt had a drowned green look, bringing the island faithfully into memory. Tylo's ghost was there and the quick, uninvited sob came to her throat. She saw him waiting for her, beside the tree, his ears cocked, one paw lifted.

None of that, now.

None of anything but this. An hour at most of this.

She drove down to the pavilion.

Oh, very much as I expected; the room with the log-fire lighted; the drinks ready on the sideboard and Noel lingering over the jig-saw before she turns. The green Russian blouse, the narrow green trousers and the yellow sandals; also to be expected. She holds out her hand. We shake each other's hand formally.

I say "I like the cherub" and you say "He came from Perigord" and take him off the wall, putting him into my hands before you go to the sideboard and pour my drink. You pour the drink and give it to me. You kick the logs into a blaze; the sparks shoot out. It is no good, I love you.

"This, I'd have you know, was not my intention."

"Nor mine," Rab said, "or maybe it was."

"And yet you have never done it before."

"Never."

"I believe you. Some wouldn't."

"Why do you?"

"Because, if you had, you'd have said 'yes' – once. The routine reply. Watch out for it next time, next person."

"Won't be a next person."

"Rash talk."

"Talk rash to me – I need it."

"Nothing would induce me to talk rash to you."

"Why not?"

"Because if I fell in love with you, I'd be sunk," Noel said.

71

"*You'd* be sunk . . ."

"Certainly. I have been warned."

"By Lisa?"

"Not by Lisa."

"Well, then —"

"Never you mind. Not by anybody, except me."

"I can't imagine your falling in love."

"Well, don't try, there's a good chap."

"They're all in love with *you* – even the ones who don't know they are," said Rab sleepily.

"They have crushes, you mean."

"Same thing."

"What nonsense you talk. Couldn't be less the same thing. They begin by staring and being sorry for me; then I show off and they think I don't give a damn. That usually fixes them."

"Do you really not give a damn?" was the question Rab wanted most to ask; she said, "Do you fix them on purpose?"

"I wouldn't honestly know."

"Did you try to fix me?"

"What is this, the catechism?"

"Well, did you?"

A pause before Noel's voice said, sounding amused, "I just thought vaguely 'That would be nice', but my intentions were honourable till I saw you sitting on the step of the truck."

"What happened then?"

"I was so pleased to see you it shook me."

"And then?"

"And then alas for vows of good behaviour. Idiotic to make them in a war, anyway, life's too short."

"Think we'll be killed?"

"Shouldn't wonder. If I'm killed," Noel said, "Come and walk by my grave. I'll watch you walking and I'll like that."

"Me walking . . . why do you like it? I slouch."

"Well, come and slouch by my grave. Promise?"

"I don't want to think about your grave."

"Very good. You might remind me to cut it out of my will, though."

"Cut your *grave* out of your will?"

"Foolish gesture," Noel murmured, "One makes them – in wills."

"What are we talking about?"

"Nothing. Couldn't we stop talking?"

We could. And this, though I drown in it, is me all alone. It is for you, but it is still me all alone while you gently give me what I like and want; and what I do for you is somehow still not enough. Does it matter my lying here, thinking that now, first gently, then fiercely, you are as much alone as I? Ought I to be thinking at all?

Afterwards, a part of her mind was soothed, with her body. "Right now the only guilt I feel is to poor old Brousse and her nice supper . . . Deserted for a pot of red caviare, for the wine and the talk and your bed."

Lying here holding hands is closer than making love.

"Goodnight, darling," Noel said and kissed her eyebrow.

"You don't sound sleepy at all."

"I'm not."

She switched on the lamp and climbed out of bed. Her naked body passed beyond the range of the lamp. It looked polished and slim and hard before she covered it with her dressing-gown.

Now your arms were around her neck, you were hugging her as you would have hugged Paula; at ease with the soft skin and the scent as once the child was, with Paula coming to say goodnight.

"Don't worry if you hear me prowling around."

"Why prowl? Couldn't you sleep?"

"No use trying without pills. And I'm damned if I'm taking a pill."

"Why not?"

"Too much on my mind," Noel said, laughing.

"What sort – on your mind?"

"Never did anybody ask so many questions. It's like having a child about the place."

"Well, I can't go to sleep if you can't – seems so rude."

"Who taught you the pretty manners? I suspect you of coming to my bed because it would have been discourteous to refuse."

Why do you have to say that? It isn't true. "Do you prowl *every* night?" she asked.

73

She saw the crooked face smiling down at her before Noel switched off the lamp. "No, sweetheart. And just in case there's another 'Why not?' coming up, the answer is I don't do this every night."

One had come to the end of the reverie. This was most apparent. Rab stared at the truth, here in the same place, in the stable yard. The rain had ceased; it was a mild, bright morning: Sunday morning. Exactly five hours since she had escaped from Noel's bed.

She was loading stores into the heaviest of the trucks, christened the Mammoth or the Big Bastard according to choice, and due at St. Anne by afternoon. The *foyer* at St. Anne was none of Rab's business; the loading was none of her business; she was helping Marny because she had nothing else to do. Poor silly Marny (who had run Lisa's car into the lamp-post, Marny with the mouse-coloured hair and the puppyish face) seemed grateful.

The reverie was over. The haunting invader of solitude was gone. When she looked back she saw a woman sitting up in bed; the springy hair, the naked shoulders and the two-sided face . . . the hand blowing a kiss.

"Bless you – thank you. *À bientot*," Noel had said.

"How can I love her and hate her at the same time? Let me not hate her, it was my fault. Childish to feel that this is the end of honour."

So it is. You went deliberately hunting after an adventure that could have been left where it belonged, in your mind.

She crashed the last box into the back of the Mammoth and heard a yelp from Marny: "Watch it! What's the matter with you?"

Everything is the matter with me. I am ashamed, excited, confused, I have to think this thing out. I have to choose: choose between Noel and Thomas. It's as simple as that. Choose between stopping right here —

– You can't do it. Not yet.

Be the best thing to do.

That's the argument of a Girl Scout.

I needn't see her today. Lisa will be back any minute now. They'll go into their official huddle. There can be a whole day without Noel; it's happened before.

Yes; and you have been disappointed, finding the day dull.

Shall I ever get back to there?

Of course. This is a beginning, not an end.

Then why does it feel all wrong?

Because you are scared of the choice, guilty and awed and excited and miserable, hating and loving.

The end of honour . . .

Rab sat down on the step of the truck. She glanced through the arch, but the Mammoth was out of line: she could see only half the lyre-shaped staircase. She tried to play the cigarette-trick, flipping it up from the back of her hand. It didn't work. She could hear Marny tramping about inside the truck. Idly she wondered who would be driving with Marny; there were always two of them detailed for the trucks.

"I could go, couldn't I? An easy out, that would be."

Marny climbed down, put up the flap, and said mournfully "Well, thanks a lot." Then she stood still, looking at her feet, a deject, dumpy shape in the unbecoming overalls.

"Who's with you today?" Rab asked.

"Roberts – of all people."

"Don't you like Roberts?"

"She's as scared of this brute as I am."

"Scared?"

"All very well for you," said Marny, sniffing. "You aren't scared of anything."

It was a godsend. Rab said loftily, "Who put you two forceful characters on the job?"

"Miss Groves. It's an order. I knew she'd do something like this – just because I told her I was nervous sometimes – when I have my period. And now of course it's the first day —"

– "Don't for Pete's sake tell me about your period – I don't want to hear about anybody's period ever. The biggest bore there is."

Marny said sulkily, "You sound like Miss Noel."

"Do I, though? Listen, dopey, I'll take Roberts and you stay home; how's that?"

"But we *can't*," Marny wailed, "This was an order."

"The hell with orders."

"*D'accord,*" said Noel's voice, "the hell with them. But careful, when teacher's listening." She might, Rab thought, have shot through a trap-door. She was wearing sneakers, that was why they hadn't heard her come. She was out of uniform, dressed in a light jacket and trousers. She carried a parcel under one arm. With the demon side of her profile turned towards Rab, she stood looking at Marny. "What seems to be the trouble?" she asked gaily.

"Nothing," said Marny at once.

"Yes there is. Marny doesn't feel well, so I've offered to drive to St. Anne with Roberts."

"But Miss Groves said —"

"Miss Groves is held up in Paris," Noel interrupted, "She won't be back till tomorrow morning. I just spoke to her on the telephone."

(Though she is saying this to Marny, her eyes are giving me the message; she looks wickedly pleased.)

My will has a knife to cut your will. Or I hope it has.

"You'll agree," said Rab, "that if they're *both* scared, it's damn' silly." She saw Marny's look of hatred and Noel cocking her head on one side. She reflected, not for the first time, upon the contradictory signs of leader and rebel that merged in the puzzling nature. She could think about this as though last night had never happened.

"Point One," said Noel. "Remember not to call any order from the Commandant damn' silly. Point Two, nobody who's scared of this beast ought to drive it." She patted the Mammoth affectionately. "Point Three, time marches on. If you aren't well," she said to Marny who – as one would have guessed – began to say "It's only—"

"I don't care what it is. Sign off and send Roberts over."

"Yes, Miss Noel." Marny bumbled away under the arch.

"Well, good morning," said Noel. "Fine situations you get yourself into."

"Meaning the Mammoth?"

"What else? How long will the job take you?"

"We'll be late back. Ten-ish, I'd think."

"So would I. Mind if I paint the door without you? Looks as if there'll be rain later."

"The door; no, of course I don't mind."

"Rather sad, though," said Noel, and laughed. She held up the parcel. "I brought the cherub. I'd like you to have him. Put him in your room, shall I? . . . Don't look so miserable."

"I'm not miserable."

"That for a story. Because of your boy? We'll talk tonight. Come straight down. Doesn't matter what time."

My will has a knife to cut your will.

"And if you decide not," said Noel, "Then not. I shan't be angry. I'll watch the clock, finish the jig-saw and in due course take two pills. Or possibly three. And sleep sound."

You are making me feel very young and stupid.

Noel swung from foot to foot, whistling *"J'attendrai."* Then she said, "Above all, don't worry. Worry's the killer. Here comes the drooping Roberts. Off you go; drive carefully." She waved her hand, sauntering away under the arch.

THE UNWRITTEN NOTEBOOK

"IN HALF AN HOUR, THEN," HE SAID AND SHUT THE DOOR. I didn't know his name. All I knew was that he would take me in his cart, a distance of some miles beyond the village. Then he could steer me by the cross-country route once night fell. After that I was on my own. I had the map, but it wasn't much of a map; some yellowing pages torn from a departmental guide.

I made it into a game; the holidays were beginning and I had decided to hitch-hike from the North of France to the South just for the hell of it. I worked at this pretence while I sat on my bed, watching the last of the rainy sunset through the small window.

Nobody could be travelling lighter. Not one of my original possessions remained to me except my boots – and this was lucky because I've always had what Brigstock used to call Awkward Feet, Between-Sizes, like. The boots had been stained black and I'd oiled them well. Very kind and sensible of the family not to throw them out. They had burned the rest of my uniform, piece by piece, in the rubbish heap.

I still wondered about my watch. I could remember the Germans stripping me of everything else, but they'd left me my watch. Somebody around here had helped himself to it and I missed it. When the Grandmother gave me her lecture about no-sense-of-property she'd remarked "Even your watch looks all wrong on your wrist." So she would approve.

There might, I mused, have been some truth in the lecture. Apart from the watch I found myself quite content to own nothing. I couldn't feel I owned these clothes; a greyish cotton shirt and trousers, a pair of patched underpants, the canvas belt and the socks:

a coat of sorts, shapeless and rather too long; or else rather too short, neither jacket nor overcoat but a compromise between the two. It had large pockets; nothing in the pockets. There was a pouch in the belt for the money the doctor had left me.

Half the money, to be exact. A thousand francs. I'd given the family the other thousand.

On the doctor's last day he had suggested I might take up the loose floor-board where he used to keep the drugs. "I'm missing a cuff-link," said the doctor, "I shall be grateful if you have the time to search for it."

That was his goodbye. When I got the board up the envelope was lying there, with the two mille-franc notes inside. The family would tell me nothing about him except that he was not coming back. I didn't press them. I'd seen them growing afraid, changing almost hourly until they seemed as far as Rab, as finally departed as the doctor. They still called me Emile, but I had ceased to be what Emile was at first; an achievement and a joke. The jolly gendarme, a relative of the family, was in on the joke.

I was the feeble minded nephew, everybody knew me. This poor bugger Emile, too cretinous for military service; helping on the farm as usual when one of the *Fridolins* took a pot-shot at him. He fell straight off the *cultivateur* and cracked himself to pieces. Emile's own fault, of course; he shouldn't have stuck his head up out of that cornfield and called them those rude names. If he'd only kept his muzzle shut, he might have passed as a scarecrow. *Pauvre cretin:* but tough, my God, tough; he always had the build of an ox and the health of a horse or he'd never have made such a quick recovery. A pity the shock hadn't brought his brains back: *ça peut arriver, vous savez.*

This was the game we had played together.

I've always thought the French a race of natural actors. And I've wondered what makes them act so well. Their passion for their own language, their concentration, their all-of-a-piece-ness – or what? I remember discussing this with Miles. Miles said it was the caginess that gave them all something to hide as soon as they'd saved their first ten francs. Being married to a Frenchwoman, he said, there was nothing I could teach him. One blessing, said Miles – they were so

79

damn cagey they hadn't time to mind other people's business, too busy with their own.

A thing I've noticed in France is that nobody behind a counter ever dreams of giving you as much as a packet of razor-blades without wrapping it up, even if you say Don't bother. I'm exceptionally bad at making parcels, it was my worst thing when I worked at the shop in Ebury Street, so I always say Don't bother. But they pay me no attention. The thing you've bought is your own business and must be hidden from curious eyes.

But caginess alone doesn't make for good acting; it couldn't. There has to be an outgoing quality somewhere: a sort of abstract sense of humour making them able to clown; to fool for the sake of fooling.

I found I didn't want to think about this, either; not now. The joking-time, the acting-time, was over. I had joined in it with a will. We were all, I think, in a state of slap-happy shock. I'd given them an immediate preoccupation and I was also a link with hope; a sort of talisman: part proof of their especial destiny. Throughout the days of mourning, they had kept a mystical belief in their own good fortune. They told me, with tears, how this one small triangle of land, from the village to the hill behind the farmhouse, had escaped the fury of the fighting. "You were the only bombshell that dropped on us," they said, "and luckily one of British manufacture." Unlike the fellows in the truck, these people didn't blame the British. They called them "ces phénomènes-là" and their best moment of the day – like mine – was listening to the news from England on the radio. We had to be very careful about this. The hostile tribes (I still called them that) forbade it absolutely.

Though the family agreed that my only hope of getting back was to head South and aim for Gibraltar, they tried – at first – to keep me here a while. I must have papers. The jolly gendarme would fake the papers for me in just a few more days. I wasn't to worry about eating their food. The food situation would improve; Pétain had promised; so had the Mayor. Rationing was temporary. The doctor too advised waiting for an identity-card that would establish Emile beyond any doubt.

The change came suddenly. It walked into the house; a fog of fear.

Everybody stopped talking. They stopped trying to get England on the radio. One morning I found the radio itself had disappeared. Something was happening in the village, two miles away. The jolly gendarme never brought the papers, because he never came back to the house. He vanished, like the doctor. The man who had come this afternoon with the map did talk a little, not much. Of the doctor this man said *"Il est Juif – c'est tout."* and when I asked if I was now a real danger to the family, he told me Yes, a very serious danger. They hadn't said so; but their eyes had. Out, their eyes said, and quickly.

It was almost dark; I could see just one pale, rainy streak on the horizon. I got off the bed and paced the floor. Time for another night-walk, I said to myself, lucky your legs are sound; you aren't quite the man you were, but very nearly. Pain still stabbed my shoulder from time to time and the shoulder itself gave an odd sort of click with certain movements of my arm. That was all, except for a fuzzy feeling in my head. At the doctor's last visit he had told me I was just about fit for my usual summer holiday on the Riviera. I remembered the melancholy smile. I would go on remembering.

I said a prayer for him and one for me.

The quiet footsteps came to my door.

Down in the kitchen the two of them were sitting; silent, worried, no smile any more on either face; his face like a carved head on a walking-stick, hers a mousy mask. The small bundle on the table was for me. She pointed at it. Then they were rigid, waiting for me to go.

HOLLYWOOD AND BERMUDA

"ONE CUBA LIBRA, ONE ROB ROY, PLEASE, PAULA. HOW come you're acting barmaid?"

"On advice from my psychiatrist. I couldn't stop dreaming about the griddle. Frying all my friends, too: damn' serious."

"You don't say?" He believed her. He was top accountant for a big studio: which made it all the odder that you could sell him anything.

The new helper installed at the griddle gave her a wink; the new helper guessing there was a joke around. He couldn't know how feeble a joke, though his English was improving. He came from Poland, a refugee. His name was Michael: he was dark and slender, as agile as an acrobat. Michael made studied, selective passes at all the women in sight, including Paula. His success stopped with his employer: Sue Brown, opposed as she was to masculinity in all forms, threatened to have him neutered.

"Hi, Paula. Two Scotch-on-the-rocks, please." They were the husband-and-wife team, scenario-writers, living across the way at the Garden of Allah. "Any news of Rab?" was always their first question.

Paula found it as hard to report Rab's news as Rab herself seemed to find it. The latest scrawl was charged with a grim finality. Skipping its message, she heard herself say only that Rab was back at Vaillancourt, working for the relief committee: "Sounds like a heartbreaker. Soup-kitchens; misery everywhere; trying to fit families together again. All under German occupation and German orders. She hates it. But the end of the job's in sight."

"You'll be glad to have her home," they said.

Whatever happens, Rab had written, *I'm determined to stay on this side – get to England, come hell or high water. There at least I can go on fighting Thomas's war for him. Not that one can do a damn thing for the dead – ever, ever, ever. But I've kind of inherited the war now, or that's the way I feel. I don't think I'm fit for any other existence. Forgive me, please.*

Unbearable. But so was everything else. Oh, you kept going, because you had to; you made your striving jokes, saw to it that Ann Meredith's Beauty Shop did the right things by your face and hair; you bought a summer dress, you sewed new curtains. You clutched and seized upon the smallest signs of life within yourself; you needed stimulants other than alcohol. Michael the Pole was a stimulant and if that was disgraceful that was just too bad. You knew more about yourself than you used to know.

This was time on a tight-rope. Six weeks today since France fell. Invasion-talk was hot. All Hollywood knew the date for Hitler's invasion of England. September the Third, when the war would be one year old.

August, now.

"Hey, Paula, time's up." Sue Brown was even more bossy in these days. She seemed, also, to be much bigger. She moved in behind the bar like a ship coming into dock; curved and gleaming, majestic as ever on the first two drinks. (Hair in a glossy, complex twist, suggesting French bread; face an enamel dumpling with hot, angry eyes.)

"Go on, sweetheart. Give yourself a drink first. Cigarette?" She held out her case, the white metal case with the tricolour badge; you saw them all the time: sold for British War Relief. The word 'Allied' was, of course, no longer in service, though some people still used it absent-mindedly.

"Drink up and then scram," Sue said.

"Nothing to scram for. Philip's coming straight from the studio. He ought to be here by now."

"How is he?"

Paula shrugged. What could one say about Philip? He was the worst aspect of her current nightmare. Thank God he had two more pictures lined up when this one finished. Thank God he spent his leisure with the British Colony. He had even reverted to cricket. Accepting the fact that she herself was no longer a consolation,

Paula still found cricket an insulting substitute. Cricket, the Actors' Orphans, Red Cross committees . . . Shaky and dazed, Philip clung to these things.

Better so. Better than walking round the glass-topped table where the snapshots lay, staring at Thomas, talking about Thomas, making Thomas into the darling of a lifetime – the thing Thomas had never been. (There was the insane, cruel temptation to say 'You've been grumbling at him since Nineteen-Twenty-Six, remember? *I* was the one who was crazy for Thomas.')

Poor Philip: hating Hollywood (except for the British Colony) hating all things American with a new, pointless hatred. She would conduct long arguments with him in her head; never aloud:

"You were the one who struck roots here; you were the one who settled down, who turned Hollywood into home. I never did. I'd have gone back to Europe any time, at the drop of a hat. Even without the dogs, yes, I would, too. You know it. You were sold on this place till war broke out. Oh yes, you were homesick now and again, all talk, professional homesickness you called it once. Damn it, you were in love with America. You'd have been a flop all your life if you'd stayed in England – you said that too, remember? No, you won't remember. You're so plunged in misery you can only go on making things worse for yourself – just like a kid. You won't even have me for a friend. If anything could hurt more than Thomas being dead, that does. Not my friend any more, not you. The one thing I need – friends. How right Miles was about that. But I don't believe I ever had an honest-to-God friend till you. There was just the bunch."

There was still the bunch. This place where she worked, these people, made sure of it.

"Quiet tonight," Sue was saying.

The temporary lull in the short orders drew Michael away from the griddle. "Some use can I be, please?" His eyes were on Paula as he asked the question. Sue said indifferently, "Stick around. See if you can help the boys in the pantry. Get lost." She stared after him, murmuring "I was born allergic to magnetism." She added "You look fine."

"Are you kidding?"

84

"I am not. And don't imagine I don't know what it costs you to keep on keeping on."

"Oh well," said Paula. She found a curious obligation to say this regularly, as if it kept something of Thomas alive.

"Here's your date." Sue went into action, greeting Philip. She worked at it, taking trouble with him. He leaned gracefully on the bar and accepted his free drink without argument. He looked no more ravaged than usual. There were moments when he seemed to Paula to be a frightening travesty of the man she had met and married; not Philip Weston, movie-actor, but a broken version of Philip Adair, the gentleman Pierrot. Here were the blazer and the faithfully-worn Gunner tie; here sounded the old lofty drawl. And here was the tricky, dodging movement of the eyes. The eyes slid away from her own face and slid away, even more rapidly, from Michael the Pole. He concentrated himself on Sue, with her story of what St. Peter said to Hitler at the gates of Paradise. He liked it. Then he signed off good-humour abruptly, saying to Paula, with the dirge in his voice, "Well, come on darling, I'm awfully tired, let's eat – if that's all right with Sue."

"Certainly is. Take the order, Michael, and then tell Josie it's time for her stint at the bar."

Even the sound of Philip's feet was charged with melancholy, Paula thought, as they went to their corner table. He stared frozenly at Michael bringing the salad. He wasn't, it seemed, going to say anything about Michael – or not yet.

"I just talked to Sarah," was his opening.

"You did? Called you at the studio, did she? I thought Bermuda was censored or rationed or something."

"I called her. I got the Consulate to fix it. That fellow's very decent, really. I was worried – *days* since we heard anything." He looked aggrieved, as though she should have worried too. Since Sarah was with Gerald and Mary in Bermuda, worry seemed an unnecessary expenditure, like the telephone-call.

"She's fixed it all up. Got the house, perfect house, she says at Darrell's Wharf. Cabled the family. The owner cut the rent as soon as she knew they were evacuees. Makes one feel better. English-woman, of course."

Of course. And Sarah's efforts on behalf of the unknown British family made him feel better too.

"Sarah's going to wait for them, and see them in. She sounds quite happy about it. In so far as any of us can sound happy about anything."

Yes, you have to say that, implying I have no part in it. And I mustn't ask you which day Gerald arrives. You'll only begin cursing him again – or give me the 'Don't mention Gerald's name' treatment.

Automatically Paula found a new sympathy for Gerald in operation. He had turned into somebody who cared, whose heart was wrung; offering to fly out from New York at once and be with Philip. Who didn't want him. "I despise him," Philip said.

This view found strong support among the male contingent in the British Colony, aflame with armchair patriotism. In their regular court martial round the card-table, Gerald stood condemned. That he was to star in a war picture condemned him the more. The British Colony's praise, like Philip's, was reserved for the boys who cut short their acting careers and went off to train in Canada.

So she must hide the truth; that she was counting the days till Gerald got here. Every telephone-call, every letter from Gerald sounded a new note of sympathetic understanding; an adult note. He was shocked and miserable, but his pity was not for himself.

"I said don't *you* think it's a good idea?" Philip repeated plaintively.

"Sorry, darling, what?"

"You weren't listening. Sarah's idea."

"For the British family?"

"*No*." Philip drummed his fingers on the table. "For Nanny and the grandmother. A little house in Bermuda." He went on about that. Though she did her best to sound agreeable, Paula knew he was well aware that she thought it ludicrous. When he said "And they can bring all their money out," she was tempted, thinking of Brigstock and Mrs. Murray, to ask "*What* money, for Heaven's sake?" Still he made the plan sound final, clear-cut. "Sterling area; no problem. Wonderful place for them to live. I can't imagine a better."

He had never been to Bermuda. Among Paula's sharpest memories of the island were precipitous rides on a bicycle and huge fuzzy spiders.

"Would you like your coffee now or later?" Michael was asking.

"Later," said Philip, and added, "I should hope." Michael smiled at Paula.

"If the little bastard looks at you like that again —"

"It's high time somebody looked at me like that," she interrupted him. He sagged. "What on earth do you mean?"

"I enjoy it. And it hasn't happened in a long time."

He gave her one sad stare before retreating to his own gloom as palpably, as deliberately as though he went into his study and shut the door.

"His King Lear act," Gerald's voice murmured from long ago.

The worst of the evening still lay ahead. He would take another drink. He would walk round and round the glass-topped table.

Then it would be time for the ritual she had privately, cruelly christened the Letter-Jag. The letters lived in a black, glossy folder. He would sit, as though alone, reading them one by one.

There was the old treasure ("Thank God I kept it") the note Thomas had left in the car for all of them long ago: *Nobody need worry and nobody, please, must stop me doing this* . . . There was the letter from Uncle Percy, the letter from Thomas's Company Commander and Nanny's letter. The longest letter was read last of all.

Dear Mr. Philip Weston,

I should have written to you before, but I've been in hospital a long time and my wits didn't come back till lately. I remembered nothing for a while. I was one of the last off the beach at Dunkirk and I got my wounds on the way. I have since had one leg amputated and it doesn't look as if the other will be of practical use to me again.

Forgive the preliminary news-items, please. This letter is about your son. I was with him in the truck. I can promise you that he was killed instantly. I saw it happen and I'm sure the bullet got him before he hit the ground. It was a brave effort. If he hadn't jumped when he did, I know I wouldn't have made my own break when we got to the cross-roads. His action alone decided me to have a stab at it.

I found my way back to our lines because I'm a countryman born and bred. I first learned the arts of dodging from a poacher when I was ten years old.

Lt. Weston was the only officer I ever admired. I admired him reluctantly at first. I'm not an easy type and it took me a while to admit to myself how fair he was to me, fair and understanding. Always. He had a kind of natural justice in him. And I couldn't go on being mean with somebody like that.

When I say I wish I had died instead, I mean it. Not because my life isn't going to interest me much now, but because men like your son *ought* to live. Humanity needs them, as it could never need somebody like myself – even if I were all in one piece.

You have my sincere sympathy.

John Rayner.

Philip had sent Rayner food-parcels and magazines as well as a signed studio-picture of himself. None of these offerings were acknowledged. Philip went on writing to him regularly but Rayner never wrote back.

Sarah came up from the beach, by the path under the pines, beside the hedge of morning-glories, to the pink house on its knoll of light, velvety green. Mary's house: very much Mary's house, not in the least Gerald's house. It was a wedding-present from one of her earlier husbands and it bore some exterior resemblance to a wedding-cake. Within, there was luxury of a carefully casual sort: just a holiday place, Mary said.

Sarah crossed the patio and made for her bedroom on the ground floor. The swim had accounted for the hot, dusty, tiredness of the day. At Darrell's Wharf the house was now almost in marching-order for the evacuees from England. In Hamilton she had conducted her last interview with the bank.

All over, signed and sealed. Cooling off, she could think about it with a pleasurable sense of shock: as though she were a child again, having done something secret and outrageous, to be confessed later on. Much later on. No need to tell Mary; impossible to tell Gerald. She would, she supposed, have to tell somebody, sometime. Philip might, perversely, approve. She didn't really care.

The bank-manager had said, "This is extraordinarily generous of you, Mrs. Butler."

But it wasn't. Like the first part of the transaction, it was merely a lightening of the conscience. "Honour is satisfied and I am tired," Sarah quoted.

The evening ahead would have its tiring aspects; with the drinks, and the guests and the silence of Gerald. Gerald frightened her. His cold, brittle façade was nothing new. Always it had been on call, but it was now permanent wear. She herself might be a stranger to him, with the rest of the strangers.

"Does he hate me because Thomas is dead? Why?" She had not said this to Mary. Mary, the tenderest, most tactful of intermediaries, said it was Gerald's express wish to be left alone. So one left him alone. Taking her shower, putting on her dress, giving her routine grimace at the craggy, furred spider pressing against the window-screen, Sarah thought, "Everybody's alone around here, except Mary."

She went up the stairs. Voices and laughter came to meet her from the long room where the colours were all greens and blues and yellows. One wall was just a great window looking out over the pines to the ocean. An all-purpose room. Here lived the bar and the bookshelves; the card games, the backgammon and Diamino boards: Mary's needlework; frames, silks and canvas. Here was the radio; the war came into the room every hour on the hour.

And here were the guests: three of them. The British boy who worked in the Censor's office; the brown little woman who grew orchids, and a new one; a bony American diplomat with silver hair.

He was holding the floor. He had the right, being just returned from Europe. Gerald, looking lacquered, bronzed and two-dimensional, stood by the bar. Sarah joined the close circle.

Paris deserted; Paris with the Nazi banners hanging in the Champs-Elysées; slow return of the refugees who had choked the roads in June; this man had seen it all. He had seen the conquerors settling in; he knew the curfew-hours, the rationing regulations, the billeting-rules. Forecasting the powers of the new Vichy Government, he was as full of authority as a newspaper. Like some newspapers he interleaved his facts with little first-hand snapshots: "So happened I was on my way to the Embassy when —"

One could always put down a newspaper.

Every time Mary, or the British boy, or the orchid-woman interrupted him with a question, he would say "Wait a minute," or "I'll come to that." Gerald asked no questions. He stayed where he was, looking more and more slitty-eyed, refilling the glasses.

The interminable, spell-binding yet maddening saga rolled on; to the treatment of prisoners, to the Red Cross, to the *Comité de Quatorze*, now in a state of imminent collapse. He had known the head of the *Comité*, "a dynamiter, a woman called Noel." Maybe her genius might have found a way to carry on. But she was dead, the relief-work was at a standstill for lack of funds and the days of the American volunteers in France were numbered. They would be coming home via Lisbon, all of them.

"Not Rab," said Sarah, "She'll stay with the war."

The voice of authority assured her that this was impossible. Rab would never get a permit for entry to England. The voice went into minute particulars, shifting its field of knowledge first to London and then to Washington. Having shut the door on Rab's chances, he accepted another Scotch. Mary moved into the moment of silence with "How did it feel, having to mix with the Germans – be polite to them? I assume you were polite."

"Well now, fortunately I have fluent German."

"That," snapped Gerald, "would surely make it much easier to be rude."

The others laughed: the pundit gave him a condescending smile: "On an assignment like mine, I couldn't afford the luxury. Not that

I was seriously tempted. Their behaviour – as anyone over there will tell you – was admirably correct."

"I've heard so. It's nice to hear," the orchid-woman said, "isn't it?"

"There I certainly took off my hat to them," said the pundit. "Remarkable. Very remarkable indeed."

For a frozen second Sarah saw the British boy – presumably acclimatized – giving her a wink. Then she was on her feet, strolling, glass in hand, towards the seat of authority. She did not throw the glass. She had meant to, but now that she was right beside the diplomat she found it more consoling to pour the whole drink straight down over his head. She saw an ice cube bouncing off his nose; she heard him sneezing; she turned and made for the door. As she set her glass down carefully beside Gerald, Gerald said in a stunned voice, "Do you know, that's the most beautiful thing I've seen since Chartres Cathedral."

She was outside the door. She was running down the stairs. Gerald came running after her. He didn't speak. He seized her hand. They were running together, away from the house, over the terrace, down through the oleander bushes, by the steep steps to the little stone jetty. Here lay the speedboat, *Mary Castle II*, the blue and white toy much prized of its owner.

They looked each other in the eyes: they began to giggle. Shaking, giggling, still speechless, they jumped aboard. Gerald started up the engine with the roar of an aircraft and they shot away across the Sound. Too much noise for talking, too furious a speed. Thud-thud-thud along the Sound's flat water, screen of rainbow bubbles arching overhead, a wet wind slapping down your eyelids, a wet wind tugging at your hair. The glimpses of Gerald's profile showed him grinning and grinning, the brown lips pulled back from the white teeth in a joyous anger, like her own anger. They thundered through the water in their rage; past the green and sandy shores, the pine-trees and the coloured houses, on and on.

Soaked with it, strangled with it, never let it stop, she thought, and Gerald cut the engine. They rocked to a standstill.

Here was the warm and gentle air again; the boat once more a harmless toy bobbing on pale oily water. Gerald brought her in, to the landing-stage. He made her fast. They came up through the pier-shed and out on to Hamilton waterfront, a line of haphazard buildings, shabby, variously painted, with the crowds strolling and the scrimmage of bicycles. Still whirled along in his private hurricane, Gerald grasped Sarah's elbow, racing her through the bicycles to the door of Twenty-One. He dashed up the stairs ahead of her.

The bar was full. But she saw that Gerald's celebrity-pose was off: for once he didn't notice being noticed. With the minimum of graceful thanks, he hustled an obligingly pop-eyed couple from their seats beside the window. "We're just leaving, Mr. Weston – it *is* Mr. Weston, isn't it?" He didn't answer. He hurled Sarah into the vacant seat and flashed away to the bar. Now he came flashing back. The lacquered set of his hair was destroyed by the sea wind; it stood up jaggedly; it streaked his forehead. There were spatters and splashes all over his beautiful grey silk shirt. A shaming drip hung from one nostril. As he threw himself down beside her, Sarah said "You need a handkerchief, excuse me," and Gerald rubbed the back of his hand across his nose.

"I'm extremely obliged to you," were his first words. "Not 'arf," he added. "Cor lumme. Struth and stap me."

"Fi-gu-ray voo," she replied automatically. The awful childhood jargon, lost for years, came rushing back.

"Rabin-bin-bindranath Tagore."

"Tagore or not Tagore."

"That is the question."

"Mute the camel."

"Mute the poor bloody old camel."

"I say, Gerald."

"I say, Sarah."

"I say, I say, I say."

The waiter, bringing a bottle of champagne in an ice-bucket and Gerald carelessly dropping a five-pound note on top of the folded bill reduced her to silence.

"Imported," he said. "Please note vintage. The last bottle but one in the bar. I've taken out an option on the second bottle. How do you suppose German champagne will taste? Correct?"

"Admirably correct," said Sarah, "And I shall certainly take off my hat to it, I shall indeed."

His eyes were fixed and glowing. "Was it bliss – doing it? God, I envy you."

"Pretty average bliss. Lovely when he sneezed."

"Did you think ahead? Or did it just happen?"

"I can't remember."

"No, of course you can't. How I love you."

"Because I did that?"

"I love you anyway, fool."

She stared at him over the rim of her glass.

"However much you hate me," he said. "And I don't blame you for hating me – oh no, not for one teeny, tiny second. I'd hate me if I were you."

"Gerald, what are you talking about?"

"Madam?" he said and arched his eyebrows.

"Why on earth should I hate you? You've been frightening me to death, that's all. You always have, rather . . ."

The lines on his face deepened; they were almost middle-aged lines when they did that.

"Is it because I frighten you that you don't want to talk? That you want to be left alone?"

"Good God," said Sarah, "Is this what Mary told you?"

"Yes, dear. Why the double-take? Isn't it true?"

"Well, of course it isn't true. She said *I* was to leave *you* alone."

He gave her one stony stare before he burst into laughter.

"I thought you were hating me," she said.

Gerald's face writhed out of laughter into the mask of Mephistopheles. Then he drained his glass.

"Masterly technique, hasn't she?" he observed, lifting the bottle out of the ice-bucket.

"I don't understand."

"You wouldn't, you wouldn't. God forbid you ever should. And my lips are sealed, do you hear? Tightly, tightly sealed. Mute the camel – till the cows come home."

"But why should she —?"

"Ha – it's so easy to explain. If I dared explain. Highly stupid of me not to guess before. I just assumed – not without reason – that you hated me for being here – safe – alive, on my way to Hollywood, when the old boy's gone and got himself killed."

"She didn't *say* that?"

"Put your mind at rest; she'd never say anything so unkind. Gets her results just the same, doesn't she? Stop me. Stap me. For Mary everything must be for the best in the best of all possible worlds. Which is the world of Mary Castle. And that will be all for today, Madam. Give me your glass."

Outside the window the spectacular, tourist-value sunset had begun to light sky and water. The fiery plumes spread wide. In here the red-gold reflection touched their glasses; touched Gerald's mocking face. He wagged a finger:

"One thing. You won't hear a word against your dunking the diplomat when we get home. No matter what time we get home. Or in what condition. All will be civilized, smooth, smoo-oo-ooth and charming. She'll Understand," he said in block capitals. "It's her strong suit. One of them. And I'm off to Hollywood. Understands that, too." He said, "Could you keep the smallest possible secret? I wonder."

Sarah's mind was zig-zagging slowly towards the truth. She said, "I think I could."

"Well, then, the minute my picture's finished, I'm going to Canada. To train for the R.A.F. Keep tiny trap shut, yes?"

"Mary doesn't know?"

"Not yet. But she will. And she'll be wonderful about it – mark my words. Bloody bleeding wonderful. The bravest war-widow on Broadway. Singing 'Johnny has gone for a soldier' very softly at parties and breaking people up – or do I mean down?"

He refilled both glasses, stood the empty bottle on its head in the bucket and waved opulently to the waiter.

"She'll know it's best for me, when the time comes, you see." The lines were now making his face look like a brown, squeezed lemon. "That's what she always knows. She knows it's best for you and me not to agonize each other, sit up late talking about Thomas, crying into our drinks." He narrowed his eyes to examine the label on the second bottle.

"'Be crying into our drinks any minute now," said Gerald. "And about time too."

Sarah felt her head swim. Deciding the champagne was not responsible, she said bemusedly, "And I've never imagined *you* being afraid of anyone."

He looked so bleak that she thought this had angered him. He was silent, spinning his glass between his fingers, stirring the bubbles out of the champagne.

"You are afraid of Mary, aren't you?"

He looked her straight in the eyes. "No, my darling. It's myself I'm afraid of."

After which he lowered his eyelashes and looked away from her in a movement that reminded her perfectly of their father.

"But why, Gerald?"

He shook his head and murmured, "Mute the camel." Then he said abruptly, "Old Thomas knew that, I shouldn't wonder. He knew an awful lot, the funny little fellow. Never thought he'd get killed, *never*."

"Didn't you? I did."

Gerald propped his chin on his hands. "Only if he wanted to be killed. Always did what he wanted. I wonder . . . How much did Romney's death really shake him, the inquest and all the brouhaha?" The inappropriate affectation of the last word gave offence to Sarah.

"I don't know. Those are things I try not to think about. I hurt him, you see; remember?"

"Yes dear, well, if it makes you feel any better the last time we met I called him a bloody little prig."

She said, "Thomas didn't want to be killed, how could he? Apart from anything else he'd know what it would do to Brigstock. And the rest of us. He was always so damn' sweet to everybody."

"Cry away," Gerald said gently. "Don't worry. I shall too when I've had another glass."

"He was in love with Rab. He was going to marry her. Anyway he did have one day with her, he got that. Why the *hell* should he want to die? Sorry. Sorry."

"All I meant was," – his voice sounded entirely composed, "I'd have trusted Thomas to beat the whole world, if he wanted to. He always could. Perhaps I'm ridiculous, but I think I relied on his magic as well as his guts. To get him out of trouble. Well, here's to you, Lord Thomas, my son.

"You said his magic."

"Well, whatever it was."

"Whatever it was failed him with Romney," she said miserably.

Gerald didn't answer. He went on drinking and staring past her shoulder. "As for you, Madam, you're probably having the worst time of any of us," was his verdict.

"My own making," she said automatically.

"Oh yes?" It was the imitation-Brookfield face, the clipped voice: "Don't, I beg you, give me remorse, darling. Why not go home?"

"Because I want them to be safe. I want to bring them here."

"Who? What are you up to? Bring who here?"

"Brigstock and the Grandmother. I can pay. I've opened an account for them. I put a lot of money into it. And a lot more for the Parrys, the family that's coming. And I've sent all the rest back to England: so's I won't be able to touch it."

She had shocked him. "You always were the silliest girl," he told her.

"Well, it's better than cheating. You know about the Treasury regulations."

"Oh darling Sarah. Is your conscience really racked by sinning against the Treasury? Yes, I see it is. Struth and stap me. Figuray-voo. Well, don't tell Father you're penniless, he'll come all over King Lear. How on earth are you going to live?"

"I've kept seven hundred dollars. With any luck I can get a job in the Censor's office. Some sort of job anyway. And look after Brigstock and Granny."

"You really believe they'd come? Oh my poor darling chump. When did you write?"

"I didn't write; I cabled."

Gerald said, "And can't you just see their faces when they get it? Granny saying, 'I don't think I'd care for the Tropics – the Tropics – the Tropics – let me see – where *is* Bermuda precisely?' And Nanny making 'tht-tht' noises. 'It's just her nerves. Mrs. Sarah was always the nervy one of the family.'" He frowned suddenly: "I presume it's a sterling account you've opened for them here . . . Yes, well, has it occurred to you that if they decide against coming, you won't be able to turn those pounds back into dollars for your own little self? It has . . . I salute your insouciance, Madam. True 'Moonrakers' blood in your veins."

THE UNWRITTEN NOTEBOOK

DAWN AGAIN; THE NOISE OF THE MICE NIBBLING IN THE hay; another hand shaking my shoulder. No matter whose hand, it managed, infallibly, to shake my bad shoulder, the right one; I suppose because I slept on the left to dodge the pain. Another face grinning through the greyness, bidding me goodbye. Another fine morning, by the smell of it.

I headed out of the yard and down the track, stiffly as always at this hour, studying to recall the directions learned by heart overnight. A hazardous day, today; I had come to the last page of the departmental guide. I was to circle the Cathedral town by the thin red line they had drawn for me, and after that . . . There had been too many After Thats . . . Too many terrors, too many near-misses: too much I would rather not have seen, too many things I won't, can't think about: though they run after me in the dark.

Living by night at first I had made slow, tortured progress. Night-living had changed me into some kind of animal, creeping, hungry, afraid. I knew what it was to be the fox slinking along the ditch, the rabbit with staring eyes crouched close to the earth, and my old friend the clumsy, blinded owl. But I came to the end of the longest night-walk yet; and still they hadn't caught me.

Day-living was better. How many days? Hard to keep count. Days were years again, as in my childhood. And this wasn't France. Perhaps it would turn into France sometime; for the moment it was a dream landscape that I myself had invented, with rough likenesses to France, such as I sometimes recognized in dream landscapes; peopled by the figures out of a dream, the nameless friends and the hostile tribes.

I came off the track and out on to the edge of a main road, only darkly discernible for what it was. I stood memorizing the map. The thin red line was about the size of a hyphen-mark on this road, no bigger. This road was dangerous. After the hyphen, about two hundred metres away, I would see a house standing back from the road on the other side. The path I wanted began there.

"You should praise the good God for your short legs; short legs make a good marcher." I couldn't remember which of them had said that: the families and the sheltering houses mixed into a *montage*. How much had the blow on my head really addled my wits? I began to wonder. At moments I was conscious of no other identity than that of Emile the cretin. Emile seemed to take over every time a German or a gendarme came my way. And by daylight nobody stopped Emile to ask what his business was; nobody demanded Emile's papers. The hostile tribes would stare at him and he would grin foolishly and nothing else happened. One moment, yesterday, had been a heart-stopper; a hostile tribe pulling up on a motor-bicycle; but he proved only to have lost his way. Emile, mumbling unhelpful directions, was cut short by an exasperated 'Scheisse!', and the tribe shot off again in search of more promising material.

Short legs . . . My father used to mourn my having short legs; his own are long. Gerald and Sarah have long legs, too; I'm the only small-sized Weston. This, coming to mind as I walked along the hyphen, was quickly pushed out again. On risky ground I always kept my thoughts away from my own truth, my own self. I wore the protective colouring inside as well as outside. No memories, no harking back, just Emile till I came to the next likely place; if there was one. (How long would the likely places last? How soon should I walk blindly into the trap? And how would it be, the trap? Would it be manned by the hostile tribes, or would it be just a village poisoned all through, like the one to the North – far away now? Unless I got hold of some papers, which began to seem impossible — switch off . . . Emile, you're Emile.)

There was the house, standing back from the road on the other side. I crossed quickly and found the field-path, as they said I would. Somewhere in the house a dog began to bark. I was used to the blind terror of that noise. "He's barking at Emile, you know; he would," was the formula I applied. The barking followed me only a little way.

By noon I was doing well. I had covered thirteen miles. I could no longer see the tower of the Cathedral, bleach-white on the blue beyond the poplars. I stood in a field of stubble, with the road before me. I could risk this one; not even a secondary road, but the lowest grade Michelin. The red line ended here because it had to. I tore the finished map into shreds and heeled the shreds into the ground. Then I lay down to eat my lunch. It was a hunk of bread with a thin slice of cheese. However short of food they were, they always gave me something to take along. When I tried to pay them they refused. I'd developed a trick of pushing fifty-franc notes under clocks or saucers for them to find afterwards.

On we go.

Since his accident Emile likes to sleep an hour or more in the afternoon. He feels the need now, but not seriously, having eaten so little. He drifts along at a slower pace than usual. An old woman comes down the road; the pattern of all the old women who work in the fields, stooped and lovable; she carries a bundle on her back. But she could be a witch, careful, just smile at her and go by. She wants something: what? She wants a cigarette, bless her, but Emile has none. Now she is telling him to be careful, as though she knew. Perhaps Emile imagines things. No, she is serious. "Les jeunes," she says, "Il y a de danger partout pour les jeunes. Soyez prudent." Emile gives her his foolish grin.

Nobody else in sight; nothing on the road, on he goes, praising the good God for his short legs, through villages that are all shut-faced in the sun, through a maze of little low hills, by an orchard where he steals an apple, by a stream where he drinks; on again, the afternoon light beginning to mellow, the legs still trudging in obedience; misty roofs of a town far to the left in the tree-plateau, this road takes in no towns, nobody here but Emile.

As the sun began to sink, I could let him go. I could allow myself a few minutes off-duty, back in my own head. At first, as always, it felt more like being *on* duty, recalled from leave of absence.

This road (they said) comes out at the Route Nationale, and I am headed due South, through Burgundy, through the Bourbonnais. I must keep on going till I reach the demarcation-line. When I have crossed into Unoccupied France there will be no more hostile tribes. But nobody knows exactly where the demarcation-line is: nor do I know how I shall cross it, unless I get those papers.

First on-duty period over: a waste of my mental *liberté*. I prayed a bit. Of course Emile prays, too, but always in rather low gear, like a child whose mind is on something else. ("Think of what you're saying, Thomas" – Brigstock's instructions long ago as I kneeled by my bed.)

I prayed for Brigstock more than for anybody else. I couldn't know what she had heard of me by now; that I was missing, or a prisoner; perhaps she had heard nothing at all. If I got beyond the demarcation-line I could surely send a postcard, couldn't I? It must get there somehow, sometime. I hoped she had moved out of London; gone with sister Mary to a safe place; if there was one. He shall give his angels charge concerning thee – and in their hands shall they bear thee up.

Nobody else seemed to be travelling with me. Rab was quite shut off, as though she had slammed a door in my face. The family were kind memories, not companions. And my own life . . . the Army, the Battalion, the platoon, where were they? I didn't know. The box-like world in which I had made myself fit for war had ceased to exist. It didn't even look like prep school; it was further back in time than prep school. Certain figures out of the period made themselves remembered now and then, notably Rayner and Lucas. But the machine itself, the machine of which I was one small part, had ground to a halt somewhere in the wood, by the ruined château.

If I got through, the machine would reclaim me. This was, I reminded myself, the reason for the journey. ("Is your journey really necessary?") I must get through: and I must go back. But here and now the whole meaning of the Army was hidden, lost. When I got to there in my mind I came to the German boy, standing in the doorway, eating his cherries: the sitting duck.

I couldn't rationalize him. I couldn't persuade myself that shooting him would have been useless. It was the fact, of course. I was trapped, I was surrounded; the betraying shot might have killed the German, but it would have brought the others straight to my futile hiding place.

It was the fact. But it wasn't the truth. The truth was my own private reason for holding my fire.

I'm no good at rationalizing; I've had to give up the struggle. I've tried it on some actions I'm ashamed of and it doesn't work. I've tried it on the lie I told in the witness-box; on the cheque I took from Romney after three refusals. My brain argues its case, for both these sins. But they remain sins. I have learned to swallow them as such and to be sorry. Which comes a lot easier than rationalizing.

No point whatever, then, in side-stepping the truth about the boy with the cherries. I couldn't bear to kill him.

Rab killed Tylo.

She is braver than I am.

On we go.

When I knocked the voices ceased suddenly. There was a profound silence. The lights in the ground-floor window remained lit: nobody was moving inside the room. Whoever they were, they sat quite still and waited for me to go away again. I didn't think I could walk ten more steps. I stood lurching from one tired foot to the other. Behind me in the grove of trees at the gate an owl hooted.

I was too hungry to sheer off and find a sleeping-place somewhere among the outhouses. I hadn't eaten since I stole the apple: before the apple there was only the hunk of bread and the thin cheese. For the last hour or so I had been feeding myself on huge imaginary helpings of roast lamb with peas and new potatoes; I'd made excursions into Zanchi's Dining Rooms, my old London standby, for sausages and mash, for stew and Savoury Pudding.

I knocked again. This time there was the sound of a footstep and the lights went out at the windows. A moment later I heard the key turning in the lock; the footsteps moved quickly away.

This hadn't happened before. And because it hadn't I was entirely at a loss. I could have cried; mainly from hunger. I went bumbling away round the side of the house and found the farmyard smells waiting for me. I stood still, sniffing the smells, gradually making out the shapes of roof and barn and stack with the stars behind them.

So I'd come to the end of my little run of luck. Longingly I looked back to last night: to the soup – and the wine. I wanted to wash my feet; I wanted oil for my precious boots. I wanted somebody to patch the newest rent in Emile's cotton shirt and somebody to give me news of England from the forbidden radio. I wanted the kind questioners, the nameless friends. But I wasn't going to get any of these. Not till morning anyway. Oh well.

The first door I pushed was the door of a pig-sty. The pigs made whistling grunts and I felt rather unkind for thinking of them purely in terms of ham. I lurched off across the cobbles, turning back to look at the house: all the windows stayed dark.

The next door swung open on to a smell of dried grass, bran, sawdust; the authentic rabbit-hutch smell that a barn has. Out of the dark a man's voice said *"Qui est Ça?"* sounding sleepy, cross. I said it was Emile and shut the door behind me. The small glow of a torch came up from a hummock in the middle of the dark; it made a halo round the hummock. A head was there.

"Evadé?" the voice said.

I answered him yes.

"From the camp? Which of us, then? Emile says nothing to me." He fired off a string of names, and I said No to them all. I sat down to take off my boots. He played the torch over me for a moment; then put it out.

"You haven't any food on you, I suppose?" I said to him.

"They fed us at the house. Must go to the house if you want to eat. Who are you?" he said again.

"Doesn't matter. I'm on the run, like you. But I wasn't in any camp."

"You were lucky." It was a young voice; the regional accent was one I didn't know. "Hungry, eh? Go to the house," he repeated.

"I did. They've locked up. They did that as soon as I knocked at the door."

"Pity." I could hear his yawn. "Probably thought you were after us. We told her it wasn't likely, we're miles away by now. But she's nervous, the little one with the face of a rabbit. She's alone here with her brother, just a kid. However, they've plenty of food."

"Well don't tell me about it, there's a good fellow."

"Who sleeps, dines," he said.

"That saying has never proved itself as far as I'm concerned."

"Ah well. In the corner you'll find a stack of old rutabagas, if you have the taste for them. Don't tread on Johnny – not that he'd wake up."

Johnny. Johnny, not *Jean*. This puzzled me for a second but I was too half-witted with weariness to go on puzzling. "Permit me to direct you to the rutabagas," he said, using the torch briefly. Its beam steered me past the second man, who was curled up in the straw with his coat pulled over his head.

"If you want water for your feet there's an outside tap – to the left of the door."

I went to the tap first. The rutabagas were, naturally, solid as wood, with a crumbly coating of earth; I gnawed at one dispiritedly for a minute or two before I flopped down. I remember my head aching violently for a few minutes and then it all went away.

The mice had begun to nibble. There was a door creaking open: I wriggled free from the hurting and the dreams. In the routine greyness I could see the figure of a boy carrying something. I smelled coffee. Blearily I watched two shapes up-heaving, shaking themselves out of their straw.

"Three of you," said the boy.

"He calls himself Emile. You might have given him some dinner."

"I'll bring some more bread."

"Coffee, Emile?"

"Better help yourself first or I'll drink the lot."

"Here – bread."

"Who the devil are you?" said the second man. I couldn't see either of them clearly. Last night's one looked to have a long face and long legs. With the straw in his spiky hair he suggested a dim sketch out of an old book, a Dickens book; he was, perhaps, Jacques from *A Tale of Two Cities*. The second one was hunched up like a monkey.

"Who the devil?" he repeated.

A different sort of accent.

"Just Emile," I said.

His shadowed profile gave me only a forelock, a pointed nose and a growth of beard.

I put my lips to the can of coffee; I tore the bread into small pieces, meaning to make it last, but as usual I found this too difficult, so ended by cramming all the pieces into my mouth at once. For days now I'd understood why dogs ate like this and then looked around for more.

"Just Emile, eh? No need to be discreet with us. Is there, Philippe? What regiment? Not a legionnaire, are you?"

He grabbed the coffee can, gulping, peering at me as he gulped. Now I could see his eyes, light slitty eyes that went up at the corners a little. He went on peering at me.

'Johnny,' the other one had called him.

Yes, I thought, yes. The pointed nose, the eyes that slant and the small bony face. When the hunched body uncurls and he stands up, he'll be about my size, though he's much thinner. And he'll have that odd, springy movement as if his heels were wired.

"Seems to me I've seen you before," he was saying.

"You have." I spoke English. "Lots of times. At Sawcombe. And in London. And you got me a job in an advertising-agency."

"Jesus Christ!" said Johnny Stevens.

"Thomas Weston, more," I replied, as a mild strike against blasphemy. It may be the Grandmother's influence or it may be Brigstock, but I'm not one for letting blasphemies go by. Uphill work, it's been, since I joined the Army.

"Old Thomas – the white-eyed Kaffir."

"Pas d'Anglais, pas-même ici," Philippe hissed.

"Ta gueule," said Johnny. I said, "Last I heard of you you were with the International Brigade."

"Not much of a step from there to the Legion."

"Beau Stevens."

"Bo to a goose and f—— you," said Johnny. Out of our childhood I said "Ditto, ditto, Brother Smut." and we both began to giggle. Philippe turned into one of the grown-ups, telling us to be quiet.

Johnny Stevens is an old friend; but only if I count the years. He isn't really anybody's friend; he has a way of bobbing up in people's lives, including mine, and then taking off. He's the youngest of a huge Anglo-Indian family: there were five brothers and four sisters and then – a long time afterwards – Johnny. The runt, Gerald called him at Sawcombe. Morris Ward called him Daddy's Last Drop; I remember asking what that meant and Gerald quickly saying it meant he'd been dropped on his head, that was why he was a dwarf.

He isn't a dwarf, but there's something dwarfish inside. The outside of Johnny is tough. He made himself into an athlete because people were always kicking him around: the reason he's a good boxer is simply that. He also likes to make everything difficult and dramatic – driving all night from Scotland to catch an aeroplane for Paris and be back the same evening. It's a sort of Ruritanian character he's created for himself.

When he was twenty-one, he inherited some money; part of a family trust, and this, he said, would enable him to live dangerously. He bought a fast car; he willed me his job in the advertising-agency and took off. I hadn't seen him since. I'd only heard his news from my friends the Tarrants.

We had to go back to talking French: Philippe insisted. Philippe also insisted it was time they were moving, but Johnny lay still in the straw and talked. He talked like an old soldier. He had been with the Legion when they made their last stand on the Loire. After that he had gone down the roads in the mob while overhead the Dorniers dropped their bombs and swooped low to fire their machine-guns. He was taken prisoner in Montargis, a month ago now. The escape from the camp had been organized three days back. Frenchmen at work on the outbuildings made it possible; smuggling in clothes for Johnny, Philippe and two others; staging a mock brawl to cover the getaway. Those men had, in all likelihood, been shot, said Johnny. He tried to sound as though he didn't care. And very nearly succeeded.

"Where are you headed for?" I asked him.

"South. Like you, I imagine. Any plans?"

"None. Have you?"

"Naturally. There's a Legion depot at Sathonay, near Lyon. Philippe's headed for Clermont-Ferrand, so I lose him tomorrow." He sounded thankful.

"What about the demarcation-line?" I asked.

"We'll cross that river when we come to it." said Johnny.

Philippe interrupted; angrily this time. *"Filons,"* he said. He didn't want me along. Three were more noticeable than two. Johnny laughed at him. Three good proletarian Frenchmen on their own soil, what was wrong with that? We could always split up later, couldn't we? No, said Philippe. "It's because you're English," said Johnny, "Pay no attention." But Philippe went on arguing until Johnny lost his temper. *"Va te faire foutre, espèce de con. . .* Get going."

He was laughing as Philippe went.

"We'll catch up with him and pass him. He's too slow for me. What's your mileage per diem?·'

"About thirty," I said.

"Not bad," said Johnny, patronizingly.

He became the leader, taking over. Unlike myself he was equipped with useful things: all carefully stowed. He had a knife, maps, a compass and a razor. He had a watch, too. And money. And a cigarette-case he was planning to sell. It was the gift of the *marraine* who, according to Legion custom, had adopted him when he joined. "But she isn't the orthodox *marraine*, she's one of my old girl-friends," said Johnny – "If we could only get as far as Aix now —" He nodded to himself in his grinning, secret, way.

"What would happen at Aix?"

"Mourri would happen. She lives there."

"Mourri? Is that her name?"

"Mourri," he repeated. "There was a young woman called Mourri . . . who with *passion* was more or less *pourrie*. On our way, Emile."

•   •   •   •   •

Now Emile changes a little; or perhaps he becomes even more himself, stupider than ever beside his bright, agile companion. When I dismiss him and take time off, I take it aloud; meeting Johnny in the childhood places; giggling, composing French versions of "Ditto, ditto, Brother Smut," playing the Hostile Tribe game, running back to Sawcombe for the memories that are happier, safer than this Now.

On we go.

He had said "Cross that river when we come to it," splendid in theory; a consoling kind of shrug at any problems that might face us on the demarcation-line. Now it was here we had both got the wind up. Fear took us differently. It turned me broody and quiet; Johnny was full of don't-care gestures, Ruritanian brags and some protests that he could manage it easily.

We had to swim for it. There were hostile tribes manning the bridges and patrolling each side of the canal: on the other side there was a *zone de securité*, three miles deep, where they were likely to pick up anybody whose clothes were wet.

We lay under the trees, smoking and waiting. After midnight was the best time. We had fed well. Our hosts had sent us to bivouac in this walled garden: the gate in the garden opened on to a path that led straight down to the Canal and reached it at a likely point, half a mile from the bridge. It was a manservant who'd accompanied us, while daylight still lasted, to show us the place.

This was the first big house and the first rich family we'd met: an elderly couple with a young son – demobilized before he ever saw a shot fired. He remained silent, plunged in gloom. The father and mother were kind; *de-haut-en-bas*, Johnny said, *grands seigneurs* befriending tramps. My only disappointment was their not listening to the English news on the radio. He took a dimmer view: "What's the betting they've sent their butler off with a message to the Hostile Tribes?"

"I don't think so," I said, having thought.

"Why don't you think so?"

"They aren't agin us. They're ashamed, that's all. At least the son was. I'm sorry for him."

"If I hear another charitable word out of you I'll throw up. God knows what you're doing in a war anyway."

"This ain't a war. It's just a summer hitch-hike. And pretty spiffing, so far."

"You know," said Johnny, "I believe you're right about your brain being affected."

I said, "Oh well."

"What the devil are you going to do when I turn you loose?"

"Thought you'd decided not to turn me loose. Last night you were going to present me at your depot as a Legionnaire who'd lost his memory. Brilliant stroke, you said."

"All my strokes are brilliant," said Johnny.

There were so many of them that I found it impossible to keep up. One minute he was going back to the Legion; the next he was going to desert. His British passport was still filed with the Legion H.Q. at Marseilles. "Straight to the consulate with it and Bob's your uncle: they can get me shipped to Gibraltar." Another favourite ploy was Spain. "Spain's my wash-pot. Over Spain do I cast out my shoe."

"Thought you were on the losing side."

"*Je t'emmerde*. If I can get across the frontier to Figueras – it's no distance – then I'm safe."

"How?"

"Friends," he said, shrugging and grinning. "Reckoned to be staunch supporters of the Régime. In fact they've spent a very happy year double-crossing it."

"What can *they* do for you?"

Johnny would only smile and look mysterious. I never knew how much to believe and at this moment any scheme – his or mine – came under my old heading "After that . . ." To be shelved, because it was a waste of time to think ahead.

"How's the shoulder?" he asked me now, with the usual tinge of exasperation in his voice.

"Not bad today. Aches a bit, that's all."

"Never mind. Another weeping Maman will give you a rub, once we're across. God's gift to them, you are. Lord, I'm tired of Mamans."

I asked him, as I'd wanted to ask before, "Don't you like *anybody*?"

Fatal. It was just the kind of question he enjoyed. "Well now . . . I'm sick to death of the French, I've always disliked the Hostile Tribes and I've a thing against the Irish because my grandfather was Irish. From what I remember of the natives in Bombay when I was a toddler, they were quite disgusting. My main worry about getting back to England is I've always loathed the British. Particularly if they happen to be aristocrats or true cockneys. Oh, I forgot my pet hate – the Spaniards, and there I speak as an expert."

"If you hate them why did you go to their war?"

"It was the only war there was," he said reproachfully. When I laughed, he grew furious: "You just don't know. You've never lived. War has this in common with the bull-fight, – it becomes an Art form."

"I never did hear such balls – even from you."

Johnny said, "Listen – you haven't had the chance to find out. Office-work and pay and quartering aren't war. All you've done so far is transport a lot of worthy oicks from Dover Harbour to the alleged Front. Where they sat on their arses till the order came to retreat. That's all, isn't it? Well, okay, not quite all. Being you, you had to get yourself in a little jam, you and nobody else. Typical Emile – Emile *Schlemiel*; oh that's another hate of mine – Jews." He sat up and scanned the dark. "Possibly," he said, "you'll hear a shot fired in anger tonight."

I said, "Oh well."

Silence came down on us both. Presently he asked me, "Are you in a trance?"

"Sort of."

"Remember when we used to put you into trance and make you talk? At the University?"

"Yes."

"Impressive, you were. Ever do those tricks now?"

"No, never."

"Quite a boy for magic at Sawcombe, too. Obviously in need of

110

a psycho-analyst. The supernatural can always be interpreted psychologically."

This was so pompous I could have crowned him. I said "If you believe that, you'd believe anything. Magic's nothing to do with psychology."

"Oh no?" He peered at his watch. "Well, suppose you while away our last half-hour explaining it. Why can't you magic us across this fornicating canal? Go on. How do you work it?"

I said, "Sorry, Brother Smut. I've given it up."

This delighted Johnny. "Back to Sawcombe again. You and me and that ugly little girl, what did you say her name was? Well, go *on*, what was it?"

"Her name was Rab. And she wasn't ugly."

"Yes, she was. The grown-ups were having a party on the loggia. We were playing jungle games in the garden, don't you remember? And you told us you'd given it up."

"No I didn't."

"I distinctly recall."

"It was magic that had given *me* up, that time."

After a moment he said, "Well what's the difference?"

"You wouldn't understand. Any more than you understand about God."

"Oh God, don't let's have God," said Johnny.

I lay still and pretended to sleep. I could hear him fussing around with his possessions; taking everything out of his waterproof bag, talking to himself in whispers, counting his money. He never parted with a *centime* if he could help it. He despised my trick of putting notes under clocks and saucers when we left our night's lodgings. Proof of a common little mind, he said. Once, when he had drunk Pernod, he told me I was smudging what was left of the glory of France with my common little mind.

Presently I heard him say, "Wake up. Come on in; the water's lovely."

We went out of the gate and down the path in the thick, lime-scented summer darkness. At the edge of the Canal we sat down to take off our boots. We tied them round our necks by the laces. I hung my belt round my neck too, because of the money in the pouch.

"Next stop – the Promised Land," Johnny whispered.

The manservant had pointed us out the house on the other side, the nearest to the bank. We must hide up there till our clothes were dry. Our clothes . . . something of a euphemism, said Johnny.

We separated, as agreed. After a few minutes I could still hear him crackling and splashing, fifty yards away, sounding as though he were making a hell of a noise on purpose. He might be. Despite his line about the butler informing the Hostile Tribes, despite the "shot fired in anger," I knew he was fundamentally sure we'd get over. Scared, but sure. "The buggers aren't organized yet," was one of his talisman phrases.

The water felt warm and rather sticky. My shoulder bothered me: I could only use one arm; the boots and the belt around my neck were a bore. I didn't quite know what I expected; the white beam from a searchlight hitting the water close to my head? And then? Shouts and bullets? I went on wondering. I was more than halfway over when the load about my neck shifted suddenly. One bootlace had snapped; the burdensome boots slid off me like the albatross. I didn't dare dive for them, what with my useless arm and having to hang on to the belt in case that went too.

I was over.

I crawled up the opposite bank, making for the house. It was very slow, nasty going in my wet socks. I kept telling myself I was in the Promised Land, after which I would remember the *zone de securité*. I had to keep sitting down to pull prickles out of my feet.

That's cooked it, I said to myself, losing the boots; that really has cooked it. Worn and battered as they were, they suited my Awkward Feet and it was doubtful I'd find another pair to fit me. I remembered my first ordeal-by-army-boots. There was a rather nice Corporal in the Quartermaster's Store who kept taking them back and giving me a different size to try. But I went around for weeks feeling as if they were soled with red-hot concrete.

Really the boots were much more important than the money-belt. I sat in my wet clothes and mourned for them.

. . . . .

Had it not been for my losing the boots, we might have missed the bicycles. Johnny consoled me with this thought. I didn't feel right about our taking the bicycles; I'm not sure Johnny did; but they persuaded us, just as they persuaded us to accept new, dry clothes and leave our sodden rags behind.

It had been a fair feasting. We were the first escaped prisoners to get to that house and they'd broken out the best they had. Afterwards we slept four hours in a feather bed. They gave our hangovers a huge breakfast in the usual yellow-grey dawn. The only boots that would anywhere near fit me were a pair of old felt ones, with cork soles, belonging to the grandfather. It was the eldest son who offered his bicycle. What about a second? *On va s'arranger.* We sat around smoking and awaiting results. The Maman clipped our hair. Johnny, with a few more curses at my common little mind, finally put a mille-franc note under a plaster statue of St. Thérèse while nobody was looking. I added five hundred, leaving myself two hundred.

In fact, they told us, we'd be better going by road than across the fields, where German patrols on horseback were liable to hunt near the river. The town was a mile and a half away. There was a Centre d'Accueil set up for *militaires errants.* "But they'll keep you hanging around forever. The Commandant is a stickler for rules and regulations, he'll want your papers."

"He can go f—— himself," said Johnny. "On wheels we can be in Lyon by tomorrow. *Can* you bicycle, Emile, by the way? I forgot to ask. You can? You surprise me. Just as well."

The eldest son came back, victoriously pedalling. There was a ceremony of removing the departmental Saône-et-Loire plates from the bicycles: a wise precaution for later on. There was a ceremony of presenting us with bundles that contained food and cigarettes. We all hugged one another and Maman wept. Johnny and I walked off waving, pushing our machines through the farmyard, scattering the hens. This reminded me of the departure of Pigling Bland, with Alexander, for the market. Johnny said, "You're awfully like Pigling, come to think of it. Emile Pigling. Pigling Emile." "Alexander Smut," I said.

It was really splendid, even with a hangover and the hazard of grandfather's boots. The morning was fine; the news from England was still fairly all right; bombing had begun, but the radio made little of it; we had clean shirts and trousers. Maman had given me a stamped postcard of the Tuileries for Brigstock, though I mustn't send it off from here.

The hostile tribes vouchsafed us only incurious glances. We saw one patrol riding toward the fields, then two tribes on foot, loitering at the outskirts of the town: young, bewildered conquerors, they looked. Like Emile, Johnny made a habit of grinning at them politely, and this time we waved as well; because, damn it, they were the last. We were in the unoccupied, the promised land. We waved with a will. They seemed pleased. Their solemn faces widened with their smiles. A master's gratitude, said Johnny, for the affection of the slaves.

And now South. South, South. Towards the enchanted coast, *France heals all wounds*, I remembered, and thought she could not heal her own this year and was sad and then tremendously happy again. I couldn't get it through my head that the enchanted coast would be different from the place I used to know. There lay all the golden memories and I went flying down the road to find them.

LONDON

THE LATE BROADCAST ON THE SHORT WAVE TO AMERICA presented its announcer with the same problem every week. (You could, if you liked, call it the early broadcast. It went out at four-fifteen a.m.) Dick Abrahams, the B.B.C. announcer concerned, reviewed the choice ahead of him.

"What's the time?" he asked his assistant; a rather too jolly young woman who said that now the air-raids were really beginning she felt so much better.

"Five to six," she told him.

"One of two things may happen."

"The sirens, you mean?"

"No. Just a Jewish story."

"Pardon?"

"Well, the frame of a Jewish story. I was trying to decide what to do with my night."

"Oh I see."

She didn't. He chanted at her, "One of two things may happen. Either I stay up till three-thirty and drink too much or I go to bed. If I stay up and drink too much, I have nothing to worry about. If I go to bed one of two things may happen. Either I sleep in a cot downstairs or I go home and set my alarm. If I sleep downstairs, I have nothing to worry about. If I go home and set my alarm one of two things may happen. Either the alarm will go off or I'll stay awake waiting for it. If it goes off I have nothing to worry about. If I stay awake one of two things may —"

— "There's always the chance of a direct hit, isn't there?" the jolly young woman interrupted, "You're on the top floor, I mean, and no Shelter. Our Shelter's nice, except for the dart-board being crooked. If I were you I'd stay where you are."

"From now till four-fifteen tomorrow?" Dick asked as the door opened to admit a hand with some envelopes.

"Here's the script back from the Min. of Inf.," said the jolly young woman.

Dick leafed through it, picking up the accustomed marks of the Ministry's blue pencil. They would not please tonight's celebrated speaker. "If there *is* such a thing as a Stock Exchange after the war" was deleted as revolutionary. "As my Nanny used to say" was deleted as being snobbishly upper-class. "The Right hand," Dick murmured, "seems a touched confused about what the Left is doing."

"Shall I retype it, Mr. Abrahams?"

"No need, ducky. What else have you got there?"

"Fan mail. *His*," the young woman said, having obviously no respect for the celebrated speaker. "Oh, and one for you." She studied the envelope. "From Bermuda. Who do you know in Bermuda?"

"Perhaps if you let me have it, I could tell you."

"My cousin's sending her children over there," the young woman said, "*I* think that's idiotic, actually. When they grow up they'll be absolutely wild to think they've missed all this." She went on chattering while Dick mentally restated one of his qualifications for a wife: *she will never speak to me while I'm reading a letter.*

After a time the chirpy voice reached his ears: "Not bad news, I hope?" He said "Quiet, there's a good girl," and began to read the letter again from the beginning.

Dear Dick,

Hearing your voice on the air last night was the most consoling thing that's happened to me for months and months. I pray this will reach you. Father sent me on the letter you'd written about Thomas, and I meant to answer, but I couldn't. Forgive me. I still can't say anything about him, I find. I try to believe he's better out of all this; he would have hated to see France collapse and surrender, he loved it so much.

You sounded extremely placid and most enviably like yourself. If that observation seems silly it is because (as well as being altogether useless and pointless) I don't seem to be me any more. That is to say, not the person you knew last year, the one who loved Romney and ran away to America because he was dead. (I wonder sometimes if he's moving through as unfamiliar a world as I am.)

I came to this island to settle some English evacuees into their new house. And am staying under my sister-in-law's luxurious roof. It's hell in triplicate since Gerald went to Hollywood. And rather more hellish now I know my Grandmother and Brigstock (Nanny, if that name's unknown to you) refuse to come here. I'd picked a house for them and got the money arranged and I meant to look after them. But they won't hear of it.

Oh *Lord*, that sounds as if my feelings were hurt; it's the last thing I mean. They're not; they couldn't be. Of course I expect them both to do what they want. I'm only miserable because I worry about them in London. Uncle Percy and Aunt Flavia go to see them and send hearty little bulletins, but they're so damned hearty about everything.

Would it be too much to ask you to telephone Granny – and perhaps, if you have time, go round there and see if they're really all right? Telephone-number and address herewith. I can send them *anything* they need. And I'd be much more ready to believe a word from you – however brief – than from Uncle P.

It suddenly occurred to me to ask you, hearing your voice. I hope you don't mind. Write to me, please, if you do write, to the New York address above. I'm going there in ten days' time to work for British War Relief, in an office. Tried for a job here; but none going.

You are in my prayers, like everybody else in England. And I'll never forget how wonderful you were to me the day Romney died. It's odd to wish one could get back to there.

Affectionately and gratefully,

Sarah.

Dick lit his pipe and brooded. She was indeed far off; no further, he reminded himself, than she would always be, for him. But the last sentence in the letter worried him profoundly.

"May I go now?" the jolly young woman was asking.

"Yes, do. Goodnight."

"Have you decided —"

"Not yet," he said "Goodnight."

The sensible actions would be to take a drink at the pub on the corner, return to eat dinner in the B.B.C. canteen and then commandeer a cot for the first part of the night. The sensible actions ... Weren't these a waste of time, when time might have a stop any minute now?

He folded the letter, putting it in his wallet. He picked up the telephone. "See if you can get me Kensington 1837," he said to the operator. If, as was likely, the afternoon raid had disrupted the lines, he would take the sensible actions instead. (Wouldn't he?)

"Can't get Kensington at all at the minute, sorry."

"Oh well, if you're going to be like that, I shall take a chance," Dick told his God: a strictly non-Jewish God, though not a Christian God either. A gambler's God, by and large; a wayward personal overseer with no other clients. His task was simply to thwart or reward Dick Abrahams, according to his own private whim.

On occasions, such as this, one could outwit him. In the matter of win-trebles he was, of course, the boss.

Down in the lobby, Broadcasting House had become, to Dick's-eye-view, a fortress designed by Gilbert and Sullivan. The sentry, the special constables, the system of showing your pass whether you went out or came in; the sandbags and the blast-doors all combined to overstate the importance of what happened here. Dick sneered at the overstatement, and knew why he sneered. The reason was simple enough. He despised his job. He wanted to be in uniform, R.A.F. uniform for choice.

Outside, in the evening sunshine, a taxi with one window splintered was just delivering Peregrine Marlow, the gossip-writer turned war-correspondent. Having greeted Dick with "My dear, the *noise* – and the *people*!" Peregrine pranced off towards the studios; Dick collared the taxi and gave the Kensington address.

In a moment Sarah was beside him, the image of Sarah, restored.

"You see," he was saying to her, "There's nothing dramatic or frightening about this – yet. Everything goes on much the same as usual. Yes, the streets more deserted than they used to be at the rush-hour; yes, the brick shelters; yes, the barrage balloons, like huge airborne boxing-gloves, aren't they? Rather decorative when they shine in the sun . . . Yes, the traffic lights masked; just those little crosses of red and green. One gets used to them. One gets used to driving a car with only one half-headlamp lit. One gets used to it all. I'll look after you. I think you'll be happier now you're home; even though it's going to be much worse very soon: over London any-way. We must learn to salute the prospect of death after dinner," he said, showing-off to Sarah.

Kensington; the Boltons; the house. He had met the Grandmother only once, at Sarah's wedding. An intimidating old lady. One would not ring this doorbell uninvited on an ordinary day. Ordinary days, he reminded himself, were off.

It was Nanny who opened the door; a legendary figure for him, Nanny; the beloved Brigstock; Brigstock, beloved of Thomas. He had seen her too at the wedding. She looked a little smaller and a little grimmer; naturally. The death of Thomas hit him again, hard. *But who shall return us the children?* he thought; looking down into the lined face, with its prominent nose and firm little chin, its clear blue eyes. Her grey hair was neat under a hairnet. She wore a black dress with a white lace collar.

Her vocation had struck him before as one demanding the most and rewarding its faithful with the least. He knew this again now, as explaining himself, he reminded her that Thomas was a friend of his, that they had worked together. Her smile began when her tears began; there was only a precarious hint of each, then her expression became merely polite. Of course, she said, she remembered him: she was sure Mrs. Murray would be glad to see him. "Please come in, sir."

"Hadn't you better ask her first?"

"Gracious no, she's only got Mrs. Flavia with her, you'll do her good," said Brigstock, "Cheer her up. This way, sir." She held back a bead portière, and marshalled him through it, saying briskly, "Here's Mr. Abrahams to see you, M'm. You remember him at Mrs.

Sarah's wedding, don't you?" Still Nanny, Dick observed: almost he expected her to tell Mrs. Murray to stand up and shake hands with the nice gentleman.

Mrs. Murray sat in a tall armchair whose arms curved about her; she looked to be enshrined. Silver-haired, heavy-boned, strong-throated, it was a regal head surmounting an enormous pair of blue rompers that fastened with a zip; the 'siren-suit' designed when war first came; lately favoured by Winston Churchill; the old lady must, Dick reflected, be rather too hot.

The room was warm and scented; he was aware of a profuse, grandiloquent clutter all about him; of the old lady studying him through a tortoiseshell-rimmed lorgnette; of the second person in the room, "Mrs. Flavia"; she had fair, fading hair and a startled-Pekinese face; she wore the green uniform of the W.V.S.

"Of course I remember you," said Mrs. Murray. "Mr. Abrahams – my daughter, Mrs. Trumbull." Done with the handshakes, Dick saw her still examining him through the lorgnette.

"But you are better-looking than you were," she said.

Mrs. Trumbull gave a little nervous laugh.

"Am I?" said Dick, "Now am I?" He glanced into the mirror that hung over the crowded mantelpiece. In the gold frame there was the face he knew and did not know; not being greatly interested until somebody said something like this. There was the suggestion of a goat's face, knobbed forehead, slanted eyebrows, amber-coloured eyes; one of the more delicate Jewish noses and a well-curved mouth. He studied the reflection, item after item, with detachment. The startled Pekinese was looking positively pop-eyed when he turned from the glass. He heard "Mother always says what she thinks", and the nervous little laugh again; saw a scramble of knees under the green skirt, a hand shooting out for a cigarette.

"That's quite untrue," said Mrs. Murray. "And if true would – rightly – give me a loathsome reputation, Flavia dear." She went on looking at Dick: the gravely charitable stare reminded him of Thomas.

"It takes some people longer than others to find their faces," she told him, "Two years is it, since we met? Almost . . . Well, at the time you hadn't quite found yours – yours – yours. Do sit down.

Help yourself to a drink first. There's some rather inferior sherry – yes, Flavia, it is, I warned you and I think you'll be sorry. Half a bottle of gin. A whole bottle of Italian vermouth, for some reason. French vermouth and some whisky. Soda-soda-soda. All on the sideboard." Dick found the bottles and glasses ranged before a huge wooden statue of the Virgin and Child. The lilting yet determined voice pursued him. "Are you still working in that tradesman's place – Sarah's husband's place, what was it called? Butler's, yes. Of course it would be, wouldn't it, that unfortunate fellow." Mrs. Trumbull's voice said, "Poor, Romney, poor little Sarah," in a quick, ritual tone, wound off with a small ritual sigh. Dick said, "I'm in the B.B.C. now." "The B.B.C.?" Mrs. Trumbull sounded sprightly and re-assured. The old lady said, "Rather too lively, I should have thought. You for it, I mean, not it for you." This brought the nervous laugh, the scramble of knees again and Mrs. Trumbull sipped her sherry busily. Dick sat down on the large, undulating velvet sofa.

"I do find it extremely boring," he admitted.

"I should have thought at *this* minute – and such worthwhile work, I mean, where would we all be without —"

"It can still bore him," the old lady interrupted, "I expect you did your best to get into uniform, didn't you?"

"Well, yes. From Munich onwards I rushed into every recruiting office there was. Shouting 'Plucky little Abrahams here – anybody want him?'"

Bad taste, said the wan smile on the face of the startled Pekinese. Mrs. Murray gave him a pleased, pearly grin. "And nobody did – did – did."

"My eyesight ruled me out. I'm hoping they'll become less choosy with time. I hoped they would after Dunkirk. I had another shot. But being a Civil Servant now, of course I'm in a Reserved Occupation."

"You're just as likely to be killed in the B.B.C. as anywhere," said Mrs. Murray on a pure, fluting note of consolation. "More likely, really."

"Oh mother."

"It is what he wants to hear."

"Percy says morale has never been better," cried Mrs. Trumbull passionately. She aimed the cry at Dick, adding "Percy's my husband." Finding no adequate answer, he smiled and nodded. "The War Office," she said – "And he's quite right, you know. I've noticed it myself. Morale *is* wonderful. Even in St. John's Wood."

"'Even . . .' Well, now, is St. John's Wood a recognized military objective? More than, let us say, Bayswater?" the old lady asked. It became increasingly obvious to Dick that, while she was enjoying herself and Mrs. Trumbull was not, this was a game regularly played and somehow necessary to each.

"Of course not, mother, how can you be so ridiculous?"

"I thought perhaps the residence of Percy –"

"Oh really – if you like to be sarcastic —"

"Well why do you say '*Even* in St. John's Wood'?"

"We have so many Jews," mourned the Pekinese.

Here it was. Once again: presenting him with the eternal problem. Silence-in-the-cause-of-good-manners? Statement-in-the-cause-of-integrity? He had long ago ceased to lose his temper when it happened and this made the decision more difficult. (Deciding to speak, you still had a bewildering variety of choices before you. Words, tempo, line of attack . . . There was the gentle sort: "Now, now, you mustn't say that to me, you know." There was the lead-on-to-make-them-say-more-and-worse. There was the jocular "Jews like me, you mean?" Oh there were dozens; lightly wounding shafts exchanged by the adult for the heavier weapons wielded in youth. Not one of them would give you pleasure. Not one but would abruptly spoil the pleasure of those present. And if you kept quiet? You couldn't; you never had. You must drag your weary gun to the defence for the simple and possibly childish reason that to let it go would be a coward's choice. Nor could you ever rationalize your silence with the comfortable reflection, "It's none of their business." It was, alas, yours.)

Having skimmed over this familiar and depressing ground, Dick had just begun to say, "The name is Abrahams, remember?" when Mrs. Murray said limpidly, "Flavia, dear, the name is Abrahams, Mr. Dick Abrahams." The Pekinese turned a rosy purple, almost matching the shade of the blouse worn with her green uniform. Then there was a flounder of apology, knees scrambling and half-finished sentences from which the words 'refugee' and 'German' frequently emerged as proof of purity in original intention, followed by Heavens-Look-At-The-Time and a breakneck hustle. She was gone. The bead curtain swayed from agitation to calm while Dick and the old lady gazed at each other in silence.

It was a silence with the hint of a giggle on the way.

"I interrupted you, I think, excuse me," said Mrs. Murray at last. "What would *your* comment have been?"

"The same as yours."

"Really?"

"Really."

"Temperate," she said, "Considering . . ."

"Oh no. It never makes me cross, happens far too often. I only wish there was an absolute rule for reply. Something as obviously correct and indisputable as 'No thank you' when one doesn't take sugar," Dick explained.

She looked at him severely. "How could there be? When the remark itself should not be made?"

"It *is* made, though. Always has been, always will be."

"More often in England than anywhere else, perhaps, what do you think?"

"Possibly," said Dick.

"Flavia's silliness has, of course, accelerated since the war. She and Percy have no children." Was this, Dick wondered, a sequitur? Apparently it was. "Unmarried women," said Mrs. Murray "can remain childless without becoming silly. Married women, particularly those of Flavia's type, cannot. My daughter Isobel, Gerald's and Sarah's mother –" (was she deliberately banning Thomas's name?) "Isobel had few brains but a far more sensitive approach to life. Which is possibly why she died. May she rest in peace," Mrs. Murray added, crossing herself majestically while Dick tried to imagine the mother of Thomas and only succeeded in bringing Brigstock to mind. He was interrupted by the old lady saying "You look as though you *needed* something – is it a cigarette?"

"Would you mind if I smoked my pipe?"

"Do, do." She was pleased. "I tried to smoke a pipe myself at one time. I couldn't keep it alight, but the taste was enjoyable." She watched him filling the pipe. "Groups – groups – groups," she chirped.

"Groups?"

"Identifiable groups. Jews. Roman Catholics. Negroes. The Irish. What others? Homosexuals, perhaps. Under a more general heading, Foreigners. The sin, everyone knows, is to be different. But different from what? What is the desired, unidentifiable, respectable norm? In other words what does Flavia think she is, that's the interesting question. Or would be, if Flavia were a person of more weight – weight – weight."

"Jews can be boring about being Jews," said Dick. "I used to be. Now I study to avoid it."

"Flavia," said Mrs. Murray, "can be quite boring about being Flavia."

"It isn't the same."

"No, of course it isn't. Xenophobia," said Mrs. Murray, "begins at home." After which she looked at him as though he had only just walked into the room; "And what can I do for you?" she asked.

"Sarah wanted me to come and make sure you were all right, you and Nanny."

"Sarah . . ."

"Yes, I had a letter from her."

"Do you think it was unkind of us not to go to Bermuda? We really are too old, you know, Blanche and I. But I hope I sounded grateful. 'All right'," Mrs. Murray reflected. "Tell her we are quite all right. Please. Try to explain how much more all right we are than anyone three thousand miles away can imagine."

"I wish she'd come home."

"You care for her." It was a statement, not a question.

"Yes," Dick said.

"I'm glad."

"Why do you think she stays over there?" he asked humbly. "She sounds so miserable."

"Tell her to come back. Tell her to come because it is what you want."

"That," said Dick, "would take more nerve than I possess."

"Well, she won't do it for her own sake, you may be sure. How did she express it to me? I remember. *'I've lost the right to be selfish. If indeed I ever had it.'* Now when one gets to there . . ." the old lady appeared to lose the thread, chirping, "There – there – there," in a vexed way. "But perhaps I am wrong. Sarah must work it out on her own terms. She will." A pause: then, sounding a little tremulous, she asked, "Did she speak of Thomas in her letter?"

"She said she couldn't."

"Nor can I," said Mrs. Murray rather fiercely. "I think of him endlessly; indeed I think of little else these days. But not aloud. Which once again proves the foolishness of poor Flavia, believing I always say what I think. It is her euphemism for 'Mother always says what oughtn't to be said'." She brought the lorgnette into play again suddenly. "You are much too intelligent to wonder why I can't talk about Thomas."

"Would it be impertinent just to tell you I loved and admired him?"

"No," she said, "No. You must come here as often as you like. And never when you don't like. Never as a guilty obligation. But I don't imagine you suffer from unnecessary guilt, somehow."

"I wanted this war – desperately. I feel guilty for that." He meant to say "Because Thomas was killed" and substituted, "when I think of all that's happened since May."

"Don't tell me you think we're going to lose?"

"No. No, I never think so for a minute. Though I can't imagine why not."

"Peace," said Mrs. Murray, "is merely further off than it was. From 'tomorrow' it's become 'the day after tomorrow'. Try to imagine afterwards. Try to practise saying to yourself 'Oh, that was during the war.' Very useful, I find it. You might suggest it to Sarah, when you write."

"Is there anything you need? She said I was to ask you."

Her face became stony, thoughtful.

"Nothing. Nothing that the hand of man can give me. Blanche would say the same, I know. It is the same for her." Then she was silent, so profoundly silent that he himself sat rigid, his mind becoming a blank, his eyes beginning to cloud with the effort of watching that still, grief-stricken face.

"I refuse to believe he is dead!" It came as a shout. After it, she moved her head from side to side, blinking her mauve, papery eyelids. She looked lost and puzzled for a moment. Then she smiled at him. "Do you know, I haven't said that to anybody. Not to Blanche, it wouldn't be fair . . . I wonder why I say it to you. I wonder how close a friend of his you were."

But as soon as he began to speak she hove herself out of the armchair, an awesome sight in the blue swaddling-clothes. "Forgive me. I like to see to the stirrup-pump. And the buckets. And the shutters. And Blanche will be bringing her things down from upstairs. And do please feel at liberty to stay," she added in a final gesture of dismissal.

THE UNWRITTEN NOTEBOOK

NOW, SUDDENLY, I COULD FEEL THE TIME COME NEAR FOR Johnny and myself to part. It wasn't said in words; it was all over the air.

We had learned our way about the Promised Land: on the whole, we'd learned quickly. No more hostile tribes, but the local gendarmerie – anywhere – had established themselves as a sub-hostile species. And we were warned to beware of German agents in plain clothes. "Just *how* does one beware of them?" Johnny asked ironically. Nobody knew the answer. The best we could do was to dodge any check-point where papers might be required. All well, so far.

I had seen the city of Lyon pushing up through a dawn mist; the tall city, an endless smoky web of towers, steeples and chimneys, arching high above the double river-line. We made bouncy progress along the cobbled quaysides; by the river there lay the wrecked and rusty corpses of German tanks. Past history.

Present history was shrouded, baffling. Present history we found in the sad little house of Johnny's friends; in the mournful, secret faces. At one remove there were different faces; we saw them on the streets; ample, cigar-smoking, business faces. The city, turning itself into a vast supply-base for the Reich, was embarked – we were told – upon profitable trade. Here the Promised Land felt more dangerous than the land I'd left behind me. We slept in the cellar. My poor postcard stayed in my pocket. I had written "*Tout va bien*" and signed it "Emile." Across the top I had printed *Carte destinée pour ma vieille gouvernante domiciliée en Angleterre.* (An old governess seemed to me more likely for a Frenchman than an old nurse.) But Johnny's friends begged me not to post it. Unofficial agents, unofficial censorship, might point the way to me, and to them.

Johnny himself laughed at my disappointment. "What makes you think Brigstock could guess who Emile is?" "By my handwriting, fool." "But it'll never get there – they've told you. Even if it doesn't make trouble, it'll never get there." "I shall try, all the same; further on." "Well, for God's sake wait till we see Mourri; she'll probably tell you to tear it up."

Mourri, the girl-friend at Aix, had become Johnny's target. So, for the moment, she had to be mine too. Here in Lyon, he was the absolute commander; he had contacts within the city and beyond it, friends out of his early Legion days. The theory that his regiment was stationed at Sathonay blew up; all the same, he returned from his recce in swaggering form. The depot was now, said Johnny, the finest brothel he'd sampled since war began. I cut him short on the details. The tension between us tightened.

"Anyone would think you were a virgin."

"Not a virgin, but not a voyeur either," I said and added, "Brother Smut."

"But you just don't know. It was marvellous. I can't tell you —"

"Don't try."

"Sometimes I hate your guts," Johnny said.

"Have *all* the Legion depots turned into brothels?"

"Big funny joke. Ha-ha."

"Well, have they?"

He grinned all over his face. "The regiment's at Fuveau. That's only twenty miles the other side of Aix. Luck, talk about luck . . . we'll get to Mourri first."

Aix-en-Provence: one of the golden memories; one of the gateways. I remembered all of us piling out of the car for coffee and hot *croissants* at a place called Le Café de L'Orient. We stopped there because Miles claimed to have had a love-affair with the proprietress. (He told Paula this; I wasn't supposed to hear.) My father thought the café a mistake. Squalid, he said. I loved it.

"Do you really want me with you – at Mourri's house?" I asked Johnny.

"Not a house, my friend, a palace."

"Well, anyway, do you want me there?"

He cocked his head on one side: "Have you the least idea what you'd do with yourself if I said No?"

"I'd keep on down the road."

"Where to?"

"To the camps of known desire and proved delight."

"Sounds like Sathonay."

"Kipling, more."

"Might have known it," said Johnny exasperatedly.

Now Emile sinks deep into his own identity, the slow silent one who smiles as he pedals along. He is beginning to join hands with a boy from the past, another slow-witted traveller, looking about him in wonder and liking the things he sees. The red-topped milestones give him pleasure. With every one he passes, Emile is heading closer to the playground beloved of the boy; he is easy with this thought; it is enough.

I am happier when I am Emile.

On we go.

We cycled through the night from Lyon; we met no checkpoint; no sub-hostile species lurked. Our machines were fitted with new lamps and new Lyonnais plates: Johnny the commander had seen to that. By morning we were at Montélimar. Sleepy, aching a good deal, I insisted on buying some nougat, because Miles always did and it was a good surprise to find the same shop still there. Johnny, for once, approved the expenditure.

It was almost the last thing he approved.

The check-point just outside St. Cannat was one of many irritations on a day that had been irritating from the start. We saw it from the crown of the hill; an ominous little line of vehicles held up, a glimpse of uniformed figures moving along the line. As we turned off the road I said, "Thank God we saw them in time," and Johnny said he'd like to know where God came in. God, he supposed, had sent the punctures, the foodshops all shut and the old chum who'd vanished from Lambesc, leaving a locked, empty house behind him. God's other gifts, Johnny said, included a saddle-sore crotch and a stomach so hollow he was catching a cold from the winds blowing straight up his oesophagus.

I was luckier. I wasn't saddle-sore. And I was too thankful, having dodged the check-point, to care about anything else. We looped our way in the dusk, through low hills and groves of pine, aiming on Eguilles; after Eguilles, we would reach Célony. After Célony we would join up with splendid Nationale 7 again. If Johnny's map-reading was right, and it usually was, we should find the road that ran to Mourri's palace branching from Nationale 7, about two miles north of Aix.

At the palace – he promised – there would be a banquet. He had managed to get through to Mourri on the telephone. Her parents were away. She was killing the fatted calf, in defiance of local orders, Johnny said: a new unofficial rule was terrorizing the owners of live-stock. Farmers everywhere had been forbidden to kill their own beasts for food. He'd picked up this information from one of his buddies and it seemed to be true. In a light-headed vision I saw Mourri, a willowy blonde wearing a coronet, cooking the calf, while a plain-clothes agent sniped at her through the windows of the palace kitchen. The whole prospect seemed more improbable than any fairytale. Particularly the feast.

Custard, I said to myself strenuously, *custard with skin on top; dried figs; tripe*. It was a useful game we'd invented. Instead of imagining all the glorious food we longed for, we constructed a menu made up of all the things we loathed: and this really did help to keep hunger at bay.

"Liquorice All-Sorts," I announced.

"Hot milk," said Johnny.

"Hare soup."

"Pigs' trotters."

"Prunes."

"Chocolate blancmange."

"Brains."

"Parsnips," said Johnny.

Sometimes we came to a point of disagreement; we had come to one now. "I love parsnips; I could eat a ton of parsnips," I told him.

"You're crazy."

"Brigstock's favourite vegetable."

"You can't love them just because —"

–"It isn't just because —"

– "Yes, it is."

"No, it isn't."

"Look —" said Johnny. "Peaches. Aren't they?"

They were. A sudden little peach orchard, close to the road; and down in the dip below the orchard we saw the lights of a house coming on, yellow against the purple, bloomy dusk.

"Shall we try the house?"

"No," said Johnny.

So we stayed in the orchard and stole the peaches. Peaches aren't exactly what you want at this stage, but they were a great deal better than nothing.

"Give us squitters, I shouldn't wonder," said Johnny. "Go slow."

"I am going slow."

"And you'll leave a hundred-franc-note, weighted down with all the stones, won't you, now?" He was lying flat on his face, gobbling from the palm of his hand. As he spat out a stone, I remembered the German boy with the cherries. I hadn't thought of him for days.

I went on thinking.

"That's enough for now. *Filons,* Pigling."

"Oh let's have a sleep."

"There isn't time."

"Just ten minutes." It was splendid, lying here; the crickets had begun to whirr in the trees; I watched a star pricking into sight through the purple veils high up.

"*Espèce d'imbécile,*" said Johnny. "We've nearly forty kilometres to go. And I don't know this road any better than you do. Get a move on."

Nothing I wanted less. "Oh well," I said, scrambling to my feet, "*Pass then, pass all, Bagdad ye cry and down the billows of blue sky, ye beat the bell that beats to hell and who shall thrust ye back, not I.*"

"Next time I do this trip remind me to leave my walking anthology behind."

"I can't imagine *not* having poetry in my head."

131

"At least you've plenty of room. Not much else in it." He plucked a few more peaches. "Room in your saddle-bag too, haven't you?"

"Plenty. But do we need these?"

"If your God sends us another puncture we'll be glad of them." He put them into my hands. "If I'd an inch of space I'd take them myself. But I haven't. Not now." He paused and repeated, "Not now." He had something on his mind: I was aware of his hovering beside me, full of a secret. I wasn't interested. I began to push my bicycle down the rough, grassy slopes.

"Haut les pattes! Je tire!" he whistled after me. Turning, I saw the metallic sheen of something he held in his hand. He was laughing: he came up with me and waved a revolver under my nose.

"Where on earth did you get that?"

"Been carrying it since Lyon."

"Loaded?"

"Certainly. A Luger. Laurent pressed it on me the night we left. He got it off a dead Hostile Tribe."

"What's the point?"

"This is the point, see. This is the butt, at the other end."

"Big funny joke. Ha-ha."

"Souvenir for Mourri," he said.

"Wouldn't it be a hell of a thing to get caught with – at a check-point?"

"My poor Emile, I don't propose to get caught at any fornicating check-point." He played with it lovingly before he put it in his saddle-bag. "Last time I had one in my hand I got him running at fifty yards. Beautiful shot, though I says it."

"A hostile tribe?"

"No, one of our chaps. But it was a good feeling just the same."

"Why the devil should you shoot one of your chaps?"

"Colonel's orders. And rightly. He was heading out of the un-pleasantness at a remarkable speed. On the Loire, that was."

Probably, I reflected, Johnny had loathed the job as much as I myself would have loathed it. He was flashing his torch over the road-map. "Fine feeling," he repeated, "Very, very fine."

"Oh balls."

"I mean it."

I said, "You keep that sort for Mourri, now."

"What's the matter with you? Wouldn't you shoot a deserter on the run? You'd bloody well have to, wouldn't you? No choice."

Because I was sleepy and tired, he annoyed me more than usual. I said, "One always has a choice."

"*There* speaks the little soldier."

"If you want to know, I did have the choice."

"When?"

"Day I was caught."

"A deserter?"

"No. A hostile tribe."

I could have told him before, having no shame about it, but the incident now belonged to time shut off, to Thomas Weston and not to Emile. Emile had buried it. If it hadn't come back when I saw Johnny spitting out the peachstone it might, I suppose, have stayed underground.

I was ready to move, still talking, but Johnny stood motionless until I'd finished telling him. He didn't say a word. I could feel waves of fury coming at me through the dark.

"That's all," I said to the waves.

"*Filons.*" His voice was a thin squeak. We came out of the orchard. We rode on and on in silence. Except for an occasional word, grunted as it became necessary, he didn't utter. This suited me. Those twenty-five miles felt like a hundred and twenty-five. There began to be nothing of me left but sweat and aches and dizziness.

"*Nous voici!*" Johnny's triumphant shout came through the queer spirals of smoke inside my head. When we turned into the branching road, he flung himself off his bike and pointed. "Up there, where you can see the lights – that's the house."

"Hang on a minute," I said to him. I lurched to the side of the road, and waited to be sick. It didn't happen. As the kink in my stomach straightened out and I wiped my forehead, Johnny came over, thrusting his flask at me.

"No thanks. All right now," I told him.

"Take a swig."

"Don't need it."

"Oh yes you do. Something to say to you before we get there."

"What?"

"Do yourself a favour and keep your trap shut. Not only to Mourri. To everybody. Keep that damned trap shut, will you?"

"What about?"

"*What about,* he says," Johnny apostrophized the stars: "Listen, little Sir Galahad. D'you imagine you can expect help from anyone who knows you wouldn't kill a Boche because he was eating cherries?"

"I haven't thought. Maybe not."

"I only wish to God you hadn't told *me*."

"Why?"

"Soft, you are, all through."

I said, "Oh well."

Johnny took a swig from the flask: "It makes a difference," he said, having swallowed.

"What sort?"

He muttered, "Tomorrow looks like the end of the ride, Emile."

"Yes," I said. "I've seen that coming. *T'en fais pas,* Brother Smut."

It had been a long, long night. Every time I awoke, I revelled and kept my eyes shut: it was so very good. There was no pain, no chill, no horror behind the dark. No hard floor grinding my bones; no straw that smelt and tickled; no mice nibbling. I was clean. I was warm. I lay in a gently rocking cradle that was soft and broad and buoyant . . . *safe from all the winds that blow; port after stormie seas; and the hunter home from the hill.*

Nothing hurt any more; not even my shoulder. I went on sleeping and awaking and turning my face from the light when the light came. My body would have liked to go on doing this forever but gradually my head cleared, my thoughts began. For once, it seemed, I had slept enough.

I sat up. There was hot sunshine in this room that was not a room at all. Between pinkish columns of stone I looked straight out on to a landscape I loved. Here were dark cypresses, green umbrella-pines, mimosa trees and the old backcloth of blue sky. In nearer perspective, there stretched a paved garden of some elegance: white doves fluttered around a lily-pond.

I remembered.

They had put me on the loggia to sleep; on a wide day-bed, an opulent piece of summer furniture that swung by chains from the roof. I remembered their piling the pillows up and my sinking down. Before that, there were only the dimmest of pictures; a long, shadowy dining-room and a feast I couldn't finish; going to sleep after the soup; a bathroom somewhere on this floor; going to sleep in the bath; Johnny slapping me awake. Johnny and Mourri very lively, with wine-glasses in their hands. All of it fading out.

I slid off the day-bed and went to find the bathroom. I was naked on top. I only recalled the fact of the pyjama trousers when I saw them on my legs; white silk, of all improbable things. They belonged to Mourri's father; the jacket had been too tight across my shoulders.

Somebody had left the bathroom door wide open in an obliging way, so I didn't have far to look. It was a very grand bathroom, with tiles and a glassed-in-shower. The towels were huge. There was a dressing-table under the window; a razor, a packet of blades, shaving-lotion, toilet-water, new toothbrushes and tooth-powder were all waiting for me. I hadn't shaved since Lyon. I was scraping the last of the beard away when Johnny shouted and banged outside.

I didn't remember "End of the ride, Emile" until I opened the door and he looked past me instead of at me. He too was freshly-shaved; the face with the light, slitty eyes was somehow cat-like this morning. A cat who'd swallowed the cream. He was dressed in Riviera clothes, most surprising to me, clothes belonging to a time out of mind and as strange as any mediaeval costume would have been; though they were only a yellow singlet and rust-red trousers. The trousers were much too big for him, swaddling down over his bare feet.

His shyness made me shy too. I didn't know where we went from here. He said, "There's breakfast in the dining-room," and added, "Mourri's looked out some clothes for you, but I suppose you'd rather eat first."

"What's the time?"

"Lunchtime. We've got to have a conference. Those bloody parents are coming back tonight." Again he looked past me.

"Have to put *something* on," I said, "For breakfast; surely."

He twitched a white towelling robe from its hook on the door. "That'll do for now," he said. I followed him.

It took me some time to believe that any of this was happening. Emile had no place in such a room, at such a table. Last night he had been too tired to take luxury in. Now he met it; he blinked and gobbled. A man in a white jacket waited upon him; bringing eggs and bacon, pouring coffee from a vast silver pot. The colours of the room were blue and gold. Emile saw wall-lights made of crystal; he saw an original Utrillo, a Cezanne and a Degas; he took a cigarette from a horn-and-silver casket. He strolled out, replete, beneath sun-blinds striped with red, to join Mourri and Johnny on the terrace. And stopped being Emile. It was I who felt their conspiracy come to meet me.

They were sitting close together, in blue wicker chairs. Mourri let go of his hand, pushing back her chair. She was a very different girl from the girl I had imagined cooking the fatted calf. I don't know – since Johnny had never given me a description – why I had pictured one of those ethereal ash-blondes. The real Mourri was a squarely-built young woman, with a tanned skin, black eyebrows almost meeting above her nose, and a determined jaw. She had a big mouth; nice, lively brown eyes. Her hair was cut as short as Rab's (and as I noted it, I was aware again of the flat, far-off quality Rab now possessed for me). This hair shone in the sun, looking like a black satin cap. Mourri was dressed in white: white shirt, white trousers, white sandals.

"Council of war," she said and at once began to talk; with interruptions from Johnny. I hardly talked at all.

She was awfully bossy.

"Marseille's out of the question. You'll never get past the checkpoints on the Route Nationale. And if you did – you'd be picked up and interned long before you got the chance of finding a ship to take you to Gibraltar. The city's in chaos. And swarming with agents, German agents. The little monster," here she gave Johnny an affectionate pat, "has the right idea. He can join up with his regiment at Fuveau; they'll legitimize him with papers and give him leave of absence and he can take it from there. You," she looked me up and down from my head to my bare feet – "Well, you really are in trouble, my poor friend. You'll have to put your faith in me. Understood? Now – for the moment – you must both stay here."

Immediately I knew I didn't want to. Mourri smiled at Johnny, put a cigarette between his lips and embarked on a portrait of her father. *"Archi-complaisant"* was her description. She added, "So would you be if you were negotiating a million-franc contract to make German parachutes. My mother will be gracious and charming – in so far as she dares. She's terrified of him, but they're both, thank God, just a bit frightened of me."

"You trade on frightening people, don't you?" said Johnny.

"It's a practice I've studied, little monster. As I told you once in Barcelona."

I began to recognize the sort she was. One of those bright, wholly cosmopolitan young women; who has been everywhere and seen everything. They used to drive up to Miles's restaurant on the Vence road. They always came swooping out of enormous cars, with a gang, to demand the best table and make a lot of noise among themselves, never noticing anybody else. Usually they had just arrived from somewhere spectacular (Athens, Ragusa, or New York). Usually they were going on somewhere in somebody's yacht. The party would as a rule be fluent in at least three languages and they would sprinkle names over their talk, names and titles. Miles used to do imitations of them after they went.

Mourri was the first person I'd met who took the French defeat for granted and remained quite detached from it as she spoke: maintaining, I suppose, the hardened world-traveller's point of view. I'd seen those who cursed, those who wept and those who were simply stunned automatons, enduring. Mourri was more like a radio-commentator. I found her rather shocking and – at the same time – rather comforting. Her knowledgeable talk had the flavour of truth: it wasn't Johnny's show-off assurance: I really believed she knew the answers, or most of them. For a little while.

"Spain?" she was saying to him, "Are you mad, you? They'll

slap you into a prison-camp for the duration. Spain's going to stay neutral all through this war and she won't be entertaining any allied troops – not even Legionnaires – except as internees. Part of her agreement with Schweinhund Hitler. If you want to cross that border you'll have to be very clever indeed."

"I am," said Johnny and blew her a kiss. He looked at her all the time; never at me. They went on arguing about Spain.

"Am I depressing you?" she asked me suddenly. She wasn't; she was merely exhausting me. There are some people so strong and violent in personality that they seem to take up all the oxygen. Mourri was one of these.

"What are *you* going to do?" Johnny cut in, capturing her hand. "You can't stand this kind of life for long."

"*Moi? F—— le camp, naturellement,*" said Mourri. "*Suis toujours rébelle,*" she assured me, "*Depuis mon enfance, rébelle.*"

Johnny got up and kissed her neck.

I broke their lovers' silence, saying heavily, "Excuse me." The two heads turned.

"If I can't get anywhere in Marseille without being arrested, where can I go?"

"You're staying here for the moment, I told you. While I make contact with my friend in Cannes. I've got to be careful. And the telephone service is terrible. But I'll get him. You'll be all right so long as you're patient."

"Jolly kind of you, but what can your friend in Cannes do?"

She began to explain him; in a cloud of idiom; he was dynamite: he was half-Greek and half-American. His name was Andreas. He owned a boat. "He can run you straight to Gibraltar. He had it worked out weeks before the Armistice. Like me, he saw all this coming. You'll find plenty of rats on the Riviera, but Andreas isn't one of them. It's simply a matter of getting in touch. You don't believe me? You must believe me."

"But could he get me papers? Otherwise I don't see —"

"Ah Christ," said Johnny. "Can't you just pipe down and put your feet up for a bit?"

I didn't answer him. Mourri said more gently, "You've earned a rest. It'll only be for a few days."

I stared at the splendid view, mumbling something conventionally grateful and beginning to thresh inside.

"Can I send a postcard to England?" I asked her. I told her about the postcard while Johnny in his turn stared at the view. She said, "You could try. I don't think it'll ever get there. Wait for Andreas."

"Could I send one to America?"

"Yes. That ought to get there. Eventually. Provided one of these unofficial snoopers doesn't turn suspicious; depends what you write. Wait for Andreas, I should. Don't do anything in a hurry."

"It's the first time I've seen him show any tendency to hurry," Johnny murmured.

"What about a drink?" Mourri asked. She turned and clapped her hands in the direction of the *salon* windows.

I felt the awful approach of a rage; I fought it down; the hot fury inside my head was, I told myself, quite unreasonable. But it went on. Lounging around in the sun wearing only a bath-robe, taking a drink immediately after breakfast, I thought, what the hell am I doing? I must get out. None of this is any good. Johnny, I suppose, will enjoy a few nights in her bed, a protection *de luxe* and then, in time, push on to Fuveau, fair enough: for him. But not for me. I'd seldom felt more baffled, more horribly tied by the heels.

"Clothes, you must have," said Mourri, patting my knee. Her bright brown eyes were busy, looking into my face. She guesses some of it, I said to myself: Johnny would guess if he looked my way.

We left him beside the drinks, which were wheeled out on an elaborate trolley. Mourri carried her drink into the house. In her own small study ("my only refuge from the parents") we made the inspection. Her maid had washed and ironed Emile's clothes, that dated from the house by the canal. They had also been well patched where patches were required. Grandfather's boots were still operative though Mourri said she would find me some decent shoes in Aix. On a chair I saw an array of coloured shirts, singlets like the one Johnny was wearing.

"But they may be too small; you have enormous shoulders, haven't you?"

Venetian blinds were drawn at the windows. In the barred sunshine she was looking at me steadily. "Here are the trousers; my father won't miss them. Think they'll fit?" They were all in different colours, too.

"You're very kind. But I'd better wear my own."

"They're awful. Try some of these."

"No, really, thanks very much all the same."

"You were wounded, Johnny says."

"Yes. But I'm all right now."

"It won't do you any harm to take it easy, will it? Just for a few days?"

I asked her the full name and address of the all-powerful Andreas. I was surprised when she went to her desk and wrote this down.

"I'll try to get through to him this evening. He's out all day," she said. She put the paper into my hand.

"Thank you. I'll get dressed now – join you in a minute."

She took a cigarette from a box on her desk. It was hard to understand why she stood there, smiling at me, until she said casually, "You know your way around, don't you, in this part of the country?"

"Yes; very well. I've driven all over here, with Miles."

"I thought so." She wasn't smiling any more. "You're planning to run out on me, aren't you?" said Mourri.

There was no point in lying. She wasn't the sort of person you could lie to, and anyhow I've never been good at it.

I nodded.

"Idiot," she said.

"Oh well."

"Is it because you've quarrelled with Johnny?"

"I haven't quarrelled with him."

"What's the matter between you?"

"Ask him," I said. "He's the one who's angry. But that isn't my reason."

"What is your reason?"

"Sorry. I don't think I can explain." Explaining is another thing I do badly and the only simple answer was "You make me feel I'm in a trap," which would have been rude.

She turned back to the desk. "You'll need money."

"Please don't give me any."

"Why not?"

"Because I'd rather not take it."

"That's idiotic, also."

I could feel our two obstinate wills lunging at each other. It reminded me suddenly of my attic room in Ebury Street; Romney holding out the cheque. "Sorry," I said again. "I don't want to seem ungrateful."

"Do you hate me so much?"

"It's nothing to do with you. It's because of something that happened to me about a year ago."

"Crétin."

"Yes, you may be right. The name's Emile," I said.

"Do you really believe in this Andreas fellow?"

"Not sure."

"Sounds too cloak-and-dagger to be true."

"Oh well; no harm in trying him out, is there?"

"*If* you get to Cannes."

"*If* I get to Cannes."

I was conducting this dialogue with myself; on the lower slopes of the Esterels; navigating a corkscrew road that ran through the pine-forests. Abruptly I realized that I was talking aloud. Forty-eight hours of solitude, sunshine and starlight weren't, I decided, improving my wits.

> *I remember going crazy, I remember that I knew it*
> *When I heard myself hallooing to the funny folk I saw.*

The walking anthology . . . For all our fights, I missed Johnny now. And it was odd that the sinking down into Emile's identity should become more difficult alone. Or perhaps it wasn't odd. I knew these roads well; I was back with myself as I headed for the sea.

We hadn't said goodbye. Mourri, bossy to the last, had told me this would upset him too much. I rather doubted it, but I let her have her way. While he took his afternoon sleep I was dispatched from the pink palace; the bicycle all clean and polished, my saddle-bag stocked with supplies. She had given me a large-scale map, stolen from her father's library. She had lingered in the road, under the rosy arch of the wall, with the fluted tiles on top: a still white figure watching me go.

"Do you really believe in this Andreas of hers?"

The question nagged. I was getting tired. I had eaten sparingly, so as to make the food and the wine last out. I had slept *en plein air*; I was dirty, unshaven, achy-boned. I had made slow progress today and the afternoon was wearing on. My shortest cut from Fréjus to Cannes would have been to keep on Nationale 7, but a gendarme had frightened me off it; not that he looked hostile, or even sub-hostile, a sweaty man in khaki, pushing his bike uphill; he looked, in fact, like the gendarme who had come to the rescue in these parts when Miles got gear-box trouble. Rab and Miles and I were joy-riding in defiance of some edict or other from Paula. Time was at a premium. Rab and I hadn't cared. We sat in the shade of the pine-trees while the gendarme and Miles were sweating and cursing and tearing the car to pieces. There was a royal row, I remembered, when we finally got back to the villa.

I remember the fourteen-year-old Rab; she is alive and laughing; but the other one? Where is she? She has vanished. And I begin to get used to this feeling – almost to trust it. Why's that, do you suppose?

Perhaps because of the sharp tree-shadows across the track, perhaps because my thoughts were away ("Don't dream, Thomas!") I never saw the gully. It was deep. It was the dried bed of a stream and my front wheel dived straight down into it. We fell with an almighty crash, the bike and I. And of course I landed on my bad shoulder. I wouldn't have thought it could hurt so much. I was winded too and that always hurts. Everything went smoky and fuzzy with the pain. I lay on my back, swearing. Then I crawled into a patch of shade: to take stock of the damage; not so much my damage as the bicycle's. One glance was enough.

A frieze of spokes stood up from the buckled front-wheel, looking like a demented umbrella-frame. That was a torn-off pedal lying over there, and the shell of a broken handle-bar close to my foot. Scattered about the gully there lay the pump and the tools.

I couldn't have disposed of my steed more thoroughly had I tried.

Oh the poor thing, I thought, it deserved better than this. Riding from Ghent to Aix . . . or rather from Aix to Cannes . . . poor old Roland. But I couldn't pour down its throat my last measure of wine. Probably Mourri's wine-bottle lay smashed inside the saddle-bag. I went to look. No; by lucky chance it still survived, with a pair of socks wrapped round it. I took the last measure but one myself. I walked sorrowfully to and fro, picking up the pieces. There was nothing to be done. The bicycle was dead.

Well, by my calculations, I wasn't more than ten miles above the coast. This road would bring me out (unless I'd made a nonsense of the thin yellow squiggle on Mourri's map) at the Bay of Agay. A downhill walk. If grandfather's boots could take it, so could I.

The familiar landscape was reassuring. The problems of the present faded: check-points, sub-hostile species, the Andreas person, even England at war lost all reality. From here, Agay felt like home.

But I was terribly sorry for the bicycle. I didn't dare wait to give it decent burial. I picked up the saddle-bag and set off downhill: slithering and stumbling, cutting straight through the trees wherever I could, short-circuiting the loops in the road. The pine needles made it slippery going. It was rather like a ski-run without skis. Sometimes I slid on my bottom, doing no good to Emile's patched and fragile trousers. I kept losing the road and bearing to my left, steering by the sun that sank lower and lower. The pain in my shoulder was fierce.

Grandfather's boots were taking no end of a beating. By tonight I should be barefoot.

Left; keep left; keep going; keep going on. Can't. Must. Pines are thinning out. Is that the sun shining through?

No. That's the sea.

Thalassa, thalassa, peak in Darien, here we are, here we are, riding on a shooting-star!

I stopped to pull out the wine-bottle, drink the last swallow and toss the bottle away. I coasted out of the pines; I tore through a patch of grey olives; I slid down a long stretch of red scree; and there I was.

Well, not exactly where I'd expected to find myself. Better still. I was standing right in the shadow of the tumbledown tower, at the loop of the road below the Twenty-nine villa.

Nothing was changed. Nothing could change this place. I crossed slowly to the seaward side and stood there, with the Twenty-nine Summer smell in my nostrils and all my ghosts keeping me company.

It was magic. Magic had brought me here, I said. Through the twilight, two men bicycled past, giving me not a look. Perhaps I had become invisible. The sea was white and the huge red-gold sun was balancing on the white rim, far away; the crickets whirred in chorus. All the red rocks were purple-shadowed and the olives looked like puffs of pale smoke on the hill.

Down this road, to the little hotel of last year: to find old Matthieu . . . That was the notion, wasn't it?

No it wasn't. The villa first.

Idiotic, but I had to.

Light-headed, dry-mouthed, filled with a furious, unreasoning excitement, I turned. I shuffled along through the scented, solemn dusk. I came to the wall. I saw the pines and the oleanders, the mimosa-trees growing high. The wire netting was still in place above the wall. Had I the strength to get the loosened staple out, to play Miles's trick, I was wondering, when it became suddenly apparent that the gate was open. A dog ran through and stood in the road.

The dog was an outsize black poodle. In the dusk he looked as big as a bear. He pranced, wagging his tail, glancing this way and that, tossing his head. Pleased with himself, I thought.

Then he sniffed me and turned my way. He had an impressive head; the ears made him look rather like a judge wearing a black wig. He had a broader muzzle than most of his kind: very large, grape-bloomy eyes, I saw, as he came trotting to meet me. A yard away, he pulled up; giving a short experimental kind of growl that ended in a bark. There was a human twitch to his eyebrows: he seemed to be raising them separately, as Romney used to do.

He growled again. An intimidating act, except that he'd forgotten about his tail, which still wagged. He rolled his eyes, showing their whites; less like a judge now than like a nigger-minstrel.

"Teruel! Teruel! Where the devil are you? Teruel!" The high-screaming voice came from inside the gate. A woman galloped out, still screaming. She was a big woman, swirling in a dress of harlequin pattern; her legs were very positive and athletic as she dashed at the dog.

"You opened that damn' latch again – not funny *or* clever," she told him, grabbing his collar.

Then she saw me and gave a great jump.

I could only goggle at her. First because she spoke English; next because she was living in the villa. Despite Mourri's talk of the Riviera rats, I'd never imagined anybody living here.

The dark was coming down quickly, as always on this coast. I could make out a crown of pale hair, a rather jolly, foxy face, ear-rings that sparkled, a full-bosomed, imperious kind of shape. A hockey-playing goddess, if there could be such a thing.

"*Allez-filez!*" she said. "See him off, Teruel. Oh you *sissy*." She slapped the dog but not very hard; he was still wagging his tail. "*Filez,*" she said to me again.

"Oh need I – please? Couldn't I just come in and sit down?"

"English. You're English? What's an Englishman doing here – dressed like that?"

"Sorry about the clothes. I'm on the run. Might I just sit down in the garden? I know it's stupid, but I thought the villa would be empty. Usually I loosen that staple there."

She glanced at it, interrupting me sharply: "How do you know about the staple?"

"Well you see, I spent a summer here once with my family. Now I make pilgrimages. I come and swim from the rocks and then I go away again." Here my throat dried. "Would it be possible to have a glass of water?" I croaked at her.

I couldn't stand up any longer, so I sat down by the gate. Above my head I heard her screaming in French towards the house. The dog came to join me, huddling close in a melancholy-comrade way.

"*Look* at those boots," I heard her saying, and then "Would you be the one who came last summer? With a girl?"

"That's right."

"The friend of Miles?"

"That's right," I said again.

> *"I've studied the desk and it isn't antique*
> *That's not a real diamond comb.*
> *That's not alabaster,*
> *Goodnight, Mrs. Astor!"*

"*Always* out of tune – aren't you?" said the girl on the other side of the long table. "So funny."

"I don't find it funny," said Sarah.

"Well, yes it is because you sing all the time."

"Just keeping my spirits down."

"Don't you mean up?"

"No. Down. They're down so I'm keeping them down."

"I don't get it."

"It's of no importance," said Sarah. She opened the next letter:

"Dear Mary Castle,

I can't expect you to remember me, but I played the Daffodil Girl in 'Come Into The Garden' 1937–38. You were most awfully sweet to me the night I sprained my ankle. I hear you're doing wonderful things for the children evacuated from England, finding them homes and so on. And I understand there's some special arrangement for theatre people. So this emboldens me to ask if there's any chance for my sister's two little girls? She's Emma Pardou of the Carl Rosa Opera Company and the first thing I want to make clear is that she can *pay every penny in sterling*. She wouldn't dream of being under any sort of financial obligation.

Is there such a thing as a 'legal' dollar swop, I wonder? One hears such different stories.

Now I must give you some details."

147

"Not now, you mustn't," said Sarah, drawing the 'Hold' file towards her. After only three weeks she was developing an assiduous brutality. The girl on the other side of the table was, by Sarah' christening, one of the War-Swooners. When she sang (in tune) she sang "*There'll Always Be An England.*" When she came to a letter that moved her deeply (and this happened every half-hour) she would look up with tears on her lashes, saying "You just *have* to hear this." The girl's name was Boodie. Sarah found her good for morale. The best scaffolding for morale nowadays was a touch of pure hatred. They had disliked each other on sight and continued to do so.

The room where they worked was not, strictly speaking, an office. It was a room in Mary Castle's apartment on East Sixty-First Street. Files, packages and stationery crowded it to the corners. The walls were conscientiously decorated: Winston Churchill, the Union Jack, bulldogs and battleships, along with some authentic posters from U.K. Careless Talk Costs Lives; incitements to buy Savings Certificates; maxims by Billy Brown of London Town; a printed card declaring that This House Was Not Interested In The Possibilities of Defeat, But Only of Victory.

There were two typewriters on the table. The room had its own private telephone-line.

"You *have* to hear this one," said Boodie.

"Can't. I'm up to my eyes. And Mary has to sign all these before she goes off to the theatre."

"I can take the cheques in, if you're pushed for time" said Boodie promptly. Boodie was, as might be expected, a devout Mary-worshipper. Mary was godmother to her revolting little boy.

"Okay. You do it."

Sarah lit a cigarette, feeling the air expand pleasingly when the door shut and left her alone. She counted the cigarettes remaining in the pack: thirteen. On the present rationing system, these would see her through till tomorrow. Nothing would have been easier than to help herself from the endless supplies in the apartment, but the scrupulous rules of Now forbade.

"Mary," said Boodie, sounding deflated, "wants to see you. I told her you were terribly busy, but she says it's quite important."

No need to feel this pinch of reluctance, was there? Relations with Mary never failed in their smoothness: Mary saw to that. ("All for the best in the best of all possible worlds. Meaning the world of Mary Castle.") It was a kind of genius, Sarah thought. Mary had not forgiven the disastrous Bermuda comedy, nor the rollicking return with Gerald in the speedboat; Mary had simply behaved as though there was nothing to forgive.

Gerald's last letter included a sudden, chirping postscript: "How are you making out with Miss Honeymouth?"

Once again, she was disarmed: Mary in her beautiful bedroom, wasn't signing the cheques: dressed in an apple-green pyjama-suit, she was doing press-ups on the floor. "Hi, sweetheart," said Mary. She rolled over and kicked her feet in the air. Then she settled as cosily as a kitten in the middle of the huge bed. On the bedside table a tray with a bowl of soup and some toast awaited her attentions.

"Dwight put the rehearsal back one hour; so I'm ahead of myself," she said. "And it's time for a talk." The most charming face in the world was alight with strategy: "Handle this carefully with Boodie, will you darling? I'll tell her myself before I go, but I wanted to tell you first. Drink? No? Tea? Nothing? Sure? About these cheques, Sal. I'm giving you my power of attorney for the War Relief account. You'll have to stop by and see the vice-president at the bank tomorrow; give him your signature – that's all he needs. Those," she waved one lovely hand "can wait till the morning. Then you sign them. And that's the procedure from here on out."

Now, of all moments, was Sarah's first thought. The gentle voice went on: "Easier all round . . . You'll take care of everything . . . Salaries, too, yours and Boodie's . . . and expenses, don't forget your expenses; just draw the cheques as you need them. Means a lot less work for me . . . important, once we're in rehearsal . . . All right with you?"

"Wouldn't it be better if Boodie had the power of attorney?"

"Why, darling?"

The only truthful answer was, "With just three hundred dollars in my current account, I don't want my hands on all that money."

She didn't make the truthful answer. She said, "I think Boodie's the one to do it."

"No, sweetheart, she isn't. I want it to be you. Want to keep it in the family . . . Please don't say no, Sal. What's on your mind?"

"Nothing, truly . . . Of course I'll take it on if you'd like me to." Sarah, perched on the stool in front of the dressing-table, met the clear, kind eyes.

"Losing weight, aren't you?" said Mary: "Do you eat properly? Evenings, I mean? Wish I could persuade you to move in here." (The wistful laugh.)

"Sweet of you." (The routine reply.) "But I like my place, I really do."

"Well don't think me an interfering bitch, but I've a favour to ask. Go to my doctor and have a check-up. Will you do that, please?"

"Mary, I'm all right; really; I promise."

But it was no use fighting. Mary's doctor would perform the check-up (and send Mary the bill). He would prescribe vitamins and sleeping pills. He would sympathize, he would try to cheer her, as they all did, saying England would come through. "Natural enough to worry; dammit, who wouldn't? But remember you're being far more useful here than you could be over there." They all said that.

But of the craziness down below, they knew nothing, could know nothing. You kept your secrets throughout this nightmare time-table.

Reading the front-page headline, "London Heavily Bombed." Looking at your watch, adding five hours, feeling the night move in over England, the bombers on their way. You stayed awake, keeping watch with London until its morning came.

Nobody knew about that; nobody must know.

Sooner or later, alone in the apartment, you began to do the crazy things.

You sat down and wrote little notes to all the family, telling them you were leaving next week. You wrote a special note to Mary, telling her you had borrowed the money from the War Relief account for your passage home. (And now, today, that door stood wide open, did it not?) You had to tell Mary that the flamboyant gesture of turning your dollars into sterling had left you flat-broke. (You could just get by, paying fifty a month for the dreary little walk-up in the Village. Dreary, not Cute: your visitors were careful to say Cute.)

Among the notes there was one to Dick Abrahams, announcing your return, trying to sound as witty and calm as he sounded; sometimes you added "I think you love me, don't you? I don't think I need to be loved, but I *know* I need somebody to love." This note was always the first to be torn up next day.

Now and again you couldn't face the apartment, waiting for you. You went the other way; uptown to Yorkville, because it was the German section and you liked to parade the British War Relief badge pinned prominently on the lapel of your suit. You loitered there, half-hoping for trouble. Once, you had visited the German movie-theatre and booed the propaganda-pictures. Along the row, somebody laughed, but there was no other reaction: anti-climax. And you duly received your reward for the pointless gesture. It was the German newsreel that gave you the most persistent of all your nightmares: the British boat torpedoed in convoy.

Every dream of that ship was the same. She was tilting, going down. You were beside the rail, with the waves sweeping up to you. Thomas and Brigstock were there too; you saw them caught away by the dark roaring waters, saw the waters close over them and knew it was your turn next.

Crazy. This was the crazy time, the crazy place. Even the wallpaper in the apartment was crazy: there was one piece of the pattern that looked like Romney's eyebrows. You saw Romney's eyebrows, arched and reproving, regularly spaced. The eyebrows mocked you; they said, "I wasn't afraid to die. Are you afraid to die – and come to me? You wanted that once, you know. Are you afraid now?"

"Yes."

The bitterest of the truths: your own fear that lived in this room. Nobody knew about that, either; nobody must know.

It was the last ditch you came to; at three in the morning (with the bombers on their way home). You said it aloud, to make sure; to let yourself off nothing.

"Even if I had the money to go, I'd still be afraid of the sea-journey. Not of the bombs: I can't imagine them, so they have no terrors for me. But afraid of the sea, yes. Afraid to sail on the ship in convoy from Montreal. There is the end of it. That is the truth. I can't go home, because I haven't got the fare. Thank God I haven't got it."

Then you climbed out of bed; you tore up all the notes and drank a glass of milk and wept for your own cowardice before you went to sleep. But by the next evening you were on the prowl again. You poured out a meticulous ration of whisky; you drank it and at once you would feel brave. You were going home. Next week.

"Got a date for tonight?" Mary was asking.

"I have, yes."

True, up to a point: a date with the self who was no worse company than a crowd would be. Alone, or in a crowd, the dead, lost Sarah drifted. She remembered Walter Ash saying, "One day, or another day, you'll wake up and find you're alive again." The day was, surely, long in coming.

The telephone at Sue Brown's lived on a ledge above the bar. When it rang, Michael the Pole went to answer it. "For you," he said to Paula, and whispered, "May I tell you how beautiful you look tonight?" He then gave a nervous glance in Sue's direction, but Sue was busy, halfway to the door, briskly disposing of an institutional drunk. This encouraged Michael to stand in front of Paula, making his lips into the shape for a kiss.

He had ceased to be a diversion. For Paula he now rated with a mosquito, heard pinging at night just above the pillow; with heartburn; with getting something in her eye. She swept past him to the telephone.

"I don't think," said Philip's dirge-voice, "I'll come to Gerald's. Awfully tired; not really up to a party."

"It isn't a party," said Paula, "He just asked us to look in for a nightcap."

"Well anyway, give him my apologies. Say I'm absolutely bushed. He'll understand."

He would; indeed he would . . . "Just take the dogs around the block, then I'll turn in," Philip was saying.

"All right, darling. I shan't be late."

"Have a good time."

I will, oh I will. Or at least a short reprieve. Gerald's near-neighbourhood was the current blessing (though Philip wouldn't call it that). He was occupying a suite in the Château Marmont. Looking at the clock, she called, "On my way, Sue."

"Okay, darling. You look lovely. New dress?"

"Heavens, no. Vintage Bergdorf."

Sue said something about old fiddles playing the best tunes. Paula said a chilly goodnight to Michael who would soon be telling the latecomers the story of his escape from Poland. Reverence for the story still obtained; though Poland was a touch out of date. Poor Michael; history moving too fast. One ought to be sorry for him. All the same, out in the cooler air, she caught herself indulging a yawn; a huge noisy yawn of the kind that had infuriated her all her life and still infuriated her when other people did it.

Then, as she walked the two blocks to the Marmont, she wondered at this sharp gratitude for a sense of freedom. There had been a time – hadn't there? – when one took freedom for granted.

"Oh well," Paula said, aloud and deliberately; the tribute to Thomas. She crossed the lobby. The elevator took her up to the place of escape; the place where life was enhanced and one's failing batteries recharged.

She found pleasure in Gerald's company for the reason that aroused Philip's fury, and the British Colony's to-a-man distaste. Gerald's façade showed him always in good spirits and a good temper. Paula didn't care to search below the façade. He was the friend she needed. With Rab still far away and Philip painstakingly remote, even at her elbow, she thanked God for Gerald. She dressed up a little for him; she felt younger when she saw him. (And better-looking, which was absurd.)

Here he was: standing in the open doorway, waiting for her. Behind him in the room she could hear voices. As Gerald kissed her she was engulfed by a cloud of French toilet-water. He had taken off his jacket and lashed himself into a red and gold dressing-gown.

"Only Geoffrey and Morris," he told her, with a movement of his glossy head in the direction of the voices, "They're just going. Have you mislaid King Lear?"

"He sends his apologies."

"Anything wrong? Foolish question. Any special variety of doom? Just the routine reluctance to cross my threshold, would you say, Madam? No, you wouldn't say. Come in, my darling."

Morris Ward and Geoffrey Bliss greeted her. She had never taken to the pussy-faced Morris but she rather liked Geoffrey. He stood, holding her hand, saying in his warm, actor's voice "We need a woman's view of the argument." He was tall and loose-jointed; his blue eyes went down at the corners. He wore an expression of distrustful amusement. He was making a wartime thriller, called *Colonel Shakespeare*. Geoffrey had written the script, played the lead and was busy telling the world the picture was terrible. He stressed, particularly to women, that he was too old for the part.

"What's the argument?"

"Murder most fair," said Geoffrey Bliss, his eyes taking in the vintage Bergdorf.

"One says one could do it," said Morris heavily. "But it's only talk. Murder's the one action we're all too civilized to commit."

"How do we know – yet?" Geoffrey asked limpidly.

"Our contention being," said Gerald as he brought Paula her drink, "that if any of us knew a really foolproof way of killing without discovery we should – sooner or later – proceed."

"Who are your victims?" asked Paula.

"Our lips are sealed," said Gerald, posturing by the piano.

"I've nobody under serious review," said Geoffrey. "But there was a time – oh certainly, there was a time . . ."

Perhaps he meant his wife who had, by reputation, stopped his fun for years. He was a widower now, wasn't he? Paula thought so. Once again, in Gerald's room, there was a light-hearted discussion going on, without reference to bombs or Britain. Once again she was grateful.

"If one analyses it honestly," said Morris, "One doesn't want to *kill* one's *bête-noire*, one just wants him never to have happened."

"Retrospective birth-control. Hardly a practical solution," murmured Geoffrey. "Whose side do you take, Mrs. Weston?"

"Murder most fair," she repeated, "No. Not really up my alley. If I wanted somebody not to be there, I wouldn't have to kill him. I'd just get up and go. I'd quit."

"Forever?" Gerald gleamed at her, his smile crooked and knowing.

"Why not?"

"And talking of quitting," said Geoffrey with a glance at his watch: "The only thing that saves one's reason in this outpost of damnation,"

– "Degradation,"

– "Disintegration,"

– "Is having to get up early. Otherwise one would just sit around all night quenching one's melancholia."

They went, Morris lingering to ask "How's Philip?" in the tone reserved for chronic invalids, and to gaze rather wistfully at Gerald before he shut the door.

"What old Bliss is too much of a gentleman to reveal —" said Gerald.

"His wife?" Paula interrupted. Gerald, who never seemed to mind her interruptions, said "Well, that too possibly. But he's pining to slip his mother an overdose. If it weren't for her he could go home. Brought her out in a moment of misplaced chivalry and —"

– "Well, he could leave her here, couldn't he? What's wrong with that? He could quit."

Gerald, his eyes alight, said, "You seem to be in a quitting mood, Madam."

"Well, who isn't? Around here? Name one."

"I can. Morris. He trembles in his tiny soul when he thinks of war. He'll stay on this side till it stops. In fact" – he began to fuss with some beauty-roses on the top of the piano – "I'd rather have poor old Morris's admission of plain funk than a lot of the phoney attitudes." He looked at her warily across the roses. He added, "Including my own, perhaps."

"But you *are* going, aren't you? Soon as your picture's finished?"

Gerald said, "Of course," in his clipped, Brookfield voice. He added, "And you'll keep on keeping it to yourself, please." He came to sit beside her on the sofa. He said, "I have to go, because I owe it to Thomas." He laid his hand on hers. "I'm sorry things are being so devilish for you. They are, aren't they? I'm not employing my famed powers of deduction to the wrong end?"

"No. They are devilish right now."

"Like living with a permanent November fog, it must be . . . My poor darling. He'll get over it. Father always gets over things – used to be his one speciality. I thought," said Gerald gaily, "that having me around to hate would cheer him up."

"Poor old boy," said Paula, "I'm damn' sorry for him, even though I could knock him cold. He can't help himself."

"And you can't quit."

She was surprised to find how much the lightly-spoken words shocked her. "Good God, no . . . You don't seriously think I meant —" It was Gerald's turn to interrupt: "You told me once you always did – when you wanted to."

"Oh, when I was *young*, yes. I don't remember telling you, though."

"I was that affected little boy at Sawcombe, in '26. With a nice taste in ties." He gave her another crooked smile before he went to the piano, where he strummed *The Last Time I Saw Paris*, singing low. She liked it. Philip never touched the piano in these days. Gerald switched suddenly to *Bye-Bye, Blackbird*.

"Sawcombe," he reminded her. "All of nostalgia. I only play it when I'm happy." Here he cocked his head on one side. He took his hands off the keys. He waited for her to comment. When she said nothing he pleaded, "Oh, you can't just leave that lying there. Can you?"

"Not one to pry," said Paula. "And you know it. Want me to ask *why* you're happy?"

"It isn't – mind you – more than a selfish little plank I'm walking. It doesn't stretch beyond this room."

"No," she said, "No."

156

"Out of prison – for a while."

"I see."

Gerald said, "So you should. Blinding glimpses of the obvious." He swivelled around on the piano-stool. He looked paler now. "Murder most fair," he enunciated pedantically: "So it would be, too."

"You hate Mary," said Paula. He burst into laughter. He swivelled back to play one crashing chord. "I love you," he called, keeping his back turned to her, "Straight to the heart of the matter. No ladylike, tentative approaches." He spun around again. "Yes darling. Put your mind at rest on that point. I hate her. I hate her more than I ever thought I could hate anybody."

It was not, Paula decided, astonishing. "Since when?" she asked mildly.

"That's not to be told." He crashed another chord; he chased it up the scale, then shut the piano with a slam. He slid off the stool and bowed to her. "Congratulations, Madam. You're the first person to hear the news. I managed to keep it from Sarah – just – only just. I think she knows."

"Does Mary? Seems to me rather more important, somehow."

She saw Gerald's forefinger pointing, quivering: "Does she *know*? Miss Lynx-Eyes? She knows everything. And rises above it – on her bullet-proof, bombproof, heavy-duty, guaranteed, anti-aircraft rainbow . . . Miss Rise-Above-It, Miss Honeymouth, Miss Keep-It-Sweet-And-Smiling . . ." He loomed over Paula, tying his face into knots. "Do I make myself clear? May I just add that if I saw a car going over her gracious, exquisite little stomach, I'd jump on the running-board to add to the weight."

He was at the end of his act. He slumped down beside her: he leaned forward, putting his face in his hands. "Oh God," he said, "I hate me, too. How I hate me."

"Sheer waste of time," Paula snapped.

Still he kept his face hidden. His voice was muffled. "Am I really such a shit? That's what wakes me up in the mornings – every morning. And the answer's Yes. And *why* am I? Thomas was an absolute angel, Sarah's an endearing ass. It's only —"

"Ah, skip *you*."

157

"Don't I wish I could?"

"Better ask her for a divorce. Only answer, isn't it? Reno or bust," said Paula.

Gerald gave a long sigh. He lay back, with his head on the sofa-cushions, his chin pointed to the ceiling.

"Scared of her?" Paula suggested.

"Yes. I think so. Humiliating, I find it."

"You're going to war just to get away?"

"Probably."

"And figuring you may be killed so it's not worth a showdown."

"Very like, very like."

She touched his hand. "Tell you something I learned a long time ago. From my father. If there's anything on your mind that makes you think, 'Oh I don't have to say it yet,' and you feel better for putting it off – then say it right away."

Seeing his twisted smile, she said, "I'll leave you with that one," and kissed him goodnight.

❋ ❋ ❋

Alone, Gerald opened the piano; he sat playing softly, singing low: *The Last Time I Saw Paris*. He was waiting for Mary's tele-phone-call. (Her turn tonight, and the magic of precarious peace would not revisit this room until afterwards.) Here it came.

Once more the good actor was acting beautifully. All the lies rippled off the tongue, from "Can't tell you how I miss you," to their appointed last words, "Love you always."

He hung up; drew his inevitable breath of relief and lit a cigarette. He did not return to the piano. He sat on the sofa, laying out his pack of miniature cards on the coffee-table for a game of solitaire.

He wasn't thinking about Mary. It was his custom to wipe her from his mind as soon as the talk ended. He was thinking about Sarah.

Miss Lynx-Eyes – as usual – could be right.

"What's wrong with Sal . . .? Like a ghost, these days . . . Does her work wonderfully, don't know where I'd be without her. But

the way she looks . . . Some private worry . . . Not just the war."
(Dear Mary) "I've a feeling it's money . . . She *didn't* turn those
dollars into sterling, did she? . . . Sort of thing she might do on
impulse . . . I don't like to ask her . . . Has she told you anything?
She hasn't? Well, I've just taken a step that may help her to relax a
bit."

Red Seven on black Eight.

"As though Sarah would keep herself on your bounty, Madam.
Not if she were starving." *Black Queen on Red King*.

"What an ass, though, bless her. The great patriotic gesture. And
now she's broke." *Red Two on black Three, looks as though it's coming
out*. The usual superstition walked in, saying "If it comes out . . .'
But he hadn't decided what wish to make. He contented himself
with "If it comes out, everything will be beautiful."

Beautiful for whom?

Not for Sarah.

Sarah trapped, he thought; trapped by her own silliness. Trapped
now by Mary. The only thing Sarah wanted, since the Grandmother
and Brigstock refused to come to Bermuda, was England. Trapped
in New York, working for peanuts.

Ace goes up; Four on Five; and there's that perishing Jack; at last. "If
it comes out, I'll —"

The idea presenting itself awed him so much that he held off
turning the next card.

"Because of course that's why she stays – the silly sausage. She
hasn't got the fare home."

He turned the card. *Yes, here we go.*

Still he hesitated on the gesture that would really hurt him, the
thing that was so hard to do. Until Mary's words came back:
"Don't know where I'd be without her." And this decided him.
"You'll know," he said, grinning wickedly. Only one card now lay
face down, imprisoned, and as he moved black Four on to red Five,
he set it free.

Gerald swept the cards into a heap, sprang from the sofa and rushed
to the writing table. It must be done now. If he waited till tomorrow it wouldn't be done, for all the vow he had made to the
Solitaire.

He sat with his cheque-book in front of him. Make it big, said his conscience; make it a thousand. Go on, you mean, penny wise bastard – just for once.

He took a sheet of paper and thought of writing "Blood from a stone, my darling," but wrote instead "I feel this may ease the situation, Madam," before he filled in the cheque.

'Pay Sarah Weston One Thousand and 00/100 Dollars.' Highly improbable, it looked, as he signed it. He addressed the envelope, stamped it and walked out to the mail-chute, giving himself no chance to repent the gesture.

"There now, that was a kind thing to do, wasn't it?" Brigstock's voice; he saw Brigstock beaming approval at him, saw the kind blue eyes and the little thin lips that smiled, even the sparkle of the garnet brooch set in her collar. "Mrs. Sarah'll be so pleased," Brigstock was saying.

THE UNWRITTEN NOTEBOOK

I AWOKE IN DARKNESS AND AT ONCE A PICTURE FLASHED across my mind's eye. It was the picture of a tiny, fragile woman dressed in black, with a lace mantilla. A red rose, somewhere. She was dark and mysterious; her small, olive-skinned face wore a look of rapt devotion. It was the image that had come to me last year, when Miles talked of his Spanish madonna, the Countess who fell in love with this villa. General Franco's friend, he had said, and the salt of the earth. ("Gambling her only sin" I remembered, too.)

I was wide awake and frightfully hungry. I could hear a clock ticking. I groped for a bed-side lamp, found it and switched it alight. The clock, a big one in a black wooden case, hung on the opposite wall. A quarter to two. I couldn't remember what the time was when I sank into this large bed. I could just remember refusing to let the Countess give me my bath and her telling me she was a qualified nurse.

The shape of the room was entirely familiar; Sarah's old room, on the seaward side of the villa. The furnishings were all new; rather grand, the room looked now: newly painted white, with shiny scarlet curtains. The chairs and a tall dressing-table were of black, carved wood. There was a silver crucifix on the dressing-table. Something quite different, though; what? Yes, the archway cut where the door used to be; no door unless you counted that black ironwork gate across the lower half of the arch.

I had barely assembled my wits when the archway blazed with light. The Countess rushed in crying, "Are you ill?" She was accompanied by the black poodle.

I gazed at her, still aware of my little image that was quite wrong.

She must have been nearly six feet tall. Big all over, too; a well-proportioned goddess. Blonde hair, sweeping up high off her forehead; the jolly, foxy face was still made up; her earrings swung and sparkled. True, she was wearing a dressing-gown of peacock colours, but she seemed as wide-awake as I – more so. She put a large brisk hand on my forehead.

"I feel all right," I told her. "Just sort of bruised, and rather hungry. I didn't wake you?"

"Heavens, no, I never sleep before two. I was just telling Teruel his bed-time story. Sure you're all right? Did you say hungry? Wait." I began to assure her – untruthfully – that a biscuit or a piece of bread would do nicely but she had billowed out again. She left the iron gate standing open. The dog remained beside it, staring at me as though he couldn't believe his eyes.

I could hardly blame him. At Mourri's palace I had been surprised to find myself wearing silk pyjama-trousers. What on earth had I got on now? A sort of huge nightgown, long-sleeved, slipping off my shoulders; it was open to my waist and down below there was any amount of it, all twisted up round my legs and feet.

I began to giggle. Light-headedly, I saw stretching before me a lifetime of passing out before dinner and waking up in strange beds wearing other people's night-clothes. I don't suppose it was as funny as it seemed, but I went on giggling. Not Emile's form, this, I said to myself; he was the boy for the barns, the straw, the hard ground. Here I caught myself wondering where poor Emile had found his night's lodging. And I don't suppose that was funny either, but it struck me as excruciating.

"Hysterical," said the Countess crossly; then she barged into Teruel and nearly dropped the tray she was carrying. She turned her crossness on him: "You're a dog, remember, not a roadblock . . . of course he isn't really a dog at all," she added, placing the tray beside me on the bed. "Pull yourself together."

I pulled.

"You're obviously very weak, still. I'm sorry there's nothing hot for you. I did keep a cup of onion soup, but one of those bloody servants has drunk it. I should have taken it into my room."

On the tray there was a plate of hors d'oeuvres: ham, black olives, sardines, hard-boiled eggs and a few unrecognizable things: with bread and a bottle of wine. Quite splendid. I began to tear at the food saying my Thank-yous with my mouth full.

She turned up more lights.

"You look rather better," she said, settling herself in one of the straight-backed chairs: "I thought you were going to die."

"Goodness no, I was only tired. I'm frightfully strong."

"Oh so am I. But I'm accident-prone." She lifted the skirts of the dressing-gown and examined her large knees, each encased in pink sticking-plaster. "It comes of not being in a state of grace," she mourned.

I couldn't think of anything consoling to say to that, so after a decent interval, I asked her about the nightgown.

"It's mine. I had to open it down the back with a pair of scissors, don't you remember?"

"Awfully kind of you," I said, "I hope it can be mended."

"No need to worry. I have far too many nightgowns. About forty, I think." She sat fondling the dog's ears, watching me eat. The dog watched too. Presently the Countess began to sniff the air; she had a well-shaped nose, though the nostrils were rather too big.

"Can you smell burning?" she asked urgently, "You can't? I can. Wait. No, not you, Teruel." She rushed out again and was gone long enough for me to finish the hors d'oeuvres. Teruel watched every bit going down. I slipped him an anchovy. I drank the wine and began to feel absolutely wonderful.

"Nothing's burning!" she screamed from the salon. She reappeared. I raised my glass to her. She smiled abstractedly. "You'll be very acid after the wine, what did you say your name was . . . Thomas yes, of course. Remind me to give you some Bromo-Seltzer; Thomas. You must call me Dorothea. Do you want a cigarette? In the box, by the lamp. I'll have one, too. Are you feeling strong enough to explain yourself?"

I wanted to say "I'd much rather you explained you," but it was politer to oblige. I told her in shorthand, as you might say. I couldn't, I found, bring the last weeks into life or perspective. It was like

163

reporting a journey made by somebody else. But throughout my dull gabble, she kept her big brown eyes fixed on me. So did the dog. They seemed to find it fascinating.

"Oh but you were guided. Guided all the way. To this house, of course it was all meant," she said. "It may even have been the reason for my deciding to buy the villa, who knows?"

Here I suddenly recognized her as a chump. I can't complain of chumps, being pretty stupid myself on the whole, but I think their words are against them. There are the words, and their habit of swallowing everything whole but digesting very little. They seem to keep all their beliefs in a sort of crop, like birds, for easy two-way access. Gerald had called Sarah a chump, but this is incorrect. If anything, Sarah *over*-digests.

"And now, what next? Or don't you know?"

"I have to get myself to Gibraltar somehow."

She looked puzzled. "Gibraltar? Why Gibraltar? Oh, oh, I see. You want to go to England."

"Well, of course."

"Back to the war. Well, so you shall." She gave me a jolly self-indulgent smile, rather as if I'd said I wanted a pony for Christmas. "But must it be Gibraltar? Can't you go via Lisbon? Then you could travel with me." That made me blink. She said, "You're the first person I've ever seen whom white eyelashes really suited."

"When are you going to Lisbon?"

"Next week. I'm catching the Clipper to America. I should be in New York ten days from now. What's so astonishing about that? I'm an American citizen."

"If I gave you a letter for my family —"

"They're in America? But of course. And I'll telephone them," said the Countess. "There you are, you see, it's all meant, every bit of it. And you can come on the train with me. Miles will meet us. At the Spanish border, I hope; but it's up to him. He's left Cintra, you know, sold his farm. Very busy Miles is, these days. Spying," she added. "Don't drink any more wine, you're beginning to look very flushed."

"Did you say Miles was spying?"

164

"Well, selling information. Selling *something*, anyway, he'll tell you all about it."

I tried to pin myself down as firmly as I could to the fast-vanishing realities. I said "But look – I can't go anywhere, cross any border, without papers. I'd be arrested and interned."

"You can have papers. André will see to them."

"André?"

"A very good friend of mine. I'll talk to him tomorrow."

"You don't mean Andreas, do you?" I asked, remembering Mourri's Greek. The Countess looked at me haughtily. "I said André. Andreas wouldn't be right for him at all. André's wrong, too." She appeared to be giving it deep thought. "He should be called Félix; or Fabien. You know," she added, "You don't look in the least like Thomas. Thomas . . . it won't do. Aquinas? A'Becket? Doubting? No, no, no." She shut her eyes. "Justin!" she said in a loud voice, still keeping them shut: "I shall call you Justin."

It was the second day of being Justin. The first day had been wasted by my running a temperature and having to stay in bed. The Countess had nursed me within an inch of my life. Now I was sitting on my own rock, at the edge of the pool. Nothing here was changed. The Countess had smartened up the villa considerably and rather chaotically. (The indecent cherubs, for example, were still at large on the ceiling in the salon; at odds with the crucifixes, primitives and Spanish leather screens down below.) All the rooms were self-conscious, over-elaborate, somehow contriving to be bare and fussy at the same time. It wasn't the Twenty-nine villa any more.

She could do nothing, thank goodness, to the balustrade, the broken steps, or my loved rock-pool. Here was the familiar reddish jumble, then the weed lifting at the edge of the bright water: here were the sea anemones and spiky clusters of *oursin* growing on the pale, angled slope of rock that lay out under the surface. I watched the little, busy fishes flickering through.

I felt dazed and floppy. "Still half a point above normal," said the Countess, shaking the thermometer. Before she left, she had insisted on my wearing one of her big straw hats. "Don't go in the water" was her last instruction. I had disobeyed it, briefly, swimming naked. Yesterday she had cut Emile's trousers off to the knee, hemming them into the likeness of shorts. She kept a very noisy sewing-machine in the room that used to be Gerald's. She made all her own clothes. She would make some shirts for me.

She was also an artist ("I dabble in everything") so I was provided with a good sketching-block and crayons. I was sketching Teruel. The old trick of drawing with my left hand came in useful, because my right shoulder still bothered me; rather more since the Countess gave it a rub with some green liquid that stung horribly.

Teruel was posing on the high rock, pointing his muzzle towards the sea. At intervals he gave me a questioning stare as though he suspected I wasn't taking advantage of the pose. I wasn't. I'd got his head quite well, and the look of the judge's wig about the ears; I'd done a prancing sketch, and one of him flat on his face, nose between paws: what the Countess called the Disney Pluto Position. It was fun to be drawing again. She had said she would buy every one of the sketches and frame them.

Just how crazy was she? Feeling a little crazy myself, I couldn't be sure. On the subject of Teruel she was certainly nuts. Crackers . . .

"America's the only possible place. The only place where he can be decently fed. People on this coast are starving already. 'Can't live on carnations, poor things. Nor can Teruel. Thank God I'll be away before the tins run out. We shall have to take some with us, of course, for the journey."

"What sort of tins?"

"I've been hoarding dog-food since September. Down in the cellar. Not only dog-food, though that's the most important. I'd far rather live in Spain than go back to America but the food situation's ghastly. He was losing weight, that's why I came to France . . . You don't know," she had said, "what it's like to have a dog dependent on you. Particularly these days."

"These days," was – to date – her only reference to the war. As far as she was concerned, it meant nothing except a threat to Teruel's health and some personal inconvenience. She had no radio: she could give me no news.

I longed to talk to the two servants: they lived in a little house among the trees, on the landward side; they might have a radio; but the Countess had forbidden all communication. According to her, I was none of their business, so she had told them I didn't speak a word of French. The result was a splendidly outspoken dialogue while they served my luncheon. By the dialogue I learned that I was her lover, who had come all the way from Switzerland, meeting with a railway-accident in the process; hence my battered looks and absence of luggage. They thought I was too young for her.

She claimed to be thirty-eight. Last night had been given over to her life-story. A Countess in her own right: "I keep the title because it's pretty." An heiress: "I've never known what it was *not* to be rich and I don't want to." A convent school in Ireland: from which she had escaped out of a third-floor window to marry an American. She hadn't seen him for twenty years. "But naturally divorce is out of the question, I mean – what is one a Catholic *for*?" Her true love-affair with a man younger than herself, in Spain: "Marriage, naturally was out of the question, but we were happy. I quite understood when he had to marry somebody else. We are great friends now." The long love-affair with Spain itself . . . "It's the only place where I can be what God meant me to be." (She didn't explain precisely what this was) "Latin blood in me somewhere . . . I know there is. If you've never lived in Spain you've never lived at all. And that always makes people start about bull-fights. Don't you dare. They're utterly beautiful – and ordained – and as right as Spanish architecture."

The life-story skidded a good deal, helped, I suppose, by my fever. There was the mountaineering expedition in the Andes: there was the time the hotel in Florida caught fire; there were all her adventures in the Spanish war. There were her two sons "who simply hate me, and why not?" One of them had tried to poison her in Calcutta, when he was six. She didn't say how old the sons were now. She was extremely erratic on dates and afterwards when I added it all up, it made her almost ninety.

Teruel gave a yawn and then a snap. He nosed his way cautiously down the rocks; he waded into the water: only a little way. He knew where the gentlest of the slopes was: here he stood precariously, with the water just over his braceleted ankles. He kept looking back at me, wrinkling his forehead, lifting his eyebrows, plainly asking when the Countess would come back.

I couldn't tell him. For somebody who never slept until two a.m. she had made a remarkably early start. At six I had been aroused to stand on a large piece of shelf-lining-paper while she drew round my feet. By six-thirty she had gone to catch the earliest train to Nice. Here she would find me some shoes. (She couldn't promise anything good, of course; with every conceivable requirement, one would find that the tarts and the *embusqués* had got there first.) She would call at the American Consulate for her passport. She would buy me some razor-blades. (Mourri had put one of her father's razors into my saddle-bag but I'd demolished the blade on my three-day growth: my chin still felt stubbly.) She would see André about my papers; a photograph would be needed, so she would get a camera. She would send off my postcard and find me a newspaper. She would try to get a cable sent to my father, but this would depend on the goodwill of her high-ranking chum at the Consulate: the post-office simply charged you heavily for cables and then hid them in a drawer. I hoped she wouldn't carry out her promises of buying me a new suit. All I wanted was the shoes. Grandfather's boots were as dead as my poor bicycle.

It hadn't occurred to me until lately how little one could do unshod. The more I thought about shoes, the more obvious this became. "Shoes," Romney had said to me, "are security-symbols." He was talking in advertising terms. More than symbols, I said to myself, much, much more. I felt there was something to be learned here; in terms of war at least. Bomb all boot-factories and you could immobilize a nation.

I looked at the Countess's bathing-shoes; lying on the ledge of rock beside me; black rubber and a little too narrow; long enough, her feet were huge. But I couldn't trust them to take me down the road to see if old Matthieu were still at his little hotel: as I should have liked.

Now the sea was beginning to turn white; it was the hour I loved in the place I loved. (Place where I dived for Sarah's gold pencil, place where I asked Rab to marry me; place of childhood memories a long way further back than those.) The difficulty, I thought, is not to realize I'm back but to believe I ever went away: and none of the past can hurt, nor does my mind awake to the present; I am here and that's all; a dazed and comfortable successor to the person who used to be here. Justin . . .

Teruel gave a sudden tremendous bark; he dashed out of the water, stopped to shake a shower all over me and went headlong up the rocks to the terrace. A moment later the Countess appeared. She came charging down, waving a small box-camera. Her face was all shiny; her hair was much blonder, and stood up much higher; she had had something done to it: she wore the Harlequin dress and some perfectly colossal earrings, like horse-brasses. I stood up and raised her own hat to her.

"How are you, Justin? Has Teruel been good? You haven't been in the water? Bad boy. I knew you would. So much to tell you. Can you work this, do you think?" She plumped down on Sarah's rock, handing me the camera. It was an ordinary box Brownie. "Mine was a Leica," she said, "stolen last year, out of the car. I rather suspected Miles: trust him to get the best possible price for it. I don't know what one does with these."

"Quite easy," I said "Look. Only one thing to press."

"That's what André said. I think it makes it much more difficult. I mean how do you focus, and get the light and speed you want?"

"You just look in the view-finder."

"Well, it's got to be a close-up. Passport-size. I think we'd better wait till the morning."

"This light's good enough."

"All right. Take off that ridiculous hat. Stay still." Under my direction she snapped the lever twice. "We must pray they come out. Only those two films left and impossible to get more, it's André's daughter's camera. She'll develop and print them. He'll take it back with him tomorrow; he's coming to lunch. Pouf, how hot and horrid I feel. That filthy train, full of hoi-polloi . . . Do you mind if I swim with no clothes on?"

"I'll turn my back."

"You needn't."

"It feels more polite."

"When there are parties here we all swim naked."

"I think it's easier in a party," I said, but already she was stripping at speed: right in front of me so I gave up the effort to be gentlemanly. She was beautifully built and almost entirely unself-conscious. Almost. The jolly, foxy smile was a little exaggerated and she kept her eyes on my face all the time as if I were a wild animal whom she needed to hypnotize. She took off her earrings last. Only the ample sticking-plaster on each knee remained.

"André and I have the most wonderful idea for you," she said, putting the earrings into my hand, "oh and I've got you some shoes, very common, imitation lizard-skin but they were the only ones in your size. A man was selling them on the Promenade des Anglais. I expect they'll fall to pieces. And my dressmaker's husband's getting clothes for you. He's a dry-cleaner and he'll help himself out of stock. A lot of people haven't come back for their clothes. I left your measurements." Followed by Teruel, she waded slowly into the water, saying, "I must be careful of my hair." She paddled about the pool with a quick breast-stroke, her head raised high. Teruel watched her anxiously. She didn't stay in long.

"Did you pick up your passport?" I asked when she came wading out again.

"No, I couldn't. My friend wasn't there today, and I was damned if I'd line up in the queue for some idiot underling. May I borrow your towel? I left a message for him to telephone me. It's a day's work, telephoning from here. I do wish somebody would tell me why everything in Unoccupied France is so difficult. If it was Occupied, one would understand. And the way they all *whisper*," she added impatiently, rubbing herself down: "Everybody whispers and looks over one shoulder to see if there's a spy within range." She put on her earrings, then her bust-bodice and her knickers. She was deflected before she reached the dress by remembering what she had to tell me.

"I've got it all worked out. You're going to cross the border as Miles's son. I thought of it. André was terribly impressed and I've invented lots of details since. Now, listen, this is brilliant. You were working as a waiter here when war broke out. The hotel closed; you've had odd jobs since. Now you're penniless and you must get back to Lisbon, to your father. What's that face for?"

"Miles only got married in 1928. I'd have to be twelve, wouldn't I?"

"You're *too* stupid: you can be illegitimate, or his son by his first wife or something. Half-Portuguese and half-Swiss – if that isn't neutral," said the Countess, "I don't know what is. And you'll be absolutely safe with me. Once we're across the Spanish border, nothing can go wrong. I have – as Miles may have told you – great influence with the Government. They're all my friends. The General himself – you're not listening, why not?"

"Can André produce a passport? They'll want that, won't they?"

"André can do everything," she said crossly. "What's the matter, Justin? I thought you'd be pleased."

"Sorry. I am pleased. And I'm awfully grateful."

"No, you're not. And I couldn't get a newspaper, they were all sold out, or any razor-blades; and of course as my friend wasn't at the Consulate I couldn't send your cable. But I *did* send your post-card." Her large eyes were full of tears; Teruel, pressed against her leg, seemed to be crying too: "André says it won't get to England, but he's not God, after all . . ." She jumped up and pulled her dress on over her head: "I won twenty-six *mille* at the Casino and that's always a sign. On the *Huit*, of all unlikely numbers." Here she discovered the block with my sketches of Teruel and began to scream with delight. Her screams were interrupted by the man-servant leaning on the balustrade to call *"Madame la Comtesse est servie!"*

"Merde," said the Countess, "It's all cold, isn't it? It can wait."

"There's always the soup," he reminded her. The Countess compared the soup with something else in Spanish and told him to leave it on the stove. She was furious now. She was accustomed, she told me, to dine at ten; she couldn't bear this bourgeois hour; she couldn't stand the exigent slaves wanting to wash up and get away. She only

171

compromised for the sake of the electric current, which was a chancy matter.

"But we can dine by candlelight; I've got seventy boxes of candles in the cellar. Teruel loves the candlelight. I think I must have his eyes tested as soon as I get to New York." She began to sniff the air: "Do you smell something funny? Something dead? I do. Let's go in."

She came to the dinner-table wearing a huge Spanish shawl, white and red; she brought another one, yellow and green, to drape my bare knees. "I know it's cold in here. I'm always hot because I take so many vitamins. How are the shoes?"

"Fine," I said. They fitted. I couldn't thank her enough. The black and white lizard-skin worried her more than it worried me. "I might be able to dye them, perhaps." She looked rather splendid in the shawl and she had changed her earrings for a pair of red sparkly ones.

I remembered our family meals in this room long ago: we used to sit round a big table in the middle of it. Anything we left on the table, before the cloth was laid, had to be piled up on the piano and retrieved afterwards. No piano here now: and the big table was gone: its narrow black substitute stood in the window-bay. With the candles lighted, the rest of the room drew off into the shadows. Teruel, at a snap of the Countess's fingers, went under the table and lay still. I had to be careful not to kick him.

"What's the cloud on you, Justin?"

I answered her truthfully: "I don't quite know. Still feeling rather cheap, I suppose."

"Take some wine. But it isn't physical, your cloud. Something's worrying you. Tell me. No, don't tell me. If one lets worries out into the air they achieve more power. I find I can conquer worries by breathing. Deep breathing, like this." She laid down her soup-spoon and inhaled. "I say to myself 'Be free' 'be free'. In-out-in-out. Be-free-be-free. True freedom," she added, "can only exist within a frame of discipline. That isn't an original remark. It was made to me by a priest."

I was diverted. "Would you count the Army as a frame of discipline? It made me feel I was back at prep-school."

"Have you ever felt free anywhere – any time? Wait a minute. Do you hear a funny noise? A sort of knocking? I do. Under the floor." She inclined her head, listening carefully: "It's stopped now. What were we talking about?"

"Freedom."

"Yes. Well, what is freedom, anyway? What do *you* mean by it?"

I tried to think. My head was still hazy. "Well, complete loss of freedom would surely mean having to live by rules you thought were all wrong," I said.

"Is that what you thought about Army rules?" She sounded cross.

"No, it wasn't." A memory from the past had walked in to help me. "I once left a job in advertising because I was asked to do something I couldn't stomach. I believe that's what freedom is; never having to do anything one can't stomach."

"Absolute nonsense. A cannibal can stomach a missionary. Do you find him a desirable example?"

She was angrier still when I began to laugh. "Sorry . . . I meant something one's soul can't stomach."

"That's just integrity."

"Oh well. Couldn't it be the answer?"

"No," said the Countess. "And *I* understand freedom. Because I was brought up in the church: the only frame of discipline that makes human sense. The fact that I can lapse proves my point."

It didn't. Or not to me. "I can see it gives you something to be free from, if that's what you want."

"How could I ever be free from it?"

"I thought you said you were."

"I said no such thing. I said I'd lapsed, moved away . . ."

"Well, but where are you going?"

"I'm on my way back to it, naturally."

She made this sound axiomatic. She said, "And don't ask *why* I lapsed."

"I wasn't going to."

"Well, I'll tell you. It began when three priests running told me dogs couldn't get to Paradise." She glared at me now as though I, not the priests, had told her. Then she sighed: "I was at my most devout during the war. Once the war was over —"

"*Over* . . . ?"

She pealed with laughter. "I didn't mean this European thing. I'm talking about the war in Spain."

Down below I felt the stirrings of a rage. My voice sounded scrapy when I said "Would you mind telling me —" She cut me short: "I know exactly what you're going to ask. You're going to ask me why the Bishops blessed Franco's guns."

"No, I'm not. I want to know why this war means nothing to you?"

The jolly fox was far less jolly now. She squinnied up her eyes and her nostrils flared. "Are you suggesting it should mean something to me?"

"I haven't said so."

"You imply it, Justin," she told me with immense hauteur.

I didn't say, "Sorry." I wasn't sorry. I waited.

"If you want an answer – the answer's obvious, or I should have thought it was." She ate a mouthful of cold veal. Then she said, "It means nothing to me because it means nothing to Teruel."

"And did the Spanish war mean something to him?" I managed, when I'd got my breath back.

"How can you be so stupid? He wasn't even born," said the Countess.

I shall always think of André as the man with the brown shoes. They were the best shoes I had seen since I started running. Brown shoes, well made and highly polished. Shoes of doom, walking in across the clean bare floor and the Spanish rugs.

It had taken him two days to get here. When I said something about hold-up, he looked bewildered: "But it was always for today. I told Dorothea I couldn't manage yesterday."

This, after the fuss she had made, staggered me. Nothing to the shock that was coming, though.

· · · · ·

I've never been moved to hate anybody. Even dislike comes hard as a rule; I suppose I'm too lazy in my head. But for twenty-four hours (it seemed much longer) I'd felt like strangling the Countess. She was driving me crackers. I think this began with our talk at dinner; but stayed underground until morning when I awoke with what Kai-Lung called a deep feeling of no-enthusiasm. This soon hotted up into a frenzy.

Everything about her was suddenly unbearable; her jolliness, her screams, her petulance with the servants: her religious chump-talk, her fussing over Teruel. I couldn't stand her regular inquiries for my health and when she went on about my shoulder, the shoulder seemed to hurt more. She told me she thought there was still a bullet in it, lodged under the blade. The number of times she smelled something funny, or heard a knocking noise, increased. It maddened me. Her earrings maddened me. Her smile was an irritation, 'Justin' was an irritation; even the sticking-plaster on her knees became an irritation.

While we were waiting for André (uselessly, as it turned out) she again told me all about her little boy trying to poison her. I didn't, I decided, blame him. Lunch was served at three. After it she tried to get André on the telephone; I had to remove myself from her yells at the obstructive instrument, so I set off to see if I could find old Matthieu. Galloping and screaming, she caught me before I reached the gate. "You idiot! A gendarme could pick you up. I saw two go past – five minutes ago." She couldn't have seen anything of the sort from the salon.

I got away, to the rocks; down she came after me, wearing a white swimming-suit and a tall Phrygian cap of white rubber. She'd just remembered something. Hadn't I refused to go to America when I was ten years old? Run away, jumped out of the car? Miles had told her. She wanted all the details. I couldn't make them entertaining; I was too cross. She kept saying, "Well, go on," and "Teruel's listening to every word." Then she said, "It was much better the way Miles told it." I grew sulkier and sulkier. I got the notion that she was driving Teruel crackers, too. He made odd faces at me. When we came up from the rocks he ran after me into my bedroom and climbed on the bed. The Countess pulled him off, screaming. He had never climbed on anybody's bed before; she took him out on to the terrace to give him a brushing and he bit her. This made for a to-do with iodine and more plaster: she decided he must be sickening for something. He had never bitten her before. She engaged in another long fight with the telephone; she failed to reach the vet.

I asked if she could acquire me a razor blade from the man-servant. She said No, because a friend of hers in the Argentine had got dermatitis from doing precisely that. When I pointed out that it couldn't be 'precisely' that, she lost her temper.

She tried to read my palm before dinner. As soon as I said No, she kissed me, saying we were so much alike I might well be her brother. At dinner she began to exhibit a tedious curiosity about my sex-life; on my taking evasive action she became quite clinical as to the dangers of celibacy for men. I went to bed immediately after dinner, but the iron gate across the archway was, naturally, the poorest of defences. She kept rushing in, hearing things, smelling things, or wanting to know how I was: eager to give me laxatives, or sedatives: full of prognostications for next week. She was telling our fortunes with a special pack of Spanish cards. Everything would go smoothly. At last I pretended to be asleep.

It was mean to feel like this; ungrateful and beastly. I lay awake for hours, wondering how I should be able to stand her company all the way to Lisbon.

More fool me.

"She never listens, that's her trouble," said André. He smiled at me: "You've come a long way, haven't you? My congratulations." The tone was reminiscent. "*You're* getting a big boy, aren't you?" it echoed. He patted me on my bad shoulder.

He was, I judged, about fifty years old. His slicked-back hair was grey, his face deeply tanned. He had small dark eyes and a beak of a nose; a chin with a cleft in it. His shape was tubby and compact; his suit was light blue flannel, lush-looking, somehow; and then the shining, beautifully kept shoes.

I said I had been lucky, that it was really no cause for congratulation. He complimented me on my French. At once I remembered the Countess forbidding me to use it. This made him smile, "She'll lift the ban. *À force*. My English being very poor. Where is she?"

"Giving Teruel his bath."

"My God, that dog. Always that dog . . . Every time I come here to eat I feel it is the dog whom I should thank on my departure. You find it annoying? But no. As an Englishman, of course, you are a dog-lover."

"I like Teruel; he's an elaborate character," I said.

"Like his mistress," said André. He was giving me a piercing stare. To any well-dressed man I must, naturally, look a scarecrow, with my stubbly chin, my old shirt and improvised shorts. (The dressmaker's dry-cleaning husband was, so far, a dead loss.) He stared particularly hard at my lizard-skin feet.

"Do you listen to the war news? No, not here, you wouldn't. Extraordinary, isn't she? Simply doesn't care. London's being badly bombed. The invasion's announced on the Boche radio for next week. *C'est de la blague*. They aren't nearly ready to invade." He could give me no details about the bombing, though I clamoured. All he would say was that the B.B.C. made little of it. Last time I'd heard the phrase it encouraged me. Not now. I plunged down into the dark of my old nightmare, running through the ruins, searching for Brigstock. It swirled up inside my head. I heard my voice saying abruptly, "I must get back. You're going to help me, aren't you?"

"Am I indeed?" Vizor down at once. Obviously because the manservant had come in to lay the table. I stalled, asking if he knew Mourri's friend, Andreas, at Cannes? I gave the name and address.

"Never heard of him. Is he another of Dorothea's illusions?"

"Illusions?"

"*Mais oui.*"

"What do you mean?"

He looked at me steadily.

"*Mon pauvre gars,*" he said, after a moment. He glanced in the direction of the servant, then took my arm and piloted me swiftly out on to the terrace.

"You mustn't believe a word she says, you know. You hadn't realized that?"

I shook my head.

"*C'est une manie*. It's the way she keeps herself going. I suppose she's told you she's off to Lisbon next week. Taking that beast with her. On the Transatlantic Clipper." His little eyes shone.

"It isn't true?" My voice sounded as croaky as Sarah's.

"Oh she'll get to America. Eventually. With money one can do most things. But her passport's held up while they communicate with Washington. She'd let it run out; of course she hasn't lived over there for years." He was smiling all the time: "That's the least of the delay. Pan-American would never let her take the dog. Not in the cabin with her. She insists on that. And if they would, which they won't, there's a queue for the Clipper about three hundred names long; the flights are irregular, she could easily wait for months. I'm a travel-agent, as she may have told you. Pretty profession in the year 1940, *hein*? At least it means I know what I'm talking about. Dorothea will have to go by boat – when she does go. There's a tremendous waiting-list for the boats, too. *Figurez-vous, donc – Psstt —*" he cut himself off quickly.

"My very dear André, I had given you up for lost." She was carrying an enormous towel and dragging Teruel, all skinny and shivery from his bath. She enveloped him in the towel: this became a struggling tent which emitted snarls. The Countess fought it masterfully, talking to André over her shoulder. The camera was waiting for him. What steps had he taken? How soon would he be able to deliver my passport? "*Voila, mon amour, c'est terminé,*" she added, releasing Teruel, who bounded off into the sunshine.

André stood silent, looking down at his shoes.

"Well, tell us what's happening, can't you?" cried the Countess. (She was wearing the harlequin dress again, I noticed blankly: and the horse-brass earrings.) "Why didn't you turn up yesterday?" she nagged him. She towered above him like a huge Caryatid.

"Because I was invited for today," he told her.

"Rubbish. Excuses. I'll forgive you if you've been working for Justin."

He looked up into her face.

"My dear Dorothea. My very dear Dorothea. Whatever miracles I may be capable of —"

"You are capable of all, you know very well."

"I am *not* capable of faking a passport."

"What nonsense, of course you are. Why tell me you are if you aren't?"

"I told you it was possible that this might, in time, be done. By somebody. I didn't say by me. I offered to have the photograph printed for you."

She shot him a baleful look, squinnying up her eyes. Then she clapped her hands and screamed to the servant to bring the Cinzano. "We'll drink out here. Here we can talk. Luncheon won't be ready yet; a slight misunderstanding with my private lobster-supply." As soon as the glasses were filled, she said, "Now then. I know it's common to talk about money, particularly before luncheon, but I must remind you, you have but to name your price."

"*Ah, ça,*" said André sadly.

"What does that mean '*ah, ça*'? You're a travel-agent, are you not?"

"I was."

"Don't talk these stupidities, you are a very influential, knowledge-able man."

"It's a pretty thought. As a travel-agent *je suis foutu, naturelle-ment.*"

The Countess banged her glass down and it broke. "What is this act? Are you trying to impress Justin with the difficulties? (Mop it up with Teruel's towel, Justin; don't cut yourself.) Really, André . . . I can't understand you. When I think how co-operative you were on Tuesday."

"On Tuesday," he said "it was yourself who did the talking."

"*Madame la Comtesse est servie!*"

She sighed heavily.

"Better get it over," she said, "Luncheon, I mean. Not a word till afterwards. Even when they're out of the room. They listen behind the door."

André winked at me. I couldn't return the wink.

For once I had no appetite. I sat in a black stupor, while the two of them swopped stories. André had endless stories about the Riviera rats. His favourite character was a woman, a devoted gambler, who had been hoarding coffee systematically since the Munich crisis. She was now making a fortune by the sale of half-pound packets; her stipulation was that she should be paid in Casino chips.

"Why?" asked the Countess, "Why can't she just take the money and change it into chips?"

"She refuses to be called a profiteer."

(I should have known, I was saying to myself, all the time, I should have known.)

I thanked God the Countess couldn't follow us into the bathroom. I didn't apologize to André for going in with him, nor for locking the door. He showed no surprise.

"You said you knew where it *could* be faked, the passport? Didn't you? Where? How?"

Even here I noticed that he gave a quick look over his shoulder before he answered: "I know only one possible place. There is a family living in Marseille."

"I'll go to Marseille. I'll go now."

"If she'll let you."

"My God, don't you see —"

– "I see perfectly. But I warn you, not to do anything precipitate. Don't rush off like a madman. Dorothea's wise to keep you tethered. She has her own reasons, perhaps. " He flushed the lavatory and winked at me again. "But it's the course of common-sense. One unsatisfactory encounter with the police and you'll be for the Fort St. Jean. Under parole, too. It doesn't even need the police. I know quite a few people on this coast who'd be only too delighted to hand over an escaped British soldier. This will become worse. Wait till our damnable government gets on its feet. Badly phrased, that. Don't wait, of course. On the other hand, don't hurry."

"Who are these people? Will you *tell* me?"

"I will," he said coolly, "If you keep your temper." He lit a cigar, offering one to me. The Countess had begun to hammer on the door.

"Une petite minute, voyons . . ." said André: "Can you memorize? I'd rather you didn't write it down. And remember I promise nothing. But when you get there, if you get there, mention my name. They are my cousins. They own a restaurant." He gave me the name and the address. I repeated these after him, twice. "Nothing may come of it, understand? If they say no, then you simply go away again. *Surtout, il ne faut pas insister.*" He frowned. "Remember, it is dangerous, that city. Perhaps I can devise some method of getting you there. I'll think about it. Patience. Patience is your best wisdom."

The Countess had tired of banging at the door. When we emerged, she was out in the sun, giving Teruel a beauty-treatment. I halted André in the salon. "Is it all lies? Every bit of it? About being met by Miles – and her influence with the Spanish Government?"

He cocked his head on one side; he stroked his chin. "Like all habitual liars, Dorothea occasionally disconcerts one by telling the truth," said the man with the brown shoes.

The only way to keep my sanity was to keep quiet: I'd been telling myself this ever since André and I walked out on to the terrace together. I'd left him with the Countess; I'd run down to the rocks and hurled myself into the sea. When I got back there was no sign of her.

She couldn't, I thought, prove the truth of his *exposé* better than by leaving me alone; how grateful I would have been for this yesterday . . . Oh, well. I was grateful now, differently. What could I say to her?

I didn't believe one thing she'd told me. Not one damn' thing. If it hadn't been for Miles, and his account of her last year, my anger might have set her up as a Nazi agent. I kept trying to tell myself she was just a chump who'd misled me through sheer silliness.

I swam too long for the good of my shoulder. Which was why I sprawled on the bed for a rest before I went down the road to see if I could find old Matthieu. (Because that was where I would go; André and his precepts be damned. I wasn't staying here. If Mourri's house had felt like a trap, the Twenty-nine villa now felt like the Château d'If.)

I dozed, without meaning to doze. For a moment I dreamed I was back in London; at Ramillies Terrace, having tea with Brigstock. I saw her most vividly. She was pouring out the milk and saying, "You *have* been away a long time." As soon as I awoke I wanted to cry.

Scrambling off the bed, I heard the Countess yelling, "Justin, Justin!" She dashed in through the archway, followed by Teruel.

I was stark naked. She didn't even notice. She said, "I bicycled up to the station, to see if your clothes had come. Look!"

From cowardice, gratitude, or good manners, I couldn't begin to fight. She laid the clothes on my bed. There was a blue shirt; a pair of grey linen trousers and a suit. The suit was the Riviera-old-gentleman sort, made of tussore, shantung or whatever it is: General Stevens, Johnny's father, used to wear a jacket of this stuff.

"Try them on – quick, quick!" the Countess was screaming. I pulled on my under-shorts, with my back to her.

The shirt and the grey linen trousers just fitted me, though the shirt was a little tight across the shoulders. The jacket of the suit was wide enough; the trousers sagged like elephants' legs; the old gentleman must have been as broad as he was long.

"Don't take them off – stay where you are!"

I stayed, holding them up. Teruel averted his eyes. The Countess came rushing back with a china box full of pins. She pinned the trousers on me most expertly and then took them away. Soon I could hear the sewing-machine thumping its head off.

Because of the clothes, I knew I couldn't run yet. It was silly, I suppose. I found some sheets of writing-paper in the drawer of a tall, painted desk: I found a pen. I took these to my room. It was difficult. My brain wouldn't work. The best I could achieve was, "I'm well and safe and I'll send another letter soon." I wrote this

twice, once for my father and once for Brigstock. There should have
been a third message for Rab. There wasn't. The same door stayed
shut; she was nowhere; I couldn't get near her in my mind. And this,
for some reason, hurt me less and less.

No envelopes; and no stamps. (And how, seeing that the Countess
might be here for months, could I know they would get there at
all?) I was in the middle of perplexity, counting my cash, finding I
had exactly forty-five francs left, when the manservant came
through the archway and peeped over the top of the ironwork
gate.

"*Monsieur est servi.*"

I discovered that I was hungry.

Here was the candlelight again, and the Countess sweeping in
wearing the Spanish shawl; here was Teruel diving under the table.
Here was some of the lobster left over from luncheon, served hot,
with a sauce. Here was the wine.

"I'll have that suit finished after dinner," she said, smiling at me.
"Fill your glass. André didn't depress you, did he? It's just an act
with him. He became quite co-operative as soon as you'd left us
alone. Very wise of you, that." She lifted her glass to me.

"I don't think," I said heavily, "I am very wise."

"Well, you read the Gospel for the Feast of St. Justin. You'll soon
see."

I couldn't wait to discuss the Gospel. "Why didn't you tell me the
truth?" I asked her. "Why did you say 'New York in ten days'
time'? You won't be there. You won't be there for ages."

She was silent, squinnying up her eyes.

"You're just pretending, aren't you? I wish you'd told me. I wish
you hadn't said André could do those things."

Still silence.

"You made me think it was all easy; that we'd be out of here next
week."

She watched me.

"It means," I said, "I'll have to try something else."

In a rather smaller voice than usual, she said, "Please don't."

"Sorry. You've been very kind. Don't let's talk about it any
more."

She swirled suddenly into fury. "You fool, you *stupid* little boy. It's your war you want, isn't it? Nothing else. Nothing else matters. Nothing in the world."

I fought to keep my temper. I said, "Oh, well. We've all got something that matters to us, haven't we?"

"Naturally, you smug, pompous little beast."

"And yours is Teruel."

I wasn't prepared for the scream: "Teruel! What do you know? What do you understand? Nobody understands. Nobody knows what I'm going through – all day, every day, all night, every night." Her voice broke; her eyes filled up with tears. "It's driving me mad. Even with the pills I don't sleep more than two or three hours. And when I do sleep, I dream he's starving – or he's run away – or that somebody's got into the cellar after the food, and when Teruel attacks him, he shoots. I see Teruel lying there dead —" The tears were running down her cheeks. "You idiot. If I didn't try to keep on hoping – keep on believing, I should lose my mind."

She seemed to turn off the tears like a tap. She wiped her eyes, drawing herself up in the same full-bosomed, imperious way as on the first evening I saw her. "Excuse me, Justin. I cannot expect you to understand."

She had shaken me a little. I said, "I do understand about loving a dog. I really do."

"How could you, possibly?"

"Because of a girl I used to know."

She pounced: "*Your* girl?"

"It doesn't matter what girl. She had a dog she loved. And when she had to leave him —"

– "Why did she have to leave him? If she loved him she couldn't possibly have left him."

"That's what she decided."

"So?"

"So she shot him." I said.

A pause.

"Was he in pain, suffering?"

"No. It was to prevent his suffering. He would have been miserable without her."

A long silence followed. Then the Countess asked in a bright, matter-of-fact voice, "And did she shoot herself afterwards?"

I controlled a giggle. I said, "Of course not."

"*I* should have. It would be the only thing to do."

Forgetting my manners, I said "Oh don't be such a chump."

That finished it. She rose from the table. Teruel, padding after her, looked back at me once with an expression of dignified reproach.

"Justin, will you kindly tell them to send the rest of my dinner to my room," said the Countess.

She did not reappear. I heard the sewing-machine thumping away for a long time.

I roamed about the salon; I inspected the books; not many books and nearly all of them in Spanish. Presently I pulled out an old missal. With some vague idea of atonement for rudeness, I began to look for St. Justin and his Gospel. The pages were tattered; the print was small; it was hard to read by candlelight.

I didn't get as far as St. Justin, because my eyes stopped on another page.

I wished and understanding was given to me; and I called and the spirit of wisdom came upon me; and I preferred her before kingdoms and thrones and esteemed riches nothing in comparison of her.

There was something eminently satisfactory here. I felt my mind give a nod, as though it recognized a friend. The spirit of wisdom ... A clue. Clue to what? Feeling accompanied, I went out and walked on the terrace. The mad sound of the sewing-machine had stopped. The shutters were drawn across her window.

Certainly I should apologize. And I was, on reflection, too sorry for her to be angry any more. There was another thing: her reaction to my telling her the tale of Rab and Tylo had somehow exorcized that issue. It added up only to the obvious fact that Rab made more sense about Tylo than the Countess made on the subject of Teruel. Why should this clear my head?

I walked up and down in the moonlight. It was some time before I realized that I was, at last, talking to Rab; confidently and affectionately, as I used to do. I was telling her that the next time we met I would be different. No more rages, I promised; and if you came to me for judgment, I would be gentle and not judge. "We shall be older; we shall meet in the spirit of wisdom," I said. At first the conversation was one-sided, myself speaking to her across distances. Then, as I leaned on the balustrade, she was beside me.

I kept my eyes on the dark outline of our rocks and the long silver sea, cut by the pine-tree silhouettes. Here, in the place where we had known love and fun together, some thought of hers came flying; and touched my thought

It was a curious communion.

She knows what I know; that childhood is far past, that youth is over; that we two, as we were, will not meet again. We loved each other as a boy and a girl, not as a man and a woman. Our love was still part of our childhood going on. And this is over.

There was no shock of surprise. It was like the minute when I knew I couldn't pull the trigger and kill the man eating the cherries. The knowledge was only the logical completion of knowledge already begun.

We have parted. And in parting with you I have parted with a whole sequence of myself. You have done this too. That is why we cannot meet; except here, for a moment, to say the goodbye that has been said before. Goodbye, until —

I saw the image of mountains towering ahead of me; with Rab somewhere on the other side of the mountains and rough weather coming after that . . It will be a long time, I said to myself, a long time

> *Before the daggers of our offence*
> *have the colour of innocence . . .*
> *and nothing is vowed, and all is vowed*
> *and we have forgotten how to be proud.*

The bright flash of her company was gone. The forbidding mountains faded. From the past and the future I was dropped back into the present.

I stood on the terrace of the Twenty-nine villa. I was Justin again; Justin who had lost his temper and laughed. I no longer wanted to laugh. To love a dog so much, I said to myself, may be what Brigstock would call an "obession"; but it is love and so to be respected.

Presently a shutter moved and I knew she was watching me. I stood under the window, calling "I'm very sorry I was rude." She didn't answer. I said it again. Then I said "Goodnight and thank you for everything." No reply.

I didn't expect to sleep, but I was down in the darkest depth of it when a hand touched my shoulder. For a moment I thought I was Emile again; Emile back on the road somewhere: it was time to be moving: I struggled awake.

"Please love me, Justin."

I couldn't say a word.

"I am so terribly unhappy. Please love me." She was lying right beside me in the bed.

After a moment I said, "I'm sorry, but it won't be love, you know. It can't be. Not real love."

"Never mind," said the Countess.

I thought, Oh well . . .

I did my best.

When I awoke the room was light. I had left the shutters open. The clock on the wall pointed a quarter past six. I was alone; the scent used by my companion of the night clung to my pillows.

The first thing I thought was, "You don't sleep with a woman just because you're sorry for her." I climbed out of bed. Here at my window was the old, authentic Riviera morning; I saw the pines, the red rocks and the sea. All the bright colours, veiled a little, tore at my heart. Mine, I thought, mine.

Out, and into it.

She had finished altering the tussore suit. It hung on the back

187

of a chair. She must have brought it before she climbed into my bed. Intimidated, I put on the blue shirt and the grey trousers. It wasn't much of a drop from this window to the terrace. I went that way so as not to cross the salon; I didn't want to wake her (though she was more than likely to wake, thinking she heard a funny noise. I ran around the side of the villa, through the garden, to the gate.

I opened the gate. I shut it behind me.

Nobody here; just the great hush of this hour, broken by the one whirring cricket whose sound (as on the old mornings) seemed to be less a sound than the actual silence going on and on. A long time, it felt, since I walked up this road.

I walked down the road.

On my left I saw the stretch of red scree, the tumbledown tower and the olives. Here came the Twenty-nine Summer smell, fainter always at this time than in the afternoon.

Behind me I heard a clank, then a pattering like the sound of dry leaves. Teruel was running after me. He came dancing up, frisking around me in circles, wagging his tail: pleased with himself for succeeding in the trick his mistress deplored. "Aren't I clever to open that gate?" was his whole message.

"You'll catch it," I said to him.

The nigger-minstrel roll of his eyes might have meant, "So will you."

"Go back, you ass."

Not he. We went on down the road together. I looked for the faded board that advertised 'Hôtel de La Corniche' and the legend below, explaining that the proprietor *'fait lui-même la cuisine'*. It wasn't there. The hotel was; the tiny two-floor structure, clinging to the rocks. I leaned on the sea-wall. I stared straight down at the red-sanded terrace, seeing it at an angle; with its aloe like a branched candlestick jutting from one corner and the pine tree growing at the other corner. The two small iron tables still stood on the terrace.

"This is where I stayed, last time," I said to Teruel. He inspected it gravely; contracting his forehead, raising his eyebrows.

While we watched, old Matthieu came out, carrying a watering-can, moving to and fro, giving the sand a sprinkle. I thought he looked even frailer than he had looked last year; a skeleton-shape in his same grey clothes, with the black beret stuck to the side of his narrow birdlike head. I whistled to him. He looked up, shading his eyes. He dropped the watering can.

When I reached him on the terrace he put his arms round me and kissed me; then he cried and I rather wanted to cry too. Teruel stood off, wagging his tail, but looking anxious.

Matthieu blew his nose. *"Comme vous êtes matinal,"* he said.

At one of the iron tables we drank thin, bitter coffee: the bread was awful, but I ate it most happily. Teruel lay under the table, giving an imitation of a black rug. Matthieu brought out a packet of Caporals, saying he had kept it for a day of good news and that I was the good news.

I told him everything: in shorthand once again. Oddly, perhaps, I didn't mention the Countess; or perhaps this wasn't odd. She seemed not to belong to the journey. I ended, saying "And now – what? There's this fellow at Cannes – or so I believe. Or there's this family at Marseille."

"Go to Marseille. I tell you that because you could drive with Jean-Louis in the *camion*. You remember Jean-Louis, my nephew?"

I said I thought so. Matthieu had innumerable relatives; they all used to come to lunch on Sundays.

Jean-Louis, he told me, was a brave type, he had fought with the Chasseurs-Alpins; in these days he was a skilled *débrouillard*. He had brains, that one. The petrol for the *camion* was a privilege, because he carried cheeses and other farm produce from the Dauphiné to a fat Fifth Columnist (a traitor, did I understand? One well in with *les occupants*: living halfway between Marseille and Istre.) "You could go with him and come back by night, when you have made your contact. He always drives back by night. You'll be safe with him; he's up to all the tricks. And he stops here," said Matthieu, "to bring me one or two things his *patron* will not miss."

"When does he come?"

"What is the time? Ah, you have no watch . . . I should say in about half an hour."

"You mean today – I should go today."

"He only passes once a week. You're lucky," said Matthieu. Here Teruel sat upright and looked at me with an expression of acute anxiety.

"Let us consider," they said – for what seemed to me the two-hundredth time. This had been a long day and it was ending in some frustration. I might have known it would. I found my thoughts swinging back to the Countess: she had been much on my mind. So had Teruel. Was he all right? Had Matthieu delivered him safely, along with my message?

The message, purposefully vague, now seemed to me a mistake. With her gift for tantrums, she was probably assuming I'd run off because she had come into my bed. All day I had imagined her, feeling rejected and furious: she would not, I knew, be placated by my return in the *camion* after midnight.

"Let us consider."

The room was their private sitting-room above the restaurant. There were three of them, a married couple and the wife's brother. The husband was a big jolly type; his thick black eyebrows looked as though they were painted on his forehead. He reminded me of Tubby Whittington, who used to play the piano in my father's Pierrot troupe. The wife was small and dark and hyper-intelligent; a mathematician, she said, which surprised me. Her brother was cut to the same narrow pattern; he never sat still for a moment; when he wasn't wriggling and threshing his legs he was darting around the room, snapping his fingers and interrupting.

The room itself was formally discreet; thick net curtains covered the windows. The horse-hair sofa on which I'd been sitting throughout eternity, was hard as a plank. Two plants in china pots, strung on wire, vibrated rhythmically when traffic passed outside.

"Let us recapitulate."

It had been a highly academic conference but these facts emerged. They approved the notion that I should assume the identity of Miles's son. They could produce a passport for me. (*"Ça se fait de plus en plus, vous savez."*) They were relieved to know that André would provide the photograph. The only photographer they could trust was one who operated down on the Cannebière. (The restaurant, with these rooms above it, stood at the corner of a narrow street, high up at the back of the city, in the shadow of Notre Dame de La Garde.) They refused to let me set foot outside.

So . . . I would return next week, with Jean-Louis in the *camion*, bringing the photograph. But then (let us consider) should the Countess not be able to conduct me through Spain, was I prepared to proceed to Lisbon alone? The railway-ticket was no problem: they would buy it for me. It was myself who might find language-difficulties at the Spanish border, myself who might – by some slip – let us consider . . . The marionette brother said the Spaniards were, if such a thing could be conceived, more pestilential than the Germans.

"How much will it all cost?"

Oh . . . as much as I could afford. Let us consider – let us say – a prolonged calculation with paper and pencil: heads together.

"Mettons dix mille, à peu près."

I had no idea how to get it. In my pocket now there was the thousand-franc note pressed upon me by Matthieu. (Perhaps I'd been cured, once and for all, of my reluctance to accept money. I could still hear his voice saying *"Mais ça me fera tant de plaisir,"* still see the look in his swimmy old eyes.)

But I couldn't possibly ask him for another nine *mille*; I couldn't, in decency, ask the Countess.

They were on to this at once. I must not worry. As soon as I got in touch with this man, this Miles, all could be arranged, could it not? How soon did I expect to hear from him?

That was another tough one. Certainly I no longer believed the story of Miles travelling around Europe as a spy; and I would have to tackle the Countess tonight (tomorrow, rather). Had he really sold his farm? If so, where should I find him? At once I imagined her losing her temper, refusing to answer the questions.

Again they told me not to worry. "Now you will descend and dine in the restaurant, as our guest, naturally, while you await your friend."

It was ungrateful to be so glad it was over; to be happier still that the wife and the brother were remaining here for a rendezvous (concerned with problems not unlike those with which we are now concerned. A pleasure. All will arrange itself. Till next week, then. All good things to you and of course to our dear André.)

Tubby ran me down the back stairs and into the restaurant by way of the kitchen. Jean-Louis was due at eight-thirty; I had an hour in hand.

"A little glass," said Tubby. He set me at the table nearest to the kitchen entrance and furthest from the door. I liked the restaurant; it had the authentic shabby red plush and dark panelling; associated in my mind forever with good food. Here were the thick white tablecloths, the thick white lace curtains, the yellowish *lustres* and a bouquet of beautiful smells. Nobody came in while Tubby served me with *bouillabaisse*. He regretted that the resources were now so poor. In the old days, not so long ago . . .

He talked freely all the time, but he kept looking towards the door. When the door opened I saw his face become just a little jollier; there was a fractional change of manner; for a moment he was, exclusively, the restaurateur serving a client. I had my back to the door. I saw Tubby relax. Obviously, this was a trusted friend. He wished the newcomer good evening and asked him how it went.

"It goes. He doesn't come. I wait and that's all." The voice was quiet, grumbly; I didn't recognize it. The quick step and the hand falling on my shoulder brought me to my feet in a near-panic.

"Bon soir, toi," said Johnny Stevens.

The next surprise was the pleasure in his face. He stood grinning at me as delightedly as though he'd won a fortune. He kept thumping my back. "Emile, good old Emile. I swear I'll believe in your God now," said Johnny. He danced from foot to foot; he might – I thought – take off and hit the ceiling at any minute. He was wearing a purplish suit, a pink shirt and a black tie like a bootlace.

"Sight for sore eyes, that's what you are," he told me in English.

I fell back on "Ditto, ditto, Brother Smut." I was touched – and puzzled. Our last encounter (only a week ago, and as long a week as any in all my journeying) had hardly prepared me for this rapture. Why so pleased? He hitched a chair to the table and asked Tubby for cognac. He began to chatter, never taking his eyes from my face.

His life-story, compared with mine, was simple. He had got his *demobilisation-prime* from Fuveau; he was loaded with back pay. He had a railway-warrant for Perpignan; the train left tonight. From Perpignan he would walk over the mountains into Spain, taking a guide. At Figueras, his friends – as I must remember – would house him: and, in due course, convey him to Gibraltar. As usual he made it sound uproariously easy. Then he cocked his head on one side, looking at me in his old, goblin way; full of a secret.

"*Et toi*? This is the last place I'd expect to find you. It's safe and it's sensible. How did poor old Emile blunder upon it?"

I didn't feel like going into all that. I said, "So you ran away from Mourri, too . . ."

"Ran away? Her bloody parents slung me out the moment they saw me. At least the father did. The mother cried and Mourri lost her head, not to mention her temper. She asked me to *marry* her, imagine. Then she could have come with me. Over the mountains . . . All the way. Back to England."

"I call that rather brave of her."

He said, "Your trouble is you're a nice guy. It's one of the things that's been haunting me."

"Don't be an ass."

"Well I was a perfect shit to you, wasn't I? You don't know how awful I felt when I found you'd skipped. Tell me how you got here, what your plan is – if you have one. It's important, *very* important." He was drumming his fingers on the table. Tubby stood behind us, watching the door.

"I'm waiting for a *camion* to take me back."

"Back where?"

"Anthéor. I have to hang about there for a week."

"No, you don't," said Johnny: he grinned until his slitty eyes practically disappeared.

"Meaning?"

The door opened again. Too early for Jean-Louis. The man who came in was a solid dark customer with a cropped head and three gold teeth; Johnny beckoned him, introducing him to Tubby and myself, calling for another glass. The new man was a Pole, a Legionnaire like Johnny; like Johnny, equipped with his first demobilisation papers. He wasn't going on the train; he was waiting for a ship to take him to Gibraltar. "He'll get it next year," said Johnny and the Pole laughed uproariously. I saw Tubby beginning to look anxious. He looked at the clock; he looked at me. *"Pour moi, c'est mieux fermer.* I'll keep a watch for the *camion."*

He locked the door and put out all the lights, bringing a lamp for our table. Then he stationed himself by the window. Johnny said he was a brave type, but a little over-cautious. He turned to the Pole.

"So? Bernard's lost his nerve? Is that the story? One could have bet on it."

"He wants time to think. Another day or two. He stays at the Fort."

"Not surprised, it's his mother's womb," said Johnny. "Wish you could see the Fort St. Jean, Emile. You'd meet any number of our compatriots – a cosy, khaki bunch. Tried to find somebody from your regiment, but I drew a blank. They're having a wonderful time. Couldn't persuade one of them to make a run for it. Only this idiot of a Breton, and now he's funking, too. I knew he was a dead loss."

"He wants his railway-warrant back; and his money," said the Pole.

"Of course he does."

"He says you stole them."

"Nonsense. I only took charge of them. He should have met me, as arranged. Who does he think he is, keeping me hanging around all this time?"

The Pole said he himself couldn't afford to hang around much longer.

"Got any money, Emile?" Johnny asked.

"A thousand francs."

"Won't get you far. Never mind, you can write me a cheque." I said, "What are we talking about?"

Johnny didn't answer. He was busy with his wallet. He counted out notes, giving them to the Pole. "Tell Bernard he's lucky to see it again. As for the warrant – I've lost it. Tell him to go back to Fuveau and get himself another. Don't argue, that's the message." The Pole stood there, gravely rebuking Johnny. Finally he strode towards the door but Tubby turned him round and steered him out through the kitchen.

"All yours, Emile," said Johnny.

I looked at the papers on the table in front of me. A railway-warrant for Perpignan, stamped and signed "*3me Bureau d'Etranger*." A brief memorandum, giving the regimental number and service particulars of Private Bernard Morlaix. This was also stamped.

"What more d'you need?"

I went on staring at the papers.

"I owe it to you," said Johnny, "I really do."

I didn't feel he owed me anything. I felt that I myself was in debt all round; to the Countess, to old Matthieu, to Jean-Louis, to the people upstairs; to Tubby, patient beside the window. But even while I beckoned Tubby over, I knew what was going to happen. The decision came so quickly that I could only wonder. I'm so bad at choosing, always. And I had chosen.

I heard the Countess saying "Please don't." I heard André's voice counselling patience. But behind me I saw, stretching out, stretching all the way back to the start of Emile, a road that led up, led down, led nowhere.

It could lead somewhere at last. Whatever came of this leap in the dark would be better than waiting.

Tubby brought me a sheet of paper and an envelope. I scribbled the shortest of notes; I thanked her for everything, particularly for last night. I told her I was on my way. I sent my love to Teruel and I remembered to sign it 'Justin'.

It felt most peculiar to be at large and moving by legitimate means of transport. The train was the oddest thing of all. I thought about the *camion*, jolting back along the sea-road, through the dark. Jean-Louis had said I could safely spend more time with him in the cab on the homeward journey; and I had looked forward to this. But the train was pure delight. A second-class carriage, battered and shabby. We shared the space with a sub-hostile species, who slept; with an old lady who sat upright looking far more hostile than the gendarme, and a drunk who shouted in his dreams. The train was an *omnibus*. It lacked all initiative. Throughout the night it pottered, clanking to a stop whenever it could. And I went on loving it. I lay wrapped in Johnny's overcoat, half asleep, half awake. The presence of the gendarme stopped our talking. It was a typical brag of Johnny's, I thought, not to move into another carriage. Anyway I was grateful for no more questions about the Countess: arising when Johnny took stock of my clothes. This was before we left the restaurant: "No Legionnaire, even demobilised, would dress like that. *Pour le sport*. You must take my overcoat. Where did the finery come from?" When I said from a woman now living in the Twenty-nine villa, he became greatly curious.

She went with me through the night. In one half-dream she was scolding me for lying on the floor of "that filthy *camion*," for getting my new clothes dirty; for changing my name from Justin to Bernard Morlaix. Next she was preaching a sermon about Johnny, saying that he was making atonement to me and that I must never be too proud to accept other people's atonement. But in the last one, when I saw her most clearly, she was sobbing and imploring me to come back.

Perpignan consisted for me of a grim little *pension* near the railway-line; of a bedroom that looked out on the railway-line; of a long day spent waiting for Johnny. He went off to find his guide, who lived six miles beyond the town. He would come back before night bringing the guide with him. The family who would provide this character might, he said, object to my presence. They were Spaniards and extremely formal.

The mattress had bed-bugs in it.

I studied the map he had left me. I wandered downstairs and

talked to the *patronne*, a rather nice lady, who accepted Bernard Morlaix and warned him not to wander in the town. Perpignan, she said, was full of refugees aiming for the border; the police were much too busy. I didn't dare complain of the bed-bugs. Johnny had told me to get what sleep I could. After I had eaten thin soup and blood-sausage with the *patronne* I went upstairs again and tried to sleep in the armchair.

It was hot and stuffy here. And I was having one of my things about the tussore suit: I couldn't get my mind off the suit, made carefully ready for me with the aid of the pins and the sewing-machine. I should never wear it now. I was reminded of a story Sarah told me; about Brigstock sitting up late to finish an overall and then Sarah hadn't put it on, so Brigstock was disappointed. That happened at Sawcombe. Sarah said it went on haunting her for years.

The tussore suit went on haunting me.

When I get one of my things I become unbelievably miserable. By the time Johnny banged the door open I was ready to run; all the way back to the Twenty-nine villa, for the sake of the poor suit.

I was so pleased to see him. He carried a clutch of rope-soled espadrilles in different sizes, a rucksack for me and one for himself. He had also equipped us with wine, fruit and some sandwiches. He was wildly happy. The guide was an authentic refugee from Franco Spain; an old soldier; they had met as comrades-in-arms. The espadrilles were a necessity. "Knowing about your feet," said Johnny, "I bought a *grand choix*. Did I ever tell you about the shop in Bordeaux with the notice outside saying '*Grand Choix de Couronnes Mortuaires*'? I always liked it so much."

One pair of espadrilles fitted me well enough. I put the lizard shoes in my rucksack. "How far?" I asked him, "By the map I make it thirty-five kilometres."

"Should be less, but this fellow Pépé has his own ideas. I can't argue with him. He wants to aim on a village – not marked, but it's approximately *there*" – Johnny dabbed at the map with his fore-finger: "And he won't hear of our walking along the railway-track, which would save hours. According to him it's patrolled night and day. I don't believe a word of it – Good God, look at those bites!"

He studied the straight line of them running up my arm. "Bugs, eh? Poor old Bernard. Now don't you wish you'd stayed on at your *villa de luxe?*"

I said, "Oh well."

The twenty-mile walk by the light of the moon would have been more bearable had the guide not set such a cracking pace. Despite Johnny's enthusiasm I found him a disagreeable young man. I had to keep reminding myself that he could be imprisoned on this side of the frontier, shot on the other side, for what he was doing now.

Once outside the town we blundered along through an endless acreage of scratchy vines: constantly hailed and heckled to go faster. Johnny was quicker than I. Every time they had to wait for me to catch up, the guide Pépé cursed me heartily.

Every kind of poem kept me company. Bernard Morlaix would have been surprised at his own familiarity with English verse. I had no breath to speak aloud, but the poetry ran on and on in my head; prayers too, but mostly poetry: everything I knew, from Browning to the *Moonrakers* lyrics. By six o'clock in the morning I had come to 'Childe Roland' for the second time:

> *So on I went, I think I never saw*
> *such starved, ignoble nature. Nothing throve.*

Not true: the vines throve lustily. My grey linen trousers were snagged and tattered; so was the blue shirt. Kipling took over:

> *They have ridden the low moon out of the sky.*
> *Their hooves drum up the dawn.*
> *The dun he went like a wounded bull*
> *But the mare like a new-roused fawn.*

Wounded bull was about right for me. Johnny, however, could hardly be classed with the fawn. In the strengthening light I saw his face, looking back: he was scratched across one cheek; the scratch bled. The goblin mask was pale and sweaty.

198

A most bless éd relief, it was, when the guide called a halt. We flopped down under a cork tree. Pépé, scarcely sweating, sat aloof with his arms around his knees; he smoked a thin cigar. Johnny brought out the wine and the sandwiches.

Life came back.

The frontier was only two kilometres away. The air was cool. The climb ahead, through banded rock and groves of Aleppo pine, looked far less formidable than I'd expected. I watched the pale dry landscape take its colouring as the sun rose higher. A hawk flew up and hung steady above the trees. This Pyrenean country being quite unfamiliar to me, I swallowed it all most happily with my eyes; munching and drinking and pleased to be here.

"How does it go, Bernard?"

Johnny looked almost lively now.

"It goes," I said.

"Lucky, aren't we?"

"All except my clothes. I don't think my clothes are very lucky."

"Ditto, ditto, Brother Bernard. We've got to get rid of ourselves, remember," he said, "Before we cross."

"Eh?"

"I mean our papers."

I stared at him. "They won't do us any good over there," he explained, jerking his thumb in the direction of the frontier.

"I thought that was just where we needed them."

"*Au contraire.* If they found those on us, they'd pick us up. Remember what Mourri said?"

"Well, what happens if we run into the Spanish hostiles – or sub-hostiles?"

"From here to Figueras I'm a Spaniard, you're my Swiss pal and we've both had our wallets stolen, passports and all," he said confidently. "We'll hole up somewhere on the mountain and get to Figueras when it's dark."

Pépé showed signs of restlessness and had to be soothed in his own language.

"Time for off, damn it," Johnny told me, "and don't expect a path, he says: too dangerous. If you think the vines were a pest, forget it; we'll be flayed alive now."

We were. We were also extremely noisy. Tearing one's way uphill through persistent undergrowth doesn't make for quiet going. We crashed up that mountainside like elephants breasting a dry jungle: Pépé dodging his head this way and that for a sight of the patrolling police, Johnny cursing, myself run out of poetry and chanting, "*Up*-we-go, *On*-we-go," to a sort of crazy waltz-tune in my head. But the pines gave us good cover and the rock-surfaces weren't difficult. It was a scramble rather than a climb.

Suddenly it began to feel different – dangerous. We shinned up a low rock-wall and found ourselves in a clearing where some trees had been lately felled. We could see the mountain road through the trees; twisting away to our right. Pépé signalled us to stay where we were. He loped across the clearing and stood looking up the road; then down the road. Then he turned, holding up two fingers.

He waited a while; he came gliding back. He began to whisper to Johnny in Spanish.

"Two of them," Johnny translated. "French patrol. Going downhill. Probably off-duty. No cause for alarm."

"On we go?"

"Surely."

But Pépé didn't move. And I needed no Spanish to understand this argument. After a few minutes I saw Johnny give it up. They shook hands; then the guide slipped over the rock wall, vanishing downward through the pines with a movement that reminded me of Rayner.

"Won't he run straight into them?"

"Not he. But now he's alone, he'll be safe enough. He'll pray for us," Johnny added, grinning, "and I really didn't think it was worth another thousand francs for two hundred yards. He says bear left; if we go right, we'll be into the village. The road ends there."

"Can we rest a bit?"

"Why not? Once we're out of this," he added: "Feels rather naked, doesn't it?"

Above the clearing we found a ledge with a small clump of olives sprouting at the top of it. We lay in the shade, drinking some more wine. Johnny took our papers and shredded them carefully; pushing little pieces here and there under the dry earth. (How long ago did Emile tear up the last of his departmental guide and heel the shreds into the ground? I reflected that I had been Emile, Justin and – briefly – Bernard Morlaix. Now I wasn't anybody.)

I watched Johnny making water methodically on the last of the scraps: he seemed to enjoy doing this very much.

"*How* I love to pee," was his wistful comment: I had heard him say this before. He buttoned his trousers and said "Want a look at Spain?"

Here my heart began to thump. Here, for the first time, I felt the cold, authentic brush of a wing that warned me. I didn't like it at all.

We crawled quietly, slowly; Johnny leading. I kept my eyes on his rucksack as it heaved up and down. My mind was a blank now; and into so blank a mind, I knew, messages could come. I tried to think of something quite unconnected with this; I was having rather a good minute remembering a Soccer match I'd played in, when the rucksack ahead stopped its bouncing. We were on the last ridge.

We knelt there side by side, staring downwards, all the way to the plain. Johnny pointed. I saw a long white blur, looking a million miles off through heat-haze.

"Figueras." He added, "And Bob's your uncle."

"Are we on the frontier – or over it?"

"What's a hundred yards between enemies? I suggest we track along this ridge for a bit, see if we can strike a promising line down, and then hole up."

He moved, again ahead of me. Making slower progress I found, after a few minutes, that he had overlooked what seemed a promising line. It began with a chimney, not a steep one, a good snaky cleft in the reddish-white rock. I couldn't quite see where it ended, but there was a ravine sloping off to the right, about fifty feet lower down. Worth exploring, I thought.

As I called to Johnny and he turned his head, there came another call, behind and below us; on the French side. It was a wild, shapeless yell. I saw Johnny fling himself flat on his face with a frantic gesture to me to get on down.

It happened fast. One minute I was saying "This might do." The next second it had to do. I went slithering down the chimney by a series of purely nominal footholds, facing outwards and with every chance of pitching forward on my head. I braked with my hands, tearing the skin. It was the most idiotic and the most alarming of descents. Now the rock bulged out: I was for it: no, I wasn't; as I twisted, trying to face inwards, my heels thudded to a halt. I fell in a heap on a wide ledge. A moment later a stone crashed close to my head and Johnny landed.

He looked very happy; he was laughing. "That was a near one. Hurt yourself?"

"Not much."

"God, we're lucky," he said: I saw what he meant. The ledge proved to be a traverse, invisible from my outpost at the top of the chimney. Where it broke off, a tumble of solid rocks poured down into the ravine: giant stepping-stones.

Up above there came the sound of a shot.

"Purely for pleasure," Johnny said, "They can't even see us."

"But —"

"What's the but, Brother Smut?"

"Couldn't that alert the sub-hostiles on this side?"

"*They* can't shoot," Johnny scoffed: "Couldn't hit an elephant at three yards." He pushed past me, working his way to the end of the traverse. With one little jump he landed on the first giant stepping-stone.

Then the shots came. From the ravine. A quick fusillade that sent the echoes flying off the mountainside. I saw Johnny turn towards me: he swayed there, looking angry, until he crumpled and fell backwards.

I was over and down beside him.

He lay huddled in a crevice between two of the big stones. There was blood here. As I tried to raise his head, blood trickled from his mouth. He muttered, "Oh don't be an ass," and then, "Sorry, Emile," before he died.

I crouched there, holding him against my knee. His head fell right back; his chin pointed up. I began to cry. The shots were banging all around but I didn't care. When they ceased and the clattering boots came near, I still crouched where I was, holding him.

After a time I looked up; into the faces of two young boys. They stood balanced on Johnny's stone. They were dressed in khaki; they wore forage-caps with tassels. They carried their rifles slung. Two greenish faces: two pairs of dark eyes, fixed, staring at the blood and the body. They crossed themselves. Then they helped me lift him.

While we dragged him up and laid him across his stone, I could see the others coming. Four khaki figures, toiling out of the ravine. They halted, raising their rifles. I went down to meet them.

LONDON

BLANCHE BRIGGS CAME DOWN THE RED-TILED PATH OF
Number Twenty-four, Ramillies Terrace. She shut the iron gate
between the laurel bushes. She looked back at the house: "lucky so
far," in terms of the present. Paper strips, pasted in criss-cross patterns,
had saved the lower windows. Blast had taken the top ones and their
frames were boarded over.

At the far end of the street, on the corner, two houses had been less
lucky. There was little left; just the jag-tooth stumps of the walls and
some steeply piled rubble.

Nobody in sight as she walked back along the terrace to the bus-
stop: herself alone in the bright October afternoon. It was quiet here
nowadays: no children swung on the railings to call rudely after her:
she missed the naughty children. She missed the neighbours; more as
institutions than as friends. Most of them had left; like Mary. (Should
she tell Mary about the bomb on the corner, about the top windows . . .? Not yet, she decided once again. Mary's nerves, according to Frank, were still a problem, even in Gloucestershire. "Mother
never stops worrying about the house – and of course about you"
Frank had written.)

Underfoot the pavement was gritty. "As though there'd been a
dust-storm," thought Blanche, who had read of dust-storms. Since
the blitz began, there seemed to be dust everywhere. It was always
waiting for her inside the empty house. One of the reasons, as she
explained to Mrs. Murray, for her regular visits: though Mrs.
Murray would admit no reason at all. The familiar exchange had
begun today as soon as she saw Blanche wearing a hat.

"Going out, Blanche?"

"Just down to the house, M'm. I shan't be long."

"Must you go? Can any useful purpose be served? Either it is still there or it is not . . . not . . . not."

"It makes me easier in my mind, somehow. I promised Mary I'd keep an eye."

"Very foolish. A direct hit would prevent your keeping an eye, an ear, a leg or any other part of your anatomy."

"Gracious, I'll be home long before they start. It isn't as though they came over in the daytime any more."

"You're a good woman, Blanche. Foolish but good."

The old lady said this quite often, and one let her say it, knowing all the same that goodness had no part in the pilgrimage. It was precious for itself. Some secret reassurance jogged along with her in the bus to Battersea, walked with her from the corner to the gate. It came up the tiled path and over the doorstep. It lingered (with the careful dust-sheets and the newspapers) in every room. A friendly, solid feeling: not remembered from the years of living here, but peculiar to Now.

Almost a magic; almost a hope; and stronger than ever today, because of the dream.

In the dream she had come here as usual, climbing off the bus, walking up to the gate, relieved to find the house intact; seeing the boarded windows and the criss-cross strips of paper. But when she tried to open the gate, it stuck fast. Looking down, in the dream, she saw that somebody had put back the old latch. There it was, just as it used to be, the rusty old thing from years ago; always a terrible nuisance. She was saying to herself, "Now, whoever could have done that?" and beginning to struggle with it, when she looked over the gate. Thomas was sitting on the doorstep.

Thomas wore battledress. He had taken off his cap and put it on the step beside him. His hair was very untidy. First he sat there with his arms round his knees, laughing at her struggle with the latch. Then he got up and came down the path. "It's easy," he said. "If you know the way. Let me do it." The sound of his voice, loud and clear, had awoken her.

Foolish, to set such store by the dream. She was hugging it to her as though it really meant something.

And yet (she would not, of course, say this to the old lady) the faint, impossible hope still survived, after all these months: far down inside; barely acknowledged, never to be told. A mistake, somewhere. Thomas still alive – somewhere.

Here came the bus, its windows opaque with mesh, the precaution against splintering glass. The bus-conductress wore dark blue trousers; her young, round face was heavily made-up. All that black on her eyelashes . . . *really*: she was cheeky, too. She told a nice-looking gentleman, wearing the silver badge of an Air Raid Warden, to "Give the old girl a hand." (Old girl . . . what a way to talk. The Air Raid Warden didn't look a day under sixty himself and now the conductress was calling him "George.")

One must make allowances . . . the young woman was doubtless very brave. If only she wouldn't sing. "There'll always be an England," sang the bus-conductress, jigging up and down.

"I believe one's temper gets worse as one gets older," thought Blanche. "It ought to get better." Every now and again, she caught herself snapping at the old lady: which was most unfair. The old lady was wonderful; brave as a lion: particularly in the matter of incendiaries, which she liked to chase; she went plunging about the gardens in her siren-suit, armed with sand-bucket and shovel. Wonderful at her age . . She would pounce on the nasty, spitting little fire-bombs like a great swaddled cat. "Got it, Warden! Got it! Hooray!"

("She's a damn nuisance," the warden complained, "Can't you keep her indoors?"

"No," said Blanche.)

Shortness of temper was due in part, she reminded herself, to shortness of sleep. The big velvet sofa in Mrs. Murray's drawing-room was a trial; alternating deep sags with sudden hard knobbles. It was too wide for the sheets and blankets to stay tucked in. One might also find oneself lying on unusual objects; Domino-tiles, a rosary, the missing enamel ashtray or a fruit-knife that had slipped down.

As soon as the sirens sounded, Mrs. Murray, dressed for the moment, would come swooping through the bead portière. She would check the positions of sand-buckets, shovel and stirrup-pump. She would drink a glass of wine. Then she would sit in her big chair, playing Dominoes, murmuring an occasional Latin prayer and keeping a sharp watch for incendiaries in the garden. This involved opening the French windows; frequently she dislodged the blackout material. About once an hour she instructed Blanche to stay where she was and get what sleep she could.

After the All Clear there was the ritual of making tea; and with this ritual there had come to be another. Side by side at the kitchen table they would talk about the children. The adult versions of Gerald, Sarah and Thomas had no place here. These were old reminiscences, going back and back – sometimes as far as to the babies in their prams.

The day when . . . Their memories did not always coincide. ("Excuse me, M'm, we were at Dawlish, not Folkestone." "It wasn't Gerald who ate the mulberries, Blanche dear, it was Sarah." "But I remember distinctly, M'm, Thomas was with the little Stevens boy —" "That couldn't have been September because —") The arguments assumed great importance. The lively, disordered fabric of the past was brighter, closer, than the kitchen walls; the lost children would seem to be playing about all over the place.

It was a queer time.

"Well, there you are. Deo Gratias," said the old lady.

Mr. Abrahams said "Hullo, Nanny." The 'Nanny', a recent privilege, seemed a right one. His presence was now as natural as the presence of Gerald or Sarah in the old life. A comfortable person, Mr. Abrahams. Though Blanche could not agree with Mrs. Murray that he was handsome (Jewish looks being to her mind a built-in disadvantage) she liked his merry eyes. And she liked his absolute calm. When he left this room, the room went on feeling peaceful. (With the departure of Mrs. Flavia or Mr. Percy a troublesome, fussy echo would linger in the air.)

For a moment, after he had gone, Mrs. Murray sat staring dreamily into space. She was, obviously, in the absent-minded mood that came upon her more and more often. She sighed; she narrowed her eyes; she smiled a little; she nodded; as though she were listening to, and answering, somebody who remained invisible. Odd, but Blanche was used to it.

"I went to Harrod's," said Mrs. Murray at last.

"Did you, M'm? You must have been very quick."

"A taxi. I kept it waiting. A sudden impulse. I went into the Oratory too. *That* was really the impulse." Seeing her look as though she required a reply, Blanche said, "Yes, M'm."

"They have replaced that disagreeable girl." Again she paused. (Mr. Percy had remarked more than once that the old lady was in the habit of Getting Her Signals Crossed.) "At the cooked-meat-counter," she continued, "so I bought a chicken. It only needs heating up."

"Good gracious!"

"A very small chicken. And I couldn't possibly risk Mr. Abrahams finding himself locked out. Could I?"

"No, M'm."

"I imagine you're thinking Percy would disapprove the cost of the taxi. That *is* what you're thinking, is it not – not – not?"

"I was thinking," said Blanche, "there's still the rest of the stew."

"Tomorrow," said Mrs. Murray, "Tomorrow is soon enough for the rest of the stew. So would Thursday be." She then rose heavily from her chair and stared at herself in the glass above the mantelpiece for a long time. She had put on her dark blue velvet dress, with the high-boned lace collar. A great string of artificial pearls was wound four times about the collar.

"Jowly," was her comment. "I look jowly. More and more jowly. And regal. Not unlike Queen Mary. Though of course one cannot imagine Queen Mary suffering precisely my kind of . . . what is it? . . . flamboyant dilapidation. Can one?" When Blanche didn't answer, she repeated sharply, "Can one?"

"I couldn't say at all, M'm. I don't really know what you're talking about."

"Yes you do. Never mind. Wouldn't a fire be nice?"

"It's warm – for October."

"I suppose it is."

"Have a fire if you like, M'm, of course." The cleaning of the grate was an extra nuisance; there was very little wood; all paper must be kept for salvage and Blanche had a deep-rooted distrust of the gas poker. Mrs. Murray appeared to take the hint. She said "We will wait," and then, "Mr. Abrahams has heard nothing from Sarah. I'm sure those dreadful people in Liverpool lose half the letters." She resented high-explosive less than she resented the powers of the Censor's office.

"Well, it's not so long since he had a letter, is it, M'm, after all?"

"You're in a very obstinate mood – mood – mood." Blanche heard her grumbling on – something about an aura – as she went towards the kitchen. Here she saw that though the tea-tray was laid ready Mrs. Murray had ignored it.

"No tea, M'm?"

"I'll take a glass of wine, I think."

She never drank wine before dinner.

"Now, M'm?"

"Yes. Now. While you get your things." Mrs. Murray glanced at the clock. Since she confidently expected the top of the house to be hit on one or another night, the rule of "getting your things" from upstairs was mandatory. "Don't forget your dressing-gown tonight, dear," she added. Blanche brought the wine and the goblet from the sideboard. She was puzzled. If that clock, and every clock in the flat seemed to have its own individual idea, was the one to be obeyed, this was surely siren-suit time. But her employer, pouring the wine, showed no disposition for air-raid duty.

"What's the matter, Blanche?"

"Nothing, M'm. I'd better see to the vegetables before I go up."

"You look as though you had something on your mind. So have I – I – I." She went into silence again. It lasted through the peeling of the potatoes and the carrots. No sudden call or chirrup summoned Blanche from these processes; an unusual thing. Only when she reached the beaded portière on her way out, did the old lady speak. She said, "Do you dream much nowadays?"

It gave Blanche a funny feeling. But last night's dream was

her own private business and she took refuge in, "No more than usual, M'm. Rather less, really, what with these nights we're having."

"Ah. I usually dream in the afternoon. But today, of course, there wasn't time."

"You oughtn't to have missed your rest," Blanche said.

"I didn't feel like resting." Now she looked mischievous, as though she had a secret. "Run along, dear, what are you waiting for?"

The steep climb to Mr. Dutty's abandoned room was always an effort. Blanche felt the little grinding pains in her back; her tiresome varicose veins began to itch and throb. Once inside the door there was the small sense of welcome waiting: the photographs were still a wistful pleasure; she had brought Thomas's box of toy animals from Ramillies Terrace; unpacking them and setting them up – forever it would seem – along the window sill. Here the lamb, the miniature sheepdog, the cat and the rabbit kept their dusty vigil; the black bone elephant was too large to live there; she had put it on the dressing table.

"Now —" she said to herself, aloud as usual, looking about the room, "Now . . ." Dressing-gown, night-gown, face-flannel, tooth-brush. And of course the string bag with all the emergency things one never used. As she took it from its corner in the wardrobe she gave her routine glance at the notebooks, still lodged on the top shelf. She had never moved them. Unlike Mrs. Murray she remained firm in her conviction that this house was safe.

"Very early tonight, aren't they, Blanche?"

"Perhaps that means they'll go home early."

"A curious sound, is it not?" The old lady inclined her head, listening to the sirens; the rise and fall, the gathering chorus taken up: "One of the few sounds I've ever been able to *see* . . . I see it as fountains or jets of smoke: or tall plants growing up by magic all over the sky. Ah, there are the guns, that's better."

"Better than what, I should like to know?" Blanche couldn't help snapping; those great guns never failed to make her jump.

"Better than when we had no guns at all – at all – at all." Surely now she would hurry off to change into her siren-suit . . . No. She moved, but only as far as the armchair, carrying her glass of wine.

"You'd better have some wine yourself."

For the first time in Blanche's memory the automatic "No, thank you, M'm" was not accepted. Mrs. Murray glared at her: "Would you kindly – just this once – say Yes instead of No." It was an order, not a plea. It made Blanche laugh.

"I will if you want me to," she said.

"Well, well. Capitulation for a change. That is called robbing one of one's grievance – did you know?"

The sound of an engine droned, far off, far up and the gunfire shook the air. A moment later there came the different thunder of the bomb falling: the splattering crash, the rumble that echoed, spreading out, spreading on.

"Quite some distance away. The echo's deceptive. Is the kitchen light off?"

"Yes, M'm. But we haven't put out the buckets and the stirrup-pump. Would you like me to —"

"Damn the buckets – and the stirrup-pump," said Mrs. Murray, filling Blanche's glass to the brim. "Do I shock you? No, I see I don't. I appear to have given you the giggles."

"Well it was unexpected – not like you – I mean to say —"

"I *used* to swear," the old lady reflected. In this tone Blanche had heard elderly people saying "I used to be such a good dancer" or "As a girl I was so fond of lawn-tennis."

These crystal goblets were large; they held a great deal.

"Drink it, dear, don't just sip and then put the glass down. It isn't medicine. Blanche, when you dream, what do you think the dream *is*?"

The guns banged very close and the walls trembled.

"I don't know that I've ever thought about it, M'm."

"Rubbish," said Mrs. Murray. "Everybody has thought about it. And your antennae are as good as mine. Which is saying a lot – a lot – a lot."

"Would you like your coffee now, M'm?"

"You don't want to talk about him. And by him I mean Thomas. And I insist on talking about him. At least I insist on asking you one question – just one."

"Very well." Blanche could feel her lips pinching and thinning. She played with her wine-glass, turning it around on the table-cloth. The high wing of the chair hid Mrs. Murray's face from view. There was the blue velvet skirt sweeping over the footstool, one hand tapping its heavy fingers on the arm-rest; and the voice:

"You believed in the gift he had. Didn't you?"

"The gift, M'm?"

"His powers. The power to heal, for example."

"I won't discuss that horrible inquest business," Blanche snapped. "I put it out of my mind a long time ago. Whatever Thomas did, I'm quite sure he meant it for the best and —"

– "Inquests are not the point. Thomas is." The guns opened up again and Mrs. Murray poked her head into view:

"*Noise* makes life so difficult for *words*, don't you find?" The head retreated. "I'm asking you if you believed him to be different from other people?"

"Oh, is that all?"

"That is all."

Relieved, Blanche said "Yes, I suppose I did. Not like the others, he never was, nor like any child I ever had to do with. But it never worried me, somehow." She looked back: she was still trying to put her long thoughts into coherent shape when the old lady's voice sounded again. The fingers had ceased to tap the arm of the chair. The voice itself was quiet, solemn:

"And if *you* had dreamed he came to you and told you something . . ."

"If *I* had . . .? That one sounded very near, M'm."

"Well? What would you like to do? Lie on the floor?"

"No, of course not." She felt her head spinning a little. "Did you dream that?" she asked severely.

No answer. Only a sudden rueful chuckle from behind the chair's wing; followed up with a ponderous sigh. "The deliberate tarnishing of the state of Grace is nothing to laugh at. On the contrary. You don't understand, do you?"

"No, M'm. And I can't really say I want to – not that I wish to be rude."

"Well then you shall bring me the coffee here. Put it on the card table. And I want you to fetch me something from the sideboard drawer. The lower left-hand drawer – you'll find it at the back; behind the fish-slice and the tea-caddy."

"The black bag?"

"How do you know?"

"I've got eyes in my head."

"You two all right in there?" the warden's voice yelled outside the window.

"Tell him to mind his own business," said Mrs. Murray.

There came a sudden lull in the fury: it dwindled down all at once to a faint bumping like that of a summer storm on the far horizon.

Blanche groped in the drawer and brought out the black velvet bag. She found it surprisingly heavy.

"Thank you, dear. And the book, please, the little book: *Ancien Tarot de Marseille*; up in the corner – second shelf – next to the Manual of St. Anthony. Thank you. I have to be alone. Take your wine and something to read and go and sit in my bedroom. If there's a direct hit or anything of the sort, come back at once."

"I'd just like to say something, M'm."

The old lady's face turned to her; like a strong, heavy mask it was now, with glittering eyes.

"It worries me," Blanche said, "I don't know why."

"What worries you?"

"The idea of asking those old cards about —" she hesitated, "about anything that's really important."

Silence. The face looked very sad. Surely those were tears that made the eyes glitter.

"Oh well – I suppose *I* must mind my own business, too," said Blanche, striving at a brisk and cheerful tone. She went through the clashing beads into the bedroom.

She did not turn up the light. The bedroom chair was fat and comfortable: the wine had a pleasant effect though she couldn't really approve this unearned sense of well-being. She put the goblet, still half-full, on the floor. She leaned back and shut her eyes. She would begin her night-prayers, because the blitz was the ruination of her regular programme and it was useful to have this time to herself. She ought to kneel down, of course. The old lady said it didn't matter, but one couldn't be sure.

Quiet now: all quiet. Not a sound in the sky . . .

"Bless Mummy and Daddy and Sarah and Nanny and all kind friends. Take care of all our soldiers and sailors and bring them safe home, and give us Peace."

Blanche sat up indignantly. How in the world had she arrived at that one? It was the prayer she had taught Gerald in the year 1914; when Sarah was still too young to pray and Thomas not yet born. Sternly she rebuked herself. Sternly she began the *Our Father*, but the soft darkness kept coming down and although she believed she was awake the familiar words were like the rungs of a ladder, climbed slowly; climbed very slowly . . . not climbed at all.

It was a long time afterwards. Out of the dark, across distances, she was dragged back: by a voice calling her name, next by the clicking flurry of the portière and the top light switched on.

"Did I wake you?" Mrs. Murray said gently, and then, "You haven't finished your wine."

"Has the All Clear gone?"

"Not yet. But nothing's happening. Would you like to go back to sleep?"

"No thank you," said Blanche, remembering. She looked questioningly at the old lady, who smiled at her and patted her shoulder as though there were no question to be asked.

"Did it – I mean?" Heavy with sleep, she could go no further.

"Perhaps you would like to see them, just once."

"Them?"

Mrs. Murray beckoned. Tranquilly, slowly, the velvet skirt

sweeping the floor, she led the way to the card-table. She moved around it at the same leisured pace. Looking down, Blanche saw the queer cards laid out; she saw the pattern of an arch: then a triangle within the arch; then three cards aligned. Beyond this formation a whole heap had been put aside, face downwards. She heard the old lady murmuring, "Knight of Cups. The Sun. The Lion's Mouth – shutting the lion's mouth." The words sounded oddly and the painted shapes themselves were hard to see in this dim light. Hard to see, impossible to understand. She blinked at them. The All Clear, the straight noise tearing the silence, made her jump. (As bad as the guns, when you weren't expecting it.)

Mrs. Murray snapped her usual "Deo Gratias," and crossed herself briskly. She stooped over the table, breaking the pattern of the cards, hustling them all together in an untidy pile. She marched away to the kitchen. She came back, carrying a copy of *The Times*. This she made into spills, pushing the spills under the wood in the fireplace.

"At this time of night . . . And we're not supposed to —"

"One issue of one daily paper can't make much difference to the war-effort."

"Well, but isn't it rather —"

"No." said Mrs. Murray, lighting the gas poker. After she had set it in place she came back to the card-table. She sat with her chin propped on her hand, watching the flames begin. Her voice sounded tired now.

"But you will have to put them in, please, Blanche. I don't think I could quite do that myself. I've had them such a long time."

"The cards . . ."

"The cards."

"In the fire?"

"In the fire. All of them – just a few at a time. Once it's got going. They won't put it out." She began to deal them into small separate heaps.

"Won't you be sorry, afterwards?" was all Blanche could think to say.

"I expect so. Yes, certainly."

"Then —"

– "Ready now, isn't it?"

"Not quite, M'm; give the coal a chance to catch. Would you like me to make a cup of tea?"

Mrs. Murray did not answer. She had gone behind one of her private walls (as Thomas used to describe them.) She sat gazing at the cards, chirruping lightly, "Given up – given up – given up. Should have been given up long ago. All the same, I wonder . . . If I'd seen him dead would I still burn them?"

Foolish, to shiver. The room was warm; the flames were rising high. Foolish to be dumb, to have no words at all; to be shocked yet certain, to condemn inside one's head and still to believe. But that was how it was. She saw the old lady handing her the first cards from the table. She heard the quiet voice say, "Thomas is living, Blanche. He will come back."

NEW YORK AND HOLLYWOOD

"Whatever came over the Duchess of Wrexe
Reciting that filthy pome?
It finished the Pastor.
Goodnight, Mrs. Astor!"

"I wonder you don't get tired of that tune," Boodie said.

"I do. Very tired. Don't you?" asked Sarah; sweetly, she hoped. She gave Boodie a great big tender smile, modelled on the Mary Castle formula. She then went back to the open file, scowling over it.

"Oh listen – you *have* to hear this. The mother's made the little girl write herself."

"Can't," said Sarah, "I'm reading up on bloody Mrs. Seaton."

"Joan – you mean?" Boodie looked outraged.

"I mean Joan. She's due at four-thirty."

"Nobody told me."

"So?" said Sarah.

Mrs. Seaton being one of their many bones of contention, it was not surprising that Boodie should put the letters from England aside, arrange her face for compromise and murmur, "Guess we ought to see her together, Sal."

"I hadn't thought of asking you to leave the room."

"Oh —" Boodie brightened. "I'm glad. You do these things so well, I'm not worried – it's just —" She was adapting her own smile to the Mary Castle formula now – "Well, Joan's problem's a *mother's* problem, isn't it?" Boodie never seemed to get over the fact of being a mother.

"The problem would appear to me financial rather than puerperal," Sarah said, her eyes skimming the facts and figures on the page. Joan Seaton, with her two small children, had the gift of a four-roomed house in Connecticut, free schooling and a house-keeping allowance. What she wanted was a larger housekeeping allowance, regular pocket-money and a fur coat for the approaching winter.

Sullen in despair, a dark young woman without charm or grace, she stood under the poster of Winston Churchill, saying "They don't understand. One can't just *exist*. One must have *some* fun. And the coat isn't a luxury, it's a necessity. With my chest, this winter's going to kill me. I could get quite a cheap one on her charge-account. They could be a bit more generous, couldn't they? After all they're as rich as Croesus and anyway all this is only a loan. They *know* Lionel and I can pay them back every penny after the war."

Sarah was silent, achieving a Romney-like twitch of her eye-brows. She could move them separately now; she had practised the trick on Joan and on others whose problems were much the same as Joan's.

"You know, Sal," said Boodie, "I think we might have a word with Mrs. Rettlinger – see if she can't do just a little more for Joan. Maybe if Mary talked to her —"

This time the eyebrow trick had more effect: Mrs. Seaton snarling, "*You* think I'm an ungrateful bitch, don't you?"

"Of *course* she doesn't," said Boodie just as Sarah said, "That's for Mrs. Rettlinger to decide. But if I were you I'd make it a rabbit-fur lining. Macy's have them. Six-fifty. In the basement."

"Tea now?" Boodie's voice had the authentic Miss-Honeymouth ring: "Tea? Or a drink, Joan? How's about a highball? Fine. I'll get it. And then I want to hear all about the kids." She whisked away. Joan Seaton, her back to Sarah, gazed up at Winston Churchill. "What people like you can't understand is this damnable thing of feeling like a refugee. They *make* one feel like that."

In an effort after good manners, Sarah kept silence. What was Joan Seaton, if not a refugee?

"It's all very well for you," was the next line of attack – "You haven't got a husband in the Army – fighting *their* war for them."

"No, have I?"

Joan Seaton left Winston Churchill and loomed above the desk: "You're over here because you want to be. You've got friends – money – no responsibilities."

"Go on. Do go on."

"Well, all I mean is it's feeling like a refugee that gets one down."

They were bores, bores, bores. Piercing, nerve-drilling, archetypal bores. And when you were tired of hating them you could pull the opposite lever in your mind and begin to hate their hosts instead: the 'America First' apostles; the Wilkie-worshippers; the kind ladies in mink (like Mrs. Rettlinger) with their careful, contrived charity; the breezy neutrals, brushing off the war.

But – and this was the balance, the weight that steadied the scale, the last illogical logic keeping you sane – you hated none of them as much as you hated yourself.

Just as she had looked back last summer in all nostalgia for the honourable state of grief, so now she looked back to last summer; envying the wild one who had threshed, tortured herself, longed to be home.

The person who lived through these November days was a kind of skeleton. Busy, mechanical, drifting between the Village and midtown Manhattan, with no other purpose than to pass the hours, fill the time. One of the theme-songs that kept the skeleton company was "*Why didn't I —?*" Why didn't I go – before Dunkirk? Before France fell? Before the blitz began? Before the submarines made the sea the terror I cannot face?

Last summer she had told herself that all was betrayed. Not true. More was betrayed this November. Busy, mechanical, coward in your soul, you lied your way along. Thanking Gerald for his cheque, you had written, "It will indeed ease the situation here . . . More sensible, I think, to stay and work on this side of the water." (Always that phrase "This side of the water" . . . She had used the same words to Dick Abrahams.) Everybody agreed that it was more sensible. Busy, mechanical, keeping the truth hidden, you could give the sensible advice to others, here in this room:

"I don't want to seem discouraging, Mrs. Morley. But even if you can get your fare paid in sterling by Cunard at the other end, is it honestly a good idea to go back? Surely the sensible thing is to do as your husband asks and stay here with the children. Don't think I don't know how you feel . . . we'd all rather go home." Busy, mechanical, lost, you heard your voice saying these things.

And the worst of it was that you hardly seemed to mind any more. You yourself weren't really there to mind. You were dead. Because you were a coward, you were dead. Perhaps you had lost the right to be alive.

"Highballs for three!" cried Boodie. "Thought you could use one, Sal. Was I right? I was. Now, Joan, tell me – how are those two bright youngsters making out at school?"

The sparkling, chewing mother-talk was interrupted by a small mink cap and the best-loved face in America coming round the door. "Hello, everyone," said Mary. "Sal, you're not going off yet, are you? Oh, fine. Finish what you're doing. I'll be in my room" She flashed out again.

"Since," said Sarah, picking up her glass, "I can finish what I'm doing in her room, will you ladies please excuse me?"

"We'll be glad to," said their eyes.

Mary was at her dressing-table; she had taken off the mink cap and was brushing her autumn glow of hair. She said "Hi. That was the Seaton woman, wasn't it – the one with the grouch?"

"Yes. She and Boodie are busy swopping wombs. After which I imagine Boodie'll come sidling in here to ask if you can prise some more dough out of Mrs. Rettlinger. I wouldn't, in your place."

"Poor Boodie . . . You do hate her, don't you?"

"It's mutual."

Mary frowned a little. "I wonder if they could use her in the Madison Avenue office – send you down that cute kid from Vancouver – you know the one. I might be able to fix it."

"Oh Mary don't bother, please. What the devil does it matter?"

"Your happiness matters, darling."

Not to me, it doesn't. But I do not say that, I just tell her not to bother, tell her I might miss Boodie's irritation-value; and we laugh.

"Gerald's going to call at five," Mary said, "and I thought you'd like to say Hello to him."

So kind.

"I saw Charlie at lunch; he just flew in from the Coast. He says

220

Gerald's on top of the world and the rushes of the new picture couldn't be more exciting."

Gerald's last letter, Sarah thought, expressed matters differently. "Only a certain peace in solitude compensates for this detestable endroit and the insane vulgarities of this production. ("Wonderful Propaganda" – I quote.) Two more weeks of it will undoubtedly strip me of what patience or sanity I still possess. But the days are crossed off the calendar nightly and Canada, thank God, looms near. Continue to keep tiny trap shut. You're still the only one who knows, aside from Paula. I'll tell Mary in my own time and my own words, darling. Just a matter of selecting the moment."

Sarah glanced at the pale green telephone beside Mary's bed. It would be awkward, though possibly diverting, should five o'clock prove to be the moment.

"You know, you look better," Mary was saying. "Quite a spark in your eye."

When the telephone rang she stretched gracefully on the bed, lying back, cradling the instrument against her cheek. "Hello, my darling. My dearest. Oh, it's so good to hear you . . ." A long, contented sigh. ("Masterly technique, hasn't she?")

Attentive to the little crackle of Gerald's voice, Sarah waited. She saw the sweet smile fading, saw the gravely tender look come instead. No word; the lovely, listening face went on listening. The little crackle went on crackling.

Odd, to feel one's heart thump suddenly, to see one's hand shake, lifting the highball to one's lips. As though one were Gerald, having to tell her.

Now she tried to catch Mary's eye, she signalled, "Do you want me out?" but Mary ignored the signal. When she spoke at last, she said, "My darling, I think that's perfectly wonderful." The beautiful body relaxed. The exquisite legs seemed to lengthen by several inches; the glowing head fell back a little among the apple-green pillows. "Would I mind? Would I *mind* – are you crazy? Sweetheart, I want you to do what you want to do – always. You know that . . . What? Yes, I know it shoots down the January notion, so what? Ah, my darling, skip it, will you? This is something *big* . . . And I love you. And I congratulate you. With all my heart. Bless

you. Now don't hang up, Sarah's here. She'd like to – what? . . .
Oh, you have? . . . Not even time to say Hello? Okay darling. Talk
tomorrow. Love you always."

*One must, as the saying goes, hand it to her . . . I can imagine him
hanging up, mopping his forehead.*

"He's a great boy," Mary said. She sat up and glowed at Sarah:
"His agent was there, and one of the studio executives, – that's why
he couldn't talk to you. But he sent his love – sounds deliriously
happy." She stroked her silken shins from knee to ankle. "And why
not? They're signing him up for three more pictures."

"I beg your pardon?" (A phrase one seldom used. It came out
flatly, coldly, stuffily, as though somebody's parlourmaid were
speaking.)

"They're signing him up for three – count them, three – more
pictures," said the adorable face of Mary Castle, growing smaller,
somehow, dwindling away, with its little words: "Wonderful
contract – wonderful money, star-billing – he's hit another jackpot,
bless him. And he deserves to."

What was happening? Something like the moment in Bermuda
when she poured her whisky on the diplomat. But something more
savage. Something like an explosion in the centre of her skull.

"So that's why he wouldn't speak to me," were the only words
that came.

"Sarah darling – what on earth is the matter?"

"Gerald's the matter." Now, absurdly, she wanted to cry. "I
didn't realize – I thought he was telling you —"

"Thought he was telling me what?"

"He was going to Canada. To train – for the Air Force. Ten days
from now."

Through the mist on her eyes she could see a beautiful hand
stretched out; through the clanging in her ears she could hear
America's best-loved voice. "Now, darling, . . . now, darling. Take
it easy," the voice said. "Just a pipedream . . . he's talked of it before
. . . shouldn't have told you, shouldn't have made you unhappy.
You know Gerald . . . his trick of romancing, we all know it – wish
you'd said something to me at the time."

"*Will* you shut up?"

222

"Sarah . . ."

"I said shut up. Stop pouring oil on troubled waters, eh? He's a coward and a liar and a louse and no pretty words about pretty contracts are going to make him anything else. And I'm not sure it isn't your fault. In fact I'm damn sure it is. All of it. He ought to have gone to fight long ago."

"When you're feeling calmer," said the cool-honey voice, "You'll regret that. Gerald's an American citizen, remember."

"Still got his British passport – hasn't he?"

"Darling, you're tired, all het-up – living on your nerves, I've told you before . . . Aren't you? That's it, isn't it, Sal? If it wasn't for this nervous state you're in, you'd be glad for him, wouldn't you?"

"Not in a thousand years."

Mary gave a small, friendly laugh. "No, maybe that was putting it a touch strongly. You're still more of a Britisher than he is, aren't you? And I salute you for it . . . What I mean is that if you weren't having this nervous spell, you wouldn't mind so much."

"Mind – so much." Her own voice was the merest croak. "*Mind*," she repeated. Words spoken last summer, words spoken quietly, confidently, in a tone of infinite superiority, came back. "I suddenly minded," Walter Ash had said.

"By God . . . that's done it!" Sarah shouted at Mary Castle.

Gerald drove up Sunset Boulevard with Kipling in his head. He drove to his doom, chanting grimly,

> *"Then wheel my horse against the foe."*
> *"He's down and overpast, my lord.*
> *You war against the sunset glow.*
> *The judgment follows fast, my Lord."*

It was Paula's reaction he dreaded; not Philip's. Philip, after all, loathed him already. There was no shock coming to Philip, insulated by his own studied sufferings. Paula would have kept her word, kept her silence. That was the agreement. At the right minute, they had told each other, they would disarm and confound King Lear.

Gerald had played this scene many times in his head; his own arrival at the door on Harper Avenue; Philip's entrenched hate greeting him; Paula's supporting wink as he ranged himself beside the glass-topped table where the snapshots lay, and said (he had rehearsed the line), "By the way, Father, you won't have the displeasure of my company after next week. I'm off to Canada to train for the R.A.F."

This was the speech Paula expected to hear in five minutes' time.

He shot past the electric sign spelling ALBERT SHEETZ – ICE CREAM and came to the lit, fluid panel signalling GARDEN OF ALLAH between the palm-trees. If he could postpone this thing, even by half-an-hour, he would. He would park his beautiful new car outside the Marmont, dash up to the suite, take two quick drinks and let the drinks take the impact. But there wasn't time. They had kept him too long at the studio. Philip was off to play Bridge with his tedious compatriots and Paula was off to Sue Brown's. The press-release would be out at midnight. He had let twenty-four hours go by since he talked to Mary.

Turning left into Harper Avenue, he gave a moment to wondering what Sarah thought. Sarah, with her own *volte-face* after all those interminable haverings and hoverings, was surely in no position to judge him. She had written, "I envy you, going where I cannot follow. And now I think I shall always be here." She sounded so sad. But she would understand: better than Paula would.

Coming to the gate, parking the new, beautiful toy, Gerald was bleakly aware that he felt fifteen years old again.

He walked up the path. There was a chill on the air, a trace of fog in the dusk; some whisper of England – as though he needed that.

The judgment follows fast, my lord. Damn Kipling . . . Damn the schoolboy living inside, one from whom he could not escape, defying all the achievements of Gerald Weston, 1940 model. Would he never be exorcized, that one? He sat on a wall and rooted for the other side. Always he had done this. He had rooted for Morris

Ward and *The Wasp* against Mary and Jay and *Caviare*: he had rooted for a rush to England when war broke out: he was rooting for Canada now, turning his obstinate schoolboy face away from the contract, away from the cash, away from the star-billing. When one argued that one was at least free to live in truth and peace without Mary, for a long time now, he seemed not to hear. He simply glowered and disapproved.

It was Paula who opened the door. It would be: Paula with the gay, heightened, loving look reserved for him in all these weeks. He stared at her as guiltily as though she knew. But she was laughing.

"Quite a moment, you've picked," she said, "Philip's lashed to the telephone. This call must have cost Sarah twenty bucks already. Did she call you?"

"Sarah? No – what about?"

"She's going home tomorrow."

"*She's* going home . . ." The break in his voice was precisely that of the schoolboy. Paula hadn't noticed. Putting an arm around his waist, drawing him into the hall, she kissed the top of his ear; she murmured low, "What's so astounding is that it's brought King Lear to his senses. Momentarily . . . Haven't seen him like this since we heard about Thomas. You, my friend," she added, "are likely to be handed a gold medal. Endorsed by the British Colony – all their signatures engraved on the back – can't you see it? Forgive me – have to fix my face; with you in a minute." She squeezed his hand. She went up the stairs.

Gerald walked into the living-room. The chintz curtains were drawn; there was a wood fire burning and the dogs sprawled beside the fire. *The judgment follows fast, my lord.* He aimed automatically for the glass-topped table. Philip, in the corner of the sofa, waved, smiled, pointing at the drinks, crooning his affectionate monosyllables: "Yes, yes, of course, darling . . . Here's Gerald." His voice was rich and warm: "Yes, of course you do . . . Well, sweetheart, if I say I think you're damn brave and bloody foolish, will that suit you? I love you. God be with you. And don't think I don't envy you from the crown of my head to the soles of my feet . . . I can't say goodbye, it isn't goodbye. I'm going to work hard at pretending you've just gone back to school. Till the holidays, sweetheart. Talk to Gerald, eh?" He handed over and blew his nose.

Sarah sounded croakier than usual: "Listen – will you be at the Marmont about an hour from now? Right – I'll call you there." She hung up.

Gerald joined Philip beside the drinks. "She'll call me at home," he said. Philip said nothing at all; he filled his glass, filled his pipe and went back to the corner of the sofa: he whistled softly to the dogs, so that they awoke and padded after him, re-settling beside his feet. He fondled their heads.

(Paula was right – *King Lear* was off. This was the Happy Warrior, or some such character.)

"Bless her," he said, "she won't say what's decided her at last – just says time to be going. And she's right." He relaxed and glowed. "*And* – marvellous, this is – she's more than likely to find Rab in Lisbon. Rab's on her way back here. If that isn't a miracle —" he sighed happily – "but I've always believed in miracles."

Seldom had one felt so cold, so small. But the practised tongue was still in command:

"Flying to Lisbon tomorrow would certainly be a miracle. No more Clippers leaving for a month. 'Came through on the radio —"

Philip raised one hand and kept it aloft; he looked as though he were blessing the dogs. "She knows, she knows. She's sailing on the American Export Line."

"Even so, I understood Portugal to be neutral."

"Dear boy —" Philip dazzled at him, "She'll get to London from there on British Airways."

"I see . . ." Gerald emptied his glass. "Might I ask just why it makes you happy?"

Philip stared into space, toffee-eyed, infinitely good humoured, though the smile gradually slackened away and left an expression of benign bewilderment: "D'you know, I've honestly no idea. Perhaps the thought of one of us besides Thomas – just one of us – having a few guts."

And how to pick up that cue, I ask myself?

There was no need. Here came Paula to do it for him. She stood in the doorway, elegant, haggard, his friend of this time, the friend whom he had trusted with all his miserable secrets; who trusted him completely.

"I wouldn't say just one of us, darling, not yet," said Paula, "Gerald has news for you."

I want to die. No swagger, no sneer, no sardonic choice of words could help him; there was none at hand: there was only that bloody fifteen-year old, speaking schoolboy language in his ear: "Get on now, Spit it out. And then take your medicine."

"News for you," Gerald repeated, "Well, yes, I have. It's a good thing you've got Sarah to be proud of. I came to tell you I'm staying on here. Just signed up with the studio for three more pictures."

Though he spoke to Philip, he looked at Paula. She said nothing. She gave him her old, unnerving stare, straight in the eyes. Then she turned and went. His friend no longer.

When the telephone rang, Gerald felt the strong temptation to leave it unanswered. What had he to say to Sarah? With an effort, he picked it up.

"Would this be our dauntless traveller?" he asked moodily.

"This is one who has come out of great tribulation," said Sarah "Or is at least on her way out. Thanks to you."

"Thanks to *me*? What are you talking about? . . . You mean the cheque?"

"I don't mean the cheque. Thanked you for that weeks ago, didn't I?"

"Then what?"

"Tell you some day."

"Tell me now."

"Oh I can't . . . not coherently, not without sounding utterly bloody. It was just that when I heard you weren't going after all —" She paused, "Well, then the walls came down."

"What walls, dear? I'd love to think you meant the Sixty-First Street apartment."

Sarah gave a giggle. "No, not those. Walls of a black glass house I've been living in – I suppose that sounds crazy."

"Black glass house . . . H'mm . . . A touch Kafka – or possibly Frank Lloyd Wright." He leaned back, cradling the telephone, staring up at the ceiling: "Am I to take it that my unethical behaviour decided you?"

"Well, yes."

"I see. I mean I don't see . . ."

"First I was furious with you. Then I thought – Well, somebody's got to go."

The quotation from Thomas made him wince. She was still talking. "So of course I would choose the moment when it's almost impossible to get out of the country. I could wait another ten days and get a boat from Montreal. 'Might be braver. But it has to be now. Before I get a chance to think again – or be frightened."

"Fear's not *my* reason, I'd have you know."

Sarah said, "I only know it's been mine."

"Truly?"

"Truly. Otherwise I'd have gone as soon as you sent the money."

"Well, well."

"Yes," she said in a smaller voice. "Nothing to be proud of, is it?"

He didn't answer that. He murmured, "So you never did take the sensible view, after all . . . I wondered. Not in character, I said to myself. Isn't this a little *too* idiotic, though?"

"Maybe. But it seems to suit me better." Here he heard her yawning. "Sorry . . . Today's been a rat-race. Bank . . . Sailing permit . . . passport. I've got a spiffing Portuguese visa. It's called Em Transito."

"My love to Em —"

"And we sail from *Hoboken*, what about that? Fig-u-ray voo."

"You sound so happy I hardly recognize you. What will you do, precisely, in a war?"

"Couldn't say – couldn't say – But it'll make a change from the one I've been fighting inside. Oh Gerald – if you see that rather snide customer Walter Ash – could you give him a message? Tell him the day came – will you remember that?"

"'The day came . . .' I'll try to remember."

He gave himself a cigarette before he said, "We did have fun in Bermuda, didn't we – just that once?" and then, "Oh I do wish you'd stay."

"Can't," said Sarah. "All over." She began to sing, out of tune as always,

> *"I've studied the desk and it isn't antique.*
> *That's not a real diamond comb.*
> *That's not alabaster.*
> *Goodnight, Mrs. Astor!*
> *We have to catch the last bus home."*

"Two Scotch and soda, Paula, please."

"Rab coming home? That's wonderful."

"You look tired – let me take over." said Michael the Pole.

"Something wrong, honey?" Sue Brown asked.

It was a long time since the days of pure instinctive anger that came to its climax with a slap. Young anger . . . This was a more complicated fury. This was made of disillusion; with the ugly inner voice still sounding its triumph: *Told you so. Told you he'd never do it.*

But I still can't believe it. It hasn't taken yet; I have to tell myself "Gerald's not going."

No indeed. He'll be here for months. The friend who lit life up for you, the one who has betrayed you along with himself.

"Two gin-and-tonic. Two Budweiser."

If only one could remake him in his old image; make him still last summer's absentee, the clipped voice on the telephone, the slave of Mary Castle . . . Why, she said to him in her mind, did you ever come here? Why did you ever change?

He didn't change. You fooled yourself. You clutched at him because Philip was driving you crazy. Philip's the better man. Philip didn't lie to you. There's all the difference in the world between an act and a built-in lie.

Damn it, I don't want to know these things: I never did. I want people to be just what they seem to be.

And they never are.

"Come out of that trance, Paula. I said I'd like you to go home right now." Sue Brown's face came near.

"Why would you?"

"You look terrible."

"I can still function."

"Not here. Out. This is your boss talking."

(You were no good at the eye-duel tonight. You did your best, but the hot angry eyes in the enamelled face were winning.)

"On your way." said Sue.

You were on your way.

Better not to call him from the lobby. Better to go straight up and take a chance. He could shut the door in your face, if he wished . . .

She pressed the bell. She heard slow footsteps, then Gerald's voice: "Who is that?"

"Paula here."

The door swung open. He stood before her, wearing his red and gold dressing-gown: he gave her a lop-sided smile.

"You surprise me," said Gerald.

"Are you alone?"

He fluttered his eyelashes before he said, "Very much so."

"May I come in?"

"Please do. What would you like to drink?"

"Not a thing, thanks." Her mouth felt dry: she said, "Oh, make it a glass of water."

The smoky, scented room was full of something more than smoke and scent: an atmosphere just as palpable. Atmosphere of what? Of tense, unhappy thoughts lying around, piled up from wall to wall? Maybe. Maybe merely a matter of shut windows.

"Open a window, could you, please?"

"Of course."

She sat down in her usual place on the sofa. When Gerald had given her the glass he still stood above her, stiff and looming, like a waiter.

"What did Philip say to you?" (She hadn't planned her words. This became, unexpectedly, the first thing she wanted to hear.)

"Father?" Gerald's grin was conspiratorial, as though she were still his friend: "He brushed it off, to coin a phrase. After making a gentlemanly effort to congratulate me and an even more gentlemanly effort not to ask what salary I was getting . . . But he couldn't keep his mind on it for long. First he went into another swoon about Sarah and then it was time for his Bridge."

"Oh fine," she said. "Fine."

"Meaning?"

"Meaning fine for you. The let-off. You didn't tell him —"

"Tell him what?"

Paula drank the iced water: "That you'd had . . . other ideas before this contract came up?"

"No, Madam." Gerald moved away towards the writing-desk, shuffled some papers there and looked back over his shoulder. He screwed up his face into his Chinese mask, saying, "And why not? For the simple reason he'd never have believed it."

"You're right. One of the times," Paula murmured, "when I realize how much more intelligent Philip is than I am."

Gerald seated himself; swivelling the chair so that he faced her. His fingers tapped a galloping tune on the desk: he said "Go on. Let me have it. What are you waiting for?"

All she could say was, "Why . . .? Will you just tell me why?"

Not a word. He stared across the room. She watched the smooth head and the taut, wrinkled profile.

"Did you ever mean to go – seriously? Was it just kidding? And if it was . . ."

"Go on," he said, his voice harsh.

"If it was – Oh, hell, what I really want to know is – were you kidding yourself or kidding me?"

"Both. Or that's what I think now."

"When did you make up your mind?"

"Make it up?"

"Or change it. Whichever. When did you decide you *weren't* going?"

He appeared to find this a perplexing question: "When? Why – when my agent called me with the offer."

"Right that red-hot minute?"

"Yes."

"Mean you didn't have to stop and think?"

He shook his head.

"Not even about Thomas? Didn't I hear you say you owed it to Thomas?"

"Kindly leave Thomas out of this." His voice was furious for the first time.

"I won't leave him out," she said. "It's you who leave him out."

Then she let the long silence go on; a silence broken only by the little galloping tune his fingers played. Gerald was the first to speak.

"All right. I give you best. I've failed Thomas. And I'm used to failing myself, as the saying goes. Failing you is something else again."

"Is it? Is it? And what is it?"

"Paula, you've been angelic to me. Ever since I can remember. Ever since Sawcombe."

There came the sharp memory of a boy sitting beside her as she drove up the steep hill away from the shore: a boy with a secret. She heard her own voice asking crisply "What's the trouble? Sex or money?" And after this there was the picture of the boy leaping in a war-dance because she had saved him; she could give him fifteen pounds.

"Always the cash – with you," she said, "Funny."

"Funny, you think?"

"Odd. Peculiar. What's the notion? Is money all you want out of life – ever?"

The fingers ceased their tapping. Gerald said, "I'm coming – reluctantly – to that conclusion."

"Then you certainly struck it lucky, getting to Hollywood. Otherwise I'd say you'd chosen the wrong profession. Of course there's always Mary's dough – I'd forgotten."

Unforgivable. But I had to say it. I won't look at him. Maybe it's somebody's turn to slap my face.

"You go too far," was all he said.

"Yes. I can't not; when somebody I love lets me down."

And has there – ever – been anyone I loved who failed to let me down? Bar Rab, I can't think of a single instance. Perhaps it's the penalty of loving people. Mrs. Philip Weston's Great Thought For The Week.

She glanced at the still figure by the desk. There was a change in him; he had gone further away. His expression was tranquil and amused.

"In attempting to explain this whole sorry matter to myself," he said lightly, "I take Somerset Maugham's view. As expressed in *The Summing Up*."

"Oh, you do?"

He said, in quotation-marks, "I realized early that money was like a sixth sense without which one could not make full use of the other five." He looked almost happy. "See?" he said to her.

"No, I don't."

"Why not?"

"Well, mainly because I can't understand a word of it."

"Darling Paula; only an elaboration of my credo. Money's the way to freedom."

She gave a shout of laughter. "Freedom! *That's* a good one, coming from you." She got up. "I think we've said it all for tonight," she told him. He didn't answer. "Just one more thing, Gerald, and then let's cut. You've proved to me that I'm a starry-eyed idiot. It'll take me a while to get over that. But once I can persuade myself I never did believe you —"

"Come here," he interrupted.

"I'm going now."

"Come here."

"Good night."

When he stretched out his hand to her she said, "No. I can't help you. Not any more. You shot everything down today."

The hand made an impatient gesture. She said "No" again, and he grasped her wrist.

"It isn't your help I need," said Gerald.

"Then what?"

"Your diagnosis is accurate. I shot everything down today."

Against her will she was reading the letter; it lay beside his hand, in the white glow from the lamp on the desk.

"Dear Mary,

This is to tell you that I am never coming back. It *isn't* to tell you that we've both been acting our heads off for months and months; this you know already. Our marriage is the biggest bluff since the late King Hal and I want you to divorce me *quam celerrime.*"

"*Quam* . . . ?"

"Latin for 'at all speed'," said Gerald. "She'll have to look it up in the dictionary."

"Well?" Paula said after a moment, "Do you expect me to congratulate you?"

He shrugged. "It's what you wanted me to do – isn't it?"

"I suppose it is." She read the words again. They affronted her. "Do you have to be so damn clever about everything?" she flung at him, as she went to the door.

With the door shut, there came a sort of peace; a quiet, perceptible movement back to the time when she had looked at his picture on the glass-topped table and said "You louse," to it. The ugly inner voice was right. Gerald had never changed and never would.

She was hurrying across Sunset, down Harper Avenue, hurrying to reach the place that was home, hurrying – for once – to be alone with herself.

A sort of peace . . . But sad, all the same.

THE LONGEST WAY

It was impossible to sleep. The sea was calm; calmer
than it had been for many days. Sarah lay listening to the steady beat
of the engines, watching the stars cross the porthole; waiting for
dawn, prey to a vast impatience.

She switched on the light above the bunk. This brought a panic
rush of cockroaches from the plate of fruit on the bedside chest. She
was used to them now, the black shapes flickering away. No harm in
cockroaches, though she disliked finding one with her bare foot on
the tiles under the shower. This was a two-berth cabin; she had
begun the voyage sleeping in the berth nearest the bulkhead. That
berth had bed-bugs in it. ("What do you expect?" said the Captain,
"If you saw the lot we carry on the return trip, you'd sure be grateful it was only bed-bugs.")

Four o'clock in the morning. She was broad awake, too much
awake to lie here any longer.

She climbed down from the high berth. She put on a sweater and
trousers, socks and sneakers. She wandered out of the cabin. Mount-
ing the companionway, coming up on deck, she met the smell of the
sea; the salt air blown back off the walls of the land that lay somewhere ahead, beyond the dark.

She leaned on the rail, thinking, I shall remember this voyage: if I
am ever to be a writer again it will be written.

I shall remember this handful of passengers; the diplomat returning and the three American journalists – and the Scots Dietary
Expert (who won't take a drink in case he has to buy one for somebody else.) Most of all I shall remember the two Belgians; brisk,
middle-aged, smiling, but with a fixed look in their eyes, a 'keep-
off' look. They do not talk to anyone except each other; and they

walk all day, around and around the deck, talking and walking: on their way back to their country, to their country's new damnation.

I shall remember going ashore in Bermuda, just for the hell of it, because we had six hours in harbour ... taking a speedboat across the sound to Southampton, wandering through the garden of Mary's shut-up house. Loitering there alone, thanking God for this time and not that time: having a drink at Twenty-One because of Gerald, being sad for him and writing him a postcard and tearing it up; it was too jubilant, he wouldn't have liked it. And I came back to the ship, with the British sentries on guard at the foot of the gang-plank.

I shall remember (Heaven knows) the bellhop. Passes made at me in this ship come from all ranks; the Captain, the First Officer and the bellhop. The bellhop sliding around my cabin when the storm blew, saying, "What you need is somebody to relax you, not one of these short-term millionaires." I don't know what he means. I keep him at bay; but I work at retaining him as a buddy; because he's the only person on board who can find me an hotel room in Lisbon, or so he says. Lisbon is jam-packed; the crossroads of the world. And the diplomat has a room at the Aviz.

(There is Miles. But I am beginning to have my doubts of Miles. I sent him the radiogram on our first day out; ten days have gone and he still hasn't answered. I will find his number in the telephone-book and call him. Perhaps he has left Lisbon.

There is Rab. But when will she come? Or has she gone? I have my doubts of Rab, too.)

I shall remember the British boat going past in the night, so near that she almost touched us, a shape blacker than the dark, and the one light signalling *What Ship Are You?* It was the loneliest thing I ever saw, that light. I shall remember the German boat that kept her guns trained on us (they said, the crew said, perhaps it wasn't true). I shall remember the fire-drill morning, the clanging bells, when I thought, "Here it comes – this is it." Running out of the shower all wet, pulling on these clothes, finding my life-jacket caught fast – somehow – under the berth; tugging at it, muttering, "Be absolute for death" and trying to decide what to take in my pockets ... Jewellery, traveller's cheques, Romney's photograph? And ending with the topaz fish and the medal of St. Michael and my flask ...

And the steward coming to meet me as I rushed through the door: with a grin on his face. "Fire-drill," he said, "You're in the Navy now." And the enormous journey back from the imagined thing to the truth.

If I am ever to be a writer again . . .

Sarah looked from side to side of the sky. She watched the morning come. The sea's horizon was drawn sharply now, the colours running fast along the rim and the water whitening, whitening. On the western side there was still the blue dark; the stars and the moon. She grew cold, and did not stir, clinging to the rail. The colours came on from the East, the light arched up, swept over the blue darkness; the moon and the stars went out.

The colours vanished. The morning was grey-white; she saw the structure of a pale ship revealed, and a pale sea all around her. She sat on a coil of rope under the belly of a lifeboat. A sailor, barefooted, came to swab the deck.

"Hi," said the sailor. "Early, aren't you?"

"I couldn't sleep."

"You got channel fever."

"Have I? What's channel fever?"

"Just the land coming near, that's what does it."

"How soon shall we see the land?"

"Oh – afternoon sometime," said the sailor: "Know Lisbon? Not a bad town. Reminds me of Athens. Know Athens?"

By their voices and their gestures, Sarah understood them perfectly. They meant "You cannot stay here." But it was easy to pretend; to smile up at them from the coat pillow she had arranged under her head on the Customs bench. Saying "I'm sorry, I don't speak a word of Portuguese; and I'm going to sleep. I am sure Dr. Salazar would have no objection. Somebody go and ask him."

There were three of them, dressed in grey; a skinny, sallow woman and two men, all shouting at her. She lay where she was, with her luggage piled close to the bench. It was a bold endeavour and she might, she thought, be removed from the customs shed to prison. All her fellow-passengers had gone; every member of the crew had vanished, even the bellhop: the one taxi-driver who spoke French and promised to take her to Miles's address had vanished too, carrying off the Belgians. There were no more taxis. There was no telephone here. There was, according to the French-speaker, no hope of a bed in Lisbon, neither tonight nor any other night.

Her hecklers grew desperate: noisier and noisier. The woman marched to the door, where she made a precise pantomime of locking it.

"Closing-time," said Sarah, "I see. Never mind. Just leave me here. I am entitled to a foothold on Portuguese soil." She opened her passport again, pointed once more to EM TRANSITO and put the passport back in her bag. She shut her eyes.

"Are you sick or something?" The bellhop stood beside the bench. He was holding the arm of a corpse-faced man who wore a green felt hat; grasping him tightly, as though he expected the man to make a bolt. The man bowed and smiled at her. He handed her a card printed with the name L. Carillo.

"How do you do," said Sarah, "No, I'm not sick. I just thought of spending the night here."

"This bastard ought to have been on the dock. Had to chase him up. He'll find us a room," the bellhop said.

Us? She reminded herself that the crew was not allowed to sleep ashore. She uncurled from the bench. The bellhop and Mr. Carillo carried her luggage. There was a taxi waiting.

"Ask him to take us here," Sarah said, handing the bellhop the paper where she had written Miles's address. The effect for Mr. Carillo was a loud cackle of laughter.

"He says it's a canning factory," the bellhop reported, "Shuts at five. He says anyway you wouldn't want to sleep with the sardines."

They drove away from the waterfront.

What sort of city was this? Impossible to discover. It seemed to tilt in all directions. The taxi drove uphill and downhill. There were cobblestones, there were long, stretching streets and bright-lit signs. There were continual stops while Mr. Carillo climbed out, made inquiries and came back saying No, it is no good. This went on until the bellhop began to lose his temper. He lapsed into his own language: "See here, buster, if you won't play ball with me I won't play ball with you."

(It looks, Sarah said to herself, as though we'll have to take a rain-check on this ball-game.)

The bellhop squeezed her arm. "Don't worry – he's just holding out on us. Come on, now, giddyap mule. Try the Borges . . . What's wrong with the old Borges?"

The taxi was wheeling round a lighted square: surely for the third time, if not the fourth. Mr. Carillo was – as usual – pointing out objects of interest, mainly invisible statues. The taxi drove out of the square and downhill again, turning to the right. It stopped again. Mr. Carillo got out again. He came back.

"It is okay, Madame. But for this night only."

"Don't give me that," said the bellhop, "and don't give him more than three bucks," he added to Sarah.

"What about the taxi?"

"I'll settle it. You don't want to throw your money around, sweetheart; you may be here a little while."

* * *

"*Tres-Incarnada!*" called the croupiers. Sarah promptly put her finger on the yellow-brown chip covering Number Three, and kept it there. Such an action at Cannes or Monte Carlo would be unthinkable. She could imagine the reaction of the *chef de parti*. But in the Casino at Estoril there was every chance that the winning shot would be raked away with the losers. When that happened and you began to argue, every croupier at the table (hitherto understanding French or English) relapsed into impenetrable Portuguese.

So she stood where she was, with her finger on the chip. After a moment of hostile quiet, they paid. The rake sent across a pink oblong chip, a green one, and a stack of the yellow-browns (undoubtedly short by two, but it was hopeless to argue about that.) Sarah put the treasure in her bag and turned from the table.

Whereupon the croupiers glowered in unison, like angry cattle seen over a gate.

All the false and fearful legends woven about roulette by non-gamblers came true in Estoril.

It was early afternoon; too early to quit, but this was not so much gambling as taking chances with a tiger. She made it an absolute rule to quit every time she won. The stunted boy, the *changeur*, carrying his satchel, came to meet her. He seemed disappointed when she handed him the chips and took the thick mille-escudo notes instead. She walked on through the dim lobby, out into the sunshine: she had nothing to do.

> "*A pleasant place for gentlemen with nothing left to do,*
> *Morning never tries you till the afternoon,*"

Sarah chanted, standing still at the top of the Gardens. The Gardens, planted with flowers and shrubs, in a faithful copy of Monte Carlo, stretched down to the sea-front. She strolled towards the Estoril Palacio, on her left: a large, luxurious hotel, haunt of travellers with Priority claims, of mixed nationals and internationals; of spies and counter-spies. (An hotel in every way preferable to her own, the Valentin.) She had half a mind to walk in, sample the new arrivals and put through a telephone-call. The Valentin's telephone was publicly placed, at the back of the hall, affording free entertainment to staff and visitors, who listened without shame when opportunity arose.

On second thoughts, Sarah decided against the call. She could guess what the result would be: the gloomy French voice telling her there was no news: reminding her once again that in the event of Miles's return he would be given her message; then the click as Cecile rang off.

The Miles mystery was just one more frustration in this daily round of frustrations.

Sarah looked back a long way – to the first Lisbon afternoon. She had hunted down the canning-factory through dingy labyrinths between the docks and the railway-line. A mixture of French, English and pantomime had finally produced Miles's private address. She could remember how happy she was, climbing the narrow cobbled way that wound up to St. Anthony's Cathedral on the height. She remembered the lift of her heart when she saw the house: a small, clean façade, with flowers in painted window-boxes: a flutter of lace curtains.

Cecile had opened the door. Her bewilderment was understandable (eleven years since their last meeting) but her news, her manner, struck a blow in one's hopeful face. No; Miles was not in the city; no, Cecile hadn't the remotest idea where he could be reached; he was *en voyage* and that was all she knew. The shrugs, the muffled voice, the down-turned mouth declared plainly that she washed her hands of Miles.

No invitation to step inside, to sit and talk over old days; a brief inquiry for Paula, Philip and Gerald; a sign of the Cross made for Thomas. A groan in the direction of the children's voices behind her, and then the sad, fat woman shut the door.

Three weeks ago, that moment. Three weeks seeming as long as a lifetime; longer than all the useless months in America.

"*I wasted Time and now doth Time waste me*" was today's theme-song.

Sarah went down through the Gardens and walked to the Valentin by way of the sea-road; the longer route; she was in no hurry to get there. The Valentin resembled an English seaside boarding-house gone mad, furnished with a bar and run by trolls. Its clientele was made up of congenital disapprovers, British to their back teeth.

She had been directed there by the Repatriation Office after three days at the Borges. Should she run out of funds, the Repatriation Office would take charge; moving her to a cheaper hotel; supporting her at the rate of two pounds, ten shillings a week. The women at the office were the kindest of governesses. Though she visited them regularly for news of a sailing, Sarah was careful not to mention the Casino. They never lost patience. They smiled and said *Do look in again, but of course we'll telephone you the moment we have any news.*

The man behind the counter at British Airways was more of a chum, but less of an optimist. Though he too said *Do look in again,* he made it clear that she stood little chance. He had shown her the book with the list of would-be passengers. There were three hundred names ahead of hers; and ahead of those were the names marked

Priority. Even so, she took the train from Estoril to Lisbon at least twice a week. It was a compulsion. The ritual round included the Pan-American office, the Marconi cable office and the Hotel Aviz, on the search for a clue from Rab. The failure of Rab to show up in Lisbon was another mystery. It was her only way home. Neither Paula nor Philip sounded in the least disturbed.

One waited for Rab as one waited for everything else: sometimes with a furious acceleration of anxiety, sometimes in the lethargic belief that this, the latest stage of limbo, would last forever.

Lethargy prevailed today.

There was still a little heat in the winter sun: the coloured sky and sea called back the Mediterranean: the ghost of the Twenty-nine summer was walking; the ghost of an afternoon spent with Thomas on the deserted rocks beside the pool. She turned her mind from the memory wherein he dived for a gold pencil. She turned away from the sea.

The inland road ran past the Atlantico, another hotel more imposing than the Valentin, a low-built modern hotel, said by some of the English to be "very nice inside".

One did not go inside, because that was where the Germans stayed. Sarah resented even the sight of its dark red roof below her bedroom window (to the left, beyond the tall ostrich-plumed palm-tree).

She came to the gates and went up through the garden. On the terrace she saw them sitting out in their canvas chairs, getting the last of the sun: the stranded company, her fellow-prisoners, the hard core of the guests here. They were all waiting to go to England. The smaller, shifting population travelled West, by the Export Line or, occasionally, by the Clipper. These also were in a queue, but their queue moved from time to time.

"Any news?" asked the Scots food-expert. *You with your Priority, who told me you couldn't possibly be kept waiting more than two days.*

"I got another *plein*," said Sarah. She could see the woman next to the Scot stiffen a little and take a tighter grip on her novel. "At this rate," she added, raising her voice, "I shall soon be able to afford my bribe."

"That isn't very sensible talk, is it, Mrs. Butler?"

"And not very patriotic, either."

"A bribe for a passage home? Surely the height of patriotism," Sarah protested.

"Well, you know what we were told at the Repatriation Office – one can never be sure who's listening."

"But the Germans know I play roulette. Heavens, they're at the Casino every night, the bastards."

"You wouldn't seriously offer a bribe?" asked the Scot, "Would you, now?"

"I have. To the little man at the Embassy; the one with the toothbrush moustache. He wasn't in the mood. But there's the captain of a coal-boat, said to be highly susceptible. I've only just found out about him. Three more *pleins* and he's mine."

The young mother on the far side of the Scot said, "It's a pity we can't all afford to gamble."

"Nobody," said Sarah, "can afford to gamble." Deliberately she chose an empty chair away from the line, and took out her wallet, for the one consoling ritual. She spread the large, dirty notes on her knee and counted them through. (Fairy gold . . . She slept every night with the wallet under her pillow and still expected the money to have melted away by morning.)

Here the elderly lady, who wore purple and went for walks, paused beside the chair. She leaned on her stick. She had a wise-monkey face; she was the only detached, friendly person within call.

"You know," she said, studying the treasure, "I can't believe you get that from the Casino. I mean, I do believe it, but I never knew anyone else who could."

"My great-uncle who lived at *Mentony* was an extremely lucky gambler," said the woman with the novel. "He made all his expenses every winter. Just by playing the even chances. And he was always very charming and modest about it: not ostentatious at all."

"Dull for him . . . Both the modesty *and* the even chances."

The wise-monkey grinned. "In fact," Sarah told the opposition, "None of this really comes from the Casino. I earn my fortune as a fortune-teller."

"Does she *have* to be so funny all the time?" the young mother murmured to the Scot. Sarah pulled her chair close to him, and grabbed his hand. He turned masculine-coy at once. "Relax," she said, "I'm going to read your palm."

"Can you do that, now?"

"Sure . . . I see delay all around you. Either a boat or an aeroplane is much delayed. You are anxious about money. I see two women in an office-building; they may make an offer of help. You are expecting a letter which has not arrived. You are going to travel across water, but not yet. Correct? My grandmother was a clairvoyant, the gift is inherited. Excuse me, I am now going to have a bath."

This was another ostentatious gesture. The hotel kept its bathroom doors locked; a bath was a charge on the bill. The bill showed a rising *pension* rate week by week; the longer you stayed the more it cost you. (There was also a supplement-charge on Em Transito, due every ten days. The British amateur revue '*Obrigado, Portugal!*' had been staged in salute to the country's hospitality.)

Crossing the lobby, Sarah met one of the nicer trolls; José, the hall-porter. He seemed excited: "You have heard the news? A boat is leaving on Thursday. I hope you'll be lucky, Madame."

It might be true. All the more diverting. The Lisbon rule was absolute. Only the Repatriation Office would know when a ship was due to sail and the procedure had been carefully explained: "You will receive a telephone-call from here, asking you to come at once. When that happens, remember to bring your passport. But – please – not a word to anybody, not even to your friends. Above all, not to the hotel staff. Invent some good excuse for going into Lisbon. And please try, at all times, wherever you are, to avoid giving the impression that you are waiting for a boat." This last was Sarah's favourite instruction to date.

No boat had sailed for England since the week of her arrival, twenty-four days ago. Still she smiled upon the porter and told him she was unlikely to be called; her name was too far down the list

"I hope it will be you, all the same," he said, and pinched her bottom

"José, you know how much that bores me. Go pinch some o those out there."

"If you are not lucky with the boat, I take you dancing."

"How do you know about the boat, anyway?"

"I take you dancing," he repeated.

In her room Sarah rang the bell for the maid. There would be a long wait. This was a bare, anonymous room, with pale grey walls and tiled floor; a small zinc alcove held a fitted basin and a bidet. (According to rumour, the Scot had said he needn't pay for the privilege of the bathroom because the little footbath beside the basin was proving adequate.)

The grey shutters were fastened; prisoner's room: Sarah folded them back, and saw the palm-tree; the tall, tired ostrich brooding above the red roofs of the Atlantico. Damn this view. It was beginning to obsess her because it was there as soon as she awoke from the dream of being back in London . . . the vivid, morning dream.

In the dream they were all together, the whole family, even Thomas. There was an air-raid in progress, but this was no cause for alarm; it was merely a succession of little fireworks popping about on the floor while Brigstock laid the table for tea.

(Pure delight, the dream: to be broken inevitably by somebody asking, "How on earth did you manage to get out of Portugal?" At once it was over; you opened your eyes. You saw the palm-tree.)

Here was the maid answering the bell; a new maid, without a word of English or French. Sarah walked her to the bathroom door and pointed.

The resolution to teach herself Portuguese had perished in a day. The movie magazine, bought with the language in mind, still lay on the wicker table under the window; the photograph on its cover smiled broadly above the legend ROBERT TAYLOR E UM INTELLECTUALE? She was always meaning to send this to Gerald; but no letter had come from him and she hesitated to intrude upon his silence.

"Madame!" José's voice outside the door, followed by urgent knocking.

"What is it, José? The boat?"

"A gentleman for you."

"Name?"

"Will not give."

"Is he fat?" she asked, hopefully, with Miles in view.

"Quite thin. Young. He waits."

"He'll have to. I'm on my way to my bath."

"I tell him," said José.

It might be any of them; the Hungarian with the bow-tie; the Czech painter; the Jewish boy from Paris, awaiting his turn on the Export Line. The female disapprovers made chilly jokes about them all.

When she came downstairs, dressed with something of a swagger for the evening, José said "He still waits." In the brown-hued room on the left of the lobby she found a very pale young man, pacing. She had never seen him before.

"You have met me at the Casino, Madame. I am a friend of Paul; your Hungarian friend Paul. He advises me to come to you."

"Oh? Why?"

"For your help, Madame. Please to read this. I am putting it into English for you."

There was a good deal of it. Sarah sat in one of the brown chairs: the young man continued to pace. The letter, a carbon-copy, authorized the young man to write a tourist's guide to the district. The advance payable was thirty thousand escudos.

"Yes, well – what?"

"Would you please be so kind as to give me the money now?"

"How's that again?"

"I know you have money. I watch you play. I am penniless."

Sarah said, "Don't be so silly," and gave him back the letter. The young man looked deeply hurt. "You have not understood. I want to go to England to fight. I can go now, if only I have money."

"You can go now . . .? *There's* talent. Do you own a private submarine?"

"Not making jokes, please. I am serious, Madame."

"So am I. You aren't getting a nickel out of me."

"Please, Madame. For your country's sake. I write the book fast, then I go."

"Go now, there's a good boy."

The young man began to weep: "If not for me, then please for my brother who is in concentration camp. Wait – I show you his picture."

•   •   •   •   •

The boy with the fuzzy eyebrows and the long chin was attached to the British Embassy in Madrid. Here for his Christmas leave, he was refreshing company. He did not ask the eternal "Any news?" He had heard no rumours. He had no money problems and he wasn't waiting for a letter. Blessedly calm, animal from a forgotten species, he strolled beside Sarah. They had walked along the beach to Cascais; they were coming home by the sea-road. The boy carried a walking-stick; he wore a tweed suit and brown shoes.

"Mind if I ask you something? You needn't say yes if you'd rather not." He hesitated. "I was thinking of going to church on Christmas Day. I suppose you wouldn't like to come?" He sounded uneasy, half-ashamed, as one making an improper suggestion.

She said abruptly, "I've laid off church for years."

"Oh well then – of course."

"Hold it. I'd like to come."

"Oh good. Sure?"

She said, "Yes. I don't know that it's fair, but I would."

"How do you mean – fair?"

"Fair to God. I don't treat Him very well. My prayers," she explained, looking up at the puzzled profile, "are just telephone-calls. Priority. Personal. Urgent. And for all the answers I get I might be ringing the wrong number. No, that's not fair, either. At least He made me shoe-horn myself out of America. And, mind you, I'm not complaining. What I deserve is what my grand-mother would call temporal punishment. And that's what I'm getting."

He looked more puzzled than ever. He murmured, "Well, at Christmas I always think —" and left the sentence in mid-air.

"So do I," said Sarah. "And it's kind of you to ask me."

"There's an early service at the English church. In Lisbon, of course. But I can get a car and pick you up. About seven thirty."

She thanked him. She offered him a drink at the Valentin, but he refused, and she left him on the station platform, to wait for the little train. "See you tonight at the Casino?" he asked hopefully.

"Very like, very like. That's a thing I don't lay off."

"Well, cheerio. It was awfully nice of you to want to come for a walk."

Something about this time was evocative, were it possible to evoke experiences one had never known. The young men in procession, with their invitations to walk, to dance (and, as it turned out, to church) belonged surely to the pattern of a young girl's life in England: a slightly old-fashioned girl, living at home. As she walked uphill towards the Valentin, Sarah began to appoint a reverie wherein she was this girl. She put Brigstock into the reverie; Brigstock fitted in easily, saying the English boy seemed so nice after all those foreigners.

Reverie had become a frantic need. Within the conscious mind, one was forced to occupy smaller and smaller floor-space. There was so little left that one could bear to contemplate.

Dead stop. Here for ever and ever. (With a letter from Philip suggesting she come back to New York and sail from Canada in convoy; "quicker in the end," he wrote: with the persistent rumour that Hitler would soon occupy Portugal: with many small horrors, such as meeting the bellhop from last month's voyage. He sat on a bar-stool saying "So I cross the Atlantic twice and you stay here.")

A cable from the Grandmother declaring "All well with us. Hold fast. Shield and buckler," was one small consolation. But with London bombed every night one needed a cable every morning for peace of mind. Peace of mind resounded from Dick Abrahams, who had written twice; his only comment on the blitz being "These foolish foreigners keep such late hours."

Sarah walked up through the garden towards the chairs on the terrace.

"Good morning, Sarah. What a pretty coat."

"Nice walk, Sarah?"

A notable change in the social weather. They were kind to her now, less kind to one another. Some shrill quarrels were developing into feuds, their causes ranging from fraternization with the Germans to a lost, allegedly stolen, knitting-book.

There were two reasons for Sarah's up-grading. The first wa money. She cashed the post-dated cheques they drew on thei British bank-accounts. Not only were they touchingly grateful bu this had obliged them to call off their objections to the Casino, th source of supply.

The second reason was their new target for disapproval: a big red-haired English girl who had just sailed in, reluctantly, from America. She had meant to stay there for the duration: she had been dislodged only by the fact of an expiring permit. This made her, she said, "mad as hops". She spoke pure American idiom with the plummiest of British accents. Neutrally-minded in the extreme, she pleaded for "civilized behaviour" toward the Germans and had been known to take tea with some at the Atlantico. She was given to saying, "Wars don't *solve* anything," "Roosevelt's job is to keep America out" and, sometimes, "It's just selfish and silly for any woman to go to England now." She would clinch this argument to her own satisfaction, and to nobody's else's; spreading out her hands; looking from face to face, trumpeting, "If my aunt who's a trained starf-nurse can't get a war-job, well, I mean to say . . ."

She never listened to the British radio; she wasn't – the Scots food-expert now assured Sarah in a shocked whisper – going to listen to the King's speech on Christmas Day. She sat in a deck-chair, a little apart from the rest, reading a huge American novel.

"Have a drink?" Sarah said to the Scot.

"No thank you very much."

"You won't have to buy one tor me. I promise. I made ten mille last night."

He turned reddish, saying, "I'm not one for alcohol, you know that. Particularly in the middle of the day."

"Anybody like a drink?" Sarah besought the company. There was a grateful but determined chorus of "No, thank you." She went on her way to the bar.

It was a long, light room at the back of the building. You could approach it from the lobby, or from the garden by the French windows. Walled with blue, white, and yellow tiles, it contrived to suggest a public lavatory. There were a few wicker chairs and tables. No regular barman attended here. The hall-porter José was serving a young man with a drink.

The young man perched on a high stool, with one long leg at full stretch, one foot on the floor. His back view showed fair, closely-cropped hair, a faded yellow sweater and grey flannels. He slanted; he slouched. One brown bony hand was propped on the bar; there was a gold identification bracelet slipping down over the wrist.

This much Sarah noted before José's face smiled its widest smile, saying "Here she comes," and the young man leaped off the stool, holding out his arms, and turned into Rab.

THE UNWRITTEN NOTEBOOK

THOMAS WESTON: EMILE: JUSTIN: BERNARD MORLAIX OF
the Legion . . . who now? Nobody. Nobody here. That was how it
felt; that was how I made it feel, striving for a self without identity.
I would call the little roll of past selves every morning; they fortified
the anonymous prisoner in the concentration camp.

"You see? You are none of them," I would explain, "They led
other lives. They know nothing of yours. You cannot remember a
time when you were clean; when the hair grew on your head; when
you had no lice; when you ate good food. Certainly your body is
not you, it is only something that belongs to you. But to keep alive
within this body you must be the unknown inhabitant; a stranger –
immune from all that happens here."

When the sound of your own voice makes you homesick for the
things it used once to say . . . Well, that was what started me on the
pursuit of no-identity. I was rather good at the exercise now, so
long as I did not stop to think; it was like ski-ing; ski-ing in my
mind all day.

It was much more difficult at night. It always had been. And
tonight was a proper bastard.

I remember the Grandmother telling me once that I was the sort
of person who would enjoy solitary confinement. At the moment I
heartily agreed with her. Perhaps it was no worse than most nights,
but there seemed to be more noise. Three new arrivals with money
on them had got even drunker than the boys of the old brigade,
most of whom were drunk enough. The singing was continuous; it
was accompanied, sooner or later, by the sound of somebody being
sick; and not only the sound.

I reflected that I was out of practice. Before I went into the infirmary, I had learned to detach my mind, to move off, to contemplate from a distance that seemed almost silent, the hut, the singing, and my own body huddled on the floor. Eighty-five of us slept on this floor. I had been able to find a sort of privacy here, just because there were so many. I never could find it among the few. I hadn't found it, for example, in the Catalonian cell, shared with only seven others. But that was last September: just after Johnny was killed and they caught me; the time of the nightmare. The nightmare drove me as near crazy as it was possible to be.

I didn't want to start up those thoughts tonight, or I'd never sleep at all. I was failing completely at the no-identity exercise; nor could I contrive the mind's escape, the move-off. Under the raucous tent of noise I lay speculating on the fate of two absentees who had shared this corner with me; a corporal from the East Surreys and a Gunner private. They were gone from the camp. Released, according to one rumour: shot while trying to make a run for it, according to another. The little Lowestoft seaman lay next to me now, plastered as usual. He chose to sing "Charmaine" against the majority who were still at "South of the Border." On my other side lay the Dutchman, comatose, talking to himself and threshing with his legs.

> *"I wonder why you keep me waiting,*
> *Charmaine – my Charmaine,"*

sang the seaman, with an excess of tremolo:

> *"I wonder when blue birds are mating*
> *If you'll . . . come . . . back . . . again."*

Any minute now he would dissolve into tears. Yes, here they came. Between the sobs he would say "Oh God, oh God, oh God." The first time I heard him do it I tried to comfort him, not realizing he was insulated.

"*Silencio!*" from the night watchman. A chorus of international obscenities; then the singing gradually began to die down. The miserable charcoal stove had died long ago. The hut was colder than I remembered. Why not? This was winter and we were two thousand feet up in the mountains. I supposed I should be grateful for the issue of blankets, lice or no lice. (A whole new ration of lice the Irish major had explained to me in the canteen; nobody could call our Spanish hosts ungenerous.)

Oh, well . . . The infirmary wasn't exactly a picnic, I reminded myself (just in time; it was beginning to look like the Ritz.) And whatever's ahead, you can't have the last three months and twenty days again; you've done those; you're that much nearer the end of the tunnel.

If it has an end.

You can endure; you can do nothing else.

Thomas Weston. Emile: Justin: Bernard Morlaix of the Legion.

What is your name?

With that, I was back in the first guard-room; an officer sat behind a table, under the Spanish flag.

"What is your name?"

"Manuel Tomaso Miles."

Patiently I stuck to the story of being Miles's son, the penniless waiter on his way home. My wallet, with all my money and my passport, had been stolen. I gave them the address of my father's farm in Cintra; if they would let me write a letter to him —

"No," the interpreter told me – "You cannot do that."

"Supposing you send him a telegram."

"The Captain says you must think yourself a person of some importance."

I said, "If I am of no importance, why do you keep me here?"

The interpreter didn't pass this one on, but warned me against frivolous replies. The Captain, questioning me about my father, seemed to find him an improbable character. This was only natural. We had all found Miles an improbable character since Paula first imported him into the family.

"You say he is half-Swiss, half-Spanish, yet he resides in Portugal. Why do you speak no Spanish, only French?"

"He married a Frenchwoman."

This truth was greeted with profound scepticism: the interpreter turned to me again.

"The Captain says Miles is a most unusual name for somebody of these mixed nationalities."

We had all said the same for years. I made no comment. I thought of the Countess and her alleged influence with the Spanish Government. I offered her as a reference for Miles. Once again I was warned not to be frivolous. I also got a jab in the ribs from the guard's rifle.

"I mean it. She is a friend of mine. I can write you down her address in France."

This brought a speech about no loyal subject of España living in France.

"Take him away," was the next thing the Captain said.

With the British soldiers whom I found among my fellow-prisoners, I kept up my pantomime of the ex-waiter; talking in French and in broken English. I was sure I would get out. I was sure the Spaniards were investigating my story and would release me as soon as they heard from Miles. The name 'Tomaso' would give Miles the clue.

Often I could see him driving up to the jail to rescue me; in this vision he was always at the wheel of Paula's grey Hispano, belonging to the year 1926.

I was in no hurry. (That was the oddest thing to remember now.) The nightmare walked the cell, walked the yard at exercise-time and stood over me while I slept. I wrestled with it as one might with the Devil. My silences were prolonged. I could go for days without speaking. When I heard the British prisoners calling me 'The Madman' I didn't blame them. Dick Abrahams once called me the Madman with less cause.

The nightmare had begun from the moment I stood beside the Spanish frontier guards, looking down at Johnny's corpse. He lay with his arms outstretched, his feet crossed, his head fallen sideways, a crucified shape on the stone.

"War becomes an art-form." his voice echoed.

I had found myself cursing Johnny. I cursed him for what he was: for the lifelong bravado, come at last to the point where it killed him. This endured: I was obsessed with this. I could see his death only as a suicide, as much a suicide as Romney's death had been. In my worst dreams these two blended, a body with two heads, arguing that death was their choice by right. Death was anybody's right, they said.

I wanted to remember Johnny as my friend on the road: the friend with whom I had laughed, saying, "Ditto, ditto, Brother Smut," dodging the hostile tribes, playing our silly games together. But I never could get him back. There was only his body lying across the stone and myself cursing him. And then the Romney Butler-Johnny Stevens figure would take over, arguing. This happened by day as well as by night.

Until the last of the coloured dreams. It came at morning. I had lain awake for hours; then, while I was still staring at the pale sky behind the small barred window, the colours swept across. I saw the scarlet blood, the white stone and the great red flowers growing high. I looked down at the stone. It was the dead body of Christ that lay there: very peaceful, very tired. I kneeled beside Him and, immediately, the dream vanished. I awoke.

That was the end of the nightmare; and the beginning of a long, long reverie.

Now, listening to the sobs of the Lowestoft seaman, I tried to remember when I had begun to lose faith in Miles as a rescue-party. The month in that particular jail was a blurred sequence; partly because of the nightmare and partly because my shoulder gave me more pain every day. The pain was savage on the day they marched us out of jail; thirty of us, handcuffed, and roped together. We were put into trucks, headed for the biggest internment-camp in the country. I think everybody except myself knew where we were going. The camp had been built for prisoners taken during the Civil War. Some of the prisoners were still in residence.

It was here that they shaved our heads.

It was here that I was interrogated again; by an officer who might have been the brother of the first one; same narrow skull, same narrow eyes; this one spoke fluent French, so we needed no interpreter.

He asked me, "Why do you carry your arm like that? You should stand at attention. Is this a joke of some kind?"

"*Non, mon capitaine*. My arm hurts."

"What is the matter with it?"

"I have no idea."

He shrugged. He looked up some notes in a file. He told me politely that as an unwanted alien on Spanish soil, an alien of doubtful origin, whose story had been investigated and found false, I should prepare to consider myself interned for the duration.

No point in maintaining the lie.

"I am a British officer," I told him.

He replied, still politely, that it was rare for British officers to endow themselves with neutral fathers and to speak perfect French. I agreed.

"In which story do you now persist, *mon petit bonhomme*?"

I gave him my regiment, my number and my name. He continued to look amused without looking interested. Like his predecessor, he told the guard to take me away.

So I settled down into the shape of the anonymous prisoner.

There was a persistent rumour around the camp that the British would be released; and indeed they seemed to disappear, slowly, in small numbers. The French, all claiming to be French-Canadians, shared the hope that they too would be set free and deported to U.K. via Gibraltar. Some of them went: none of us knew where. After a week or two, the rumour would change its tune. No British prisoner would get out until the war ended. We were here for the duration. Then somebody knew something: the word went round; hope revived again. And in due course, turned to despair.

Whom could one trust? Answer, nobody. This was the place where your best friend (if you had one) could pick your pocket, steal your last razor-blade – or suddenly assault you in the latrine. This was the place of abominations large and small. Never had I hated before. I hated now (because it was night and the self I sought to eliminate was awake and prowling). I hated the place and all who lived here, soldier or civilian, old or young. This was an international refuse-dump: where lice bred, where thieving and fighting, drunkenness and homosexuality became natural human behaviour. If you treat people like scum – as we were treated – they turn into scum soon enough. Man is at his lowest here, I thought, and

I'm brought down with the rest; and so I came to the reverie once more.

It is the reverie of human suffering, of God made man only to be tortured and killed. I see him dying everywhere, every day. He dies in the dirt and squalor; he dies in the cruelty; he dies of a blow or a blasphemy; he dies at the hands of the Spaniards who so devoutly worship him. I kill him with my own hating.

I am haunted by the cross and the sword. By the paradox that the cross and the sword-hilt are shaped the same: the sword-hilt Cross stands bloody in my way, wherever I look.

Till I come in my mind to the figure lying on the stone; and I know that he will rise from the dead. But why do we kill him so often?

This night was interminable. There was a hell of a draught blowing along the floor, through the smells and the stuffiness. We had no beds of any kind; just the floor and the thin blankets. I always tied an old shirt round my shaven head; but tonight my chin was cold too. One of the orderlies up at the infirmary had trimmed my beard: kind of him, but I missed its tickly warmth.

Beyond the snores, the grunting and the groaning, I could hear a train rattle by. We weren't far from the railway line. There was a game I could play now, if I went about it carefully. Keeping my eyes shut, breathing deep, I dispatched myself – a free agent – by this train. I sat all alone in a clean, comfortable carriage. I was well and strong; my hair was grown; I didn't hurt anywhere. The train travelled fast on the smoothest of roadbeds. It crossed the frontier and bore me home through France; France restored, France as she used to be. I saw the vineyards and the rivers; the bright, beloved Southern landscape changing to the green of the North. The train slipped easily round the Paris *ceinture*; it stopped nowhere, it was made for me.

Silently it drew into the dockside and silently the ship that waited for me alone sailed out of harbour. I stood in the prow to see the coastline of England come. Then I could go no further.

I could go elsewhere. The deep, regular breathing had loosened the ties with my body, was sending me on my way.

Shafts of bright colour moved in through the eyelidded dark; made patterns, made pictures: until I saw a mediaeval tapestry, a neat little wood on a sudden hill, a white road curling round the base of the hill. Down the white road the gold men marched, under their flying banners, toward the city. Above them I saw the green wood and the silvery turrets of the château breaking the green. The whisper came:

Run into the wood, Thomas, run into the wood. You are still in your body and your body is still in the hut, on the floor. Rise up and out of it. Run into the wood, into the wood where the dreams are. You know the way.

I knew the way.

At first I thought I was coming up through the trees to the château, but presently I saw that the dark path was leading me to a different place. No more trees. A high stone wall confronted me and in the wall there was a solid wooden gate with a latch; rather a stiff, rusty latch; it took me a few minutes to make it work.

I walked into a paved yard. An old-fashioned carriage was standing here. It had been newly painted, with a shiny black top and yellow panels; its gleaming red shafts rested on the flagstones. Its lamps were alight. The carriage diverted me immensely. It gave me more than pleasure: it was a clue. I came on, to three steps, with a door at the top of the steps.

The notice on the door read ARTISTES ONLY. I went in.

At once I found myself in the second theatre; as I had begun to suspect I would. It was a long time since I had been here. Nothing was changed. It was still the black-ribbed hall – friendly, smoky, a little haphazard and amateurish, with its stage in the centre like a boxing-ring and the seats all round.

As usual there was a row going on about the lights. I could see the producer (a new one by the looks of him) pointing up at the network of bizarre machinery that dangled above the ring; I could hear him yelling at the men in charge. Though this place is emphatically second-best, a poor substitute for the first theatre – which one cannot find from here – I was glad to be back.

The house was pretty full. Facetious shouts greeted me as I came down the aisle. "Look who's come!" "Late again!" "Poor old Thomas . . ." "Dozy individual, he always was." "Got your script?" "Oh dear me no, he dropped his script in the river – with his boots." "You're going to catch it, you are," said my friend the London taxi-driver. I was, indeed. I hadn't lost the script; here it was, tucked under my arm: but I ought to have learned my lines long ago. I'd had weeks in which to study them and I didn't know a word.

I was, however, cheered by seeing that the new producer looked comparatively harmless. They are tricky customers. Sometimes their hostility is just a pretence; sometimes it is the real thing and then you have to watch out; they can order you as they please. This one wore khaki; cavalry uniform with breeches and gaiters. He had a red, bullfrog face and he kept hitting his legs with a silly little cane. His badgered, bewildered voice rose as I reached the ringside.

"I don't know what you fellows think you're playing at. In my young day —"

"Good Lord," I said to myself, "It's Uncle Percy." At the sight of him as producer I couldn't help grinning, though the look he gave me now was deeply reproachful.

"So there you are. About time too. What account can you give of yourself?" When I hesitated, because I hadn't a clue as to what I'd been doing all this time, he said "Oh do get on, Thomas. You know there has to be an account, that's the drill."

I said, "It never was, in my young day." The whole audience laughed and clapped: I felt I was being rather mean to Uncle Percy.

"Well, you can come up and shake hands, can't you?" he grumbled, "'least you can do . . . I suppose you've lost your regiment."

"No, not exactly. It's lost me."

There was more clapping and somebody cheered. Uncle Percy sat down on a stool by the ropes. He took off his cap and wiped his forehead with a large silk handkerchief.

"Better start with the dog scene," he said wearily, "Hadn't you?"

"He can't do that," a voice shouted from the front row, "No dogs allowed!" A chorus took it up: "That's right, no dogs!" "Positively no dogs!" "Says so on the programme, plain as plain – no dogs!" "Not the dogs!" they all chorused, "Not the dogs!"

I realized that they were on my side; they were trying to protect me from something. Which was nice of them, though I didn't know what the danger might be. But they were wrong: my script proved them wrong: it had to be the dog-scene. In fact (as often happens here when the sequence skids) the scene was already playing. Under a shaky barrage of lights, the Countess, wearing her harlequin dress, stood holding Teruel on his leash. Beside her Rab the child, the small girl who looked like a boy, the skinny ragamuffin dressed in blue shirt and trousers, was grasping Tylo by his collar. Uncle Percy had left the stool. It was I who sat here, to judge the dogs.

"Let them go, please," I said, "Let them come to me." I had a long speech after that, but I cut it because the dogs came bounding, and I hugged them close. There was a tender, exquisite pleasure in this. I sat with my arms about them. I stroked Teruel's black silk head and Tylo's feathery crown. I looked into their eyes; their eyes pleaded with me. "Two first prizes," I said to them.

"Utterly ridiculous. There can't be *two* first prizes," said the Countess indignantly.

"Sure, there can," said the child Rab, "'Got to be two. Poor old Thomas can't choose; he never could, see?"

"He *must* choose," said the Countess: she glared at me: "Your cue, Justin."

I'd forgotten my next line. There was too long a pause while I leafed through the script: I could feel the stillness of the audience waiting. I couldn't find the right page; I kept saying, "Sorry," but the notion came to me that I should be sorrier when I did find it. Now the audience began a slow handclap, shouting, "Prizes! Prizes! Two first prizes!"

"Really it's quite absurd," said the Countess.

The lights dimmed down. Behind me a voice of authority, a producer's voice, that was not Uncle Percy's any more, said, "Bring on the prizes." There was a quiet, crunching menace in that voice. I glanced up from the script to see the child Rab handing me two long wooden boxes. There were no lids on the boxes. The child looked pale and frightened; she did not smile. She backed away from me.

I had found the cue. I read the stage-direction.

"The prizes," the script said, "are two pistols." Now I had them in my hands. I looked at the dogs, lying close to my feet. Teruel gave his eyebrow-twitch and Tylo wagged his plumy tail.

"What are you waiting for?" the producer asked. He was one I knew, the executioner with the black mask; leaning upon his axe. I didn't answer him. The audience, I could feel, were ceasing to be my friends. A hostile murmur came up all over the second theatre.

I knew what I had to do. It was clearly printed in the script.

"Get on with it," said the producer. He signalled to the boys overhead. They manoeuvred the single spot until they had it focussed upon the dogs. From the dark beyond, the murmur changed to a roar. I could hear the child sobbing, "Don't do it, oh please don't do it."

"He has no choice," the producer said. He stepped closer to me; I stood up, with a pistol in each hand. Obeying the script I whistled one note to the dogs and they lifted their heads, alert for my shots that would kill them both.

"Take aim," the man in the mask was saying. "On the word of command, you will shoot. The word of command is Fire."

It was then I knew that none of this need happen. I could do a thing I had never done before. I could stop the play. The knowledge came in one triumphant blink.

"Fire!"

I hurled the pistols across the ring and out through the ropes. I picked up my script and tore it in two. I heard the child laughing; I saw the dogs bounding free; they vanished into their freedom. I stood alone.

The crowd, turned enemy, rushed upon me, roaring. As they engulfed the stage I ducked through the ropes and ran. I was singing as I ran: *"Merrily, merrily, shall I live now."* Merrily, merrily . . . Running on, running up to the back of the hall, brushing through curtains that parted upon a flight of wide blue steps – the blue staircase. I had looked for this way before, I thought, and never found it.

I was gliding, rather than running, up the steps. They led straight into the first theatre.

I was standing in the blue corridor, up at the back of the steeply-shelving boxes, in the calm glow of the house-lights that never go down. The voice of a custodian spoke to me instantly:

"How did you find the way?"

As is usual here, I couldn't see him; I merely heard his voice. I said, "It was easy, this time."

"Easy?"

"Oh well . . . not really difficult."

He was silent. I made my way into the first box and down the blue slope toward the front seats. How long since I last got here? *Far too long, and there is still the same magic, the baffling ecstasy, the knowledge that nothing awaits me – or everything.*

"Hullo," they said.

"Hullo," said I.

"For once you're in time."

"In time for the play?"

"Well . . . in time for the interval. This is the interval."

"How long does it last?"

That made them laugh softly. They are different from the ones down below; more sophisticated, with quieter manners; friendly, but a little remote. We have all known one another for years and we don't need names.

"It lasts till it stops, of course," somebody said.

"And, being an interval, it must stop," somebody else pointed out. "That's one thing you can be sure of."

I moved to the very edge of the box. There is no rail. You look down and down to the merest thin slice of the stage itself. You cannot see the play from here. If you could see, you would know the answer. It has always been like that.

"Curtain going up," a custodian's voice announced. Somebody said "That's quick." Then the custodian spoke again:

"You, there."

"Me?" I knew he meant me. My eyes were fixed far down where the curtain mounted slowly beneath the gilt border.

"You, there. Stand back."

"Must I?"

"Certainly you must. Nobody ever stands where you're standing, you know that."

"Oh, please."

"Not allowed," he said, "We can't allow it. You might be able to see."

I could almost see. It was like a magnet, the pull of the lights and the moving shapes, the faintly-rising voices. I'd never heard the players speaking before. It was the best ever tonight, and I wasn't going to be moved; not even by a custodian.

"You could fall, you know," somebody reminded me.

No . . . not fall, I thought, if I took one more step I should not fall; I should simply be down there, on the stage. I would become part of the play. I knew that this was pledged to happen to me sometime. I hadn't, so far, been aware of the pledge.

"Oh sorry," said the custodian's voice: "'Didn't realize it was you. You can stay where you are this time. It's your turn."

THE LONGEST WAY

THEY CAME OUT OF THE TIGHT EMBRACE. SARAH SAID, "SORRY to cry, it's just I'm so *damn* glad to see you" and Rab said "More than I deserve," sounding shaken, humble, most unlike herself.

"Let me look at you."

"Don't," said Rab quickly. One saw why she said that. She looked older by ten years. The body was all bones. The face had thinned and hardened. There was no *beauté de diable* left, only the enduring light in the blue eyes.

What have they been doing to you? "Oh Rab, darling Rab, however did you find me?"

"Your British Repatriation Office. Not my own idea, suggestion made by kind gentleman escort. On the train. 'Tell you about him . . . not now. Kind of a forlorn hope, I thought. Couldn't imagine you'd still be here."

"She get a boat soon," José interrupted.

"That for a story. Tell me all, all, all. I'd given you up."

"Don't blame you." Her shyness, the old shyness of Rab the child, was upon her. Sarah had forgotten it: here was the slouching withdrawal; the eyes looking away. "Excuse these clothes," Rab said, "All I possess aside from uniform: and the uniform's a dead duck. That's my luggage." She made a gesture with one foot: a bulging kitbag leaned drunkenly against the bar. "Think they'll give me a bed here?"

"They'll have to. A bed in my room, most likely." *It is the end of loneliness, it is the end of limbo, Rab has come. Thank you, God.*

"Could we drink in your room? We could? Fine. Nice knowing you, Mister," she said to José, who bowed and beamed.

Sarah sat in the chair beside her window, looking out – almost with affection – on the ostrich-plumed palm-tree and the red roofs of the Atlantico. Rab refused to sit: having swallowed her drink in one long gulp, she paced the floor, smoking furiously: "Haven't had a cigarette since I can remember. Gentleman escort's a non-smoker so I couldn't bum any off him."

"Who is he?"

"Tell you," Rab said again.

"You're so thin."

"Nothing the matter with me that a week's eating won't cure. Good food on the train, though. They pulled down all the shades in the dining-car when we got to the Spanish frontier. Too tough a sight for the starving Spaniards to take, they said. What about that? Tell about you . . ."

"What is there to tell? I'm just a victim of the great Lisbon baffle – like everyone else. I'm about the three-hundred-and-fiftieth in line for a boat."

"Not a plane?"

"There aren't any. Or not for the likes of me. When the boat does sail – if ever – it takes five weeks. Down to Gibraltar and then a convoy. For all the good I'm doing, I might as well have stayed in America."

"But you wouldn't have," Rab said quickly. "Would you now. You *couldn't* . . ." She halted in her pacing. She spoke emphatically as though she knew about all of it; about the tortured threshing, the surrender to fear, the dead person living in the black glass house.

She could not possibly know these things. Sarah said, "Why do you say it like that?"

Rab lit another cigarette from the stump of the old one. "I don't see how anybody could stand America now. I'll find out, I guess."

"When do you sail?"

"No idea. I have to stand in line, like you."

"Where have you been all this time?"

Rab puffed at the cigarette.

"*Weeks* since you wrote saying you were coming home – months – it must be nearly two months. The letter got there before I sailed."

265

Rab sat on the bed, hunching herself up, nursing one skeleton knee. She said, "All the others went home; the whole outfit folded – mainly for lack of money. Lisa Groves – remember? – wanted to keep the welfare work going; God knows it's needed. She's back in America now, trying to raise funds. And not getting any place. They can't see over there that helping France doesn't mean helping Germany. I could have gone with her. She wanted me to." Rab gave a lop-sided grin. "What a hope *she* had. All I wanted was to get to England. We fought about that. Lisa still thinks the British let her beloved French down – get it?"

"I get it. You'll hear the same now and again in New York – and points West."

"What does one do? Kick their teeth in?"

"Did you kick Lisa's teeth in?"

"I didn't have to. She yielded. She latched me on to the Red Cross in Paris: volunteer work, of course; she had to stake me. I only let her do it on account I was so sure I'd get my British permit; the Paris job was just a standby till it came through. And it didn't. I got a two-way brush-off. The British won't use me and the State Department turned down my application. So . . . well, you can guess it, can't you? I quit."

Rab always escapes; I just run away. Her own words, a long time ago . . . She said, "Wouldn't Paris have been better than going home – feeling the way you feel?"

Rab jumped off the bed. "Like hell it would. You haven't seen Paris. Keeping up *la politesse* with the goddamned Germans . . . I don't know how the others manage to make it – I can't. I ran out on it as soon as I found my chances of England were screwed. That was when I wrote to Paula . . ."

"But what have you been doing since?"

"Oh well." The echo of Thomas was loud, but there was nothing of Thomas in Rab's manner: she slouched and paced, heavy with a secret: she had no skill for this. The secret was making its statement all over the air.

"Dodging my way through France," she said at last. "Into the *Zone Libre*. Quite a trick. Though any American's safe enough: you

266

just wave your passport and your papers and make the story up as you go along."

"Good God! You were taking chances, weren't you?"

"Sure. But I had to." The flash of a smile that followed was unconvincing: "Just a place I had to get to. And I got there. And that's all."

"No, it isn't."

"What d'you mean, no, it isn't?"

"There's something more – something that hurts," Sarah said.

"So what if it does? Hurting's no problem."

"All right . . . If you have to be so grown-up . . . I rather think you have grown up."

"Let's hope," said Rab soberly: "What happened next wasn't grown-up at all. I was darn hungry; and I'd come mighty near the end of Lisa's money. So the jig was up. The only place to go was the U.S. Embassy: in Vichy. Vichy, imagine. In a German staff-car. I hitched a ride. And if you don't think I'm ashamed of *that*. One of them made a pass, too."

"Honestly —" said Sarah.

"What's that mean – honestly?"

"Just you . . . The little Turk, Brigstock used to say. How did the Embassy react?"

"Blew me sky-high. I couldn't make out if I was an international incident or just a candidate for reform-school. Anyway, I was fixed up with a Portuguese transit-visa and put on a train. In charge of the nice gentleman. He's our military attaché and a perfect sweetheart. He's flying home. Said he'd try to wangle me a place on the Clipper and lent me fifty bucks – strictly off the record. But some sort of memo about me went off from Vichy to Washington; you can be certain I don't rate the Clipper. Which is one comfort."

"Comfort?"

"Sure." Rab came to hug her. "All I want is to stick around with you."

"Something I must ask you."

"Go ahead." Rab released her and stood away, in the old childish attitude, ready for punishment.

"Was it anything to do with Thomas – the place you had to get to?"

"Ah no." She drooped, looking utterly miserable.

"*Would* you have married him, Rab?"

There was a short silence before Rab said, "He mightn't have wanted to marry me."

"Oh, don't be an ass."

"People change – in wars."

"Not Thomas."

"Ah, damn it, I'll have to tell you. Now I see you I see that."

"Tell me what?"

Rab was prowling again: "Never told anybody, never thought I would. But with you," she swung around and stared. "With you I feel . . . what? False. Under false pretences. I can't take the feeling." She lit another cigarette: "You aren't going to like me much, Sarah."

❀ ❀ ❀

"And then . . ."

Rab halted at the ashtray. The sound of her own voice seemed to have been going on a long time: with Sarah still sitting in the chair: with the next cigarette and the next walk to the ashtray, the butts piling up: with the maddening invasions from outside (the spare bed hauled in, the kitbag carried by José, Sarah saying, "What about another drink?", Sarah sending José down to the bar; herself stooping over the kitbag, lifting things out, stowing them). This was not the unbroken monologue she was used to, the monologue at midnight, alone.

And then . . .

"I didn't go down to the pavilion. I hadn't truly made up my mind, one way or another. I guess the day made it up for me. First we were delayed at St. Anne. The usual crossed wires; the depot wasn't expecting the stores for another week. They had to make room. Unloading took forever. Then the Mammoth played hell on the way back and I had to fix it single-handed; Roberts was no

268

mechanic. It was nearly midnight when we got to Vaillancourt. All I wanted was sleep.

"I knew I wouldn't have to explain, Noel wasn't one for explanations. Brousse told me she'd come up once during the evening to see if we were back. Nothing odd about it, Noel was in command after all.

"But I don't like knowing she did that.

"It was four a.m. when the racket woke me up. The fire-party had never been called out before so they were slow getting under way. I wasn't on fire-duty, I just went along as soon as they said the pavilion.

"I'll skip how it looked. We went in as soon as we could. She had never woken up at all. She was still lying in bed. The fire hadn't touched her; she was suffocated by the smoke. 'Two pills, or possibly three' – well, so you wouldn't wake up. Lisa was always fussing at her about that fire-guard. Lisa was right."

No mercy now, on the child crying inside, no mercy. The spoken verdict was, she found, as final as the verdict given alone and silently.

"I helped Noel to die. If I'd gone down she could still be alive. You needn't argue; I've had it out with myself and I know the answer."

"I won't argue. I helped Romney to die. A little, I helped. By not being there. It is the worst."

"I guess it would be, if one bore it in mind." She stooped again over her kitbag: "At the time I thought the worst was going back to Vaillancourt."

"And I thought I knew all about death . . . Why 'going back'? What happened?"

"I was sent away right after the fire. Lisa Groves posted me to the depot in Haute-Vienne. Lisa must have guessed about me and Noel. She's a clam, she wouldn't say it, but she posted me. Kindly meant. And I didn't get back till after the Armistice. Idiotic to volunteer for the clean-up job. I had to, somehow. Vaillancourt changed hands three times in the fighting and they were saying it was unrecognizable. Six of us went. It was worse than the hottest bombardment, driving across that appalling, smashed-up landscape, feeling the place come nearer. And it was triple hell, getting there."

Her hands were busy with a confusion of small souvenirs. She was looking at her driving-licence, *Carte de Circulation Temporaire*, the pink paper with a snapshot of her own face in the lower left-hand corner and the stamp, *Validité Prorogée Trois Mois*. She tore it in half.

"You couldn't see an inch of ground anywhere for the layers of filth and debris . . . Kind of battlefield in the middle of the battle-fields. We had to dig it out. I still dream about it. All the damn weapons lying around – pistols, grenades, bayonets . . . old uniforms rotting. Steel helmets. German orders, French orders, painted on walls. Doors and windows gone. Machine-gun nests built in the gardens. Filth beyond belief; stray cats and dogs flickering about. And rats – and flies. The nastiest dream is the one where I'm still cleaning those clogged-up cans."

She stared vaguely at the ignition-keys of a truck that had burned out somewhere on the road from Paris; she threw them into the wastepaper-basket. Here was a shell-splinter; here a German lighter that didn't work any more.

"All the time I felt as if Noel were buried underneath. Which was insane. The grave's on the other family estate, south of Limoges." She laughed her hard, routine laugh at the capacity of Noel for causing disruption even in death: the coffin flown by the French Air Force; the escort, all the privileged complexity set in motion by Noel's will. "That's where I had to get to, Sarah, to her grave. I'd promised. It's a good place to lie." Her hands paused in their work. She saw the walled plot and the trees; the rising ground where the new turf still made its clear-cut shape; her mind was debating, as it had debated before, whether Noel might, by some miracle, have known she was walking there. ("Come and slouch by my grave" . . . *No mercy now, no mercy for the child who goes on sobbing with its knuckles in its eyes.*)

"Nice grave," she said, "I should know. Helped to dig a few in my time. Those Germans took trouble: they even brought their own crosses along, truck-loads of them, all ready. But the French left their dead where they fell."

She put aside a pair of shoulder-flashes, red eagles on white, and a cap-badge; she hesitated a moment, then dropped them into the wastepaper-basket. "Glad Noel *didn't* change that instruction in her will. She meant to. Glad she's not at Vaillancourt. She'd be down in the vault with the ruins of the chapel piled on top. A shell blew it to bits and they haven't shifted the rubble. Maybe they will, one day."

Across distances, the voice of Sarah was saying "You are good. And brave."

"Thanks. 'Not sure I believe you, but thanks all the same."

"There's no such thing as comfort. Kipling put it better. 'There is no anodyne for pain.'"

"Sure, there is. You just stop thinking."

"Can one?"

"I can. I have." She pulled the stained, beat-up copy of *John Brown's Body* from the kitbag and slammed it on to the table. To the gentle voice asking, "Have you still got the wooden cherub?" she snapped, "Never saw it again. Guess Noel took it back down to the pavilion after all. May have had a re-think. Or a touch of absent-mindedness. Doesn't matter." She rolled up the kitbag. "*Things* don't matter. Thomas always thought they did, bless him. Still got his lion, the silver lion with one eye; he'd be glad about that. Remember thinking so, at the time."

"Where were you – at the time?"

"When I heard about him? Still on the clean-up job. Paula's cable came through the Embassy at Vichy." Briskly she reviewed the moment in her mind. *No mercy, now.* "At least he didn't have to know," she said. "Sorry you had to."

"You loved him." Only the words were accusing, not the tone.

"I loved him. I'd have loved Noel more, though, given half a chance. I have to make that clear, even if it makes you hate me."

"No hate," Sarah said, "how could there be?"

"Oh, well."

"Probably just what he'd say if you could have told him – 'oh well'. Did you get the letter Philip wrote? About his will? He left his animals to Brigstock. Gerald and I get his books. The money, whatever there is, is for you. And the notebooks, but only if you want them. He didn't have anything much to leave."

"Things," Rab said again. "Yes, I got the letter."

> *We talk of the dead, we write of the dead,*
> *We send their things to their people when we can find them,*
> *We write letters to you about them, we say we liked him,*
> *He fought well, he died bravely, here is his sword,*
> *Here is his pistol, his letters, his photograph case;*
> *You will like to have these things, they will do instead.*

She was thinking it, not saying it. Sarah might have caught the echo, murmuring "You aren't all that detached, you know. You aren't nearly as resigned as you sound."

"Who is?" Rab mocked.

"I can understand about loving a woman. I never have, since I grew up. But I can imagine it. I don't think sex is as clear cut as people try to make out. All one's first loves are for one's own sex anyway."

"Yeah, I should know. You were mine. At Sawcombe. I'd have died for you. Too bad I couldn't die for Noel or Thomas."

"Nobody," said Sarah, "can die for anybody else, more's the pity."

No. And the child inside, the child who can't take that, can't take anything, goes on crying its eyes out. And comes a little too near. Maybe because I said 'Sawcombe', I am back with her, looking at you and Gerald for the first time, at the table where Thomas and I ate ice-cream. Thinking how beautiful you are. I'm the child on the cliff, hiding in the grass, spying upon you all. I'm the outsider, the worshipper, the one who longed to be like the Westons, who knew she never could, and tried to swagger it off.

"What are you looking at?" Sarah asked.

"Looking inwards again, bad habit, legacy from April. No – partly looking at you." She stared at the dark-eyed, compassionate face before she made her plea.

"Sarah, I have to be tough, d'you understand? You're much more intelligent than I am, you always were. You can be kind of intelligently sad. You can talk about it, think about it, brood on it – maybe because you believe in God. I can't. I have to pack it

272

all away – rattle along. Remember my telling you I'd never had to get over anything? Well, this is the only way I can do it. Only way I can work. What I mean is," he took Sarah's hand, grasping it tightly, "I'm slamming the door on all that, here and now. I won't talk again – and you mustn't, d'you mind? Talk about Thomas all you like, but not about Noel. Ever."

MILES

THE FAT MAN WALKED THANKFULLY OUT OF THE STATION, carrying his small, anonymous suitcase. Six o'clock of a December evening: he stood for a moment enamoured by the return to a city of lights: Lisbon, he reflected, as the dazzle hurt his eyes, was the lucky place. He reflected further, passing a shop window full of half-forgotten temptations, that he had lost twelve pounds in weight.

At the garage, Sebastian remarked upon this.

"Well, what do you expect?" Miles asked. "There's nothing much to eat between here and Switzerland. I only had twenty-four hours in Switzerland."

"Paris?"

"Paris starves. Outside the restaurants, that is."

"Why weren't you eating in the restaurants?"

"My German friends aren't all that generous."

"But you did good business?"

"I made a bit of money," said Miles, "What's money? I always make money. I'll put that battery in myself, if you don't mind."

While he restored his car to life, Sebastian said, "Cecile was telephoning."

"You bet."

"She'll be glad you're back."

"She will. But it'll take me a week to prove it to her. How was her temper?"

"Not good," said Sebastian, "She's had a lot of worry. First there was some fellow at your house making enquiries."

Miles grunted. He wasn't going to be drawn. "Then there was this rumour about Hitler walking in. Everybody heard it."

"Walking in where?"

"Into Portugal, naturally."

"By-passing Spain on the way, I suppose. The older I get, the less anybody makes any sense." He continued his meticulous examination: the car was in good order. He checked the mileage with the figure written in his notebook: correct; nobody had been joy-riding in his absence. "But your bill is out by roughly a thousand escudos." he told Sebastian.

"No it isn't. Prices are up. Everywhere. You'll soon see. We've got a floating population of fifty thousand refugees. Or that's what the paper says. Lisbon's the cross-roads of the world, it said that too."

"Just the way it was when I left."

"Only ten times more so. For one thing the U.K. traffic's at a standstill. The Americans' fault: they went on pouring people in by the Clipper and the Export Line until they bogged down. British Airways can't get them off the ground and there's about one boat leaving a month."

"Who wants to get to England anyway? England's finished."

Sebastian gave him a look that warned him he might be over-doing his bluff; then asked, "Going to stay a while, now?"

"Going to mind my own business, like other people should, and that's a precept, not just a counsel," Miles said. He handed over the money, aware that Sebastian was much interested in his wallet.

"Don't seem to have lost any weight there," said Sebastian.

"*Até logo*," said Miles.

"You aren't going to call Cecile? She wants —"

"I'll be seeing her," said Miles. "But not yet," he added to himself, turning the car in the direction of the Aviz Hotel. There was just one hurdle ahead, before he met the gale-force of Cecile's temper. Thinking about the hurdle, he could almost look forward to the temper. He didn't blame Cecile. She had loved the farm: she despised the factory. And she was outraged by the notion of all those sardines going down Boche gullets. "So'm I, come to that," he thought, "But – like they say – the end justifies the means. Makes the money, and gives me my cover, what more can one ask?" Life treated one as well as could be expected, with a war going on. "And this war will keep right on going on till the Americans come in. That's for sure."

America brought him inevitably to the Weston family, and to Thomas – his one black grief. His heart went down. When he thought of the men come safely home via Dunkirk, when he thought of Cecile's non-stop Novenas, he felt like cursing God. It wasn't fair that Thomas should be the one to get himself killed.

While he drove he saw, sitting beside him on the front seat, the small boy wearing a tweed cap shaped like a mushroom, the small boy who had run away. Thomasinho . . . (Run forever now, away and out of sight.)

"May he rest in peace. I'm getting old. What I need is a drink. And what I *don't* need —" he told himself, parking outside the Aviz, "is what I'm liable to find." With any luck, of course, she would be gone already. But his hunch said No; and his hunches were reliable. He groaned inside. He cruised quickly through the foyer, keeping his head low. He made for the bar.

The bar gave his eyes a consoling welcome. It was decorated in dark red, it had a high ceiling, a grandiose air. On one wall a plaque recorded the beginning of Lisbon's immediate history: the first Transatlantic Clipper flight, with the signatures of pilot, passengers and crew.

The cream of the cross-roads drank here; Englishmen from the Foreign Office and the Food Mission, Embassy types; trading types; privileged travellers, their warring or peaceful nationalities instantly recognizable, Miles thought. He picked them up with his eyes, one by one, making his routine diagnoses. There were more men than women; only a few women, and the dreaded figure not among them. He couldn't help staring at the women because of their clothes; their lush, sprightly elegance. He hadn't seen a well-dressed woman for weeks. He leaned on the bar, and the barman said, "Well, well . . . Look who's here. Get your message?"

"What message?"

"At the desk, let us say." His big mouth and his little eyes were thoroughly mischievous. Miles said, "I haven't been to the desk."

"*Nao faz mal;* I can tell it to you."

"It's a drink I want."

"Excuse me. Yes, sir? What would you like?" In his maddening, obsequious way, he was giving the cream of the cross-roads priority. Miles studied this one. Tall: a thin, amiable face; square shoulders. At a guess, he would be back in uniform as soon as the British Airways plane touched down.

Miles prided himself on the accuracy of his guesses. Observation was the business of the scout; and he knew his business. A scout, as he had explained frequently (and uselessly) to Cecile, was not a spy. Spying was something else again. There was no danger for a scout, free to travel – though not by the sky-roads or sea-roads the cream of the cross-roads took.

He, Miles, was only a neutral *commerçant*, with good German connections, speaking five languages, crossing frontiers on his own legitimate affairs; watching, observing, reporting back. He reported nothing spectacular; no military secret; merely the way people were talking and living, under Nazi occupation. The picture had its uses for the British. If you were clever you could find much they wanted to know. And he was clever; far too clever for his German friends: who suspected nothing. They liked him and trusted him. The Germans, he said to himself again and again, are the stupidest people in the world.

The British customer carried his drink away. The barman grinned at Miles. "What's it to be? I advise you to make it a strong one."

"She's here?"

"She's here."

"I knew it."

"But you're only just in time. She sails tomorrow."

"Tomorrow . . . that's a laugh," said Miles bitterly. "One more day on the road . . . oh well, like they say, one can't be lucky all the time. A double whisky. She's been entertaining you, I hope. Did you say she *sails*? Not the Clipper?"

The barman chuckled happily. "Not the Clipper. Not even the Export Line. The only boat that'll let her keep the dog in her cabin is the old 'Serpa'. And if you think that's reconciled her to us Portuguese, you're wrong. She's torn the whole city apart. Not to mention this hotel. Up till today she had to sleep in the writing-room; with two other ladies; didn't mind for herself, of course, only for the dog."

"When I get to wondering why she doesn't marry that dog," said Miles, "I can only conclude it's because the dog never asked her." He gulped his whisky.

The barman said, "Well – glad you're here."

"More than I am."

"She's been threatening me with the custody of some precious document or other. To be handed to you personally. Excuse me." He dealt with a priority customer and came back. "She was on about it again before lunch. Urgent, vital, matter of life and death."

"Oh certainly," said Miles. "I can guess. An order for sardines. To be sent to some fat-arse in the Spanish hierarchy; cheque enclosed." He spun the empty glass across the counter. "You can fill that up again."

The barman pursed his thick lips: "I think it was something more serious. She wouldn't trust it to your wife. Only to me."

"Why you?"

"Well, I happen to like dogs. I took trouble with the dog's food, she appreciated that. And she said you were bound to look in here; this was your last rendezvous. Mind you, I think she's given you up."

"Fair enough. I gave her up a long time ago." He swallowed the second drink and lit a cigar. "The writing-room, you said?"

"Not any more. You'll find her in the suite."

"Which suite?"

"*The* suite . . . of course."

Miles knew what he meant. He wondered how much the Countess had paid. Perhaps it wasn't a matter of money but of pure attrition. After all, she had been here – God help the management – for three weeks.

When an idol fell, he thought, it fell with a crash and left regrettable splinters lying around. He had met this experience before, though never on quite so large a scale. He was, by nature, a prey to heroine-worship. "My little mania," he called it. As a hired chauffeur, he had found ample opportunities for indulging the little mania: the recurrent need to put one of his employers, a woman of superior class, on a pedestal; to adore her and make himself her slave. Cecile knew about the little mania. Cecile – rightly – called it idiotic.

Miles finished his drink and turned from the bar. He said a grim goodnight to the barman. His mind was revisiting past excursions.

He looked back to his first heroine: Paula Weston; Paula Lee, she was, then. As an idol, Paula had never toppled: he had merely been obliged to replace her when their lives went separate ways. After that . . . He saw a White Russian princess, with jet-black hair, in Monte Carlo. She had stolen his favourite lighter. He saw a languid lily from Georgia, heir to two fortunes; with a nice, tame-cat husband and a summer palace at Antibes. She had fallen flat on her back, drunk as an owl, leaving the Palm Beach Casino. He saw an Ambassador's widow; she had given him an unseemly commission concerned with a parcel of cocaine. He saw the wife of an English Earl. Here he got no further; because the Earl's wife was, naturally, a Countess; and this was where the last of his idols had fallen with such a hideous bang.

He would not forget the moment. It had come on the June day when she completed her whirlwind plans to buy the villa at Anthèor. (The Twenty-nine villa, in Thomas's language.) Miles had driven her up to the Château de Madrid, her favourite restaurant for its obvious Spanish association. She had insisted on his sharing a bottle of champagne before her guests arrived. She sat at the table, leafing through the monstrous bill of sale, signing here, initialling a clause there. He had watched her write "Dorothea, Countess" and she had caught him watching. She had given him her bright, foxy smile, saying "It *is* a pretty name, isn't it?"

"Dorothea – gift of God – sure, my Lady, what could be prettier?"

"I don't mean 'Dorothea', I mean 'Countess.' Do you suppose anybody's ever been christened 'Countess' before? My mother thought it was pretty – that was the Irish in her – Countess Cathleen – the Abbey Theatre – Yeats – Lady Gregory. And it amused my father because Countess was the name of his best brood mare."

It had taken Miles ten minutes and two glasses of champagne to assimilate the fact. She wasn't a Countess at all: this was no title, this was just a name. He had sat there, stunned, listening to the prattle: "Nobody knows – even my husband didn't know . . . I've never told a soul. That I tell *you*, Miles, is the proof of how much I trust you. I know you'll keep it locked inside." She added, "Wonderfully useful, I've always found it. Particularly in Spain."

It was a blow – the blow that rocked the pedestal. From that moment onwards she had begun to bore Miles to death. He was bored by her panache, by her whims, her tantrums, by all that had beguiled him as authentic signs of blue blood. She was a commoner: she was a tyrant: she was stupid. She was only another of the many rich dumb-bells whom he had deplored as he drove them up and down the coast of pleasure. On top of this she had the impertinence to be a Fascist. He could tolerate her devotion to Franco just so long as she had the excuse of her ancestry. A lot of blue-blooded fools were Fascist for this reason. Now there was no reason; not even her Faith: she had let that slide (worshipping Teruel instead? He often wondered). He could tolerate a lapsed aristocrat. A lapsed fake was another matter altogether.

She had killed the last crumb of his loyalty when war was declared: writing from the villa, "Sensible, sophisticated neutrals like you and me."

And she was without shame. Even after his discreetly insulting reply she had continued to write to him: letters that were a doom: letters that always got through, despite his pretence of not receiving them. She persisted in loading him with her pompous, autocratic plans for departure to America. *"You must meet me somewhere near the border."* As though the world were still as it once was; as though he were still at her service. She recognized no change, no obstacle. Somehow she managed to win. At the last *poste restante* where he called on his travels, he had found a fat envelope addressed in her handwriting. He felt no better for tearing it up without reading the contents.

She was still winning. Miles paused at the door of the suite, to wonder why his conscience brought him this far. She was sailing tomorrow. A bribe to his friend the barman, and she need never know he had been here. "I'm too soft – always been my trouble," he decided, "Too much heart . . . too sensitive."

He saw what he had expected to see; the glories of the suite half-hidden by the luggage that looked as though six people were travelling: four upstanding Vuitton trunks with the flower design; suitcases of brown calfskin; suitcases of white rawhide; a canvas bag; a wicker hamper; her sewing machine. At his feet an old-fashioned dressing-case stood open to reveal innumerable tins of dog-food; some were secured by the straps and sockets intended for bottles or hairbrushes.

Behind her ramparts, the Countess was sitting at a table, writing. She did not raise her eyes, though Teruel barked and came rushing to the door. Miles stood where he was and fondled the dog. Teruel gave him a series of winks.

"You can put it in the bedroom," said the Countess, speaking Spanish. "Don't excite my dog, please. He's had a sedative."

"Good evening, Madame," said Miles; he left off the words "La Comtesse" just to teach her.

She raised her head. She looked startled, then amused. Her tall crown of hair had been highly gilded. Her make-up would, he knew, be too pink in daylight; under the becoming glow from the small chandeliers, it looked very well. She was wearing a white mink jacket and the fanciest of her earrings; long swinging sparklers that reminded him of decorations on a Christmas tree.

She stared at him in silence. He saw her assume the attitudes of haughty reproof; she lifted her eyebrows, her chin and her bosom. When she spoke she made her voice light, casual; as though he had just returned from some small errand: "Oh, there you are, Miles. Will you see if you can mend the lock on the dressing-case? You'll find a screw-driver on the floor. Teruel, come and lie down. He must rest," she explained. "The treatment begins the night before." She swept into the bedroom, pulling the reluctant dog. "I want him to be at his most relaxed on the journey," she said, coming back.

"This lock is broken."

"Naturally. Or I shouldn't have asked you to mend it." She billowed towards the marble mantelpiece and took up a statuesque pose. On the surface at least she was positively gleaming with good temper.

"I'm afraid this is a matter for a locksmith," said Miles.

"Well, all right. We don't embark till two p.m. Can you get a man here before that?"

"I daresay it will be possible."

"As early as you can. All the luggage is supposed to be on board by eight in the morning, not that I'm paying any attention. Ridiculous the Portuguese are . . . like Spaniards stuffed with sawdust, if one could imagine such a thing. It would be the dressing-case – the most important – Teruel's food, you see."

"I see." He put the screwdriver down. The Countess said, "Well, go on . . . Tell me things. How was your spying?" One of her great, foxy grins accompanied the question.

Miles contrived a chuckle. "You have the strangest illusions, Madame. I was selling sardines."

"And what else? You can't deceive me, you know, I can read you like a book. Not a book I'm very fond of, at the moment. Thinner, aren't you?"

"Yes."

"Sulky, too. I should have thought it was for me to sulk. Nobody has ever treated me with such rudeness . . . Teruel, how dare you?" The dog had returned briskly, prancing, ready for social contacts. "He's thin, too, don't you think? The train-journey upset him and he hasn't been right since." She pounced upon the poodle, who growled and snapped. "In the bathroom," she pleaded with him – "you *like* the bathroom. There's a black marble tub," she added to Miles. "He sits in it." She came back, shutting the door behind her. She was carrying a scent-spray. She sprayed the air vigorously. "This suite has such a queer smell. Musty . . . I think there may be something dead under the floor. Does it smell like that to you?"

"No, Madame."

"Oh I'd forgotten, – you've no olfactory sense – all those cigars. Now, Miles . . ." She seated herself again at the table where he saw documents spread far and wide. "You're an answer to my prayers. I've spoken to your wife every day. She hates me. I'm very glad you're back. Otherwise I should have had to entrust all this to that sweet barman."

"So he told me."

"Oh, he did, did he? Well, he couldn't have said what it is because he doesn't know."

"I wondered," said Miles heavily, "why you chose him."

"Because you were bound to look in here sooner or later." She nibbled a pen and narrowed her eyes. "In fact I'd begun to suspect you of waiting around on purpose till my boat had sailed."

"No, no, no," he said, rather too emphatically, he thought: "I reached Lisbon an hour ago – less. Besides, how should I hear about your sailing?"

"Well because I wrote and told you. To the address your wife gave me . . . You didn't get it?"

He shook his head.

"Are you sure?"

"Certain," said Miles, fighting his conscience.

"A letter saying I might have an important commission for you?"

"No letter. There are always hazards nowadays."

"There shouldn't be." The Countess returned to the documents. "These are nice cigars," she said, pushing a box towards him. "The management sent them up by mistake. Do have one. And sit in the armchair, it's a much better size for you, you must be tired."

"Thank you, Madame la Comtesse." He was surprised to find himself feeling more charitable. Odd, that she should improve with presence; most of the people he disliked improved with absence.

"What will you drink?" she asked, still reading busily. "Nothing? Really? Pour me a glass of white port – Thank you. What's that noise?"

"The dog is scratching at the door from the inside."

"*Teruel!*" The scratching stopped. There was a low whine and then silence. "He hates to leave Europe," she said, "So do I, really. Christmas at sea, too, which I always loathe. But there's no alternative. America's the only possible place." She took two little snapshots from an envelope, peering at them, putting them back. Then she drank her port and looked pathetic. "You should be sorry for me. I've never had a more horrid autumn. Never. And one really terrible thing happened. Which is where you come in."

"I?"

"You."

"I'm a busy man," he said quickly. "Doesn't worry me; like they say it's good to be busy; but —"

"Be quiet," said the Countess. "Listen. At the beginning of September a young man came to the villa." She drank another swallow of port, squinnying up her eyes; he mistrusted her most of all when she did that: "He was so nice. At first I thought he was a tramp, but he turned out to be a British soldier, taken prisoner by the Germans and escaped. He'd managed to get all that way . . . to the South." She paused; her eyes were practically invisible. Miles said "*Tenez*. What did you do with him?"

"I tried to help him. He was bent on getting back to his war. Idiotic, but there you are. He had no papers, no passport, nothing. Then he ran away. After three days – just walked out early one morning and disappeared. I got a note from him, sent by hand. It just said goodbye and thank you. And I found two little letters he'd written; obviously meant for his family. But I couldn't do anything about them, there were no envelopes, no addresses . . . From that day to this I've never heard a word. Except through a cousin of André – you remember André, my travel-agent?"

"No," said Miles.

"Rubbish, of course you do. This cousin saw him in Marseille. God knows why he didn't tell me he was going to Marseille; I'd have stopped him."

(Perhaps, Miles thought, that was why he didn't tell.)

"According to the cousin, he met some man he knew – unexpectedly – and they went off together. They were planning to cross the border into Spain. Of all insanity —"

Miles said, "A lot of them go that way."

"No reason for *him* – he could have waited." She drummed her fingers on the table. "After I'd warned him – *Fool*."

"Well, but maybe he's home by now. Maybe he got to Gibraltar; sounds like the kind of fellow who can look after himself."

"No," she said, "I know he's in prison somewhere – it must be Spain, it can't be anywhere else."

"How do you know?"

"I dreamed it," she said briskly, "and I've got to find out. Or rather you've got to." She gave him the haughty, reproving look again. "You see now," she said, "Don't you? If you'd only answered my letters, managed to meet me at the border, we could have done this together."

"Done what together?"

"Searched the internment camps, of course."

Miles burst into laughter.

"What's that for?"

"Excuse me, but if Madame imagines —"

"Shut up," said the Countess. "I say we could have done it together. As it is, I've managed miraculously, considering I had less than twenty-four hours in Madrid. I couldn't see the General, maddening, but I got as near the top as I could. Which is nearer than most people could. They put me on to the British Military Attaché. I was extremely firm with him. He couldn't have been more offensive or less helpful. You know, Miles, I really can't believe I have a drop of Anglo-Saxon blood. I seem to alienate them at once. Nothing to the way they alienate me."

Miles was quiet, puffing his cigar, awaiting his moment. Now she was looking sly and pleased again.

"The Spaniards were quite charming. I don't trust them a yard, of course, but I'd so much rather be cheated with charm, wouldn't you?" She began to pick up the documents one by one: "This is the order they gave me – technically a command for his release. These are the directions. Here's the map. This is the most obvious place – marked in red – the biggest camp, do you see? There are prisoners coming in there all the time. I made the Spaniards promise to send a message to the camp direct. They promised; and I don't doubt they shelved the whole matter once my back was turned. Only natural. So —" she finished her port and lit a cigarette: "It all depends on you."

Miles grinned.

"You should start tonight – or at latest tomorrow morning. You can do the journey easily in a day. Here's your *laissez-passer*. Introduction to the Commandant. Requisition-forms for petrol – ration-card, you'll need that . . . oh and two snapshots of the young man, you'll find them useful. If you draw a blank there, they suggest two other possibilities. I've written them down. Now – money." She wagged a thick envelope at him; it was sealed with gold wax. "More than enough. And half of it's in dollars, a good wheeze." She put all the documents together and slid them into a small brief-case, bright yellow imitation pigskin, obviously brand new. "I bought that here," she said, with a sigh, "I'm afraid it isn't very nice."

"Madame la Comtesse."

"Miles?"

He said, "I'm very sorry. Very sorry indeed."

"For what? For your behaviour to me? So I should hope."

"Please listen. This is a fantasy."

"Fantasy, eh?"

"Of course. Quite apart from the fact that it's none of my concern. I am not your servant."

"I don't ask you as a servant, I ask you as a friend."

"And as a friend, then, I refuse."

He expected a tornado; all he got was a smile. He said "I mean it. This is a job for an international detective, not for a fat man in late middle-age who has just returned from a very tough trip. I have my business and my family to attend to. Immediately. They are in immediate need of me, do you understand?" Though he was trying to keep calm, he felt his temper rising; helped by her obstinate smile.

"Really," he said. "You have a nerve. It is impossible. *Epouvantable – Furchtbar –* it stinks."

"I beg your pardon?" She was still smiling.

"This assumption that I'll turn straight round and go off to Spain on a wild chase-goose."

"Goose-chase," said the Countess.

"As if I didn't know. Anger mixes my words up, that's all."

"But why be angry?"

Miles shut his eyes and ground his teeth. "Okay, okay . . . So it's logical, sensible, easy . . . When you aren't even sure this fellow *went* to Spain."

"But I am, I told you, I dreamed it. He was behind a high wall, in a yard, and there was a Spanish flag somewhere. Miles, could you switch off the electric fire? It's making those little hisses and sparks, I'm sure it'll fuse in a minute."

Miles tramped to the fire and switched it off. He stood up, hands on hips.

"We don't need to talk any more," he said. "And – repeat – I'm sorry. Nothing in the world would induce me. The answer's no."

The Countess gave him her foxy grin. "Perhaps you'll change your mind when I tell you his name," she said, "I'd have told you at the beginning if you hadn't been such a beast to me."

THE LONGEST WAY

"AND TO HELL WITH HITLER!" ANOTHER GLASS, deliberately flung, crashed against the wall. "Party's getting wild," said Rab and winked at Sarah; who winked back, reflecting that the communal Christmas luncheon at the British Bar would have been unbearable but for Rab's presence. Some surprising characters were more than merry; the Scots food-expert and the neutrally-minded English girl had their arms around each other's necks. Now they were all singing again: first they sang, then they broke the glasses.

> "There'll always be an England
> Where there's a country lane!"

The Scot was bawling, "It's no' richt, it's no' richt at a'!" A strong Robert Burns accent had come upon him. "There'll always be a Br-rritain!" he sang: he went on protesting after the song ended. A clamour of voices told him to pipe down. The English girl said, "You're perfectly right, he's perfectly right – feel exactlyersame if I was Scotch, exactlyersame, who wouldn't?"

Sarah murmured thoughtfully

> "If I should die, think only this of me,
> That there's some corner of a foreign field
> That is forever Great Britain and Northern Ireland."

"Alwaysersarcastic" said the English girl. "She's alwaysersarcastic." A little old lady who lived alone in Estoril and had been invited as a mark of respect, bobbed up suddenly, crying?, "To hell with Mussolini!" as she threw her glass against the wall. Sarah made "Out" signals to Rab with her eyebrows.

As they ran downstairs they met the owner of the British Bar running up. "They've got to stop that. It's a beastly German trick, I won't have it here."

"You'd think," said Rab, "he'd mind more about the cost of the glasses. Quite an orgy. For those stuffed shirts." She was laughing. "Fun, it was."

"Fun."

"Wasn't it?"

Sarah said, "Not for me . . . Like something in a hideous movie. Christmas Day in exile – getting all patriotic and plastered."

"You didn't get plastered. Nor did I. Far too busy eating. Me – liking to eat. That I should live so long."

Rab's surface-gaiety persisted. She gave every sign of content with this precarious interval. She was, to all appearances, the person she claimed to be; one who could bury her dead and not be haunted. For two days now, she had seemed at home, amused, happy. (If one could only learn, like Rab, to prize the hour at its exact current value, disregarding the ominous trend of the market.) She had forty-seven dollars in the world and no curiosity about her future fate. She would know it, she said, soon enough. She shrugged off all obligations. She couldn't be persuaded to write to her mother. A five-word cable, *Delayed but on my way*, was, in her view, entirely adequate. She showed no curiosity about Miles, either. "I knew he'd be up to some monkey-business in this war. 'Probably walked out on Cecile for the duration. No point in my calling her."

It would be consoling, also, to see this prison, this no-man's-land, through Rab's eyes. While they walked in the winter afternoon, Rab stared happily about her. She was – Sarah knew – looking at a landscape unmarked by war, houses untouched and safe; roads where no armies had passed. A country still itself, still free was – for Rab – a marvel. She rejoiced in the absence of the hated uniform and the eternal filthy swastika. She found it hard to accustom her ear to friendly voices, voices speaking above a whisper, people who could talk without looking back fearfully over their shoulders. She lingered like a child before the shop-windows. The food, in its abundance, was the only thing that seemed to worry her. "I look at all this," Rab said, "and then I see those dam' bakers' shops with the

shutters up and the signs outside: *Pas de pain. Inutile d'insister.* And
hate myself for eating. Crazy but there it is."

Now she stared at a brown goat, chewing turnip-roots in a
garden. "You wouldn't get those in France, brother. Your master
and mistress would be eating them. And they'd have eaten you
long ago. Lucky goat. Lucky Portugal. How's about the Casino?
Seems kind of dull to go back to the hotel, after that orgy."

Sarah hesitated, uncertain whether to tell or not to tell.

"They'd surely give you a *plein* today. Christmas present. Why
not?"

"You'll say I'm a case of arrested development – Gerald's
view."

"He's a fine one to talk. What's on your mind?"

"It was in church this morning —" Sarah began. She looked back
on that hour of nostalgic peace, that illusion of homecoming.
Already it seemed a long time ago: "I was saying thank you for the
money, the roulette money. The more I've thought about it the
more it seems like a miracle. And I promised God I wouldn't
gamble again if He'd give me another miracle."

"Which was —?"

"To get me out of here."

"Well, he hasn't come across, yet, has he?" said Rab cheerfully.

"Give Him time – And I'm not going to play."

"We're only depressed because it's Boxing Day," said the
neutrally-minded girl in a loud voice, "Boxing Day always *was*
depressing. If we were in England now, we'd all be depressed."

As a rallying-cry, it lacked something. The line of fellow-prisoners
in their deck-chairs exchanged weary glances. Sarah went on reading her letter. "Patience," Dick Abrahams wrote, "is a virtue I
neither possess nor approve; so be as impatient as you like. Have you
tried grumbling at God? I once got a fifty-to-one winner that way."
(She could see his face as he said it, the face with the knobbed forehead and the amber eyes.)

Beside her, Rab sprawled, lazily contemplating the garden. The English girl, unconscious of her effect, pressed on:

"I don't really see what we've got to complain of. We're jolly lucky. Here we are in the sun . . . The *sun* . . . Doesn't anybody want to come for a walk?"

Nobody did. Presently she remarked to the silence, "I know this won't be popular, but really we're none of us trying to make the best of it. And we ought to try. I mean – we're all in the same boat."

"In the same *what*?" Sarah asked coldly. This appeared to restore morale. At the derisive chorus, the neutrally-minded girl blushed an angry red. José came out through the glass doors. His smile, Sarah saw, was splitting his face in half this morning. He halted in front of her chair. "Mrs. Butler, I speak to you by yourself, please?" was enough to bring them all to attention.

Inside the glass doors, he said, "It is you. I am so glad. Only you."

"Only me what?"

"You go home. You have a boat."

"Come off it," said Sarah.

"Repatriation Office on telephone," said José, "Means boat."

She heard her diminished voice reminding him, "You know you're not supposed to . . ." but the words trailed away. She walked to the back of the hall and picked up the telephone.

"Mrs. Romney Butler? Would you come in this morning, please? As soon as you can. And bring your passport. Not a word now," the gay governess added, "Not to anybody. That's very important."

Turning, Sarah saw that Rab had joined José. Rab said, "Is it it?" José said "You take the train or I call taxi?"

"A taxi. And it's nothing to do with – what you were talking about," she croaked at him. "They have some letters for me."

"I am to be trusted," he told her, still grinning widely. He went to the telephone.

"Rab – quick, go and tell them a story while I get my passport. Any reason you can think of for driving in to Lisbon. Any story you like."

"That," said Rab, "is one hell of an assignment for a girl with no imagination."

"Never mind. Make it good. You'll come with me, won't you?"

In the looking-glass above her dressing-table she saw a face that had no colour at all. She dropped the passport on the floor. This was, oddly, reminiscent of the fire-drill at sea; the thumping heart and the shaking hands were here to remind her that she was still a coward. The blesséd, longed-for moment had come: bringing fear.

"You rat," said Sarah to the white face in the glass.

It was a silent company who watched her come; through the glass doors; across the terrace, down to the gates where the taxi waited. Nobody said a word. "What did you tell them?" she asked Rab in the taxi.

"That you were wanted at the British Embassy for gambling and offering bribes. Sorry – best I could think of," Rab said, "You're *green*, d'you know?"

"I know . . . Rab, how has it happened? Why me? Why nobody else?"

"Looks like God came through, doesn't it?"

Yes . . . And now, with the voyage ahead, the familiar view turned a somersault. She saw her forlorn no-man's-land assuming the look of a safe harbour: this road, these cypresses and the placid sea. She began to laugh.

"How does it feel to be brave? I wish I knew."

"Brave? Who's brave?" Rab asked.

"You are."

"Do I have to say it again? I'm just lacking in imagination. If you don't have enough imagination to be scared, there's nothing to be brave about."

"That's a myth. I never can believe it. There's a natural order of courage – like yours; and a natural order of cowardice – like mine."

"Climb out of the hair shirt, will you please? Maybe it'll tickle less when you're dodging the torpedoes."

Here was the approach to the city; the women walking by the dockside with stately steps, the flat fish-baskets balanced on their heads.

"If it makes you feel any better," Rab said, "I was scared one time, scared as all hell. On the road, in June, just before the end. Didn't take any imagination to see those bastards right over us, so low you thought you could touch them. Machine-gunning and dropping their damn whistling bombs. And the poor jam-packed refugees getting it . . . Not that I would have minded being killed, but I was scared all the same." She held Sarah's hand: "Pollyanna talk, my specialty."

"Don't I wish you were coming with me."

"Me too," said Rab. "Put me off here and I'll wait for you at the café – corner table, see?"

The Repatriation Office received one differently today; in a different room, a cubbyhole of privacy. The same brisk note of kindliness was sounding. "Your passport, please. Now, the passage will cost fifteen thousand escudos. If you haven't got it we can advance – you can manage? Sure? Only too glad to help. You've a hundred thousand . . . Well, isn't that splendid?"

"With the compliments of the Casino," Sarah explained and got a charming smile of disbelief.

"Here's the address of the shipping-office. Go down there now, show them your stamped passport and they'll give you your ticket. Your boat sails at four o'clock. That'll give you plenty of time to get back to Estoril and pack your things. Now you mustn't say a word at the hotel."

"Excuse me, but am I the only one?"

"Yes, you seem to be." Another bright smile. "I think your best plan is to say some friends have arrived unexpectedly and you're coming in to stay with them. Goodbye and good luck to you." A firm handshake, and she was dismissed.

"Does she honestly think they'll believe *that* one?" Rab asked. "Far better carry on with my story and tell them you're going to jail."

The man behind the counter at the ticket-office said apologetically, "I'm afraid you're going to be rather uncomfortable."

"Small boat?"

"Three thousand tons. You'll be sharing the cabin with two other ladies, French ladies."

"Cheer up," Rab whispered. "You can always sleep with one of the crew."

"How long do we take?"

"About five weeks. Perhaps a few days less. We usually count five weeks. Here's your ticket. Fifteen thousand – thank you. I must warn you this sailing may be postponed – or even cancelled. We never know quite what's happening till the last minute."

"And on that jolly note," Sarah said to Rab. "I'd better buy some presents. For Brigstock and the Grandmother."

They strolled past shop-windows until Rab halted before a jeweller's. "I like those gold ships, . . . the little Christopher Columbus jobs. Brooches, are they?"

"Yes, they're pretty. I was thinking in terms of useful wartime supplies. But somehow it feels like a day for gold ships."

"What's this about a boat?" "Sarah, when do you sail?" They were all crowding around her on the terrace: a ravenous reception-committee. After a few minutes it became impossible to deflect them; her own lies and Rab's lies were entirely unconvincing.

They were steering her into the bar. They were calling for drinks and wishing her well. Nobody grumbled or asked, "Why not me?" though the Scots food-expert and the neutrally-minded girl had split off from the party.

"I feel like a self-conscious bride," Sarah thought; thanking them, making poor jokes, raising her glass.

"You'll all get home in a few hours by air," she told them, "while we're still heading for Gibraltar; or possibly – let's look on the bright side – lying at the bottom of the sea."

"Telephone, Mrs. Butler. Repatriation Office."

As she went she could hear them chorusing "Cancelled."

"Your sailing," said the kind voice, "has been postponed til midday tomorrow. You *will* be discreet, won't you?"

"Wildly," said Sarah. She returned to the bar. "I suggest," said the lady in purple who went for walks, "that you make a night of it at the Casino. We'll all come up and watch you play."

Little did I think I should ever look on one more night here as a reprieve. But I do. There's a perceptible flow of relief – all over me.

"Doesn't anyone want to eat? I'm starving," said Rab.

"One more round – on me."

"No, on me."

"This one's on me."

"You're wanted on the telephone, Mrs. Butler."

"That's done it," Sarah said. This could be nothing but cancellation. She smiled at the awed, sympathetic faces. Slowly she walked out, watching – from a sorrowful distance – her own abrupt change of mood. Here was heavy, sickening disappointment, the slam of the door.

And you were afraid, you idiot, you were afraid.

"Hullo." Not the Repatriation Office. A male voice; a jolly one: "British Airways here."

"Wait a minute, I think you've got the wrong person. Whom do you want?"

"I want Mrs. Romney Butler."

"That's me."

He said he thought it was. He added that he would know that deep voice of hers anywhere.

"Well, what can I do for you?" she asked bewilderedly.

"How would you like to leave on the flying-boat at three o'clock tomorrow morning? I've got you a seat."

"I – I don't understand."

"I said . . ." he repeated his message: "Did you get that? You'll be in England by the afternoon, by tomorrow afternoon." She could not say a word. "O.K. with you?" he was asking.

"Look – if this is a leg-pull, please don't, I can't stand it, please don't."

A hearty laugh sounded in her ear. "Now, now . . . I told you I'd do something for you as soon as I could. Didn't I? Can you come in this afternoon to collect your ticket?"

Speak up; answer him, he's waiting. This is true, this is happening. It's over, it's over, it's over, Answer him, fool: don't just stand here and cry.

THE UNWRITTEN NOTEBOOK

THE DREAM WAS STILL WITH ME IN THE MORNING; A BRIGHT consoling memory. While we were marching down to the parade ground I was able to restore most of it. This was extremely unusual. I know I have been There (as I used to call it when I was a child, for want of a better name) more than once in my adult life. Waking, I have been aware of the two theatres; of some bizarre action played in the second, of the teasing ecstasy that haunts the first. The echo is always strong but the coloured fabric always perishes in daylight, An occasional shaft may touch a scene, a thought, a word spoken. bringing a sense of familiarity that is almost physical; a stirring somewhere inside. Then, as I chase frenziedly after the clue, the clue is gone.

Not today. I could remember nearly everything. I felt as though I had been given a prize. I was careful to hold it with a light hand; not to press or clutch.

The mountain wind was sharp. There was a fresh fall of snow on the peaks, a thin coverlet of snow under our boots. Our breath smoked up from our mouths as we marched. The Spanish flag streamed straight from the staff; black, yellow and red. We were obliged to salute it, with the Fascist salute, arms outstretched; even the Civil War prisoners had to do that.

On the shout *"España!"* from the officer who took the salute, we had to reply in chorus *"Una, Grande, Libre!"* This reminded me of some similar, though quieter, performance at my prep-school, Puxford. I didn't object to it much. With the rest of the British, I indulged in some variations on the next chorus: we were meant to shout *"Arriba España, Viva Franco, Viva España!"* We didn't.

Obscene language has never really amused me before. If the officer heard us, he gave no sign.

In the canteen, I joined the Irish major and the Lowestoft seaman, the Yorkshire corporal and the subaltern from Glasgow. It was the good day; the day for the Military Attaché to turn up with the British allowance; one pound in cash; some bully beef or tinned fish. A brisk trade was done selling the food to the rich civilian internees. The wine in the canteen was surprisingly potent and most people needed the cash to get drunk on. The pound didn't last long. I was always in arrears. My particular group, my friends – had there been true friends in this place – were all richer than I. They had come in with saleable property of one sort or another: watches, pens, wallets and razor-blades. The subaltern from Glasgow would always lend me money for a drink. He kept a record. When the figure mounted up, he made me write him a cheque on my English bank, using toilet paper.

"You look bloody awful," the Irish major told me.

"So would you if you'd just had a bullet dug out of you." I wondered if I would ever use my right arm again. I was really more interested because the Countess had proved correct in her theory than in any other aspect of the situation. The anonymous prisoner inside was accustomed to pain.

"Lucky to come out of *that* place alive."

"He's probably septic. Smells like it," said the Lowestoft seaman.

"That's yourself you're smelling."

"Nark it."

"What really happened to Phil and Alfred?" I asked them. (As though I'd get a reliable answer . . .) According to the Irish major they had tried to tunnel out under the wire and were shot on the other side. According to the seaman they had been released. The Glasgow subaltern gave his oath that they were each in solitary confinement for assaulting a Spanish sergeant. The Yorkshire corporal inclined to the escape theory; he had heard the shots. Nobody else had heard the shots.

The first glass of wine was hitting me hard. It always did; like the rest I had breakfasted off a piece of mouldy bread and the tepid acorn-brew that passed for coffee. I began to glow inside. I could look about me at the dirty, greasy berets covering the shaved heads, at the Lowestoft seaman burning up a louse with a match; I could listen to the voices getting loud; the blasphemies; the quarrels that would soon turn into fighting: and not care. Because of the dream I felt better than at any time since the beginning of the long tunnel. *Merrily, merrily, shall I live now* . . . Tonight, I said, I'll get back. I know I can do it again. I'll live for the nights; and perhaps I'll rediscover the whole landscape of the place called There; not just the two theatres . . . Wasn't there a lane I used to go by? And a hill; and below the hill a town where the house with the jumbled roof stands? It was gone again, as I stared; whisking away out of mind.)

"Wake up, Weston, he's talking to you," said the Irish major.

"Tell the bugger you're busy."

I blinked at the guard. He was a young one; I hadn't seen him before.

"You. Please."

"Christ Almighty, he said Please."

"We don't do that there 'ere, Ferdinando."

"Tell him to fuck off."

"This is our private recreation room," said the Irish major to the guard, with deceptive courtesy. He spoke fair Spanish and I could by now understand enough to translate the exchange. The Irish major said that no official business was allowed to interfere with the solemn ritual of getting drunk. "You will find a notice to that effect, posted on the wall."

"Yes, go and read what's written on the walls, Ferdinando. Read the whole issue. If there's anything you don't understand – come back and we'll give you a demonstration."

According to the major I was wanted in the Commandant's office. Urgently, urgently. The guard had been searching for me all the morning.

"No organization in the fucking Spanish Army – said so before."

I walked beside the guard, taking evasive action because he was bound to seize my bad arm. He didn't. He did not attempt to touch me. New to the job, certainly. Not a knee-jolt, not a cuff in the face for luck. (There was one, a Corporal, who always carried a whip.)

We trotted in silence across the frozen ground, past the endless whitewashed huts; the best part of a mile. The sun was high and the mountains were steel-clad. Far off I saw an eagle; a tiny black shape ringing up in the blue.

We came past the clumps of rusty barbed wire; to the white steps and the flagstaff. The guard saluted the sentry. It was like being back at my training-camp. This brick hut was clean. I hadn't set foot in it before.

Inside the office the heat was unbelievable; one blast of it made my head swim. A genuine stove roared under the window. I rocked on my feet. *Shouldn't have had that second drink* . . . The frieze of sacred, political and military posters danced up and down. The Commandant, sitting behind his table, danced up and down too. He was a little grey man, with purple and gold epaulettes on his shoulders, and three lines of bright medal-ribbons, all waving about on his chest. Beside him there was a junior officer standing, in the ramrod, anonymous attitude familiar from my days at Sandhurst. In a series of jumps, he steadied; with the Commandant, and the rest of the room.

"You speak Spanish?"

"No, sir. French, but no Spanish."

"I don't know why not," he said in French, sounding rather amiable. "With your connections," he added, "I should have thought —" He broke off, smiling at me. He picked something up from the desk, and handed it to the junior officer; a snapshot, I decided. They examined it together. Entirely baffled, I tried to get a sight of the documents lying on the table. This meant taking a step forward; the guard gave a hiss. I stepped back.

Still looking amiable, the Commandant now passed the snapshot over to me, saying, "You may like to keep it as a souvenir."

It took me a moment to recognize my own face; or what used to be my own face. There was hair on my head. My cheeks were positively plump. This picture had been taken in bright sunlight; I had puckered up my eyes. There was no background. It looked like an old passport photograph.

"Take him over to the Company office," the Commandant said to the guard. "They'll complete the formalities there," he told me.

"Formalities . . . What formalities, sir? What's happening?"

That made him twitch his eyebrows, like Romney – or like Teruel. "Did nobody tell you? You are released," he said, "Free."

I stumbled and lurched against the guard, hurting my shoulder. I righted myself. There was the noise of bells in my head and a voice shouting through the bells. *With wings as eagles*, it shouted, *They shall mount up with wings, as eagles.*

THE VIEW FROM THE SUMMIT

I

THE JOURNEY WAS ENDING IN MILES'S HOUSE.

He'd had other ideas for me; Nannyish ideas. He wanted to drive me to Madrid and put me in the hands of a doctor before I reported at the British Embassy. He wanted, alternatively, to aim for Gibraltar and get a doctor on the way. I wouldn't hear of a doctor. I didn't need one. I wouldn't hear of Madrid; I wouldn't hear of Gibraltar. Lisbon or nowhere, I told him. I was completely light-headed and I argued with fury, making no sort of sense. I was convinced that the Countess was still in Lisbon: we must get there with all speed, so I could thank her. I could see her waiting, I explained; she had the tussore suit ready for me and I must put it on. I could see Teruel. It was useless for Miles to say No, they had sailed already, they were gone to America. Nothing he said to me got through.

Poor old Miles. I made him drive far into the night. Time didn't exist. Everything was glorious and everything was mine. We ate and drank from a splendid hamper, packed by the Countess. Sometimes I sat beside Miles, wrapped up in a rug. Sometimes I stretched out on the back seat. Since they had given me a brisk delousing at the camp I reeked of disinfectant; Miles said it was loathsome. I said it was what Brigstock would call a nice clean smell. I couldn't stop singing – or shouting. I sang *Merrily, merrily*, for hours on end. I shouted "With wings as eagles!" I sang *Here we are, here we are, riding on a shooting star!*

I told Miles about my dream, calling it the Conqueror's Dream. I understood, and explained to him, its full significance in coming the night before I was set free. Sometimes when I'd finished telling him I would find myself back at the beginning again. So after a while he must have known the dream by heart. Later, I could remember his groaning a good deal and swearing at me in all his five languages.

We slept for a time. I slept longer than Miles did. When I awoke we were moving. Now I didn't know where I was, nor who Miles was. I thought I was being taken to another jail. I couldn't get the truth into my head. I would yell and grab his arm; and he said the roads were bad enough, dangerous enough, without that. I clunked him once, hard; and he clunked me, harder still. That woke me up.

The next stage was the stage when I couldn't stop laughing. I got silly giggles, and I could hear the Countess's voice saying 'Hysterical.' I asked Miles if he thought I was hysterical: he said No, I was just a damn' nuisance. He begged me not to behave like a fool at the frontier. So when we got there I sat still and solemn, bowing to left and right. There was no trouble whatever on either side, though Miles, who seemed to be losing heart, had warned me of indefinite delay. We fairly shot through. I said those papers of ours certainly acted like Seidlitz powders. Miles told me not to be coarse. He further accused me of interrupting his prayers.

We stopped at a town just beyond the frontier. Back in his own country (if it is his own country) he was Nanny with a vengeance. In this town there was a doctor who gave me pills. After which I passed right out and didn't wake till we were driving through Lisbon. A blue and gold afternoon: the lights were coming on. I thought I was still dreaming. I told Miles to take me to the Second Theatre.

There was nothing much wrong with me. I knew that for certain; sitting up in bed, blinking at the room. The fever was gone. I felt rather sweaty and limp: I still reeked of disinfectant. But I was clean. I was all right all over, except for my arm, which was quite numb and – when I stretched it out – shorter than the other. Oh well . . . it didn't matter. I always drew with my left hand anyway.

I stared around. There were echoes of France in the room; the huge bed, the tiled floor and the stove. (Clean room, quiet room, and a bed – of all things . . .) I could hear Cecile moving about in the room below. Hadn't Miles told me Cecile would be cross? Or was that something I'd imagined in fever? It wasn't true. As I lurched in through the front door she'd clasped me to her fat bosom; the three small boys stood around staring at us; and then Cecile had gone down on her knees. The kids knelt down, too, when she pushed them.

What the devil was I wearing on my head? To protect my shaven scalp? A sort of mob cap, Cecile's, I supposed. There was a ribbon in it. I took it off, giggling again. These were obviously Miles' pyjamas; with some peculiar kind of arrangement at the neck that suggested a tie should be worn in bed: buttons and little tapes. The pyjamas swaddled me, bringing instant memories of the Countess's night-gown, of the tussore suit before she altered it. God's blessing on the Countess. Too sad that she was gone. I owed her everything.

But she was no longer my immediate preoccupation.

> Now that I am clean again,
> Now I've slept and fed,
> How shall I remember when
> I was someone dead?

Dead, I kept repeating: they all think I am dead. Miles hadn't told me this on the drive. Or perhaps he had and I was too drunk with happiness to understand. The truth had only penetrated here in this room: and he had left me alone with it when he went off to send the cables. (Priority, he had promised, there were *des moyens* if you were Miles. But I need not expect to see him tonight. If I awoke, I must take the last dose of pills immediately. They would knock me out again. Doctor's orders: Nanny's orders.) Was he back? Not yet. Listening, I could tell that Cecile was alone downstairs: the boys must be asleep.

Dead . . .

I should, I suppose, have thought of it. But I hadn't. I'd imagined them hearing I was missing, a prisoner perhaps, but not dead.

It was the hardest of all things to realize, to understand, to picture: Brigstock thinking I was dead; and the Grandmother: Philip and Paula, Sarah and Gerald knowing they would never see me again.

303

And Rab . . .? But Miles knew no more about Rab than I myself knew; which was nothing.

I turned up the oil-lamp that stood on a black wooden chest beside the bed. Cecile had put a small vase of flowers next to the lamp. And a small ivory crucifix. I gazed at the flowers, at the cross, at the white walls with the black shadows flickering. The thought and the look of death were here.

For all of them you are dead. Not anywhere in the world. Gone forever. In their minds you are wiped out, eliminated. Only you, as you once used to be, are remembered. This you can understand. Lately, you have begun to share their knowledge; you were on your way to the same point: you were teaching the anonymous prisoner to think like that. The other selves (Thomas Weston, Emile, Justin, Bernard Morlaix) stretched behind him, but he was not they; nor anybody. You were working to make him nobody at all.

"So I know," I thought, "how it feels to remember me. But it stops there. I don't know how it feels to mourn me."

I didn't want to know. The thought of having made them sad began to drown me in misery. I climbed out of bed. In front of the stove the tiled floor was warm. I stood on my bare feet. I ached a bit. Quite well, otherwise. Hungry again, too.

"Tough, my God, tough." A voice was speaking in French, speaking of Emile: "He always had the build of an ox and the health of a horse."

I found a packet of extraordinary-looking cigarettes on a shelf. I lit one. I sat down in the chair by the stove.

"Tomorrow I'll have to do the explaining," was a burden on my mind. I was never any good at explaining. I imagined (though I can't now think what they would have been doing in Lisbon) a row of khaki figures: high-ranking types, seated behind a table; an Army Board. I saw them looking at me with sceptical faces, mistrusting my appearance and my story. I saw myself, standing at attention, trying to tell them how it had happened, and making a nonsense; with somebody like Uncle Percy in my dream saying, "Do get on. You know there has to be an account given, it's part of the drill."

I had kept, after all my wanderings, my same old prep-school dread of authority's demands.

"I say, you know, the War House isn't going to like this," grumbled an imaginary Brigadier, "Nor Records, either. You were killed, young man. That's what you were. And in our view you still are."

Oh, well . . . Time for the pills, I said to myself. I swallowed them down and climbed back into bed. I put out the lamp. After a few minutes I felt the drug take hold of me. I began to be wrapped in a kind cloud . . . a kind cloud.

> "And nothing is vowed and all is vowed
> And we have forgotten how to be proud,
> And we sleep like cherubs in the same cloud."

The words, with the darkness, lulled me: words echoing from the terrace of the Twenty-nine villa in the moonlight; when I believed that Rab's thought came flying and touched my thought.

That could be; that could be.

Telepathy, as the Grandmother said, was no stranger than wireless waves travelling through the air. The source of supply was different; nothing else.

The source of supply . . . What was magic, anyway? Peacefully, contentedly, I stared in my mind at the gift I'd possessed, the gift that came and went; but mostly went, as I grew older. War seemed to have extinguished it altogether.

And yet . . . I looked back on the journey that began in the dark, in the wood. I saw the luck of Emile when the shot failed to kill him. I saw the meeting with Johnny. I saw the path I'd taken by chance to the gates of the Twenty-Nine villa. Last I saw the dream, the Conqueror's dream. So, to the gloriously improbable and ridiculous Now; to the ridiculous me, preserved. Magic, you could say. Or you could deny. Did it matter?

Did it matter where magic hailed from, or what – precisely – it was? Cradled in peace, I looked back a longer way. To my child-hood; to the Grandmother saying it must be given up; and the conjuror, Perry Potter, saying much the same. When the swing-door opened, he said, you saw through: but nobody could tell what made it swing nor what made you see . . . I remembered the vow I took, at the age of eighteen, after the experiment. I remembered the times I broke the vow. I remembered Willie Toyne asking me to help him, and Carola, who condemned the gift. I went past their deaths and came to Romney's dying, to my own belief that the gift was from the Devil. I was wrong, I thought. I may not be right now; but I was wrong then.

These memories began to have a shape. The shape was certainty. I wouldn't find myself at odds again. The powers of healing, the powers of second sight, had been favours granted to me; favours I was too ignorant to understand. First I had prized them; then I had grown to fear them. But they were neither to be prized nor feared. They were none of my business. They were only signs on the way.

One is simply a part of magic. Magic is simply a part of oneself: it becomes absorbed: it ceases to present one with tricks or problems. It is there and that is all.

I shut my eyes, and let the kind cloud carry me.

II

This day, December the Twenty-Seventh, was uncomfortably long. For Rab it had also the disadvantage of feeling like yesterday extended: she had gone to bed at four and awoken at eight: in Sarah's room, without Sarah.

At noon a slow, polysyllabic message from the Embassy had told her that arrangements were now made for her transportation to New York. She would sail within three days by the Export Line. She was requested to call in and "finalize the necessary procedures," whatever that might mean. Rab had taken childish pleasure in saying "Okay, sometime tomorrow" and hanging up.

At the Valentin, all was changed. Since the early hours she had found herself living apart from the uproarious Britishers; suddenly they were on their way; the log-jam had broken. Every one of these slap-happy exiles would be gone by tomorrow. There was wassail in the bar. Even the neutrally-minded girl had danced a jig on the terrace.

Sarah's miracle was, therefore, no miracle. "Except," Rab said to the believer, "You did get it before anybody else, Lord knows why. And you're there . . . Where, I wonder? Where did that plane set

306

you down?" The luggage was labelled only with a W for West-bound. Rab, who had been looking at her watch all day, looked at it again. She tried to imagine Sarah made free at last of the war-shrouded island, but imagination failed. Sarah seemed to be still in this room, with the scatter of her possessions left behind: silk scarves, a fur jacket, a velvet skirt, advised for wear at the Casino, because it had pockets; there were books, scent, powder and cigarettes. "Any-thing you can't use, give away." No protest had worked against the lavish will.

"*And* the money. You pulled a fast one there," Rab said. She had found it only at four a.m., in an envelope beneath her pillow. "Don't be cross" was written on the envelope.

"That makes me want to cry. And I'm not saying one word about it to those stuffed shirts tomorrow. Penniless, that's my story. I'm taking your dough to the Casino tonight – see if *I* can't swing a miracle."

There was, she reminded herself, a miracle under way already: she was writing a letter; to Paula.

As in the other letters since April, she was at pains to sound like the person she used to be. Nobody could read between these lines. Here, she prided herself, was Rab from the days before Noel. (It seemed odd, never having been one for an act, to find this act comparatively easy.)

"And how's that for craziness? One minute a boat, next crack out of the box a plane. We took another taxi into Lisbon to pick up that ticket and cancel the first one. Sarah was in what she calls a fine frenzy – almost out of her mind. I don't blame her. This business of hanging on to the hem of Europe by the fingernails is enough to get anybody down.

When we were in the British Airways office she had a hallucina-tion. I mean it. We were waiting at the counter and Sarah saw a fellow come out of an office and heard him tell the man who was writing out the ticket to cancel Mrs. Butler's flight because a priority passenger had taken the seat. I don't mean the fellow wasn't there. I saw him too. But he hadn't said anything about Sarah. And when the other guy brought the ticket to the counter he did a double-take because Sarah said, 'So it didn't work out.'

After that – well this *is* a damn fool place. First the Repatriation Office women were mad at her for getting the plane instead of the boat. Then – you won't believe it – the shipping-office said they couldn't sell her berth to anybody else. Nobody wanted it. When you think of the mob that's clamouring to get out of here. Don't know if they're scared of boats or if the man on the job was just being ornery. He ended by telling Sarah he could only refund her half of her fare. To which Sarah says, 'Oh, good enough, I realize I've been a trouble to you' whereupon *he* says, 'My God if you're as nice as that, I'll give you the whole lot back.' And does.

Then it was a rush to the bank, swopping all those escudos she'd won for black market dollars – good rate, too – what a town! Then a church for a quick pray. And I thought that was it, but no, she insisted on stopping off at the Red Cross depot to give them the fifteen thousand she'd got back on the boat-ticket. *Honestly!* A thank-offering, she said.

And she *still* didn't believe, right up to the last minute, that she was really going – not even in the taxi to Cabo Ruivo at two a.m. Hell of a hold-up there, too. Some Pole or other had lost his papers. You can guess what it did to Sarah.

Last I saw of her she was walking down some steps in the dark, with all the others, to a launch. I could see the flying-boat, way out on the water, all lit up. It looked huge – like a fortress, kind of . . ."

Rab laid down her pen. That seemed to be the end of the news. She ought to add her own news.

The damnable finality of writing "I sail this week" was too much. She couldn't say less; and she had no heart to say more. She scrawled it; she collected the sheets together. A letter as long as any she had written since she went to war; longer; as long as the letters the thirteen-year-old Rab had written to Thomas.

No mercy on the child, sobbing "He was my friend."

Impossible to be happy, ever again. But easy to be gay. Rab commandeered a bath. She dressed herself in Sarah's clothes; one of the blouses from Saks and the velvet skirt. Being highly-coloured as well as expensively-made, they suited her not at all. Her thin neck and boy's head emerged from the scarlet chiffon looking like one of those pallid plaster dummies in a shop-window. An unfortunate piece of modelling. Who cared? There was no one around to care, and a good thing too.

She grinned at her reflection in the glass. She made up her pale, truculent face, using Sarah's powder and Sarah's lipstick. She sprayed herself with Sarah's scent. Despite four days of good eating she was still unbecomingly thin. She had to lash a belt about her shrunken middle to keep the blouse and skirt together: it was her own belt, a black one; it looked all wrong. She scrambled into Sarah's fur jacket and turned up the collar.

She descended the stairs, feeling as though she had put on a particularly hostile form of fancy dress.

In the hall she met some escaping prisoners, headed for the bar. "How nice you look," said the Scots food-expert. "If I may say so," he added, having said so. "I suppose I'm old-fashioned," he went on in a tone of deep satisfaction, "But I'm not fond of seeing a woman in trousers."

"You'll be out of luck when you get to the war, won't you?" said Rab.

She took the back road to the Casino. They had come this way last night, for a farewell visit, Sarah still keeping her cock-eyed vow. "No, one can't call it cock-eyed . . . It worked, or something did." As she came into the rooms, with their gilded walls and purple velvet hangings, she could hear Sarah's voice. "This evening one is merely surveying a site of historic interest, no more."

The gyp-joint, Rab said to herself. The rooms were harshly lighted; the air smelt of sweet oil, rank sweat and stale cigars. Not an atmosphere favouring miracles. The crowd was thick at every table. Changing Sarah's notes for chips, Rab found herself greeted by one of Sarah's indigenous boy-friends; the Czech, or was it the Hungarian? He was saying "So she went at last – you are alone." His eyes were on the money. Rab moved off. She saw the woman with the long white gloves: to be avoided as a neighbour, Sarah said: her practised elbow-movement could sweep some of your chips away.

There was the pale young man who hovered and cadged. He was

the nut-case who had tried to get money from Sarah on the strength of a book he was supposed to be writing. There were the two blondes in evening-dress; spies, according to local rumour.

"What a bunch. And the croupiers liable to steal your shirt . . . How she ever managed to win. Well, if she can, I can." Braced by the perilous prospect, Rab found a seat at the far table, close to the wall. She lined up her chips in front of her, thinking, "Here we go. 'Back myself against any Portuguese croupier." She felt a certain affection for them. The Portuguese, after all, made a link with the Vineyard. On the Vineyard they were her friends. "Maybe I could track down half their grandparents if I had a word of the language . . . This fellow at the wheel looks a tough. And has to be," she reflected as a fight began. Since the tall customer claiming that his stake had been stolen was claiming in German, Rab sided with the croupier.

It would be intelligent, perhaps, to watch the wheel for a turn or two; they spun quickly. Around the table there was much last-minute agitation; packed shoulders shoving, arms shooting out, hurried hands still placing bets as the ball rocketed on its way.

The lanky, white-haired man opposite, solemnly playing the Red, was an American. Beyond a doubt. He looked like an Embassy official, too. Perhaps he was this morning's talker on the telephone. He smiled at her after Red came up. "Maybe you wouldn't smile at me, Mister, if you knew my guilty secret . . . What was that number? Three. Sarah's pet. I ought to have backed Three."

A big, heavy arm in a dark blue sleeve descended past her shoulder. A smell of cigar-smoke came with it. The hand was large, plump and brown, flecked with dark blotches: she watched this hand spill a cascade of pink, oval chips, the hundreds, across the green cloth; covering the numbers from Ten to Twelve.

The wheel spun. She was near enough to see the ball going round, slowing up, hanging poised for a moment above the Seven, then jumping perversely into the next socket. Number Twelve. She felt her chair squeezed against the table as the winner moved in, to collect. Above her head she could hear his voice; a deep, nasal voice, speaking in Portuguese. Whatever he said was not well received. He was giving some instruction that went badly with the croupiers;

what was it? Ah, yes; he was asking them to hand him back his stake. He was getting it. Cautious character . . . just to play that one shot and then go.

She turned to watch him go. He walked with a roll. She looked at his square, padded shoulders, his squat neck and the back of his oiled, grey-blond head. As he passed the end of the table she saw him in profile. It was a fat-cheeked profile, with a narrow eye and a nose that jutted above the cigar.

She was looking at Miles.

"Miles!" she shouted, "Hey! Miles!" The shout brought a hiss of rebuke all around her. Miles turned. He yelled "Rab!" She was up from the table, scattering her chips; she had knocked her chair backwards; she had struck somebody's head with her elbow. She was charging through the crowd – full tilt into the huge embrace. It was like being hugged by a scented grizzly.

"Kiss me again," said Miles: "You never kissed me like that since you were ten years old." The fat-skull face was eyeless with laughter; could those be tears, squeezing out at the edges of the lids? He held her off, then clutched her to him again, laughing over her head. "You're strangling me," Rab told him and he let her go; she saw his green silk shirt-front and satin tie, ornamented with a Sacred Heart tiepin.

"A miracle," said Miles, "Another goddam miracle. Know what I am? I'm the Blesséd Mother's favourite boy. Bar one, of course," he added, crossing himself with his cigar.

III

The slow train clanked on its way through the dark of early morning. The carriage was cold. Sarah curled herself into the corner: there was nobody else here: she would have liked a companion, any companion, to talk and keep her awake. The intolerable heaviness of sleep forced her eyelids down. She had stayed awake all night.

Her head nodded and she pinched her arm again; the left forearm just beneath the elbow was obligingly bruised by now. She must not sleep. Because this could still be a dream; here in the misty, moving dark most easily: and the dream might break at any minute with a voice asking, "How did you manage to get out . . .?" Then there would be the window, framing the ostrich-plumed palm tree.

Have a care. It may be a dream. This, and the journey behind you, all of it a dream. Have a care.

No. I am coming to the end of the journey. I am on the last lap. I can remember all of it. If I am ever to be a writer again it will be written.

Play it back. From the beginning. That alone will keep it safe.

She played it back. The river at Cabo Ruivo and the launch that took them out into the night: the green-lit cabin of the flying-boat; the engine gunned and the slow take-off; the lights of Lisbon circling below, circling away, dropping behind. The last lighted city you would see.

Yes; you were there: on the long bumpy flight, five hundred feet above the water. You had seen dawn come, dawn off the Spanish coast. Then the clouds, and the German aircraft swooping out of the clouds, just below the wing-tip . . . the altimeter going round like a crazy clock, the tilt of the floor as the pilot climbed steeply . . . that was no terror, that came too fast. Terror came with the blue sky and the sun. You had looked out to see two black dots pursuing, one high, one low; following at speed, growing wings as you watched. (Until you thought there was no hope and shut your eyes, saying your last foolish prayer: *Thank you for getting me as far as this, please take care of them all and please forgive me;* waiting for the end to come.) You had opened your eyes to find the boy in blue uniform, bringing you a cup of soup and a ham roll. "Only our escort," said the boy, "This is what we call Rendezvous Corner."

You had felt the endless bumping; you had endured the hideous sounds of air-sickness behind you; you had stared straight ahead; sometimes you had put your fingers in your ears.

You had seen the opaque shades the boy clipped across the windows when the English coast came near; a most baffling gesture. Surely, you had said to yourself, the different bumping meant land below; you must make certain. "Just one look," you had pleaded, until he plucked off the shade, like a conjuror showing you a three-second magic; small brown fields and the dark ropes of hedges dividing them.

There had come the stillness at last; and the fresh air at last, blowing in through the open door. You had gulped the fresh air. You had pushed your way to the bow of the launch as it chugged across the silken water, slower by far than a speedboat in Bermuda, chugging steadily away from the aircraft. You had seen the aircraft recede and change, no more the carrier in which you had lived long hours, merely a flying-boat at rest and growing smaller; nothing to do with you.

You had seen Poole Harbour in the grey silence of a winter afternoon: one tall chimney painted in twisting camouflage colours, a line of sandbags along the jetty; a few loiterers staring at the launch. The engine cutting off, the hull bumping against a square rock fringed with green seaweed. You had pressed your foot hard down as you stepped on to the rock – hard down on home.

Are you sure? Have a care, now. That green-fringed rock bobs up and down in your dream, you are dreaming, aren't you? Pinch your arm, twist the skin. Sit up, strain at the fogged window, brush it with your sleeve and take account of the field beyond; a dark hump of English field, and behind it the shrouded shapes of trees. Is it true, the landscape?

It is true. It is all true. It is all remembered. There was tea served in the customs-office; there was a black teapot.

Yes, you were there. You could have kissed the black teapot and the thick white cups. You could have kissed the Field Security Officer, a colonel with green tabs on his uniform; he had sat, solemn and important, behind a table in an upper room.

"Passport, please. America. H'm . . . What brings you back?"

"The war. I wanted to come home to the war."

"I see." Not a smile; no marks for that. In fact it had appeared to annoy him: "You just wanted to come home . . . Good enough reason to get you priority on a plane, d'you think? We've no record of your name. Not listed. Not on any list. Highly irregular."

(My God, he's going to send me back – all the way back.)

"Oh please – can't I stay? Let me stay."

"Well, *really* . . ." Exasperation. "Of course you stay, now you're here. I'm just asking how it happened."

"I think it was a miracle. An act of God."

"You do, do you?" At last he had smiled: "Well, I suppose I must take your word for it. Let's get down to business. Money first. Not allowed to bring money in, English currency that is; ten pounds the limit. Ten-pound note, eh? Nice clean one. Been carrying that all over America?"

"I bought it on the black market in Lisbon yesterday. I bought these dollars, too – six hundred and twenty dollars. Do you want to see cheques, postdated cheques people gave me?"

"Good God, we're used to passengers arriving bankrupt. Where did you get all this money?"

"I won it playing roulette."

"I give up," the Field Security Officer had said.

You could have dreamed that conversation too, you know. Doesn't sound real, does it? The words echo in your ears, drift off, return, through the noise of a dream-train moving; you must pinch your arm.

I am awake, wide awake. This is an English railway-carriage, that is my luggage on the floor. I am travelling to Waterloo Station; from Bournemouth.

I can remember last night at Bournemouth; the twilight drive into the town; once the home of *Hi Jinks* or was it *Gay Cavaliers*? I stared at the town. I stared and stared because it was the same. It wasn't a heap of rubble with everyone living in air-raid shelters down below. The hotel was just as it used to be . . . music playing in the Palm Court and well-dressed old ladies sitting at small tables, having tea; smiling, ordinary, as if there was no war.

I'd got it all wrong. I asked pleadingly, timorously for a cup of coffee because – according to the Americans – there was no coffee in England. And the waiter brought a gigantic silver pot. I was hungry; I asked gaily for beef sandwiches; and he dropped his voice to a whisper. *See what he could do, rationing,* he said. I implored the hall-porter to let me send a cable to America, to my family, just one cable, as a favour; please, no matter what the regulations were. There were no regulations: he handed me a form and a pencil. I asked him how I could possibly get to London (buses, they had said in Lisbon; a chain of buses; the railway-lines were bombed out of existence.) The hall-porter picked up an A.B.C. (I could have kissed that too) and read off the times of the morning trains. He recommended the fast train with the restaurant car. But I couldn't wait. I had to take the first there was.

I am in that train now. The light is coming through the foggy windows; I have seen the smashed roofs of Southampton beyond the station yard. One hideous glimpse and we are away, we are moving on. At the other end of this line there is London. They will be there.

Are you sure? Certainly you are dreaming that telephone-call, it couldn't have happened; they all told you it couldn't, the baffled Lisbon fugitives coming away dejectedly from the telephones, saying Raids Last Night, Can't Get Through. Remember?

But there was the operator who said "Been away a year? That's a long time. Hold on, I'll try to get them," and I stood and waited.

I am not dreaming the Grandmother's voice; I heard it. "We're perfectly all right, we're very well indeed. Dead? Nobody's dead that I know of . . . No I'm not breaking anything gently, there's nothing to break . . . break . . . break. Of course Blanche isn't dead, she's scrubbing some potatoes, we aren't supposed to peel them any more, she'll come and talk to you." Yelling, "Blanche dear! Blanche! It's Sarah come home!" The crackling on the line; Brigstock's telephone-voice, careful and distinct, as always. "Hullo, darling, how lovely you're back."

No, no, you dreamed it. You dreamed you told her the time this train arrived at Waterloo. You dreamed the voice saying, "See you in the morning." That voice fades, drowned out by other voices:

"*Do look in again. Though of course we'll let you know.*"

"*Any news, Sarah?*"

"*Name so far down the list.*"

"*I know you have money. I watch you play.*"

"*My great uncle who lives at Mentony.*"

"*Selfish and silly for any woman to go to England now.*"

"*Tres – Incarnada!*"

"*I take you dancing.*"

Of course you were still there. You would never get out. Rab would never come and you would never get out.

·   ·   ·   ·   ·

Never-get-out – Never-get-out – Never-get-out.

Something was making this noise in Sarah's ears. A train. She awoke as the noise stopped. A blast of cold air came in, a door slammed and now there was a man sitting opposite her, a young man in khaki.

He said "Hullo. Did I wake you up?"

"Where are we?"

"Basingstoke."

"Oh nonsense. I'm sorry. I mean it couldn't be Basingstoke, could it?" She rubbed the window with her sleeve; she looked out and saw the small red houses with their many chimneys (one had forgotten how many chimneys) thrusting into the landscape of fields and trees.

She looked back at the soldier. He was offering her a cigarette; a Grandchester cigarette; same old yellow packet.

It is a long time since I mourned for Romney.

"What's the 'W' for?" he asked, peering at the labels on her luggage. "Haven't seen that before."

"'Westbound'. That's all they put, at Lisbon."

"You just come from Lisbon?"

He had a terrier's face, a scrubby crest of brown hair. "What on earth were you doing there?"

"Getting home from America."

His expression was disbelieving. He said, "Rather a long way round, wasn't it?"

"It was."

The soldier gave her another sceptical look. She turned to the window again. She saw a level-crossing, a thatched roof, a man pushing a bicycle; a sudden little pond and a black dog running at the edge of the water; a clump of leafless oak-trees. The view suited her perfectly. There was nothing else she needed to see. There was nothing in her mind but the sensation of a noise that had gone on, it seemed, forever; ceased now, leaving silence.

"Been away long?"

"A year – and more."

He grinned at her. "Chosen a hell of a moment to come home, haven't you? More sensible to stay in America, I'd have thought."

"Oh, much."

"Pardon?"

"I said much. Much more sensible. But I got tired of being sensible."

This seemed to disconcert him. He scratched his head and said, "Give you a tip. Don't join the Army," and then laughed heartily. "Not that I've any complaints today. Seven days leave."

"How does it feel?"

"Damn' good. London's all right."

"*All right?*"

"Why not? Oh, bombs . . . You won't notice much damage," he told her blithely, drumming his heels on the floor. "What's it like in America?"

"I don't really know."

You are disconcerted again. But I mean what I say. I don't really know because I, the I who sits opposite to you, watching the suburbs begin, trying not to talk because I would rather stare, this I was never in America. Nor in Lisbon, either. This I is a new acquaintance (or possibly an old one, forgotten) who has no fight inside and no outside forces stacked against her. Leisured, she only wants to stare out of the window.

Presently he said in a chirpy voice, "You're very quiet."

Yes, I am. You speak more truth than you know. Utterly quiet; utterly at peace. It feels rather as though I'd gone deaf.

"Family live here?"

Oh do shut up . . . No, that is most ungracious. I work at it. I tell you about the Grandmother, about Brigstock, about Thomas being killed and the rest of them still in America. I wish I hadn't said Hollywood. Now you are asking me about Hollywood; but this will not last for long. The minutes are running out. My heart has gone up into my neck and my words jiggle.

"Bloody slow train. Nearly there, though."

"Nearly there."

"I suppose there's somebody meeting you."

"Yes, I think so, I hope so."

"If they don't turn up, I'll take you and give you a drink – celebration drink. Your first day home. My first day's leave. I know a pub that's open all hours, quite nice, it is, only a step from Waterloo."

That is kind. I shall remember you. Your terrier-head, your crest of hair . . . You are part of this journey.

"Shouldn't look out of the window now, if I was you."

But I have to look: at the poor little houses by the line; the houses I've always thought so ugly. That wasn't true; that wasn't ugliness; this is ugliness; only this, the shattered roofs, the skeleton shapes with the sky behind. On and on, the blasted broken walls. I want to swear.

"Doesn't all look like that. You'll see. Houses of Parliament okay, see? Big Ben, still right way up. Now – give you a hand with your luggage."

We are there. It's Waterloo Station: dirty, battered, blessèd Waterloo Station. And it feels like the holiday train. It is the holiday train, by God . . . It is the noise of bells, it is shouting inside. He holds the door open and at my feet the platform slides past the door; slides, slows, stops.

"'Hand 'em out to you. Not a damn porter in sight, as usual. Here we are, two small ones. I'll take the big one . . .'"

Did I say I would remember you? I have forgotten you completely. I suppose you are still there, but I do not see you any more, you have vanished, with all of it. There's a face looking at me; a face with a knobbed forehead and amber eyes; a wise, affectionate face from long ago. This face comes close above mine; these hands come down upon my shoulders: they turn me quickly so that I am standing right in front of Brigstock . . . Brigstock in a grey coat and hat: the same small wisps of hair are straying loose under the sides of the hat: Brigstock with her holiday look, the look of amazed happiness, the little flush across the cheekbones; as it was in the beginning. But there is something else. She is panting, laughing, trying to speak, not managing to speak, the hand with the grey glove on it is holding out a telegram. And I see the fingers shake and suddenly, against all the odds there are, I know.

IV

"Some people," Miles said, "have no consideration." He sat on the running-board of his car. He blinked in the cold blue blaze

318

of morning: this, like the wind off the Estuary, was no good to a hangover. He stared balefully across the drawbridge, at the sunlit bulk of the Belem Tower. That was where they were: talking.

"Talking . . . when there's a dozen things we ought to be doing . . . Why I ever pointed it out, told them what it was . . . teach me to keep my big mouth shut. 'Sure,' I say, 'Run along. Climb all over it, bone up on Vasco da Gama, take your time.' Sarcasm goes right past some people's heads. 'If you get bored, Miles, you can look in at the Monastery.' The Monastery . . . as though I didn't know it by heart. What's happening? Do they want to spend all day on those ramparts? We're on our way to the Embassy, aren't we? (Or we were. 'Just keep on driving, Miles' . . .) He's got to get there; it's me who'll be in trouble if he doesn't.

"'Wants hospital treatment, too, he's a wreck. Either they'll fly him home right away or they'll put him in hospital here. And he has to have some clothes, can't go around in those Spanish hand-outs . . . shoes, he's cursing the shoes, my best shoes, there's gratitude for you . . .

"And another thing. I come in, hangover and all, I wake him up, I bring him his breakfast, I say, 'Got a miracle for you waiting downstairs' and he says, 'Would it be Rab?' just like that, not as much as a blink . . . Not the way she took it . . . at the Casino. Never saw her cry before, even when she was a baby. Hadn't occurred to me one ought to break *good* news gently . . . God, she looks terrible. Can't have slept all night. Well, they both look terrible. And not a word to say (though they must have said it by now. Look, you two – it's an hour you've been up there). Stone faces, they had. Rab says, 'What happened to your hair?' and Thomas says, 'You're thin' and then they just gawp at each other.

"I say, 'Well, well, isn't this something?' Nobody answers. I say, 'Want to call up the family in California? I can fix it easy.' Not as much as a thank you. Then it's 'Just keep on driving, Miles.' I say, 'Anybody like a drink – merits a drink, doesn't it?' Nobody answers. Then we get to the damn Tower. Off they go. Funeral march, even their backs look terrible. That awful beret pulled down over his ears . . . and why she couldn't put the nice clothes on, – old sweater

and trousers, not even the fur jacket . . . she'll catch cold. Well, s
will he. Me too, I shouldn't wonder.

"Well, so they're saying goodbye up there, is that it? *É ou não é?*

With a shake of the head he reminded himself that this was non
of his business. They weren't his two kids any more. Useless to g
on fussing like a Nanny. They were far beyond Nannies, the two o
the tower.

Thomas looked up to the top of the tower, to the flag streamin
from the staff; thought of the Spanish flag and the salute; looke
up-river and down-river, blinked at the sun; hitched himself mor
comfortably on to the parapet between the two stone shields
thought about Miles waiting, thought about everything waiting
and went on waiting himself.

Rab did not answer his question. When she spoke she said only
"You're here . . ." She had said this before. "It's like the end of th
world." She had said this too. She swung from foot to foot, keepin
her eyes on his face. "Are we *both* dead? Is that it, do you think?"

"Well, yes and no," said Thomas. She continued to stare at him i
silence: he went on talking to himself, thinking, "I was right. Yo
aren't the person I used to know, that's plain enough." He foun
himself looking at her predecessors, as – lately – he had learned t
look at his own. He saw the child who had vanished, the tough an
fearless friend. He saw Peter Pan, alone on the island. He saw th
figure like the sailor-boy in ballet, leaping down from the Blu
Train to keep their appointment in the South. "'A boy inside'," h
thought, "I understand. It's part of you, it always was. And even if i
makes for danger, you are the person I knew I would meet. Nov
you've told me, it doesn't hurt me – only you. You fell in love, you
met truth head-on. Now you know about yourself. But Noel is dea
and we are here."

"The end of the world," Rab repeated. Her eyes glittered wit
ears.

"Give me a cigarette, there's a nice kind girl . . . It isn't the end c

world, it's simply the end of being young. For both of us.
erhaps rather early in the day; but from what I've seen war's
clined to speed the growing-up process."

"You sound so placid. You always were – except in rages."

"Won't be any more rages."

"Well, no. Bless you, there won't be any more anything. Except
oodbye. We've only got two days."

Thomas eyed her deliberately and ironically, saying "Oh . . . back
o there, are we?"

"I'm one for facts. You're the only fact I don't seem able to take
n."

"And for the moment," said Thomas, "I'm the only one that
natters."

He watched the full blue river where now a black boat with a
ust-red sail ran before the wind, passing the foot of the tower. Out
o sea . . . place of farewell, he thought; and place of triumphant
eturn.

"You must see it, Rab. Try."

"Your arm," she said, "Your poor arm."

"We didn't come up here to discuss my arm."

Rab thought, "It's no use, I should have slept, I should have woken
p clear-headed, I shouldn't have let myself cry. I should have kept
ie brakes on, the doors locked. I shouldn't be dazed, stunned, going
round and around it, thinking, 'You're here, you're alive. Not
ooking like you, looking like an orphan or a refugee or something.
Sut you are you, you're Thomas.' I don't seem able to get beyond
iere."

"I do wish we could make a move," said Thomas's voice, and
dded "Miles must be wishing it too."

"All I know is you're here and I want us never to stop talking."

"Should be enough." The face was wearing its old, absent-
ninded smile. She looked at the calm eyes with the darkened lids
bove and the dark lines below; at the fringe of white eyelashes; at

the bridge of his nose, as sharp and delicate as a wishbone; at th
smile and the gap made on one side by two broken teeth. ("O
well, a lot of teeth get broken in that place, you'd be surprised."
She saw him holding his stiffened arm across his chest as though h
still wore a sling. He caught the look and said quickly, "Not becaus
you're sorry for me, though – please. I've just been knocked about
bit. You're the one who's had the tough time."

"I'm not sorry for you. That would be patronizing. I couldn'
patronize you. You can take anything, do anything, you alway
could."

He didn't answer. She stared past him, down towards the mout
of the river, thinking, "That's where the ship will come, the ship t
take me away."

"Ah, *prove* it to me, can't you?" she cried despairingly, "Prove i
wouldn't be just because I'm so glad to see you and I want to go t
England."

"Why shouldn't it be?"

"Because it wouldn't be fair."

"Oh Rab . . . that's childish. I'll accept a 'No' if you're feeling 'O
I *can't*'. Or if it looks like prison. No other argument holds."

"Not 'Oh I can't'. Not like prison."

"Well then, we're getting somewhere."

"I'll make you miserable."

Thomas grinned. He said, "My doom-clothes ready to wrap m
in? And the fire burn and the water cool and a fool beget anothe
fool?"

She was shaken: "Where did you find it?"

"You gave me the book, remember?"

"So I did, I hadn't remembered."

"I can't see you as my doom-clothes, darling. I can only see we'v
been given this meeting, against all the odds there are – in thi
improbable place. And I can't believe it was given us to say goodby
with. Goodbye was last year."

"I shouldn't have gone back," she said.

"I shouldn't have let you. I don't think now that a man woul
have let you. I can still see the boy who sobbed and said goodby
and broke his heart wishing he hadn't. I can still see the girl wh

vent. I can tell I'm not that boy any more. And you're not that girl. But I love you. Differently. Quite solemnly and truthfully. In the spirit of wisdom."

She tried to say in her heart *No mercy now* and found this edict failing her; its power spent. She turned away from him, looked up-over. Through the tears she despised she saw the higher reaches; a web of masts and rigging, two pennants stiffly flying, and a gull turned silver as it slanted. She looked at the green bar of land across the water. She thought of the island. (Somewhere back in time a small, sad voice was saying, "He'll never get to the Vineyard now – not ever.")

She saw him alone, turning his thoughts to England, going on without her, accepting it. *As you accept me; and April; and everything.*

"You believe in God and I don't," she said.

"Does it matter? Either He's there, in which case I'm right. Or He isn't. In which case you're right."

"Oh *Thomas* . . . Stone wall."

"If you don't want to be married in church, then nor do I. Probably much quicker and easier not to, hereabouts. We'll get somebody who'll make us sign our names – gabble 'Now you are man and wife' at us and then we are. If you find you can't stand being married to me, you tell me when the time comes and we'll pack it in. That's a promise."

"Then you'd be miserable."

"Oh well. I expect I should. Not really the point, is it? What I'm trying to make clear is that I don't want to *own* you. I'm not much of one for owning things. And I've never thought it was possible to own people."

"I don't deserve you."

Thomas said, "Pooh." He swung his legs, drumming his heels against the parapet: "Mark my words. To part now would be idiotic. And ungrateful. And negative. And slinking away defeated. On such a nice morning, too."

She began to laugh. He pointed a finger at her. "You like facts. Well, war's a fact. And it's going to be a long fact. Staying three thousand miles away from each other for the duration simply doesn't make sense."

While she fumbled for an argument she heard him say lightly "'Lazarus was risen once . . .' Think, do think. We stopped in April didn't we? Us as we used to be, I mean?"

"Yes."

"But this is a different us. And this is now."

"It's now. And now, right now, the only thing I want is to stay with you – and love you. But oh Thomas, don't you understand, it won't always be now. What happens afterwards?"

Thomas slid down off the parapet. He said, "Let's go and see."